LEAVING YUMA

OTHER FIVE STAR WESTERN TITLES BY MICHAEL ZIMMER:

LEAVING YUMA

A WESTERN STORY

MICHAEL ZIMMER

FIVE STAR

A part of Gale, Cengage Learning

GALE
CENGAGE Learning

Detroit • New York • San Francisco • New Haven, Conn • Waterville, Maine • London

GALE
CENGAGE Learning

LIBRARY OF CONGRESS CATALOGING-IN-PUBLICATION DATA

Zimmer, Michael, 1955-
    Leaving Yuma : a western story / by Michael Zimmer.
      pages cm
    "Five Star Western."
    ISBN-13: 978-1-4328-2704-5 (hardcover)
    ISBN-10: 1-4328-2704-9 (hardcover)
    I. Title.
    PS3576.I467L43 2013
    813'.54—dc23   2013014015

First Edition. First Printing: September 2013
Published in conjunction with Golden West Literary Agency
Find us on Facebook™ https://www.facebook.com/FiveStarCengage
Visit our website– http://www.gale.cengage.com/fivestar/
Contact Five Star™ Publishing at FiveStar@cengage.com

Printed in Mexico
1 2 3 4 5 6 7 15 14 13

For Tiffany Schofield
Helping me keep the rubber side down, six novels and counting

FOREWORD:
THE AMERICAN LEGENDS
COLLECTIONS

During the Great Depression of the 1930s, nearly one quarter of the American work force was unemployed. Facing the possibility of economic and government collapse, President Franklin Roosevelt initiated the New Deal program, a desperate bid to get the country back on its feet.

The largest of these programs was the Works Progress Administration (WPA), which focused primarily on manual labor with the construction of bridges, highways, schools, and parks across the country. But the WPA also included a provision for the nation's unemployed artists, called the Federal Arts Project, and within its umbrella, the Federal Writers Project (FWP). At its peak, the FWP put to work approximately six thousand five hundred men and women.

During the FWP's earliest years, the focus was on a series of state guidebooks, but in the late 1930s, the project created what has been called a "hidden legacy" of America's past—more than ten thousand life stories gleaned from men and women across the nation.

Although these life histories, a part of the Folklore Project within the FWP, were meant eventually to be published in a series of anthologies, that goal was effectively halted by the United States' entry into World War II. Most of these histories are currently located within the Library of Congress in Washington, D.C.

Foreword

As the Federal Writers Project was an arm of the larger Arts Project, so was the Folklore Project a subsidiary of the FWP. An even lesser known branch of the Folklore Project was the American Legends Collection (ALC), created in 1936, and managed from 1936 to 1941 by a small staff from the University of Indiana. The ALC was officially closed in early 1942, another casualty of the war effort.

While the Folklore Project's goal was to capture everyday life in America, the ALC's purpose was the acquisition of as many "incidental" histories from our nation's past as possible. Unfortunately the bulk of the American Legends Collection was lost due to manpower shortages caused by the war.

The only remaining interviews known to exist from the ALC are those located within the A.C. Thorpe Papers at the Bryerton Library in Indiana. These are carbons only, as the original transcripts were turned in to the offices of the FWP in November 1941.

Andrew Charles Thorpe was unique among those scribes put into employment by the FWP-ALC in that he recorded his interviews with an Edison Dictaphone. These discs, a precursor to the LP records of a later generation, were found sealed in a vault shortly after Thorpe's death in 2006. Of the eighty-some interviews discovered therein, most were conducted between the years 1936 and 1939. They offer an unparalleled view of both a time (1864 to 1916) and place (Florida to Nevada, Montana to Texas) within the United States' singular history.

The editor of this volume is grateful to the current executor of the A.C. Thorpe Estate for his assistance in reviewing these papers, and to the descendants of Mr. Thorpe for their co-operation in allowing these transcripts to be brought into public view.

An explanation should be made at this point that, although minor additions to the text were made to enhance its readability, no facts were altered. Any mistakes or misrepresentations resulting from these changes are solely the responsibility of the editor.

Leon Michaels

January 19, 2012

SESSION ONE

I won't say I didn't have second thoughts about this. I appreciate your belief that it's important to keep a record of our country's past. I'd even have to say I agree with it. But you've got to understand that there's more at stake here than just an account of someone else's misfortune. What that woman and those kids went through was bad, the kind of ordeal a lot of people don't survive, and I hope I don't need to remind you that some of the men who were involved in their rescue didn't survive.

But she did, and so did her children, and they've all got fresh new lives today. They've put what happened in the past, and I won't be a party to dredging it up again, or bringing their story back into the public's eye.

That said, I still agree it's important not to let our country's history slide out of perspective because of a lot of flag-waving rhetoric on one side, or revisionist nonsense on the other. I've given this a lot of thought, and here's about the only deal I'm willing to make. I'll tell you what happened down there in as much detail as I can remember. I'll tell you things I probably shouldn't, and I'll even let you record it on your Dictaphone. But I won't reveal the names of the woman or her children, and by extension, I won't tell you her husband's name or what he did for a living, either. If you can honor that one condition, we can get started right now. If not, then you might as well pack up and walk on out of here, because that's the only way I'll tell you about it. Are you OK with that? All right, then let's get this shindig moving.

I guess you could say that I'm fairly well-known, at least around the Midwest. People have read about me in magazines and newspapers and such, and a few of those publications have included little biographies, most of them along the lines of: *J. T. Latham came to Iowa with nothing but a suitcase and a dream.*

I won't even comment on the inaccuracies of such a statement, but if you've ever read one of those articles, you've probably noticed they tend to ignore my life prior to my coming to Davenport in '07. Which is fine, since nothing I did before then really has any bearing on what I've accomplished since, but I suspect it's going to surprise a lot of people to learn that I once rode on the wrong side of the law, and that I spent some time behind bars in the Territorial Penitentiary in Yuma, Arizona.

Although I seldom talk about those days, I'm not ashamed of them. Sure, I might have broken the law on a fairly regular basis in my youth, but I was never a cold-blooded killer or a rapist. I never robbed banks or held up stagecoaches or rolled a drunk, other than that one time right after I got back from living with the Yaquis. Escaped from them would be a more accurate description—but that's getting ahead of myself.

The account of my going into Mexico to ransom—let's call her Abby, Abby Davenport—actually begins in the Yuma pen, which is why I brought it up. I figure it was my last day there, one way or another, because if Del Buchman hadn't come along when he did, the odds were pretty fair that I wouldn't have lived to see the sun come up the next morning. It's not a stretch to say I was reckless in those days, and prone to poke the tiger more than common sense would dictate, but probably the dumbest thing I did in Yuma was to get crosswise of a thirty-to-life convict named Elliot Walsh.

There was a hierarchy to Yuma back then—to most prisons, I expect—that varied depending upon which side of the bars you viewed the world from. For an average con like myself, the head man was the chief turnkey, a stone-hearted son-of-a-b---- named Chuck Halsey. After Halsey came three or four of the prison's toughest guards, then Elliot Walsh and his boys. The rest of the hacks, and even the warden, came behind Walsh, that's how much influence he had on the day-to-day operations of the joint. At least behind the scenes, in that unhinged world very few people realize exists.

Other than a handful of prisoners who were what today's doctors might call psychotic, and should have been in an asylum instead of a h--- hole like Yuma, Walsh was probably the meanest man on the Hill, at least when I was there. This is the same guy who murdered that family up on Grouse Creek in the summer of '99, which you might recall, since the incident was in all the papers at the time.

I was sprung from Yuma more than thirty years ago, but I can still see Elliot Walsh's face on my last day in the pen, as expressionless as a chunk of wood while his boys had me cornered behind the prison laundry. He looked like someone about to toss a smoked-down cigar into the gutter, rather than watch his men stomp the life out of another human being—but I guess that's getting ahead of myself.

At Yuma in 1907—which is when all of this took place—after the evening meal and if we'd behaved ourselves during the day's labors, we'd get a little free time in the exercise yard. Most of the cons used that hour or so of fading daylight to chew the fat or play some kind of game like stick ball, or just wind down as best they could under the watchful eyes and cocked Winchesters of the prison's hacks. Although there were rules against gambling, we all did it. The guards knew about it, too, but they wouldn't say anything if we didn't cause trouble.

I reckon Elliot Walsh liked to gamble more than he liked to play stick ball or talk. The way he acted, you might think he preferred it to eating or sleeping. He probably also liked the money that gambling brought him, and not just from his own wagering. When I was there between '03 and '07, there weren't many games of chance that Walsh didn't have a hand in, one way or another. He had a number of slab-faced flunkies he'd gathered around him over the years. You know the type—big, dumb brutes, willing to shove an iron spike through a man's heart if Walsh told them to. The fact is, there were a lot of guards who were just as afraid of Elliot Walsh and his goons as the rest of us were.

I didn't care for Walsh, but I liked to gamble as much as the next guy stuck behind thick, windowless walls and locked doors, so one evening after mess I rolled the dice with him and a couple of cons I sometimes hung out with, and within half a dozen tosses I'd won forty bucks. Back in those days, forty bucks was a month's wages for most men. In a place like Yuma, it was just about a king's ransom.

My two buddies could see where this was heading and backed out real quick, but I was young and brash, and hung in for another throw just to see if my luck held. Walsh was betting wildly by then. He glared a warning as he slapped the dice in my hands, but I didn't pay him any heed. It was my roll and I shot an easy six right off the bat, then just squatted there on my calves staring at the dice. H---, even I was starting to wonder if the game was rigged. Grinning, I said: "With this kind of luck, maybe we ought to try breaking out of here tonight."

Even on a good day, Eliott Walsh didn't have much of a sense of humor. My remark brought him instantly to his feet. I stood just as quick, shoving my newly won cash into a pocket.

"It was a fair game, Walsh," I said. "I just had a run of good luck, is all."

"Nobody has that kinda luck, Latham."

"It happens."

"Like h--- it does. You cheated. I don't know how, but you did."

Being right-handed, I was keeping my left side to him, my arms down with my fists clenched and ready to let fly. "That's not true, and, even if it was, I wouldn't be fool enough to do it eight times in a row."

"I want my money back," he snarled.

"That ain't how it works," I replied.

"It is tonight."

I shook my head. You might consider me foolish to refuse his demand, but you have to understand that life functions differently inside a penitentiary. Show the yellow feather just once and you'll drop to the bottom rung of prison society like a rock down a well, and that isn't a life I'd wish on a rat.

Walsh's eyes flitted briefly to the mess hall entrance, where a trio of guards were watching us. I knew what he was thinking. Whether most of the hacks were secretly afraid of him or not, they couldn't ignore a fight right out in the open. They'd lose their jobs if they did. Walsh knew it, too, and he suddenly relaxed, rolling his shoulders as if to work out some of the stiffness. "Yeah, you're right, Latham. Besides, I'll win it back the next time, right?"

"Sure, it was just a fluke." I took a sliding step backward, not yet willing to take my eyes off his. Over at the mess hall, one of the guards was yelling for the cons to pack it up and get inside for lockdown. There was some grumbling about the short shift we were getting on our free time, but I suspect most of the yard knew what was going on.

Walsh said: "See you around, pard." Then he strode away as if enjoying an after-dinner constitutional.

My pulse was racing. I think Elliot Walsh had the shortest fuse on the hottest temper of any man I'd ever met, and that includes Old Toad, who I'm going to tell you about later on. As for Walsh, I guess I should have taken his personality into account before throwing dice with him. That ol' boy was just plain crazy mean, and, with a sinking sensation in my belly, I knew he'd retaliate.

It happened sooner than expected. I was over near the prison's west wall the next day, where a bunch of us were slopping mud and straw for adobe bricks that the warden would sell in town. We made a lot of bricks in Yuma. That and busting big rocks into gravel with sledge-hammers was our primary occupation. Those particular bricks were for a photography shop going up somewhere on Third Street. I was packing one of the wooden molds we used to shape the plates for drying, mud up to my elbows and toes squishing inside a pair of cheap, prison-issue shoes, when one of the hacks came over to tell me I was needed at the laundry. I didn't question what I was needed for. In a place like Yuma, when a guard tells you to go somewhere, you keep your mouth shut and go, either that or risk a hard club to the kidneys and a couple of days in the snake pit.

In the official paperwork, the snake pit was called the Punishment Cell, a ten-by-ten foot chamber carved out of solid rock on the bluff overlooking the Colorado River, where the prison was built in 1877. The cons called it the pit, and if you ever go through Yuma, take time to see it. You won't have any trouble figuring out how it got its name.

There was no light in the pit other than what shimmied down a tiny ventilation shaft in the ceiling. There wasn't a bunk or blankets or pillow, or even a bucket for waste. There was just cold and dark and hard stone, where every once in a while, if a guard or another con didn't like you, a snake might be dropped down the ventilation shaft into the cell. I knew from experience it was a place to avoid, although I'd been lucky in not having to share the space with a rattler looking for something warm to curl up against.

After cleaning myself off with a piece of burlap sacking, I headed for the laundry. I don't recall if I was surprised or not when I rounded the corner behind the low-roofed building and saw Elliot Walsh and a couple of his boys standing in the shade of an adobe wall, although if I was, I probably shouldn't have been. Glancing toward the guard's tower, perched on the corner of the main wall like a squatty birdhouse, I wasn't exactly stunned to find the hacks inside looking off into the distance like there was a circus setting up outside the prison's walls.

I remember hoping the Judas sons-of-b----es enjoyed their thirty pieces of silver, then reluctantly turned to face Walsh. Hearing a hard thud behind me, like a hand smacking the wall, I looked over my shoulder to see two more of Elliot's men coming up from the rear, big grins drawn across their faces like scars.

I wouldn't have minded taking on Walsh or one of his boys in a fair fight, but the odds now were five to one, with retreat cut off. Mister, I was in trouble, and I knew it. My heart was kicking around in my chest like it wanted to get out of there even more than I did. There was one more possible avenue of escape—through the laundry itself—although I figured Walsh probably had more men stationed inside to block off that route. I made a move toward the rear door anyway, but hadn't covered more than a few feet when Elliott whistled sharply, the laundry door swung open, and Tiny Evans squeezed through the wooden frame like sausage through a casing. Behind me, Walsh's goons were chuckling merrily, likely having set the whole thing up just to see the expression on my face when the big man made his appearance.

Tiny Evans reminded me of one of those black stone monoliths you see in the pulps of the surface of Mars, broad enough to hide a fair-size crew of little green men. He was sheathed in slabs of muscle and hard fat, a big ol' Cajun from the backwaters of Louisiana where, according to rumor, he fled after killing a kid who'd chopped the head off his pet gopher snake. Whacked the kid's head off, if what they said was true, but who knows how much to believe of a story like that? What I'd observed first-hand was Tiny breaking a two-by-six plank over his knee with just one downward swipe of the board, that plus the fact he was as loyal to Walsh as a starving dog is to a bone.

Just so the folks who might someday listen to these disks understand, I'm not a small man—even in my socks I come pretty darn close to six feet, not to mention broad shoulders, large hands, and, back then, plenty of muscle of my own from swinging a sledge-hammer and lugging eighty-pound adobe bricks around the prison yard six days a week—I just looked small standing next to Tiny Evans.

I said: "Is it just going to be me and him, Walsh? Or will I have to fight all of you?"

Walsh laughed, so naturally his boys did, too. Well, not Tiny. Tiny just stood there like that monolith I mentioned a few seconds ago, his arms hanging slack at his sides as he awaited his master's instructions.

"I'll tell you what, Latham," Walsh returned easily. "You fight Tiny, and, if you can beat him, I'll let you go."

I nodded, but I didn't believe him. Elliot Walsh maintained his control over the convict population with intimidation and threats of violence he was unquestionably capable of delivering on. Even if I did somehow best Tiny, it wouldn't erase Walsh's need to bring me under his heel. My options that day were few and dismal, and made my stomach churn with dread. I wasn't eager to meet the Reaper, but figured it was a better alternative than serving the rest of my term as one of Elliot's dogs.

Bringing my fists up close to my chest, I backed into the open where I'd have room to maneuver. Tiny came after me in his dull, lumbering stride. We made a slow circle with me in reverse, searching for an opening. Although Tiny stayed close, he didn't rush me. He just kept coming on with the hungry, almost glassy-eyed look of a . . . well, the look of a man who'd kill a kid for killing a gopher snake.

Finally, taking a deep breath, I feigned a left, then a quick right. Tiny might not have been the sharpest shovel in the ditch, but he'd been in his share of fights over the years, and wasn't easily scammed. He batted my fists away as if shooing off a pesky fly, his demeanor never changing. I nodded acknowledgement of his skill, did a partial feint with my left, then took a half step forward as if to bury my toe in his crotch.

Tiny saw that one coming, too, and was already reaching for my ankle when I abruptly pulled my foot back. For the first time, the big man's face registered something other than imperturbable confidence. His broad visage was wide open, and he knew it. Using his already badly mauled nose for a bull's-eye, I drove my fist into it with everything I had. He cried out throatily, reeling backward on stiff, tottering legs.

A collective note of awe eddied across the yard from Walsh's men. Tiny came to a halt with his massive feet planted wide and shook his head, flinging droplets of blood into the dust. A look of wonder spread across his face as he probed gently at the buckled lump of flesh and gristle above his mouth, but except for the steady dripping of blood from his left nostril, I don't think I added any new damage.

I hung back, not wanting to press my luck, and hoping, I think, that he might yet keel over. I believe the fact that he was still standing after the kind of a blow I'd given him was doing more to undermine my confidence than his size and reputation had.

Tiny stood there a moment longer, his brows furrowed as if in confusion as he studied the smear of blood across his fingertips. Then he looked at me, and I cursed softly in disbelief and started backing away. H---, what else could I do? My right hand was still throbbing from its collision with Evans's face, and my breath was coming swift and deep, as if I'd just finished a race to town and back. I needed a weapon of some kind, but a prison doesn't offer a lot of those—not handily, at least. So I kept backing up, staying on my toes and fearful of a charge I wouldn't be quick enough to dodge. As my thoughts scrambled for a plan, it suddenly occurred to me that, while Walsh and his boys might still have the two main avenues of escape shut off, the laundry was now open. I began widening my circle in a track that would take me within fifteen feet of the rear door. I kept my eyes away from the opening, fearful of telegraphing my intentions to the others.

"Come on, Evans, finish it," Walsh called impatiently. I knew what was troubling him. Those hacks in the guard tower couldn't pretend they didn't know what was going on forever; sooner or later they'd have to turn around and put a stop to it.

Tiny's eyes flitted guiltily toward his boss without actually meeting the man's gaze, like a dog that had been beaten too often. It was just a fleeting look, but figuring it was probably the only chance I was going to get, I took off for the laundry in a sprint.

Lord, Tiny was fast. Like a streak of lightning snaking along the ground, and nothing at all like what you'd expect from someone so big and clunky-looking. His fist caught me in the ribs while I was still ten feet shy of the door, and I stumbled to the side with a grunt that all but echoed off the prison's rear wall. For a moment the laundry's rear entrance kind of shrunk down like it was sinking into a pool of black tar. Before I could regain my senses, Tiny grabbed my arm and spun me around full circle, slamming me into the building's rough adobe wall. I grunted again and started to go down, but a hand as imposing as a catcher's mitt grabbed my shirt and hauled me to my feet. Wobbling like I was, his next swing only grazed my jaw, although it was enough to drop me in my tracks.

I lay on my back watching the sky do a jerky little dance overhead until Tiny hove into view, casting me in shadow. I was more than a little worried when I realized he was grinning, and impulsively brought my right leg up as if to aim a kick at his groin. He was ready for that, but caught completely off guard when my left heel smashed crosswise into his left knee.

I rolled clear of Tiny's plummeting form. Up in the guard's tower, one of the hacks uttered an expletive of disbelief. I guess my unexpected success, no matter how short-lived it was likely to be, had proved too much for their curiosity; they were leaning over the low wall like fans at a dogfight. Lurching to my feet, I spied the laundry door just a few feet away and quickly darted inside. Walsh shouted for his goons to go after me, but I wasn't running. H---, I was in prison. Where was I going to go?

There were stacks of clothing everywhere, but not a flatiron in sight. Then my eyes lit on a squat, three-legged stool, the kind you can still see at some of the smaller dairy farms where they milk by hand. Grabbing a leg, I whirled to face the door.

Brad Butler was the first of Walsh's thugs to come through the door. I hit him in the face with everything I had, dropping him in his tracks. The others skidded to a halt outside, fanning out in front of the door but wisely hanging back. I could see Tiny behind them, whimpering pitifully as he rolled back and forth on the ground, clutching his busted knee. Butler lay sprawled across the threshold, cupping his face with both hands. Blood—a lot of it—was seeping from between his fingers.

We stood that way for perhaps a full minute, and I was glad for the opportunity to catch my breath. Finally Walsh wandered over as if just passing by, although I noticed he was careful to stay well to the rear of his men. Nudging Tiny with the side of his foot, he said: "You impress me, Latham. Most men I've sent this ol' boy against don't even get in one good lick. I didn't think you had it in you."

"You want your money back?"

You might recall that I'd said I wouldn't do that, but that encounter behind the laundry had me reëvaluating my options.

Walsh seemed to mull over the offer for a moment, then shook his head. "I reckon we've gone too far for that."

One of his men turned part way around. "A couple of us could go around front, come in that way."

"Naw, the situation's changed." Walsh glanced toward the guard tower. The hacks still hadn't called for help, but we both knew they soon would. They'd have to. Scowling, he said: "Get Evans and Butler on their feet and take 'em to the infirmary. We'll deal with Latham later."

It took a couple of minutes for Walsh's men to get Evans on his feet. Walsh hung around after his men had moved off with their staggering cargo. "It's too bad," he said after they were gone. "I could have used you."

"For what, another half-baked cut-throat to kiss your a--?"

Walsh shrugged. Then he abruptly stiffened, and I tossed the three-legged stool behind a pile of dirty laundry. From beyond my field of vision I heard a voice bark: "What in the god-d---ed name of h--- is going on out here?"

Rubbing the back of my right hand, the one I'd bruised from knuckles to wrist on Tiny Evan's jaw, I moved to the door.

Yuma's chief turnkey was coming toward us like a thunderstorm on bowed legs. His name was Chuck Halsey, which I believe I've already mentioned. He was tall and slim and hot-eyed, as if he was always half ticked off about something. I hadn't been in Yuma long before I realized Chuck Halsey was more in control of the day-to-day operation of the prison than the superintendent, a burly guy named Tom Rynning. Halsey interacted with the prisoners on a daily basis, and knew us all by name, crime, and reputation. He had a pretty fair idea of what each man was capable of, too. Which ones he could depend on and which ones he didn't dare turn his back to, although I noticed he never really trusted any of us completely.

Coming to a stop about ten feet away, he spent a long moment just glaring at us. Walsh and I remained silent and kept our eyes averted. We didn't ignore the man, but we were careful not to look directly at him, either. Living behind bars can be like walking a tightrope sometimes. Finally turning to me, Halsey said: "All right, what happened here, Latham?"

I shrugged. "I'm not really sure, boss."

"You're not sure? What kind of idiot do you take me for?"

Now there was a question rife with possibilities if ever I saw one, but Ma Latham didn't raise no fool, so I kept my mouth shut and my gaze on a middle button of Halsey's shirt.

"What about you, Walsh? What have you got to say about this, since those were your boys I saw heading for the infirmary spilling blood all over everything?"

Affecting a friendly grin, Walsh said: "Butler and Evans? They ain't my boys, captain. They're just friends. As far as what happened, I wasn't a part of it, but, from what I could see, it looked like Latham was coming out the back door of the laundry just as Tiny and Brad were going in, and they accidentally ran into one another. Although what Latham was doing over here when he was supposed to be framing bricks is. . . ."

23

"What are you doing over here?" Halsey interrupted, and Walsh's smile faded. Without giving Walsh time to fabricate a new story, the turnkey turned back to me. "What about it, Latham? Is that your story, too, that you and Tiny bumped into one another in the door?"

"Sounds about right to me, boss."

Halsey nodded curtly. He knew we were lying. Swiveling at the waist, he pegged the guard's tower with a smoldering look. Both hacks were standing smartly at attention by then, their Winchesters at the ready. It was pretty clear from the expression on Halsey's face that he knew what was up with them, too, and that they would be in for an a-- chewing before the day was out. But not right away. Turns out Halsey had other business to deal with first.

"You come with me, Latham," he said. "The warden wants to see you."

Being a smart con, I stayed two paces behind Halsey all the way to the main yard, where the turnkey stopped me in front of the kitchen's side door. Squinting at the still-oozing cut above my brow, he said: "I would have liked to have seen the fight that put Brad Butler and Tiny Evans on their a--es."

I shrugged. I didn't really believe he was trying to trick me into confessing to something I'd already denied involvement in, but it never hurts to keep your mouth shut when you're not sure what to say. I've found that to be true in most situations, but especially in Yuma.

Jutting his chin toward the kitchen door, he said: "Go clean yourself off. You look like the bottom of a spittoon."

Ignoring the gray-haired cons inside, sitting at a long plank table peeling potatoes for that night's supper, I filled a tin basin with water and scrubbed off as much dust and blood as I could with my bandanna. Although Halsey didn't seem particularly impressed with the results when I came back outside a couple of minutes later, he kept his opinion to himself.

"Come on, they're waiting for us," he said, jerking his head toward the sally port.

Rynning's office was located not too far outside the prison gates. This was my first visit to the office, and what caught my attention as soon as I walked in was how cool it seemed. Even though it was only early May, it was as hot as a chile pepper outside, and my gray and black striped shirt—yeah, just like in the picture shows—was dark with sweat.

We entered a small outer office, where a trusty named Harold Warner sat at a drawerless desk shuffling through stacks of papers. A sign above a second door in the far wall read: *Private*. Halsey rapped firmly on the thick wood, and a voice from within bade us to enter. Halsey motioned me inside first, but, as I started to slip past him, he grabbed my arm and whispered: "You mind your manners in there, Latham, or I'll hand you over to Walsh myself."

He'd do it, too. Chuck Halsey was a fair man if you treated him right and minded the rules, but he could be a son-of-a-b---- if you crossed him. I spent four days in the snake pit my first week at Yuma after telling him to go to h---, and learned a valuable lesson for my impertinence.

Thomas Rynning was an ex-Arizona Ranger who had been appointed to the position of superintendent only a few months earlier. There was no welcome in the warden's eyes as I was ushered inside. Hearing the door close behind me, I knew I was on my own.

There was a second man in the room, a burly guy deep into his fifties by then, with thinning gray hair, thick brows, and a heavy gut. His cheeks and nose were finely threaded with broken capillaries, and there was a watery weakness to his eyes that I recognized. Over the years I'd met a lot of men with too much fondness for the bottle, but I'd never expected Delmar Buchman to be one of them.

"Hello, Latham," Del said in a voice like a mean dog's growl. He chuckled at my disheveled appearance. "Been making new friends?"

Oh, I had more than a few remarks I would have liked to have shot right back at that old b------, but I'd been a guest of the territory long enough by then to know when to keep my lips sealed. Focusing on Rynning, I said: "Chief Halsey said you wanted to see me, sir."

"That's correct." He tipped his head toward Buchman. "You know Acting Deputy Buchman?"

"Yes, sir."

"He knows I'm the one put him here," Buchman said with a spreading grin. "Like a rat to a trap, ain't that right, champ?"

"Refrain yourself, Mister Buchman," Rynning said curtly. "Prisoner Latham is no longer in your charge."

"Well, he might soon be again," Buchman replied, but the smile had slid off his face.

Eyeing an open folder on his desk, Rynning said: "You've already served a third of your sentence here, Latham. According to both your records and Chief Halsey's assertion, you've been, overall, a fairly disciplined inmate. If I were a betting man, I'd say your chances of getting out early are quite good. Possibly even before we make the move to Florence." [*Ed. Note:* The Territorial Penitentiary at Yuma was officially closed in 1909, with operations and prisoners moved to Florence that same year.] He looked up, eyeing the cuts and bruises Tiny Evans had planted around my face. "Assuming you can continue to stay out of trouble," he amended.

Buchman snorted and looked away. After an irritated glance in the old lawdog's direction, Rynning continued: "I want you to understand, Latham, that you are under no obligation to accept Mister Buchman's offer. If you would prefer to remain here and finish out your sentence, you may do so. Is that clear?"

I nodded like it was, like I knew what the h--- he was talking about.

Rising effortlessly, Rynning said to Buchman: "You've got five minutes . . . champ." Then he stepped around his desk and left the room.

I stayed where I was, as rigid as a soldier under inspection, my eyes trained on a spider making its slow way across the wall. Pushing to his feet, Buchman shuffled behind the desk to commandeer the warden's chair, dropping the last few inches with a faint grunt. Opening a top drawer like he already knew what he'd find inside, he took out a slim Cuban panatela, bit off the tip, and spat it into a wastebasket, then placed the cigar in his mouth. With a match lifted from a little iron box atop the desk, he calmly lit his pilfered smoke, then leaned back to jet a slim blue cloud toward the ceiling.

"How they treating you in here, Latham?" he asked, then chuckled when I didn't reply. "Teaching you some manners, anyway, huh?"

I waited patiently, and it wasn't long before I could tell my silence was starting to aggravate him. Prisoners everywhere have to toe the mark pretty closely, but we have our ways of getting back, too, exacting a little revenge whenever the opportunity presents itself. And I didn't like Buchman, for reasons that had nothing to do with him being the cop who'd arrested me in Moralos in '03—but I guess I'm getting ahead of myself, again. I seem to be doing that a lot tonight.

Anyway, back there in Rynning's office, I glanced at an ornate clock sitting on the warden's desk, its small white face embedded in the side of a bronze elephant. I didn't know how long Rynning had been gone, but the implication was clear, and Buchman's cheeks reddened.

"I hope you take my offer, Latham," he rumbled. "I'd surely

27

like to finish the training they started on you here."

"Just what offer is that, Buchman?"

The brows above the old lawman's eyes started to wiggle like a pair of woolly worms preparing to do battle. I could tell it bothered him that I referred to him by his last name, rather than sir or boss, but I didn't care. I had to jump through enough hoops in that place, I'd be d---ed if I'd start doing it for a man like Del Buchman.

"I've got a proposition for you," the lawman said, reaching into his jacket to pull out an ivory-colored envelope that he tossed casually across the desk in my direction. "Go ahead, take a peek."

I hesitated only briefly, then picked up the envelope. There was a single sheet of paper inside, marked with the official seal of the Territory of Arizona at the top. I scanned the document, noted the governor's signature at the bottom, and a line next to it for a second signature. Typed above the second line was the name *Delmar C. Buchman,* followed by the title: *Acting Deputy Sheriff, Pima County.*

"Play your cards right, champ, and that's your punch outta here."

My gaze drifted back up the page to a title printed all in caps: *DOCUMENT OF PARDON.* I heard a sound like escaping steam, and only belatedly realized it was my own exhalation.

"Interested?"

I nodded cautiously, returned the paper to the envelope, then the envelope to the desk top. "What do I have to do to earn it?"

"I got a party of men wants to go into Mexico without being recognized. What they call incognito. You know what that means?"

"I know what it means. Where does this party of yours want to go?"

"Sabana."

"My old stomping grounds."

"Yeah."

I thought about that for a moment. "You could take a train to Tres Pinos. It's a five-hour ride from there to Sabana. You could be there and back in three days."

"A train ain't an option. We're going in the back way."

I couldn't help smiling at that. "Through the *páramos?*"

Páramos, by the way, means "badlands". Or more correctly, "barren plains", although the *páramos* Buchman wanted to take his party through were anything but flat.

"You figure you can find your way?" I asked.

Buchman's eyes narrowed. "I could use you, Latham, but I sure as h--- don't need you. I could walk outta here right now and we'd still make it. Only difference would be that you'd still be locked away in here like a monkey in a cage, spending the next eight years of your life thinking about what a fool you were to turn down my offer."

Well, he had a point there, but he was wrong if he thought he could lead a party of men through those desert lands south of Moralos without a guide. I told him as much, then added: "You couldn't carry enough water for you and your men. You've got to know the water holes, and those are mighty few and hard to find."

"It can be done," he said stubbornly.

"Not by white men, it can't."

Buchman's eyes turned flinty, his fingers tightening around his cigar until it jutted from his fist at a nearly forty-five-degree angle. "If you ain't interested, Latham, say the word."

I held his gaze a moment longer, then glanced at the pale envelope sitting on top of Rynning's desk and sighed loudly. "No, I'm interested. Tell me the rest of it."

Buchman leaned back in his chair, his grip relaxing around the panatela. "Six days ago a train on its way to Hermosillo was

29

stopped by bandits. Seven Americans were taken off. Four of 'em were shot on the spot, but a woman and her two kids were taken away. Now, here's the kicker. On the very same day them three were pulled off that train, her husband gets a proposal from a bandit chief named Chito Soto that ain't nothing but a ransom demand wrapped in fancy words. This Soto claims he's a major in something called an Army of Liberation. He wants the ransom delivered to Sabana by May Sixteenth, which is eight days from today. They're threatening to start carving on them kids on the Seventeenth if they don't get the . . . their ransom on time."

"You keep saying ransom, instead of money."

"That part of the deal doesn't concern you. Listen, we're running outta of time here, Latham. You know that country better than any other white man in the territory. You can get us down there in time to save that woman and those kids."

"And if I do, I get the pardon?"

"That's the long and short of it. Edward Davenport . . . he's the gal's husband . . . he packs a lot of sway around here, and he's got some pretty good friends up at the capital, too. He's managed to wrangle you a full pardon, on the condition that you co-operate fully, but, if you ain't already noticed, that paper is one signature shy of being worth anything more than paper for the privy."

"Yours."

"That's right. It's a stipulation I insisted on. You help us get that woman and them kids outta there, and I'll add that final signature. You'll be a free man to go wherever you want. But I'll warn you right now, if you double-cross us, champ, this ol' world ain't gonna be big enough for you to hide in. I've already talked to Davenport about this, and he's agreed. He's vowed to post a five-thousand-dollar reward on your head, along with a description sent to every newspaper between New York and San

Francisco, London to Johannesburg. There ain't gonna be nowhere in this country or any other that you'd be safe in after that. Savvy?"

I walked over to stare out the window. Buchman probably thought I was thinking it over, but I wasn't. I'd already made up my mind to go the moment I saw my name on that pardon. What I was thinking about was all that country between Moralos, where we'd likely jump off from, and Sabana, way down deep in Sonora. I was fairly confident I could do it. I knew most of the water holes and trails through those *barrancos*—meaning those steep-sided cañons that can be nearly impossible to find your way through—then over the Sierra Verdes into the green Sabana Valley, but it was going to be d---ed hard. That was Yaqui country down there. Yaquis and whatever bandits were tough enough and mean enough to carve out a chunk of it for themselves. For most of the way we were going to be totally on our own, for it was a place where the *soldados* didn't often venture, or come back from when they did. And with just eight days to make the journey, we'd have to move light and fast.

Turning away from the window, I said: "What's your position with Davenport?"

"I reckon I'm what you'd call his agent."

"So it'll be you and me?"

"And others."

"How many?"

"That ain't your concern, Latham. You're coming along as a guide only."

"I'll need to know how many men and horses there'll be before I can decide which trails to use."

Buchman's eyes suddenly narrowed. "You might not want to ask too many questions, champ. The only thing that's important to you is this." Reaching across the desk, he flicked the pale envelope containing my pardon a few inches closer to where I was standing. "Savvy?"

I stared at it for only a few seconds, then met the old lawman's eyes. "Yeah, I savvy. When do we leave?"

Buchman smiled coldly. "Just as soon as I can get you sprung."

SESSION TWO

I won't waste too much space on your disk with the details of how I was processed out of Yuma. That's not the story you came here for, and, besides, the way the wind is howling out there, we might not have electricity much longer. I will say it didn't take as long as I was afraid it would, since I didn't want to spend another night inside those stone and adobe walls, dodging Eliott Walsh and his boys. Fortunately Buchman was able to get me out that same day.

It was probably after four o'clock when Halsey escorted me in my cheap new suit to the sally port in the prison's north wall, and I've got to admit my heart started thumping a little faster when I thought about those twin, strap-iron gates swinging open for me. You can imagine my resentment when I got there and spotted Del Buchman waiting on the other side with a pair of polished steel manacles dangling from his left hand.

Standing with Del was Warden Rynning, a deep scowl pulling his eyebrows down in the middle like a funnel. Knowing Rynning's reputation as a martinet, I suspected his annoyance was at my circumventing a duly administered prison sentence with a reprieve from the governor. I'll confess I didn't give a hoot in h--- what had the warden's britches so steamed. I'd rattled around my cell most of the previous night calculating the probability of surviving eight more years in that cess pit with Walsh and his goons stalking me. The odds weren't too favorable, in case you're wondering. Then there I was, not even twelve hours later, about to walk through those gates a free man. Or pretty darned close to it.

Halsey's parting words were poignant. "Watch your a--, Latham. Walsh is saying that if you ever come back, you'll be dead before you can be assigned a cell."

"I won't be back."

Halsey grunted like he doubted my promise, but I intended to honor it. I stepped through the inner gate alone, then waited while it was pulled closed and locked. Then the outer gate was unlocked and I stepped outside into the Arizona sunshine. I think I was grinning wide enough to hide my ears.

As soon as I was clear, Rynning signed off on a final release form, handing that to Buchman and accepting one from the lawman in return. Passing me on the way in, Rynning said: "Good luck, Latham." It kind of irritated me that he didn't stop or offer to shake my hand. I'd kind of figured he would.

Buchman tossed me the bracelets—like handcuffs but with a longer chain—then pulled his jacket back to reveal a large-framed revolver in a shoulder rig under his left arm. "Put those on," he said, nodding toward the manacles.

I wanted to protest, but Rynning hadn't completely closed that outer gate yet. He seemed to be waiting for my reaction. Laughing, I fitted the cuffs over my wrists and Buchman locked them in place. Returning the key to his pocket, he said: "This can go real easy, Latham, or I can make you wish you'd stayed inside those walls. Savvy?"

"Let's get out of here."

We started down the dusty road at a swift walk, the echo of the outer gate clanking shut drifting over our heads. Despite the cuffs on my wrists and the lawman at my side, I was feeling pretty chipper. Like I wanted to whistle. That good cheer lasted about a dozen yards, when Bachman veered toward a four-wheeled contraption parked at an angle under the prison wall, its narrow, rubber-shod wheels chocked with stones to keep it from rolling downhill. It looked sort of like an army ambulance, only it had a steering wheel in front of the wooden bench seat and a metal cowl out in front that reminded me of a blood-hound's cold black nose. My pace ebbed noticeably, and Buchman's eyes narrowed. "What's the matter, champ, ain't you ever seen an automobile before?"

"Yeah, I've seen them. Are we going to ride that thing into town?"

He laughed. "I'll be d---ed, the mighty J.T. Latham, scared of a panel truck."

I gave him a dismissive look and didn't say anything else, but, yeah, I'll admit it. My mouth was cottony and my palms itched, like they do even today when I get antsy over something. You can go ahead and laugh if you want. Knowing how it all turned out, I don't blame you. But the fact is, although I'd never ridden in an automobile at the time, I'd been around a few, and I considered them nothing less than snorting, belching deathtraps, no safer than a crateful of dynamite bouncing around inside a tub of burning fuses.

"Come on," Buchman said. "We ain't got all day."

Although I kept my mouth shut, I won't deny a hefty dose of relief when we passed the panel truck and made for a sleek black buggy with the words, *YUMA CAB CO.* written in block letters across the low sideboards. An old sorrel mare was standing patiently in the traces, swatting flies with a tail grown thin from age. Del released the snap on the sorrel's halter and tossed the tether-weight under the seat, then we both climbed in, the buggy swaying wildly on ancient springs.

We followed the road from Prison Hill south to level ground, then west into town, the lowering sun nearly blinding us. Yuma had changed over the years. When I came through there in '03 to begin my sentence, I don't recall seeing any automobiles.

Now there were cars and trucks in every direction, probably a couple of dozen between the Hill and downtown alone. There were numerous bicycles, too, and the streets through the business district were festooned with electrical and telephone wires.

Buchman's first stop was the Yuma Livery, where he returned the rented buggy. Then we walked back downtown to Hunsaker's Department Store, a two-story brick building on the corner of Third and Jefferson. Hunsaker's was where a lot of the cons went after their release to replace the cheap suits they'd been issued inside with more suitable clothing. Frankly I was hoping for something a little less scratchy in the crotch.

We entered through a side door, where we were met by a young man sporting a Teddy Roosevelt haircut, complete with mustache and thin-framed eyeglasses. He noticed my cuffs right away, but didn't seem alarmed.

"What can I do for you gentlemen?"

Buchman hooked a thumb in my direction. "I need to get this jasper outfitted for an extended trip into the desert. Can you do that for under twenty bucks?"

"I believe we can," Teddy replied with the flash of a smile that paled in comparison with the real thing. "Follow me."

He led us to a back room, where a long wooden table was piled high with used clothing. Shelves along all four walls were lined with shoes, boots, hats, cheap pasteboard suitcases, and a number of smaller items like spurs and gloves.

Never having been accused of being a stickler for fashion, I didn't waste time looking for fancy. I picked out a pair of sturdy, copper-riveted jeans, some low-heeled work boots that would do nicely for the saddle, and a couple of plain wool shirts, shaded in the same light tan as the desert we'd be crossing. For a hat I chose a silver-belly Stetson that time, weather, and the previous owner's hands had transformed into something uniquely its own. Its brim curved slightly upward both front and back, and its crown was lumpy from handling. An engraved leather hatband was saved from being labeled ornate by hard use and sweat. I also picked out a light blue bandanna, leather gloves, a corduroy vest, and a heavier canvas jacket that came down over my hips.

Hunsaker's didn't carry socks or underwear in their used clothing department, so I had to purchase those new. Then Buchman had the clerk add one of those new screw-open razors with the flat blades, a bar of Castile soap, a towel, a sodbuster's knife—its little four-inch blade the largest Buchman would consent to—and a palm-size sewing kit because, believe it or not, most of the men who roamed the frontier in those days were pretty handy with a needle and thread, having to rely on our own resources if we ripped a shirt on an ocotillo or popped a button wrestling with a balky mule.

Buchman paid the man out of his own wallet. I didn't mention the $20 I had in wages from the prison, or the $45 I'd taken off of Walsh while shooting craps. Afterward the clerk escorted us to the same side door we'd entered though, as if wanting to steer us away from the more genteel clientele up front, where the latest fashions were on display. Being older and a bit more traveled myself nowadays, I can appreciate the clerk's sentiment; at the time I just didn't give a d---.

We went to a bathhouse run by a Chinaman named Charlie Ye next, where I got my first hot bath in nearly half a decade. I'll tell you what, there are few indulgences I prize more today than a regular bath with hot water, good soap, a soft washcloth, and a little electric heater in the corner if it's chilly. Living like I did back then makes a man treasure some of the things folks today take for granted.

I left my cheap prison suit in a heap on the bathhouse floor. Our next stop was the Acme Saloon, where Buchman bought me the first honest-to-God beer I'd had since my arrest in '03.

It wasn't cold, but it was cool—Yuma had its own ice factory by then—and I drank it down fast enough to give myself a headache. Buchman laughed and bought me another and told me to take my time, as it would have to last me a spell. Del was still working on his first one, and, as I watched his face in the backbar mirror, I noticed how he kept eyeing the whiskey bottles lined up behind the bar. Buchman was a man in conflict, and I had a good idea what was gnawing at him.

Later on we stood on the boardwalk in front of the Acme and Buchman offered me a cigar from an inside breast pocket of his jacket, courtesy, I suspect, of Thomas Rynning's top desk drawer. The sun had dipped below the horizon and the sky was streaked in shades of red, gold, violet, and turquoise. For a moment, all I could do was stare. I've traveled some since those woolly days of my youth. I've been to the Metropolitan Museum of Art in New York a couple of times, and spent a day touring the Musée Du Louvre in Paris, along with shorter excursions through London, Rome, and Berlin, but I've yet to see anything in a gallery to match the grandeur of a desert sunset. On the Hill, the guards always made sure we were locked down well before dusk, so this was the first eventide I'd seen in nearly four years.

"Delmar," I said, taking a pull on my cigar, "you're turning out to be more of a gentleman than I figured you for."

"I told you if you minded your manners, we'd get along."

"I'm guessing Davenport is paying for this?"

"Uhn-huh, although he doesn't know it yet. I've got a letter of credit lets me pull cash outta the bank whenever I need it. You got a rough road ahead of you yet. I figure you might as well enjoy a few amenities before we leave all this luxury behind."

I glanced up and down the dusty thoroughfare. There was a canvas-topped automobile rattling and popping on the street, spewing noxious clouds of exhaust into the air. Closer, a couple of dogs were copulating in the mouth of an alley, and half a block farther an ox was voiding itself in front of a feed and grain store. Not exactly Paris, but I knew what Del was thinking. Once we got into Mexico, Yuma was going to seem like a metropolis.

We went to the Moorhead Hotel next and ordered a supper of flaky fried chicken, mashed potatoes and gravy, baked corn, green beans, strong coffee, then peach cobbler with cream for dessert—my mouth still waters when I recall the perfection of that meal. Afterward we paused on the boardwalk out front for Del to light another cigar.

"How many of those things did you steal?" I asked as he struck a match.

"No more than the d---ed government owes me," he growled, sucking furiously on the slim panatela until he had the tip glowing to his satisfaction.

I didn't ask him what he meant by that, or point out that the cigars he'd taken had probably been paid for out of Rynning's own pockets; in my limited association with Yuma's newest warden, he hadn't seemed the type to abuse the prison's annual budget.

Del—and yeah, I was starting to think of him as "Del" then, rather than Buchman—tossed his match into the dust, then pulled a silver-plated pocket watch from his vest. He studied its face in the dim light, then snapped the lid closed and returned it to his pocket. "We've got tickets on the eleven-forty to Gila Bend," he told me, expelling a thin cloud of smoke toward the sky. "It's just past seven now. We've got four hours to kill."

"I wouldn't turn down another beer," I said. "We can swing past a hardware store on our way to the Acme, and I'll pick up a rifle." I held my cuffed wrists up where he could see them. "Might be time to get rid of these, too. I ain't likely to abandon a tit as generous as Davenport's."

Failing to see the humor in my comment, Del said: "You ain't getting no rifle, so you can just shut up on that subject right now." Apparently coming to some kind of decision, he started down the street at a brisk stride. "Come on, Latham," he barked over his shoulder. "You're wasting my time."

The last of the light faded from the sky as we hoofed it toward the Southern Pacific depot on the morning side of town. Figuring Bachman intended to sit out the remaining hours on the platform waiting for the eastbound to arrive, I was more than a little surprised when he turned off a block before the station. Our destination was a two-story frame house on the outskirts of town, with a picket fence and rose bushes lining a gravel walkway. We paused at the gate, and Buchman yanked me close. "You try anything funny in here, Latham, and I'll have your a-- back on Prison Hill before they turn the lights out in the cells tonight. Savvy?"

I stared back silently. I don't know if it was the cooling breeze coming in off the desert, or the look in Buchman's eyes, but my scalp had started to crawl.

Del nodded as if satisfied with my response, even though I hadn't spoken a word. "Let's go."

We climbed the steps to the small porch and Del removed his hat, telling me with a look and a tip of his head to do the same. He pulled on a knob beside the door, and deep inside the house a bell chimed, announcing our presence. A colored woman answered the ring.

"Hello, Emma. You remember me, Del Buchman? I'm here to see Miss Goldie."

Emma gave me a quick once-over, and I noticed she didn't miss the exposed link of the cuffs holding my wrists together, even though I had it mostly hidden with my coat and hat.

"Miss Goldie expecting you, is she?"

"Yes, ma'am, she is."

The dark-skinned woman gave me another disparaging glance, then pushed the door open far enough for Buchman to grab the frame. "You can come on in," she said. "I'll tell Miss Goldie you's here."

You've probably guessed by now where we were. I'd known Goldie Werner when she ran the Dove's Roost in Tombstone, and I could tell from the decor that she hadn't changed her occupation. The wallpaper was ruby red and heavily flocked, and there was a mix of lithographs—manly scenes of huge bucks and rutting buffalo bulls, scattered among more demure prints of cavorting nymphs splashing about in woodland pools and tiny cherubs watching over nearly naked maidens reclining upon plush sofas—that filled the imagination as much as it did the empty spaces on the walls. A richly polished wooden staircase led to the second floor, and I could hear the gentle clack and roll of ivory across the green felt of a billiards table from the rear of the house. There were neither waiting customers, however, nor scantily clad whores batting their eyes for our attention. It was just me and Del, standing there with our hats in our hands like a couple of farm boys on our first trip to the city.

I think Goldie's presence swept into the parlor a full second before the actual blood and bone specimen made it. She was a large woman with a heavy bosom, dark-rooted blonde hair, and gray eyes, one lid slightly drooped. She was painted as if for business, although rumor persisted that she hadn't been upstairs with a customer in over ten years. Not a paying customer, at any rate. Her eyes grew wide when she saw me standing next to Del.

"Why, J.T. Latham, I thought you were. . . ." She looked at Del. "Is this the jasper you . . . ?" Then she laughed and gave Buchman a friendly poke in the ribs. "You are a card, Delmar, I'll swear if you ain't. You're the one who locked this poor boy up, and now you've gone and sprung him and brought him here to. . . ." She stopped, her eyes taking on a faraway expression. "Why, you old Cupid," she said, smiling knowingly. Tipping her head toward the stairs, she added: "At the top, first door on the left." She winked at me. "We'll talk later, J.T., there's someone upstairs who's going to be real happy when she sees you."

I hadn't said a word the whole time, but that was Goldie, and I didn't feel slighted.

"Move out, Latham," Del said gruffly, thrusting his chin toward the bannister and giving me a not-so-gentle shove in that direction. He sounded irritated, as though he hadn't cared for Goldie's ribbing, but knew there wasn't anything he could do about it. That cat was already out of its bag.

I didn't protest the rough handling. Ol' Cupid might not know how to respond to Goldie's teasing, but he'd d---ed sure put a kink in my tail if I tried something similar.

We paused at the top of the stairs, and Del checked his watch. "It's seven-thirty," he announced. "I'm gonna be knocking on this door at eleven sharp, and you'd d---ed well better have your boots on and your pants buttoned when I do, 'cause I'll haul you over to the depot buck naked before I waste ten seconds waiting on your sorry a--. Savvy?"

He handed me the watch with its lid still open, then reached past me to bang on the door. It immediately opened, as if whoever was inside had been listening at the keyhole. She was a little sprite of a gal, with dark hair, alabaster skin, an upturned nose, and wistful blue eyes. She squealed when she saw me, and launched herself into my arms as if jumping off a high bank into deep water. Or at least she tried to. My cuffs prevented us from becoming too intimate right there in the hall.

"J.T.!" Selma Metzler cried happily. "I thought you was locked up, honey."

Del brushed past me to grab Selma's arm. He backed her

into her room, dragging me after him with his free hand. "You listen sharp, sister. I've already warned this boy, and I'll do the same for you. Latham is under my authority. If he ain't here when I get back, or, if you've tried to help him escape in any way, I'll by d--- lock the both of you up and toss the keys into the river. You savvy what I'm telling you?"

"Hey," Selma protested, trying to twist free. "You're hurting me."

"I'll do worse than this if he ain't here, you just remember that, girlie." He gave me a look that said he fully expected me to try something stupid, yet felt duty bound to see his end of the bargain all the way through. I don't know who he'd made that bargain with, unless it was his conscience. "Eleven o'clock," he repeated.

"Sure, I'll be here," I said. I meant it, too. Those new clothes, a hot bath and shave, beer and a meal, and now this—I had no intention of mucking up any of it. At least not on purpose. But I was getting tired of those manacles. Raising my hands, I jangled the chain linking the cuffs on my wrists.

"Not on your life, champ," Del growled. "Them cuffs stay locked until you prove to me you can be trusted, and you ain't done that yet." Then he backed out of the room, pulling the door closed behind him.

"Geez, what an a--!" Selma exclaimed, rubbing her arm where Buchman had gripped it so hard. Then, smiling, she came up against me, allowing me time to raise my arms over her head so that she could slip inside my embrace.

And that right there is as much as I'm going to say on the subject of me and Selma Metzler, and it's a lot more than I would have brought up at all if not for what happened at about 10:55.

I was sitting on the side of the bed, happy as a lark and as sleepy as a fresh-fed kitten. I was still wearing my shirt and vest because of my manacles, but was naked on south of there. Selma was over by a dresser in a short silk robe, rummaging around in a cedar box sitting on the dresser top. When she came back, she was carrying one of those elastic garters all the fancy gals wore back then. This one was black, with a little red rose embroidered on one side.

"I've got something for you," she said. I reached for the scrunchy band, but she pulled it away. "Nope," she said, dropping to her knees in front of me. "This goes on your leg."

I laughed. "If you think I'm wearing a woman's garter out of here, you've gone daffy."

She looked at me with a wicked grin. "Just wait until you see how it fits."

I could feel my smile starting to slip. "I don't care how it fits."

"You will," she said, lifting my right foot in an attempt to slide the garter over it.

"Hey," I said, jerking my leg back.

"Dang it, J.T., just let me do this. You'll like it, I swear you will."

"Get that thing away from me."

She threw the garter on the floor. "I just wanted it to be a surprise," she said, pouting. Rising smoothly, she went to the dresser to pull something out of one of the drawers. I recall uttering a startled exclamation when she returned.

"See, you've got to learn to trust me," she admonished, handing me the gun. She kneeled in front of me again, and this time I didn't resist when she slid the garter over my ankle. "Do you know how it works?" she asked.

I nodded, turning the pistol over in my hand, examining it from every angle. It was a nickel-plated semi-auto, long and awkward in my hand after a lifetime of handling revolvers. There was a rearing mustang embossed on each hard rubber grip,

44

with the word Colt above it. From information stamped on the slide I learned it was a .380 Semi-Auto, Rimless and Smokeless, which meant it fired a .38-caliber slug using the newer, less corrosive gunpowder.

"Goldie gave me that about a month ago," Selma said, leaning back on her smooth white calves to regard the garter's positioning with a practiced eye. "She took it off a railroad dick that was roughing up one of the girls. Goldie gave him a tap on the noggin with a sawed-off baseball bat to teach him some manners, then took this pistol and a wad of cash from his pockets. She claimed it would enhance the learning experience. She also tossed his pants on the garbage heap down by the tracks, then had Tony . . . that's Goldie's man, the one she hired to take care of things when customers get too rowdy . . . anyway, she had Tony haul him to the depot and dump him in the middle of the platform." She giggled. "I surely would have loved to have seen his face when he woke up." Mocking a stern expression, she lowered her voice to as close to a masculine rumble as she could. "I'm the head bull on the Southern Pacific, and if you don't think my word carries plenty of weight around here, you don't know who you're dealing with, missy." She laughed and looked at me, and then her eyes turned misty. "It was me he roughed up, J.T." She worked a shoulder experimentally. "Wrenched it something frightful, he did."

I leaned forward to run my fingers gently through her hair. "What's his name?"

She hesitated, then shook her head. "I won't tell you. If I did and you saw him, you'd do something silly and get yourself thrown back into that h--- hole." She smiled. "It's OK, though. Tony managed to drop him a few times while carrying him to the depot in a wheelbarrow. Goldie says she reckoned he's learned his lesson. He sure ain't been back here since that night. Goldie says, if he ever comes, she'll kick his hind end over the line into Mexico and let the bandits have his hide. Goldie takes good care of us."

"She's a good woman," I agreed. "How long have you worked for her?"

"She left Tombstone the same year you got sent to the Hill. I came here a few months after she got set up." She took a deep breath, then plucked the Colt from my hand. "This here thing over the barrel moves backward, see?" She quickly went through the instructions for cocking and firing the semi-auto that someone had obviously recently given her. Then she handed me the pistol and a single, seven-round magazine. "I'm giving you this, J.T., only I don't have any extra bullets. Just what's already there. I want you to have it on account of you was always real nice to me when you came through Nogales. You was real nice to all us girls."

Right about now, you're probably thinking I'm some kind of monster for frequenting whores with enough regularity to be recognized and liked by them, but you've got to understand that things were different in those days. It was a simpler time, before we all got caught up in prim and proper. I'm not saying I'd do it now, but I'm sure not ashamed of having done it then.

I'll say this, too. I never roughed up any of the girls I visited along that border region. I treated them with respect and as much understanding as a rough-necked ol' boy like me could muster. Selma wouldn't have given me such a means of escape if I hadn't. Unfortunately I had to refuse her gift. Setting the pistol on the bedside table, I said: "I thank you, but I can't take it."

She looked surprised. "Why not?"

"Because the first thing Buchman's going to do when he comes through that door is search me for contraband."

Selma thought about that for a moment, then got a big grin on her face. "Then let's give him something to find." She shoved to her feet and walked around the bed to a dressing table. She came back toting one of those old, single-shot Philadelphia Derringers, the kind you loaded through the muzzle. I laughed when I saw it.

"Where'd you get that thing?"

"I've had it since I was a little girl. Don't make fun of it, J.T., it works just fine."

"What are you going to do with it?"

"I'm going to tuck it under your shirt so Delmar can find it." She hurried on when I started to shake my head. "He'll check your boots and pockets and around your belly first, but he won't think to check halfway up your leg. When he finds this," she tapped the Derringer with a slim finger, "he'll figure he's got you cold, and won't look no more."

Glancing at the garter, made for a slimmer leg than mine and already digging into the flesh just above my knee, I had to chuckle. "So that's what this is about?"

"Uhn-huh, Mister Smarty. Ain't you glad you come to see me, instead of one of them other girls?"

I told her I was, and didn't mention that this was Buchman's doing. I did wonder, and still do to this day, if Del had known about Selma and me back in Nogales. Although I never asked him, I always kind of figured he did, that it might've been something that came up when he was nosing around about my habits, before slipping below the border to arrest me in Moralos.

I slapped the magazine back into the grip-well and chambered a round. The action worked smooth as silk, and I was still smiling when I slid the pistol under Selma's garter. I shifted it around to the inside of my lower thigh, and made double-d---ed sure the hammer was lowered to the safety notch. Then I pulled my pants up, and dang if they didn't cover the pistol's budge pretty well. Those old Levis had baggier legs in those days. I slid my suspenders over my shoulders, tucked the Derringer behind the waistband at my back, then stooped to pull on my boots. I was just stomping my left heel into place when the door burst open.

"Stand back!" Del barked, startling a quick squeal out of Selma. He had his revolver drawn and his eyes were shifting rapidly as he stalked into the room.

"My, ain't you all big and bullish," Selma said in that breathy little voice she sometimes used when she wanted to charm a man.

"Save it for the rubes, girlie," Del growled, his eyes boring into mine.

"Howdy, Del. Did you have a good time, too?"

"Don't get cocky, Latham. I ain't in a mood for it. Stand up."

I did as told, automatically raising my hands and turning my back to him to be searched. He chuckled as he returned the revolver to his shoulder rig. "They taught you pretty good up there on the Hill, didn't they?"

"They were insistent," I replied mildly. I was trying to keep my tone light, but I knew it would be only seconds before he discovered Selma's Derringer hidden under my shirt, and I wasn't sure how he'd react. I was hoping he'd overlook a little pea-shooter like the muzzleloader—judging from its bore, I'd say it couldn't have been larger than .32 caliber—but if he found that Colt, I'd be lucky if he didn't send me straight back up the Hill into Rynning's custody. I'll tell you what, at that moment I was strongly questioning my decision to try to smuggle a gun past an old lawdog like Del Buchman.

Well, I was lucky, and I won't deny it. As Selma had predicted, Buchman started at the top and worked his way down. He found the Derringer almost immediately, and his face turned to thunder as he yanked out my shirttails and grabbed the gun. Then he spun me, chest first, into the wall, and I'll swear the whole building seemed to shudder under my impact. I started to reel backward, but he slammed a fist into my spine, right between my shoulder blades, and pinned me there. I felt the Derringer's muzzle digging into the flesh behind my right ear and closed my eyes. I squeezed them even tighter when I heard the hammer snick back to full cock.

"Jesus, Del, don't shoot!" I shouted, my words nearly lost under Selma's scream.

For a long moment the only sound I heard was the roaring of my own pulse. Then Del pulled the muzzle away and laughed. "You stupid con," he said. "There's no cap on this nipple. What were you gonna do, try to club me with it?" He pulled me around and shoved me back into the wall. "D---, criminals are dumb." He laughed again, then tossed the Derringer across the room and turned to Selma. "I ought to kick both your a--es up over your ears."

Selma was shaking her head rapidly, as if she hadn't a clue as to where I'd found the gun. I didn't fault her for looking after her own hide. H---, Del knew she was at least as guilty as I was, but that odd bit of luck with the missing cap had saved us both.

You might be wondering about that cap. I know I was. I'll swear it was on the gun when Selma handed it to me. I guess it came off either when Del yanked my shirt out of my pants, or while I was fumbling around trying to shove it under my waistband with cuffed wrists.

Thankfully Selma was right about Del abandoning the search when he found the Derringer. Keeping a firm hold on my collar, he manhandled me through the door and down the stairs, Selma's forlorn—"Good bye, J.T."—trailing after me.

Ready? Well, before we stopped for you to change disks on your recorder, I was telling you about Del Buchman finding Selma's little Philadelphia Derringer tucked inside the waistband of my trousers, and the sulky mood that put him in. He dragged me downstairs, making sure to slam me into the wall a few times along the way to express his displeasure.

Goldie showed up with a swarthy, broad-shouldered gent I took to be Tony, probably to investigate the ruckus we'd made in Selma's room, but I reckon Goldie could tell from Del's expression that whatever was going on wasn't anything she wanted to involve herself in. Goldie Werner had been running successful whore houses along the Arizona border for nearly two decades, and knew when to keep her lips zipped. She didn't say anything as Del propelled me through the door and all but pitched me, headfirst, off the front porch. Although I tumbled a-- over tea kettle across the bare yard, sweet Selma's nickel-plated Colt didn't budge an inch inside its lacy holster—bless that little gal's true-blue heart.

"On your feet, Latham," Del barked.

I stood, picking up my hat. My left cheek stung from its contact with the gravelly soil and my shoulder ached from its numerous collisions with the stairway wall, but I was more concerned with what Del was going to do next. I won't deny I was just about quaking in my boots for fear he'd haul me back to Rynning, but I guess he needed my knowledge of that country south of Moralos more than he needed to fulfill his promise of returning me to the Hill if I tried to double-cross him. I decided that was a good thing to know, but nothing I wanted to test the limits on, as we hiked to the Southern Pacific depot a couple of blocks away.

The 11:40 to Gila Bend rolled in about twenty minutes early, then spent thirty minutes taking on water and coal while the passengers from San Diego disembarked and those heading on east from Yuma mounted the iron steps to the twin passenger coaches hooked behind the mail car. Del led me to the second coach and pushed me onto a rear bench. His lips were squeezed tight as a poorly healed scar. He hadn't said a word since leaving Goldie's, and neither had I.

The rear car was nearly empty, probably fewer than a dozen passengers, all told. A drummer in a gaudy plaid suit and dusty derby asked to sit with us, but Del jabbed a thumb toward the front of the coach like a choleric hitchhiker, and the salesman took the hint.

Despite the tension between Del and myself, I was feeling good as the lights of Yuma fell to the rear. As the rails swung north, I could see the massive bulk of the penitentiary, squatting like a fat gargoyle above the town. There was a light glowing at the sally port and another in the warden's private residence outside the walls, but the rest of the giant structure seemed as dark as the souls of the men trapped inside its eight-foot-thick walls.

The tracks took us north for a while, then northeast along the south bank of the Gila. I was sitting next to the window on the river side of the car, facing forward with my cheek pressed against the frame, breathing in the cool desert air that flowed through the half-opened portal—intermittently interrupted by vagrant clouds of acidic coal smoke, laced with tiny, wind-borne cinders. But I didn't care. I was leaving Yuma behind at something like forty miles per hour, and would have ate mud if that's what it took.

We were about an hour out of the station when I told Del I needed to use the facilities. After giving me an annoyed glance, he pushed stiffly to his feet and accompanied me to the small chamber at the rear of the coach.

"I'm going to need these off," I said, holding up my cuffed wrists.

He peered inside the rocking privy, grunted at the size of the window, then loosened one of the manacles, only to close it a moment later around a brass rail bolted to the side wall. I had to bite my lip to keep from saying anything, although I'll admit it was nice to have at least one of the d---ed things off.

"You got two minutes," Del growled.

"I'm going to need five," I said, then shut the door in his face.

The first thing I did after throwing the dead bolt was to lower my trousers far enough to retrieve the Colt from its black lace holster. Although the gun had remained snuggly in place all night, its sharper edges, and especially the hammer spur, had been gouging into the soft flesh above my knee ever since leaving Goldie's. Figuring it would be too risky to carry it in my pocket, I scooted everything—pistol and garter both—down until it was cradled inside my right boot top with the butt sloping forward for an easy grab. Well, as easy as it was ever going to get, buried inside my boot and under my pant leg.

Del was glowering suspiciously as he led me to my seat—I'd lost a lot of ground with him over that Derringer—but, instead of reattaching the shackle to my other wrist, he fastened it to the decorative, wrought-iron scroll of the seat's arm.

I studied him curiously as he locked the cuff. "You ain't getting soft in your old age, are you, Del?"

"Shut up, Latham. I'm going outside for a smoke, but I'll be poking my head back inside from time to time, in case you get any more fancy notions like that one you got at Goldie's."

"I reckon I'm fresh out of fancy," I replied, grinning.

"You'd better get fresh out of that smart-a--ed attitude of yours, before I go looking for a crowbar to pry it out."

He pocketed the key, then exited the coach, pulling the door closed, none too gently, behind him.

I was tired, and after a few minutes I pulled my coat over my shoulders and curled up on the hard bench as best I could. It wasn't comfortable, but I've slept in worse locations, and it wasn't long before I dozed off.

It was still dark when a change in the train's cadence eased me from my slumber. I opened my eyes. Del was seated across from me, arms folded, his head bobbing loosely, although he came instantly awake when I sat up, his hand sliding instinctively inside his coat for the revolver. I smelled whiskey on him, and knew it hadn't been a cigar he'd gone outside for.

Sensing the train's slackening speed, Del twisted around to peer out the window. There was a light up ahead, a red-shaded lantern swinging steadily back and forth in a stationmaster's hand, signaling a stop.

"Where are we?" I asked.

"Sentinel, more than likely."

"What time is it?"

He hauled out his pocket watch. "Three a.m."

I leaned close to the window to see what I could in the moonlight. We'd come through Sentinel on our way to Yuma in '03, but hadn't stopped. It was, to my knowledge, a refueling station for coal and water, and of little use otherwise. There were a few buildings scattered around the station house, some scrubby trees, a water tank, and not much else. Then the engine began to brake firmly enough for the cars to roll forward with their customary crash of steel couplings that shook everyone from their slumber.

The conductor came down the aisle, swaying with a natural rhythm to the coach. "Just a quick stop, folks. Need to let a couple of passengers off."

I leaned back in my seat and chuckled. "Who in their right mind would get off out here?" I wondered aloud. Then my smile faded at the taut grin on Buchman's face.

"On your feet," he ordered, loosening my cuff just long enough to return it to my free wrist.

I stood reluctantly. I could tell from the way the bushes were whipping back and forth in the light from the station house that it was windy. It was probably going to be cold, too, the way nights in the desert often are at that time of year.

The train stopped and we got off, and then it pulled forward again, couplings clashing as it slowly picked up speed. I stood on the station platform and watched it grow smaller, the single lantern hanging from the rear of the caboose pulling in on itself like a rapidly healing wound. The elderly stationmaster blew out his lantern and set it inside the shack that passed for the depot, then hobbled down the steps and made his way to a small frame house, its wood siding scoured by blowing sand to the same dull gray as the rest of the town.

"Ain't very talkative, is he?" I observed as the lamp inside the stationmaster's house was extinguished, reducing the structure to a dark blob against the lighter desert behind it.

"I doubt he's got much to talk about out here," Del replied.

"You'd think he'd be curious about us."

"I expect his curiosity's already been satisfied on that subject."

There was an ungodly roar from behind the depot, then a pop like a gunshot. Looking relieved, Del said: "Grab your stuff. We're pulling out."

My stomach was already knotting up as I followed Del down off the platform. The racket grew louder, a mechanical barrage of valves and pistons, seemingly at war with each other. After a moment the gnashing smoothed out, settling into a low, steady rumble like that of an asthmatic cougar. Seconds later a hulking steel giant lumbered around the side of the station and rolled to a stop a few feet away. Huge brass headlights mounted in front of the fenders reminded me of the bulging eyes of a child's nightmare, the exposed front chassis its sinister snarl. The roar of the engine quieted to an idle, and the door swung open.

Del quickly stepped forward to shake the driver's hand. "D---it, Spence, when I didn't see you, I was afraid you hadn't made it," he said loudly, above the digestive-like sounds of the machine.

"Sure, I made 'er. I was just catchin' me some shut-eye out back, where the old man who runs this s--- hole couldn't give me the evil eye." He was of average height but thickly built, with a head like a rock fixed to the top of a three-foot section of cross-tie instead of shoulders, his face a battered map of past brawls. He wore a linen duster over heavy wool trousers and a red-and-green striped sweater. A pair of goggles hung from around the stump that was his neck. Eyeing me with the scrutiny of a horse trader judging a possible purchase, he said: "I see ye got 'im."

"Yeah, I got him. Rynning didn't want to give him up, but there wasn't much he could say when I showed him the governor's letter and the pardon."

"Still cuffed, though."

Del chuckled. "He got a little too ambitious back in Yuma and tried to steal a gun."

"That wasn't stealing," I protested. "It was a gift from an old friend."

"It was one of those old, single-shot muzzleloading popguns a whore gave him," Del corrected. "The dumb a-- forgot to cap it."

The driver laughed good-naturedly. "Ye've gotta cap 'em, lad," he told me. "They won't fire if ye don't."

"It was a gift," I repeated stubbornly. "I didn't cap it because I didn't want it going off and shooting ol' Cupid there in the butt."

Del swung around. "You put a cork in that trap of yours, Latham, or I'll by God cork it with my fist."

I looked at the other guy and winked. I knew I was risking a punch in the nose for my trouble, but something was telling me to push back a little, keep the old lawman off balance.

Buchman threw his gear—a leather valise and a pair of saddlebags, plus my stuff—into a wooden trunk bolted to the automobile's rear fender, then shrugged into a heavy corduroy coat with a fur collar and toggle buttons.

While he was doing that, the burly driver came over. "Spencer McKenzie," he said, thrusting a mechanic's greasy paw toward me. "I reckon ye're Latham?"

"J.T. Latham."

"Well, best we be gettin' mounted, J.T. Latham, for 'tis a long trip to Moralos, and a poor road, to boot. Assumin' we can find it."

I hesitated. "We're going to Moralos from here? Ain't that taking the long way in?"

"Aye, but 'twas Mister Davenport's orders, and I won't question a man who's payin' me seventy-five dollars a month. Come on now, time's a-wastin'."

"What is this thing?" I asked as we approached the automobile.

"She's a Nineteen-Ought-Six Berkshire!" he exclaimed proudly. "Belongs to Lord Davenport, she does, though he's hired me to wrangle the thing for him." He patted the hood as affectionately as a cowpuncher might the shoulder of a favorite horse. "She's got a thirty-five horsepower engine and a transmission guaranteed never to strip a gear, which makes me love her all the more out in these lonely parts."

What he was said makes perfect sense now, but it might as well have been ancient Greek at the time. The only thing I knew with any certainty was that I'd never ridden in an automobile in my life, and I sure as Hades didn't want to start then.

Laughing good-naturedly, Spence said: "Don't act so glum, lad. 'Tis the future ye're lookin' at here."

Well, it was the future, all right, and we all know it now, but, that night in Sentinel, the thought of crawling inside that huffing contraption had my stomach tied in knots that just kept drawing tighter and tighter.

Del was already in the back seat. He motioned me into the front. "Where I can keep an eye on you," he said, then tapped the revolver under his arm. "I'll be keeping my hand close to this, too, in case you start thinking unhealthy thoughts, like trying to jump and run."

"Why don't you take these cuffs off so I can put my coat on?" I said. "It's going to get cold when we start moving."

"You're gonna freeze your a-- off," he agreed cheerfully, and I knew he was getting back at me for that Cupid remark.

Climbing into the huge front seat, I pulled my coat over me like a blanket. Spencer got in behind the big wooden steering wheel and began fiddling with levers and pedals and knobs and who knew what all, and the next thing I knew we were moving. I remember pressing back into the deep leather of the Berkshire's seat, bracing my heels against the floorboard as the vehicle lurched over the iron rails of the Southern Pacific tracks and gradually picked up speed. Although the car was equipped with headlamps, Spence hadn't bothered to light them. With the moon nearly full and the lights of the tiny station quickly fading behind us, we didn't need them.

For the first hour or so it seemed like we were just weaving aimlessly through the desert, circling sprawling patches of prickly pear or creeping through shallow arroyos, but after a while Spence found a trail that appeared to follow the natural contours of the land, taking us southeast toward the Sonita Mountains. I knew those Sonitas pretty well, having traveled through that country numerous times before my arrest, and figured Spence intended to skirt the mountain range's barren western slopes until we could turn south to Moralos. From the southern tip of the Sonitas, the town would be no more than eighty miles away. If we didn't end up driving into a cañon and breaking our necks, we'd probably be there sometime that afternoon.

We were making good time in spite of the ruggedness of the terrain—a whole lot better than we could have done on horseback, that's for sure—and as much as I hated to admit it, I was growing impressed with the automobile's capabilities. We were probably doing twenty miles an hour over the flatter stretches, dodging jack rabbits and cactus beds with a dexterity I would have thought impossible for something so big. And the odd thing is, I was enjoying it. I was having fun. Coney Island roller coaster kind of fun, and if you've ever been to Coney Island or ridden the Loop-the-Loop, you know what I'm talking about.

The moon dropped toward the horizon and the light grew dimmer. Spence finally had to stop and light the massive head-lamps. While he was doing that, Del leaned over the back of the seat and loosened one of my cuffs.

"Put your coat on," he said gruffly. "You keep trembling like that, you're liable to force us off the road."

"What road?" I demanded between chattering teeth.

Del guffawed as I shivered into my coat and quickly buttoned it to my throat. I was already wearing the deer-hide gloves I'd picked up at Hunsaker's, and had tugged my hat down almost to my eyes. I could have used a blanket, or, better yet, a heavy buffalo robe, but I doubted if Spence had one in the Berkshire's wooden trunk.

We continued on through the night and into the next day, the Berkshire's engine humming smoothly. We almost made the border before one of the tires went flat. Spence told us not to worry and hopped out of the car. Five minutes later he had a wagon jack under the frame and was cranking the vehicle into the air. He removed the tire with tools dug from the bottom of the trunk, patched the inner tube with a piece of rubber and some glue—not the first time it had been repaired that way, I noticed—then had me refill it with a tire pump while he checked the oil and the water in the radiator. He added gas from a five gallon can strapped to a rear fender, then hauled out some sandwiches and beer for breakfast. Thirty minutes later, we were on our way.

The trail veered sharply east below the Sonitas, but our destination lay more to the southeast, across a rumpled land of cactus and rocks and a stifling heat that had us shedding our coats before midmorning. Spence had the Berkshire to a crawl as he wove through a jungle of cholla and ocotilla, the spiny plants gouging unrelentingly at the automobile's paint, peeling it back in thin curling whiskers. Spence was cursing steadily as he battled the huge wheel, while Del and I clung to whatever handhold we could find as the pitching vehicle bulled through the desert flora. When we came to a low-banked, sandy wash late in the morning, Spence wrestled the Berkshire into its middle and cut the engine.

"What are you doing?" Del demanded. "We can't stop here."

"I can," Spence wheezed, pulling a wool cap from his head and tossing it on the floor. He slumped back in his seat with his arms limp at his sides, muscles twitching.

"What if it won't start again?" Del asked worriedly.

"Then ye can shoot the d---ed thing and put it out of its misery." He lolled his head toward me. "That trail from Tucson to Sentinel was open all the way, but this bugger has nearly wrung me dry, lad."

"Got any water?"

"Aye, five gallons in the trunk for the radiator and a canteen for me own use, but there's a beer or two back there yet, and I'd prefer that, if ye're doin' the fetchin'."

"I'm fetching," I said, and jumped out.

"You stay where I can see you!" Del shouted after me.

I'd already lifted the lid on the trunk by then, shutting off his view to the rear, and I won't deny that, brief as it might have been, the idea of slipping Selma's pistol from my boot, then stepping around the side of the car and pulling the trigger, flashed through my mind. They wouldn't have been the first men I killed, either, but the fact is, although I'd already shot a number of men at that point in my life, I wasn't a killer. Or rather, I wasn't a murderer, and there's a difference. You may think me brash to admit that on a machine that's recording my every word, but I'll be confessing to a lot worse before we're through. Of my many adventures, that final trip into Mexico to rescue Abby Davenport and her children was the bloodiest.

Rummaging through the trunk, I located a couple of bottles of *Dos Equis,* wrapped inside a dripping wad of burlap. Seeing the familiar double Xs brought a smile to my face. *Dos Equis* was illegal in the United States and its territories, and wouldn't have been available if not for the smuggling that went on along the border. Taking the bottles around front, I opened one for Spence and the second for myself, and laughed at Del's scowl.

"Get your a-- back there and fetch me a bottle, Latham."

"This is all there was," I replied, tipping my head and taking a healthy swallow.

Spence backed me up. "Just the two left, Delmar. Sorry."

"Besides, you being an acting sheriff for Pima County, you wouldn't want to drink anything brought into the country illegally," I told him.

Del grumbled but didn't push it. Spence was drinking leisurely, savoring his beer, although I noticed his hand still trembled every time he raised the bottle to his lips. After several minutes, he belched contentedly and said: "Boys, I be fair bushed. I'll get ye to Moralos, don't fret yeself on that, but I'm going to have to sit here a spell to catch me wind."

"It doesn't look like it's your wind that's bothering you," Del observed.

"Aye, 'tis the truth, and then some." He set his bottle aside and raised both hands to tentatively flex his fingers. They moved slowly, quivering from the strain, and I could see the pain in his eyes as he forced them closed.

Del was less sympathetic. "We ain't got that kind of time, McKenzie." He glanced at the sun, nearly straight overhead. "It's still twenty miles or more to Moralos, and I told Davenport we'd be there by noon today at the latest."

"What ye told the old bugger isn't me concern, Delmar. It'll be a couple of hours, at least, before I can drive again. Unless ye want to wrestle this beastie yeself."

Del glared but didn't say anything. Then, out of the blue and surprising all three of us, I said: "I'll drive."

"Shut up, Latham," Del growled.

"Hold on, now, Delmar," Spence said, squirming around for a better look, as if sizing me up. "Do ye think ye can, lad?"

"Sure."

"My a--," was Del's opinion, but Spence chuckled.

"Ye may be right, Delmar, but better to give the lad a chance than while away the day waitin' for the trembles to drain from me arms."

"He'll wreck it."

"I can handle it."

Turning to Del, Spence said: "I say we give the lad a try."

Del was eyeing me suspiciously. I knew he was remembering the Derringer I'd tried to smuggle out of Selma's room. He didn't trust me, and I guess I couldn't really blame him. But he also wanted to get to Moralos as soon as possible, and sitting around in the middle of a dry wash twenty miles short of his goal wasn't going to get him there.

"If you wreck this thing, Latham, I'll rip that pardon of yours to shreds and toss it to the winds."

"You just hang onto that pardon if you want to reach Sabana without losing your hide to bandits or Indians," I replied, my temper finally beginning to stir.

Starting an automobile in 1907 was a lot more complicated than it is today, but thankfully Spence was there to walk me through it, adjusting the choke and spark and fuel mixture, then having me crank the engine like I was whipping up a batch of homemade ice cream while he coaxed the slumbering creature to life. It didn't hurt, Spence told me later, that the engine was still warm. The Berkshire sputtered to life on the third spin, and Spence quickly adjusted the controls until the motor was once again purring smoothly. I've got to admit I found myself liking the sound.

I tossed the crank under the seat and told Spence to shove over, then held my wrists up where Del could see them. "I can't drive with these on."

Del started sputtering in a fair imitation of the Berkshire engine on the crank's second spin, but Spence cut him off.

"The lad's right, Delmar. Either remove his cuffs or wait until I'm fit enough to drive again."

Del partially conceded by freeing my right wrist. I could drive, but I'd have a heck of a time explaining myself if I escaped, then showed up in a town with manacles dangling from my left arm.

Spence turned out to be a pretty decent instructor, and it wasn't long before we were hopping down the middle of that wash like a cottontail. Del was cussing up a blue streak at my neck-snapping jerks, but Spence only laughed and increased the throttle. After a bit he closed the choke, then retarded the spark, and we were soon chugging along at a good clip, although still in first gear. After about a hundred yards in low, with me primarily getting the hang of steering, Spence explained the art of shifting gears, and it wasn't long before we were fairly flying along.

We reached the main road between Moralos and Nogales around midafternoon, and Spence reluctantly reclaimed the driver's seat. I don't think he wanted to show up in Moralos sprawled across the passenger side of the car like a hitchhiker, not with Ed Davenport paying his wages. Del, the b------, snapped that left cuff back on my wrist as soon as I slid out from behind the wheel. Thirty minutes later, the little village rose into view as if sprouted amidst a forest of cholla.

For its size, I think Moralos had changed even more than Yuma in the years since I'd been away. Jorge Archuleta had enlarged his *cantina,* there was an adobe wall surrounding the well in the center of the plaza to keep the goats and hogs and such out of the drinking water, and the livery on the north side of the plaza had added more corrals behind its stables. But what really caught my eye was a new, two-story structure with the word *Hotel* painted in bright red letters above the entrance.

Moralos had grown up with its new hotel and developing businesses, but as we entered the town in a cloud of dust, rapidly scattering chickens, barking dogs, and yelling, laughing children out of our way, I noticed that it hadn't grown out. There were still only thirty or forty small adobe homes surrounding the central plaza, making me wonder where all the extra commerce was coming from to justify the village's expansion.

At the hitch rails in front of Archuleta's *cantina* was a burro loaded with dried cholla for firewood, a couple of nondescript horses swatting lazily at the few flies out and about in that kind of heat, and a two-wheeled contraption the likes of which I'd never seen before. As soon as Spence brought the Berkshire to a halt in front of the hotel, I walked over for a closer look. Del yelled for me to get my hind end back where he could keep an eye on me *muy pronto,* but I was growing weary of Del's barking, and ignored him.

The machine looked like one of those safety bicycles I'd seen in Yuma, right down to the pedals. But it also had an engine mounted inside its vee-shaped frame, and a blue, flat-paneled gas tank under the top rail between the seat and handlebars. The word *Wagner* was scripted across the tank. [*Ed. Note:* A safety bicycle is an obsolete term for a bicycle with equal-sized wheels, versus the earlier penny-farthing models with their overly large front wheel and tiny rear wheel; the Wagner Motorcycle Company (1901-1914) was founded by George Wagner, in Saint Paul, Minnesota.]

What had caught me off guard wasn't so much that I was looking at what was essentially a motorized bicycle, or motorcycle, but that I'd come across it way out there. Two five-gallon gas cans were strapped like saddlebags on either side of the rear wheel, with a bedroll and flat-bottomed portmanteau fastened crosswise behind the seat. A dented coffee pot was tied to the bedroll, and an empty rifle scabbard with elaborate floral carvings, dyed in shades of red, green, and gold, was slanted to the rear on the bike's right side. A dripping two-gallon water bag was hung off the left to counterbalance the weight of the rifle.

I stood there for several minutes just staring at the thing, and it was about then, even more than seeing all those automobiles in Yuma, that I began to comprehend the changes that were about to overwhelm the world. Staring at the motorcycle, I recalled Spence's comment from the night before: *'Tis the future ye're lookin' at here.*

It was indeed.

When I finally returned to the Berkshire, Del and Spencer had already disappeared into the hotel, and I wandered in after them. The place was still fairly new and in good repair, the lobby pleasantly cool after the blazing desert sun. A middle-aged Mexican in a white linen suit manned the register. Spotting my cuffs, he motioned toward the stairs leading to the second floor.

"*Señor* Buchman says you are to go upstairs immediately."

"Which room?"

Solemnly the clerk informed me that Davenport had rented the entire north side of the upper floor for his private quarters.

I whistled. "*Hombre rico,* eh?" I queried, grinning.

"*Sí,* very much." And still not a trace of a smile.

We were speaking Spanish, and I ought to explain that a lot of the conversations that took place after we reached Moralos were in Spanish. Having spent a good many years trading south of the border, I was fairly fluent in the language, although lacking the formality of a scholar. Mine was more a polyglot of the border Spanish that dominated that region, a mongrel collection of Mexican, American, and Indian dialects. Del and Spence could get along in Spanish, but Davenport didn't speak it at all, despite numerous business dealings in Mexico and, I'd find out later, an office in Hermosillo. It was Spence who confided in me that Davenport considered the language beneath him, and that he considered it a strength when dealing with Mexican officials to have them bring along their own interpreter.

But I'm not going to try to keep all that straight—what was spoken in Spanish and what wasn't. It would bog down the story, and probably confuse me as much as it would you. Just know that after we left Moralos, most of what was spoken to anyone other than Davenport, Del, or Spence was probably in the language of the land.

There were eight rooms on the hotel's second floor, four on the north side of a long hallway, and four on the south. Hearing the low rumble of masculine voices from one of the middle rooms, I went there first. Halting in the doorway, I found Del and Spence standing stiffly before a middle-aged man perched on the edge of a cushioned chair, pulling on a pair of expensive, lace-up riding boots. He was of average height and thick through the middle, the way some men get at that age—although he didn't look soft, at all. His hair, what was left of it, was gray and curly, with a few strays on top that caught the light from the open window. His face was square and craggy, like a sculpture inlaid with a pair of cold blue stones for eyes. Other than sideburns extending just below his lobes on either side, he was clean-shaven.

Davenport saw me as soon as I walked into the room, and his first words were: "So this is the infamous J.T. Latham, whose skills we couldn't survive without?"

I didn't like the guy from that moment on.

"That's him," Del confirmed, minus the bluster I'd endured ever since he'd sprung me from Yuma. "Although you recall I never said we couldn't do it without him. Just that our odds of getting there undetected were gonna be better if we had him to guide us."

Davenport glanced at my wrists. "Why is he still handcuffed? Don't you trust him?"

"I'd trust him as far as I would any con, and more than most, but that doesn't mean I'd turn my back on him. He tried to slip a whore's pistol past me in Yuma, so I figured another day or two in cuffs might convince him that. . . ."

"A whore's pistol?"

"Yes, sir."

"From a whorehouse?"

Del shifted uncomfortably. "Yes, sir."

"Tell me, Buchman," Davenport said softly, "what were you doing in a whorehouse?"

Clearing his throat, Del said: "We was waiting for the train and had a few hours to kill before. . . ."

"Are you also responsible for those bruises on his face?"

"No, sir, that was done before I got him released."

Davenport stood. "Is what this man says about your skills true, Latham? Do you know that country south of here like the back of your hand?"

"Pretty much."

"He was raised by the Yaquis," Del interjected.

"Were you?" Davenport asked, never taking his eyes away from mine.

"Not exactly raised by them. I spent a few years among them as a captive. Most of the land south and west of here was their home until the *Federales* chased them deeper into the *páramos.*"

The old man—and I call him that only because of his position in the group—scowled at my reply. "*Páramos?*"

"The badlands."

"Speak English, Latham. We're not savages."

See what I mean?

"Are there still Yaquis between us and Sabana?" Davenport went on.

"Probably."

"And bandits?"

"Possibly, although I'd worry more about the Yaquis."

"Can you get us around them?"

"Maybe. The Yaquis are the ones who know that country like the backs of their hands. They're the ones who showed it to me.

It'll be a hit or miss thing, but if they're nearby, they'll probably find us."

I could tell my reply bothered the old man. He wanted assurances, not conjecture. "If we are found, can you deal with them?" he asked.

I thought about that for a moment, remembering Old Toad, who was the war leader of the Dead Horse clan, and the man who had tried to teach me the ways of the People, as the Yaquis referred to themselves, for the three years that I'd lived with them. Deciding there was no point in lying, I said: "If we're caught, they'll kill us." I was looking Davenport straight in the eye when I said it, wanting him to understand the risks we'd all be taking venturing into that country. "Those they don't kill outright, they'll torture, and it'll take us a long time to die."

"Us?" He cocked a brow curiously. "All of us . . . even you?"

"Especially me," I replied flatly.

Davenport was silent as he mulled over my response. After a moment he turned to Spence. "Take the Berkshire to the livery and cover it with a tarp to keep the chickens from crapping all over the seats. Tell Pedro that he's to watch it like it's his sister's virginity, and that, if I find any evidence that it's been tampered with, I'll shoot him in the foot. Check the gas and oil, too, and let him know that if I come back and discover even a pint of either is missing, I'll shoot him in both feet."

"Aye, sir," Spence said, heading for the door.

"And McKenzie."

Spence stopped and glanced over his shoulder. "Sir?"

"Be sure Pedro understands that I mean exactly what I say, all right?"

Spence hesitated, then nodded rigidly and ducked into the hall as if eager to escape.

When he was gone, Davenport returned his full attention to

me. "Has Buchman filled you in on what we're attempting to do?"

"Not much. He said your wife and kids were taken off a train by a bandit named Chito Soto, and that we're going to slip into Sabana the back way to deliver the ransom."

Davenport graced Del with a questioning glance.

"I figured it best if he didn't know too much till I got him down here," Del explained.

"For once, I agree with you." Davenport motioned me to a table set against the wall under the room's single window. A large map of the Mexican state of Sonora was spread out across it, weighed down by a German Mauser pistol on one side and a bottle of Old Overholt whiskey on the other. A brass compass sat in the middle, directly atop the town of Sabana.

"Since you know this region so well, tell me how we're to reach our destination without becoming fodder for bandits or Indians," Davenport said.

I studied the map's crude contours, its squiggly lines that represented the steep-walled *barrancos* that could take days to find your way through, and the inverted vees that were supposed to be its mountain ranges. Then I laughed. "You'd need a better map than this for me to trace you a path."

The old man's face reddened. "Nevertheless, this is the only map available to us at the moment. If you'd like to fill in the blanks, feel free to do so."

I ran a finger down the map in a serpentine path. "Right through here, more or less. It's five days in the saddle if we push it, which we'd d---ed well better if what Buchman said about them threatening to carve up your wife and kids is true." I glanced at the older man, wondering if he knew how serious his wife's position was, how much danger his children were in. "Knowing that part of the country, I'd say the odds are good that it is. Do you have a contact yet?"

"I sent a man to Tres Pinos by rail last week to see what he could learn of the situation. I was hoping to bring the negotiations closer to Arizona. Three days later I received a wooden box in the mail containing the man's head. It was packed in sand, and had a bullet hole behind his right ear."

I swore softly. "Then, yeah, they mean what they say." After a pause, I asked: "You've got connections down here, why haven't you gone through them?"

Davenport considered my question for a moment, then nodded toward the next room. I don't think I've mentioned yet that all of those rooms along the north wall were joined by interconnecting doorways. Davenport was renting the whole side, and had the interior doors thrown open to create a cross breeze.

We went into the room next door, where a dark-skinned man sitting in a rocking chair was covering both doors with a sawed-off, pump-action shotgun. Although dressed in the traditional garb of a *vaquero*—dark trousers split up the side to show off his *calzoncillos,* or ankle-length cotton drawers, a gray linen shirt I suspect had once been white, and a dark, short-waisted jacket—he looked more Indian than Spanish to me. A sweat-stained sombrero rested on the floor beside him, and he was armed, in addition to the shotgun, with a large-frame revolver holstered at his waist. He studied me closely as I entered the room, his eyes lingering for a moment on the manacles, then shifting back to Davenport as if awaiting instructions. I'll say this for him, at least he didn't jump to his feet to kowtow before the big man like Del seemed to be doing.

Davenport, for his part, ignored the stocky *Indio* as he led me to a stack of unpainted wooden crates. My eyes widened when I read the lettering stenciled across the three largest boxes: *M1895 Colt-Browning Machine-gun.* Stacked beside them were another twelve crates, smaller but heavier, reading: *.30 Government.* Suddenly the old man's desire to take the back way into Sabana

70

made perfect sense.

"This," Davenport said heavily, "is the ransom Chito Soto has demanded of me, and which was in my power to deliver. I believe you can understand now why using the railroad is out of the question. I'm told that news of these guns is already spreading across Sonora, and that is another reason haste is so imperative. We have to get these guns to Sabana before Porfirio Díaz's *Federales* learn of our whereabouts, and ride to intercept us." He swung around to face me, pegging me solidly with those hard, blue eyes. "So I'll ask you once more, Latham? Can you get us there . . . in time?"

Excerpted from:
A Description of the Model 1895 Colt Machine-gun,
Its Use and Operation
by
Colonel Robert Percy, (U.S. Army, Retr.)
The Potomac Press
1952

The Model 1895 Colt Machine-gun was the United States' first gas-operated, belt-fed, automatic firearm. [*Ed. Note:* The hyphenated Colt-Browning designation is a fairly recent adaptation; its use in the Latham transcript is to avoid confusion with other Colt firearms referenced in his recordings.]

[It was] chambered in 6mm. Lee Navy, 7×57mm. Mauser, .30-40 Krag, .30-06 Springfield, .303 British, and 7.62×54mm.R [Russian].

[The gun's] heavy fore end was largely the result of the Model 1895's unique gas operation, which employed a swinging piston under the barrel. Upon firing, gas from the cartridge's detonation [muzzle blast] was channeled through a port approximately 15 cm. [six inches] from the muzzle, actuating the piston in a rearward swing [like a lever-action rifle in reverse], thus

72

chambering the next round as it expelled the empty brass. . . .
[*Ed. Note:* Small changes have been made to the text of Percy's
description to clarify the gun's operation for persons unfamiliar
with military/firearms jargon.]

When the gun was positioned close to the ground, this
backward motion of the piston would often dig a small trench
under the barrel, resulting in the gun's nickname of "potato
digger".

Feed was from the left side of the firearm, via a cloth ammunition belt carried in a box that mounted to the gun's frame.
[*Ed. Note:* Latham makes no mention of these boxes in his
recordings, and, in fact, seems to imply that they didn't have
them.]

Tripods were adjustable for elevation and free traverse movement . . . with a rate of fire of approximately 400 rpm. [rounds
per minute]. The gun weighed 16kg. [about 35 pounds];
standard-issue tripods added another 28 pounds to the load.

SESSION FOUR

The sun was down but it was still light out when I left the Moralos Hotel and made my way across the plaza to the stables. Spence McKenzie already had the Berkshire under wraps when I got there, and was sitting on the passenger sideboard, smoking a cigarette. Squinting at me through a haze of smoke, he said: "The old man about done making threats, is he?"

"I doubt it."

Spence shook his head ruefully. "I've been workin' for the ol' boy nigh onto two years now. 'Tis a fair job when he's away on business, though stressful when he's close by. That thing he said about shootin' Pedro in the foot, he means it."

"I figured as much."

Spence sighed and leaned back against the automobile's door, sheathed in canvas. "When are we leavin', did he say?"

"It appears we're waiting for more mules. He told Buchman he sent a man to Nogales a few days ago to pick up a couple more head." I glanced inside the livery's main entrance. It looked cool and inviting, but was empty.

"They're out back," Spence said. "Four stout mules and a half dozen saddle horses, minus what Davenport's man took with him to Nogales. The old fool's hired four of us to handle his pack string, as if two weren't twice as many as we needed."

I squatted in the dirt nearby and Spence tossed me the makings. "Who's he got?" I asked, stripping a piece of paper from the pack and shaping it with a forefinger.

"Luis Vega and Carlos and Felix Perez. I think them Perezes are cousins, though I wouldn't swear to it. Do ye know 'em, by chance?"

"I've heard of Vega."

"Aye, a good man, that one. The Perez boys hail from over around Chihuahua. Showed up in Tucson about a year ago. They're good packers, or so they'd tell ye, although I don't believe I'd turn me back on either of 'em."

I nodded as I put the finishing touches on my cigarette. After pulling the drawstring closed with my teeth, I returned the sack and the little bible of papers to Spence. He offered me his cigarette to light my smoke from.

"You said he's got four packers," I remarked casually, wanting to feel him out, to know what kind of man I'd be sharing the trail with.

"Aye, I'll be the big chief when it comes to the mules, though I kinda wish I hadn't told the old bugger I used to pack for Crook against the 'Paches."

I looked up at that. "You rode with Crook?"

"Packed for him and Miles both. I was with Lawton when he went into Mexico after Geronimo in 'Eighty-Six. All the way to the Sierra Madres and back, and not a mule lost out of me own string, although I'll allow 'twas a hard trip for man and beast alike, and more than a few that didn't come back from those high, godless peaks."

I chuckled. "I'll be d---ed. I was just a kid, living in Holbrook, when troopers from Fort Bowie brought the last of the Apaches up there to ship them to Florida. I remember the soldiers held the Indians outside of town, afraid some of the good citizen of Holbrook might start taking pot shots at them if they were brought to the depot. They might've, too. Folks around there sure did hate the Apaches."

"A lot of 'em still do."

I nodded absently, recalling that early September day when Pa took me and my brothers out to see the defeated warriors. The soldiers wouldn't let us get too close, but even from a distance we could recognize some of the more important figures. There were several, like old Nana, and I think Peaches was there, but it's Geronimo who stands out vividly in my mind, sitting with quiet dignity in the back of a wagon, guards on every side and throngs of gawkers feathering the nearby hills for a better view. It was like a circus had come to town, and it shames me still to remember the way the old warrior stared out over our heads into that vast land he had to know he was leaving forever. It was as if no other creature existed on earth but him, and I felt like an intruder watching him, no better than a peeping Tom.

"Well, 'twas a sorry business, for sure," Spence acknowledged after an awkward silence. "It did end the Apache Wars, though. I doubt there be a soul alive in Arizona today who doesn't believe the old bugger would've jumped the reservation again if he'd been allowed to stay."

"Likely he would have," I agreed, but I thought Spence was right, too, when he called it a sorry business, shipping that proud old man and his followers out of the territory like so much cattle to market.

Over by the *cantina* a tall man in a knee-length, leather duster was standing beside the Wagner motorcycle, pulling on a pair of gloves with flared gauntlets. He was wearing what looked like a leather helmet, and had goggles pushed up on his forehead. His boots were tall, disappearing up under his riding coat—additional protection from cactus, I supposed.

Spence and I watched as he straddled the machine, still up on its rear axle stand. He fiddled a moment with a pair of controls mounted to the top of the frame, then started pedaling like his life depended on it. After a few seconds, Spence chuckled. "That boy ought to get hisself a bicycle. He'd be a mile down the road by now, and no less exhausted."

I didn't reply. I'd come to the livery to have a look at Davenport's mules, but I was wishing I'd gone to the *cantina,* instead. I would have liked to have talked to that guy, find out who he was and where he was going. But mostly I wanted to ask him about the Wagner, and why he was riding that instead of a horse.

He kept pedaling vigorously until the whole bike jumped like it was coming apart, and a burst of blue-gray smoke spurted from its exhaust. The engine sputtered to life, its deathly rattling quickly smoothing out—as the Berkshire's had under Spence's skilled hands—as the rider made his adjustments. After disengaging the chain that ran from the rear wheel to the starter, he shoved the shifter into first gear to tighten the large, leather primary drive. When he was ready, he pushed the cycle off its stand, rolling crookedly until he was able to pick up some speed. With a shout and a wave to the knot of well-wishers who'd followed him out of the *cantina,* the cyclist hauled back on the throttle and roared east into the desert.

"Where do ye suppose he's headin'?" Spence asked reflectively.

"I don't know. There's not much out there except cactus and scrub until you get to Nogales, but that's a good long ways away."

"Do ye reckon he'll make it?"

"I guess he's made it this far," I replied. I hated to think what would become of him if he broke down out there, though. Grinding my cigarette out under my heel, I pushed to my feet and headed for the livery. "You say the mules are in back?"

"Aye, ye'll find 'em. The old man's are the only ones out there."

I walked down the center aisle, then out the back door. The

mules and horses were all in one corral, feeding on hay that had been recently forked into the lot. Leaning against the top rail, I studied the remuda in the softening light. Someone had chosen well, I thought, watching the animals mill around the piles of loose hay. My attention kept coming back to a chunky bay mare with three white socks and a narrow snip down her muzzle. She must have sensed my interest, because, even as she continued to eat, she would move around behind the other animals, always keeping two or three of them between us.

Her obstinacy brought a smile to my face. I liked a smart horse. They weren't as easy to manipulate as a dumber mount, but I'd never been the kind who needed to assert my authority over any animal. It's better to work in partnership with a horse if you can, especially in the desert, where a lot of times your life depended as much on your mount as it did finding the next water hole.

If not for the manacles I would have tried to rope her out of the bunch and work with her a little, just to introduce myself and see how she responded, but I knew I wouldn't be able to handle a reata with twelve inches of chain between my wrists, and decided it would set a wrong example if I tried to catch her and failed.

"*Mañana, chica,*" I called softly. "I'll see you tomorrow."

The light was dimming rapidly as I made my way across the dusty plaza. The *cantina*'s front door had been thrown open at sunset to welcome the cooling evening breezes, and the soft light and gentle strumming of a guitar seemed to beckon me. I paused in the door, breathing deeply of the familiar odors, and for a moment I experienced a vague sense of loss. Four years gone forever, thanks to Del Buchman's treachery.

Candles flickering from sconces driven into the adobe walls created pockets of light and shadow. The hard-packed dirt floor had been recently swept and sprinkled. The guitar player was sitting at a table across the room with his feet propped on an empty chair, a clay mug and bottle of mescal within easy reach. There must have been twenty or more others scattered around the room, most of them sloped forward over their tables or leaning back in their chairs, the day's weariness etched across their features. The majority of them were men, but there were a few women, mostly wives sharing a drink with their husbands. There were no whores. Archuleta had never employed any, and Moralos had never been large enough or successful enough to attract independent hookers.

A slim man in a high-peaked sombrero leaning against the rear wall caught my eye, but I ignored him and walked to the bar. Jorge Archuleta came waddling down the business side of the counter, a broad grin plastered across his sweaty face, his eyes nearly lost above plump brown cheeks.

"Ah, Latham, my old friend!" Jorge exclaimed, swinging his bulk around to face me across the bar. "It has been a long time, *hombre.*"

"Four years," I said.

"*Sí,* I remember." He nodded toward the far end of the bar. "You were standing there when the lawman called Buchman put the shotgun into your back and took you away in chains." He glanced at my wrists, his brows furrowing in confusion. "Now he brings you back the same way?"

I chuckled softly. "Some things don't change, *amigo.*"

"Still, four years is a long time. I hope you have not been wearing these bracelets since you last left us."

"No, I just came back for a visit, and to have some of your fine *Cerveza Grande.*"

The fat man's eyes sparked with unexpected anger. "*Ay chihuahua,* that beer is no more, my friend. Bandits have taken over Sabana, and hog the beer and mescal for themselves."

"All of it?" I asked in surprise.

"*Sí*. I have mescal that is locally produced and very good, but no beer. Not in over a year."

"Then I guess I'll have the mescal," I said, propping my elbows on the bar and making no effort to hide the manacles. I knew everyone had already seen them, and those who hadn't had probably heard about them. Moralos was a small town, and gossip travels fast, no matter what the language.

Bringing out a clay jug stoppered with a piece of corncob, Jorge splashed a hefty dose into a clay tumbler of the same dull color—locally made, I assumed, like the mescal.

Raising the stubby mug in a salute, I murmured—"*Arriba, abajo, al centro y por de dentro.*"—which means: Up, down, center, and in. I threw back a healthy shot, then worked hard to suppress a shudder. Lowering the mug, I stared at its contents as if I'd heard a voice from within calling my name. Across the counter, Jorge grinned knowingly.

"You see, Latham, it is not as good as what you used to bring me from Sabana."

"It isn't as good as most burro p---," I stated hoarsely. "Who's taken over Sabana, and what happened to the *Federales* who were stationed there?" I asked it casually, like I'd never heard of a man named Chito Soto, or an Army of Liberation, but I figure Jorge already suspected an ulterior motive in my question. There were too many *gringos* in Moralos not to know something was going on.

"Chito Soto controls Sabana. He took over the town more than a year ago, and told the *Federales* that they could either join his forces or be executed as enemies of the revolution. Then, to prove his seriousness, he stood the captain and two lieutenants against the wall of the church and shot all three of them in the head." He touched a spot behind his right ear. "Here."

I remembered Davenport telling me about the man he'd sent to Tres Pinos, and how his head had come back in a box with a single bullet wound in that same location. "Sounds like a mean son-of-a-b----," I said. "Where did he come from?"

"He claims to be a major in Castillo's army, but I don't think so. I think he is a thief who masquerades as a leader in a revolution that does not exist. They say that for two days after he took over the Sabana Valley, the rivers there ran red with blood." [*Ed. Note:* Despite smaller insurgencies in prior years, including, apparently, the Castillo Revolution, the historically recognized *Revolución Mexicana,* led by Francisco Madero, did not begin until 1910.]

"Wait a minute, who is Castillo?"

Jorge gave me a puzzled glance. "You have not yet heard of Adolpho Castillo?" He chuckled. "Do not worry, *hombre,* you soon will. Adolpho Castillo is *el general uno* of the Army of Liberation, or at least that is his claim. Personally I think that, like Soto, he is merely another bandit, although it is said that his hatred for Porfirio Díaz is a wonder to behold. Like lava from Colima, it scorches everything in its path. Fortunately for you, *amigo,* Castillo is far to the south, in the mountains of Durango, where he hides from Díaz's *Federales.*"

"What about Soto? How many men does he have?"

"Perhaps two hundred, although it is hard to know how loyal a soldier truly is when they are threatened with death if they do not join a cause."

There was movement behind me, and the slim guy in the tall sombrero I'd seen earlier stepped up to the bar at my side. "Fifty, I would think." He looked at me. "Fifty who would blindly follow Chito Soto into the inferno, or so I have heard. The others . . . maybe a few. Not all of them, but some."

"If given the choice," Jorge added.

"*Sí,* if given a choice." He turned partway around, smiling cautiously. "*Hola,* J.T. I am Luis Vega, from Nogales."

"I remember you," I said, taking his hand. My cuffs rattled

softly, and I noticed Luis's curious glance, but he didn't comment on them.

We made small talk for a while—horses we'd known and country we'd seen, the usual stuff—until Jorge grew bored and moved off. Then Luis lowered his voice and leaned close, so that we wouldn't be overheard. "*Señor* Davenport said that even though you were locked behind the walls of Yuma, you would come." He smiled again, almost shyly. "I see you have consented to his wishes."

I had to laugh at that. Although Luis and I had never ridden together, I'd seen him often enough around the saloons and *cantinas* of Nogales, and I'd always liked him. He was a good-natured man in his early thirties, whipcord lean and quick as a cat. He was good with a gun, but better with a knife. I'd seen him fight, and wouldn't want to go up against him in close quarters.

"Leaving Yuma has been a recent goal of mine," I acknowledged dryly. "I didn't figure it would be Buchman who sprung me, though."

"Life has many twists and turns, my friend, but I am glad you came." He gave me a sly glance. "Now maybe I will learn the location of that secret water hole you have used to your advantage for so many years."

Well, Luis had me there, although you're probably confused as to what he was talking about. So maybe it's time I told you why I was serving a twelve-year stretch in the territorial pen at Yuma. I suspect you've been wondering.

Luis and I had been in the same business since the mid-1890s, importing such fine Mexican goods as Sabana mescal, *Cerveza Grande* beer, those short Aztec Gold cigars that used to be so popular along the border, coils of hemp, pieces of silver—anything that might turn a profit on the American side of the border. It was a fine and sometimes exciting career, but the local politicians—along with the larger merchants who operated their purse strings—had insisted on calling it smuggling. Personally I never saw the harm in it. Just the opposite, in fact. The stores that bought my merchandise through their back doors were then able to pass the savings on to their customers, and they did, too. It was a real boon to the economy, or at least the poorer sections of it.

But, of course, the law didn't see it that way. Especially Del Buchman, who had been a deputy sheriff for Pima County at the time of my arrest, although I knew folks who said he generally answered more to a conglomerate of Tucson businessmen called The Brokers than he did the Sheriff's Office. I guess more than a few of those upstanding Arizona citizens had started to object to my success as an international merchant, and were particularly incensed at my not paying a tariff on the goods I brought back with me from Mexico. I think mostly they were just upset that I was allowing a bunch of smaller shops that couldn't otherwise compete with the larger operations to scrape off a little profit for themselves.

No matter the reason, those larger stores didn't appreciate the competition, and someone made a deal with Buchman to put a stop to it. Not that the law hadn't been trying to do that for quite a few years by then, but I'd been good at my job—one of the best, in fact—and, although I'd had a few close calls along the way, I'd never been caught. Not until Del slipped south of the border to wait for me in Moralos, breaking more than a few laws himself by doing so.

My attorney had pointed out these obvious infractions at my trial in Tucson in '03, but no one seemed to care. Del had caught me right there in Jorge Archuleta's *cantina*—Moralos had been my home base south of the border—by slipping up behind me and shoving a sawed-off double-barreled shotgun into my spine.

That water hole Luis Vega was talking about was what made me so successful as a smuggler. I called it Yaqui Springs, although the Yaquis called it the Cañon Where the Small Lizards Run. My name was shorter, and not as off-putting.

I'd been introduced to the place while still a captive of the Yaquis. That was in my early teens, the late '80s, when the tribe was still fairly powerful and far-ranging. Very few Mexicans knew of its location, and I'd never met a white man who'd even heard of the place. The Yaquis guarded its location closely, and would kill anyone they found trespassing on it. Of course in those years, the Yaquis would kill just about anyone not of their own nation that they caught on their land, period.

I was allowed to use the site because I'd lived among them, and because, while making my escape, I'd managed to save the life of Old Toad's son, Slayer. I'd been warned, however—with the tip of a slim-bladed dirk pressed firmly against my Adam's apple—that if I ever revealed the cañon's location to an outsider, I'd be killed in the slowest, most painful manner they could think of. Having observed their handiwork on past captives, I'd taken the threat seriously.

Toad didn't know about Abby Davenport, but I doubted it would have made any difference. That ol' boy had murdered a lot of white-eyes, and even more Mexicans, over the years, and wouldn't see a problem with us killing each other. Saved him the bother, I suppose.

Anyway, that's why I was in Yuma, and that's why Del Buchman had recommended me to Davenport. Del knew I had a secret way into the Sabana Valley, a method of slipping across better than two hundred miles of blazing desert without being detected, and that no other white man seemed to know about. I'd planned to take that secret with me to my grave, and that night there in Moralos, I figured I still might.

SESSION FIVE

I'm glad your machine is still working. The electricity doesn't go out around here very often, but with the wind as bad as it is, I wouldn't be surprised at it happening again.

I don't recall where I was when the lights went out, but I know where I want to start now. The next day, there in Moralos.

Buchman had again refused to remove my cuffs that morning, so I was forced to labor alongside Spence, Luis, and Carlos with my wrists still fettered. Looking back on it, I suspect Del's bull-headedness over my manacles had more to do with his animosity toward Davenport than it did with anything I'd done—that little incident with Selma Metzler's Derringer notwithstanding. Still, it was a growing vexation and a h--- of an inconvenience, and it was starting to make me mad. Not to mention those bracelets were beginning to chafe.

The first thing we did was sort through all the gear Ed Davenport had brought with him from Tucson. Besides the three machine-guns and a dozen cases of .30-40 Krag ammunition, he had a pretty extensive collection of camping gear, including a small tent, a half case of wine, good crystal, and a folding canvas chair like those Hollywood directors like to use.

The more crap we unpacked, the more worried I became. I could tell Spence and Luis were feeling the same way. I couldn't say what Carlos Perez was thinking; in all the time we spent together, I never was able to read that little half-breed b------.

Pausing at one point to wipe the sweat from my brows, I pointed out that it would take a dozen mules to haul all the stuff Davenport wanted to take along.

"At least," Spence agreed solemnly. "But we couldn't do it, even if we had the animals. Not with the kind of ridin' we'll be doin'." He glanced at me. "One of us is goin' to have to tell the old man he'll have to do without some of his fineries."

"You mean me?"

Spence shrugged. "He'd never admit it, but he knows he can't make it without ye, lad. Me? He could cut my pin and not be hampered in the least."

I scratched thoughtfully at my stubbled jaw. "If Felix Perez doesn't get back soon with some extra stock, it won't matter what Davenport wants. It's going to take at least three mules just to carry those potato diggers and all that ammunition."

In the end we separated the gear into piles based on order of necessity, and how many mules Felix came back with. One small stack contained just enough blankets and foodstuff to get us to Sabana if he didn't return at all, which Spence was beginning to believe was a possibility. We added a little more to each succeeding pile, but tossed the tent, chair, and crystal out of sight behind the Berkshire. I don't know what became of the wine.

We finished around midafternoon, and, leaving Pedro to watch over the gear with a fresh promise of another bullet in his foot if he failed to keep pilfering fingers away from Davenport's gear—I imagine Pedro was real happy to see us ride out when we finally got under way—we trooped over to Archuleta's for some shade and mescal. We were still there, lounging tiredly around a single table and not saying much, when a youngster's cry from outside announced the arrival of a horseman.

"Felix," Carlos declared with unmistakable relief, nearly tipping over his chair in his haste to reach the door.

After downing our drinks, Spence, Luis, and I followed him

outside. Carlos was heading for the livery, his short, thick legs really eating up the ground.

"No mules," Luis observed quietly.

"Aye, and just as well," Spence replied. "Now the old man'll have to cut his supplies to the bone."

Inside the livery we found Felix unsaddling a short-coupled pinto, jabbering happily with his cousin in a language I didn't recognize. One of the smaller tribes to the south, was my guess. It sure wasn't Yaqui, which I spoke moderately well, or Mojave or one of the Western Apache dialects I was familiar with.

Felix Perez shared the same dark, stocky build as his cousin, although he was quite a bit younger than Carlos. They were dressed similarly, too, the major difference being that Felix was wearing a sombrero made of straw, instead of felt, one of those wide-brimmed monstrosities they coated with cactus juice or goat p--- or whatever it was that made them just about indestructible.

Hearing me talk, you might be asking—*Why all this animosity toward the Perezes?*—and I'm going to tell you. The reason I noticed Felix's sombrero was because of the goggles he had fastened around the crown like a hatband. There was a long leather coat tied behind his saddle, and an extra rifle in a scabbard hanging off the horn. The scabbard was elaborately carved and dyed in shades of red and green and golden browns, and my vision narrowed when I saw it, and there was a roaring in my ears like a distant freight train barreling through the night.

"Easy, lad," Spence cautioned out of the side of his mouth. "We don't know how he came about obtainin' 'em."

"Let's go find out."

The two *Indios* must have sensed my mood, for they both backed away from the pinto when I drew near. Carlos's hand dropped to his revolver, while Felix gently fingered the mesquite grips of a *belduque,* carried in a sheath on his cartridge belt.

Carlos spoke first.

"You have a problem, *señor?*"

"Where'd your cousin get those goggles?"

"Goggles?"

I motioned toward the pair clinging to Felix's sombrero. "The glasses, and the coat and rifle, too."

Carlos smiled expansively. "I think he bought them." He glanced at his cousin, speaking rapidly in Indian. Felix replied, and Carlos nodded solemnly. "*Sí,* he bought them in Nogales. One hundred *pesos* for the . . . what you call them . . . goggles? And the rifle and coat."

At my side, Spence sighed heavily. I was staring hard at Felix, my pulse thundering. "Do you speak Spanish, *chico?*"

Felix's eyes narrowed dangerously. "*Sí,* I speak the language of the invaders."

"Then you know what I mean when I call you a liar?"

The Indian's fingers crept around the scales of his knife. "I think you would be wise to take back those words, *gringo.*"

"Did you kill him?"

He hesitated for only a moment, but it was long enough for me to read the truth in his eyes. Of course he'd killed him. Probably today, coming across the tall rider on the Wagner motorcycle, alone in the desert and likely unaware that anyone was around. But Felix denied it. I figured he would.

"I bought these items you accuse me of stealing. To say differently is to risk your life." His gaze dropped to my manacled wrists, and a smile slid across his face.

"Give me your knife, Luis," I said.

"I don't know, my friend. I think maybe the odds are too much against you with those cuffs on your wrists."

"Vega's right, lad," Spencer hissed. " 'Tis no the time to fight, not hobbled like ye be."

"I think perhaps your friends are right," Carlos added. "My

cousin, he is ver' good with the blade. Ver' good."

Felix slid the *belduque* from its sheath. It was a simple fighting knife of an old Mexican style, long and slim and wickedly sharp. He turned it razor's edge up and leaned forward in a slight crouch. Grinning, I went to meet him.

"D--- it, Latham, ye bloody, pig-headed fool!" Spence roared at my back.

I circled slowly to the left in the wide aisle of the livery. Felix countered likewise, and the others moved out of our way. The *Indio*'s knife weaved hypnotically between us. "If you wish to die, *gringo*, I can easily assist you."

I held my manacled wrists chest high in front of me, spread as wide as the twelve inches of chain would allow. Although aware of the knife, I was focusing on Felix's dark, brooding eyes, counting on reading his decision perhaps a tenth of a second before he could act upon it. That's not much time, but, in a situation like that, it could well mean the difference between a fatal cut and a near miss.

Right about now you're probably thinking that I'm either a d---ed fool or an outright liar, and I can't say that I blame you. But you've got to understand that things were different back then, and a man didn't just turn away from what he believed in, or what he thought was right. Not out there on the woolly frontier, where indecisiveness and timidity could get you killed quicker than an Apache's bullet. The world is full of top dogs and toadies, but the space in between is pretty sparsely populated.

Felix feinted and I drew up defensively, skipping back a couple of paces. Chuckling, the *Indio* said: "If you wish to leave now, *gringo*, I will allow it. As long as you do so on your hands and knees, and after you beg a little. Not even ver' much, the begging. Just enough to let Felix know you've learned your lesson."

He was feeling mighty pleased with himself, so his eyes really bugged out in alarm when I charged, bringing my arms up and screaming a Yaqui oath. Instinct drove him backward, slamming him into a stable wall and rapping the back of his head against the top plank. His straw sombrero flipped over the top of the partition and landed in the manure on the other side.

I stopped at the last second, easily avoiding the clumsy swipe of his *belduque*. I laughed and backed away, feeling pretty good myself. "Put the knife down, *chico*," I mocked, "and I'll let you crawl out of here on your belly."

Felix's black eyes sparked like flint on steel. I eased to the side, waiting for him to make his move, never doubting that he would. Anger had taken over the stocky Indian's mind, clouding out all other thoughts save for revenge, a need to erase his shame.

We began moving faster, although still in our familiar, crude circle, kicking up clouds of stable dust as we darted back and forth. Felix's attack, when it finally came, didn't surprise me. He brought the slim *belduque* forward in a quick, waist-high swipe that I readily parried. There was a clank of metal on metal as the blade tangled briefly with the steel links of chain connecting my cuffs, but he jerked the knife away before I could tighten the snarl. Dodging quickly, he lashed out with a rattler's speed, and I sucked in my gut and batted his hand away.

His lips peeling back in a silent snarl, Felix darted to his right, then immediately came back to his left; he feigned twice, then lunged. I snapped my arms up to block the knife's deadly arc, but was only partially successful. I felt the blade's chill kiss just under the ribs on my left side, followed by a wet, creeping warmth. The younger man smiled and glanced at his cousin as if for approval. When he did, I hurtled toward him. A startled squawk erupted from the Indian's throat as he gracelessly thrust the *belduque* at my midsection. I slapped it aside, then grabbed his wrist and twisted his arm up and back, throwing my weight into him, tripping us both into the wooden planks of an empty stall.

Felix grunted loudly as my shoulder rammed his chest. His face went momentarily slack. I hooked a leg behind his knee and fell, coiling to the side as I pulled him down with me. His knife wobbled in his hand and his eyes bulged as he sucked desperately for air. I leaned hard on his wrist, bending it back a lot farther than I thought it could go before he finally dropped the blade.

With my own wrists shackled, I was unable to prevent Felix from snaking his free hand around my neck and grasping my jaw, trying to unscrew my head from my shoulders. I uttered a strangled curse as he attempted to flip me off of him. Although able to resist his efforts, I was also stuck myself. I couldn't let go of Felix's right hand for fear he'd grab the *belduque* again; at the same time I couldn't reach his other hand with mine in cuffs.

Finally, with the joints in my neck crackling like autumn leaves, I rolled in the direction Felix had been trying to toss me. The move caught him off guard, and he yelped in surprise as I threw myself astride him, my knees planted solidly in the dirt on either side of his torso. I still had both of my hands grappling with his right one, but at least his knife was now several feet away, out of easy reach.

I maintained my dominance for about ten seconds. Then a fist plunged into my side as if trying to burrow up under my ribs. I gasped in agony, my fingers involuntarily loosening. Heaving upward with his legs, Felix chucked me almost effortlessly over his head. Rolling onto my hands and knees, I scrabbled for the *belduque* and almost had it when I felt the Indian's arms wrap around both my legs. Jerking one leg free, I stomped my heel into his cheek like I was packing dirt around a freshly set fence post. He howled and let go, and we both staggered to our feet, bleeding and gulping air.

Sweat was pouring off my face and my ankle throbbed where, at some point in our brawl, I'd driven the muzzle of Selma's semi-auto toward the bone. Blood soaked both my side and my sleeve, where I discovered another deep cut, although the pain had yet to become debilitating.

Expecting to be rushed, I was a second behind when Felix whirled toward the pinto. I swore and raced after him. I knew what he had in mind, just as I knew Spence and Luis would be too far away and on the wrong side of the shaggy mustang to stop him.

Felix was trying to yank the motorcycle rider's rifle free when I threw myself into his back. We both went down hard, practically under the pinto's hoofs, but this time I'd gotten a solid hold, and was able to wrap my manacles around his neck. I was hauling back with everything I had to cut off his wind, but he was bucking and twisting like a catamount, while overhead the pinto was hopping and kicking and trying its best not to step on us. Not out of any consideration for human life, mind you, but because it didn't want to plant a hoof into something mushy, like a human belly, and lose its footing.

With those flashing hoofs coming way too close for comfort, I began trying to wiggle clear of the panicking horse without giving up my hold on the Indian's neck. As tight as I was hanging on, Felix was slowly squirming free. I wasn't sure how much longer I was going to be able to stay on top when a bellow from the front of the livery blasted down the central aisle. Through the sweat and blood stinging my eyes, I saw Del Buchman storming toward us like an enraged bull.

Del grabbed my collar and dragged me backward, but I still had my chain around Felix's neck, and brought him along.

"Let go, Latham!" Buchman hollered.

I grunted a reply, the top button of my shirt digging into my Adam's apple. Had I more wind and the opportunity to use it, I would have explained to Del that I didn't want to let go of Felix until I was sure the wiry little Indian wouldn't make a dive for either his knife or the rifle. Then something hard and heavy slammed into my head, and my knees buckled.

"God-d--- it, let 'im go or I'll bash your skull in, you bull-headed son-of-a-b----."

Hot white sparks danced before my eyes, and my legs turned to soft rubber. Sensing his chance, Felix twisted free of my manacles and scrambled down the aisle toward the rifle, half canted precariously from its fancily carved scabbard. Before he could yank it free, Del spun me out of the way and palmed his own gun. He had the big Remington revolver leveled on the Indian's head, the hammer rocked all the way back to full cock, and Felix froze with the rifle still hung up in its scabbard.

"You let go of that gun, or I'll blow a hole through you big enough to push an anvil through," Del growled.

Felix hesitated only a moment, then pushed the rifle back into its boot.

Me, I just stood there on the end of Buchman's arm like the catch of the day, knees wobbling and my head feeling like it might explode if I blinked too hard. Del's knuckles were digging into the back of my neck where he still gripped my collar, and in my skittery vision I spotted a wad of hair caught in the Remington's ejector housing that I recognized as my own. That a--hole had whacked me a good one.

Then Del shoved me against one of the stalls, and I quickly flopped both arms over the top as he backed away. Moving to the center of the aisle where he could keep an eye on both of us, he said: "What the h---'s going on in here?"

Del asked his question in English, and Felix and Carlos exchanged worried glances. I knew from my own experience that it was never a good sign when someone starts speaking angrily in a foreign language, as if they don't give a hoot what your position is in the matter.

Luis explained to Del about the motorcycle rider who had pulled out late the day before, and about how Felix had shown up with the rider's goggles, rifle, and coat. Luis was about halfway through his narrative when Del cut him off.

"What the h---'s that got to do with you, Latham?" he demanded.

I'd let go of the stall by then, but was still leaning against it. "There's no way he could've bought those things in Nogales, like he claims," I rasped. "That's over a hundred miles from here."

My reasoning didn't cut a very wide swath with Del. "You dumb ox, you were hired as a guide, not a lawman. I don't give a d--- what happens anywhere except along the trail we're following to Sabana, and you'd better not, either. And you!" He jabbed a finger at Felix like it was the muzzle of a gun. "You keep that knife of yours sheathed, or I'll ram it. . . ."

Well, I guess you've got a fair idea where Del threatened to shove Felix's *belduque*. He included a similar threat to me, although more in relation to what he was going to do to my head, rather than my hind end. Returning the Remington to its holster, he squared his shoulders and glanced around at the others.

"You boys had better turn in early. Davenport saw this *muchacho* ride in without the mules, and has already assumed the worst. We're pulling out at sunup." Motioning to Felix, he added: "You come with me, champ. Mister Davenport wants to know why you couldn't find one d---ed pack animal to bring back. You'd better have a good reason, too, or that ol' boy is liable to pin your ears to the wall and leave you hanging there when we ride outta here in the morning."

SESSION SIX

If Davenport wanted to get an early start the next day, he sure didn't act like it. Spence and I and Luis and the Perez boys were all up before dawn, packing mules and getting things ready to roll, but there wasn't a light burning in any of the hotel's upstairs windows by the time we'd finished.

With the mules packed and dawn creeping in from the east, I dropped a rope over that bay I was telling you about and led her out near the Berkshire to saddle. I did that because the night before, after Del had taken Felix and Carlos with him to see the old man—Carlos tagging along to translate for his cousin—I'd pulled the motorcycle rider's rifle and scabbard from the pinto's saddle and hidden it, along with a full cartridge belt I found tucked under the Indian's bedroll, beneath the canvas Spence had stretched over the automobile.

The Perezes had searched high and low for that rifle after they got back from their a-- chewing with Davenport, but they hadn't approached the Berkshire. Probably because of the old man's promise to shoot anyone he caught messing around with it.

I took my time saddling the bay, fairly stoved up after my little altercation with Felix. Besides the usual aches and pains you'd expect from a brawl, Spence had taken stitches on both of the cuts I'd received from the wiry Indian's *belduque*—five in my side and another three on my arm, the scars from both of them still visible to this day.

With the bay decked out in a worn but sturdy Texas rig, canteen and bedroll already in place, and my gear stowed inside a pair of used saddlebags, I slid the rifle from its hiding place and slipped over behind the bay.

"Ye be playin' with fire there, laddie," Spence remarked when he saw me. "The mood Delmar's been in lately, he's liable to hang ye from the rafters with ye own cuffs."

"Del can go to h---," was my response.

Luis chuckled. "It wouldn't be a far ride from where we're going."

"Just over the next hill," I agreed, laughing.

I was aware of the dark looks the Perez boys were giving me, but ignored them. They could go to h---, too, as far as I was concerned, although I knew I'd have to watch my back around them from there on.

I slid the scabbard under the off-side fender with the butt sloping forward, along the bay's shoulder. I'd taken a peek at the gun the night before. It was a Model 99 Savage, a hammerless lever action with a rotary magazine located under the chamber. The headstamp on the ammunition marked it as a .303, which was basically a .30-30 with a little extra punch. It wasn't a firearm I would have chosen for the journey we had to make, but it was a definite improvement over Selma's semiauto, still tucked inside my boot.

I had the scabbard secured to my saddle and was readjusting the angle of the toe to a more comfortable position when Del came out of the hotel and spotted me. You'd have thought I was threatening to blow up an orphanage, the way he came stomping over, the Remington already drawn and his face about as red as an Arizona sunset.

"There ain't no way in h---!" he roared, thrusting the revolver in my face with one hand and yanking the Savage from its scabbard with the other. "If you think I'm gonna let you carry a gun, Latham, you're a bigger fool than I had you pegged for."

"What the h--- do you expect me to do if we get jumped by bandits?" I flared.

"You can go howl at the moon if you're looking for someone who cares what you can do," he replied. "I ain't giving you no rifle. Now shut up about it."

"D--- it, Del," I grated.

He cocked the revolver. "I ain't telling you again, champ."

My jaws were grinding hot enough to crush rocks, but that was about all I could do with a gun in my face and cuffs on my wrists. But the battle wasn't over, I swore as I led the bay away. Not by a d---ed sight, it wasn't.

With our horses saddled and the mules packed, all we could do was wait. I took a seat on the front steps of the hotel and rolled a cigarette from the cloth sack of Bull Durham I'd bought from Jorge the night before, along with matches and paper—but no .380s for the semi-auto. Moralos' small general store didn't carry such oddball ammunition yet, either, just shotgun shells and the more common rounds for revolvers and rifles.

Del had gone back in to see if Davenport was ready. He returned a few minutes later with the look of a man who had just gotten his butt chewed ragged by an ornery wolf. Walking stiffly over to where Spence was holding the reins on a leggy roan, he said: "The old man's gonna be a while. When he gets here, tell him me and Latham went on ahead to check the trail."

Spence winced as if he'd swallowed something sour. "Shouldn't ye be the one tellin' him that, Delmar?"

"You've worked for him longer than I have, you tell him. And God d--- it, do what I say for a change. I'm getting tired of everybody questioning my orders." He turned a baleful eye on me. "What are you waiting for, Latham? Get on your horse."

I laughed at Del's spitfire mood, then turned to my saddle. Del rode over a couple of minutes later astride a powerfully built buckskin. Jutting his chin toward a cart track winding through the ocotillo south of town, he said: "Let's go. You're up front."

Smelling the whiskey on Del's breath, I wondered if he'd slipped a drink before talking to Davenport, or after.

I'd thought my muscles had given up protesting after we got the mules packed, but I discovered a whole new batch of aches as we rode out of Moralos at an easy jog. My back, especially my neck where that bushwhacking Indian had tried to unscrew my head, was sending spasms up and down my spine, and the base of my skull was throbbing. Yet for all the pains, I couldn't deny an unexpected thrill to be moving out across the desert, a good horse under me, and a cooling desert breeze buffing my face. I think, for the first time since leaving Yuma, I began to feel like a whole man again. Like maybe there was a future for me, after all.

The trail started climbing soon after leaving town, winding through a maze of dry, broken ridges, hided over in rock, cactus, and sparse clumps of grass that you wouldn't have thought would have kept a goat alive. The air grew still and warm, and the semi-barren slopes seemed to trap the sun's rays, reflecting in every direction. It was a desolate country, yet I knew a lot of wildlife not only lived out here, but thrived. Back in my smuggling days, cougars and wolves had always been a concern at night, although there had been an abundance of antelope and desert bighorn to keep the large predators fed.

Jack rabbits, coyotes, and javelinas ruled the underbrush, along with horned toads, Gila monsters, scorpions, and more snakes than you could count in a lifetime. The flora was as rough and unforgiving as the landscape—spiny cholla and ocotillo, sword-like yuccas thrust into the sky, rabbit brush, prickly pear, and scattered stands of saguaro. Mesquite, catclaw, and an occasional *palo verde* grew along the dry streambeds, providing what little shade a man was likely to find in that country.

We were still following the cart track we'd picked up outside of Moralos, although it was growing more rutted as the miles passed. I suspect Del thought the road might actually lead some place significant, but it didn't. There was an old silver mine a half day's ride to the south that had never amounted to much. According to Jorge, the place had been abandoned for more than twenty years. The only reason the trail still existed was because there was water inside the main adit, and sometimes a few villagers would go up there to hunt for meat, or to graze their sheep or goats. Del was going to be mighty disappointed when he discovered the road we were following ended abruptly at the mouth of a shaft that only went back into the rocky hillside for one hundred feet or so. [*Ed. Note:* An adit is a horizontal entrance to an underground mine, as opposed to a vertical shaft.]

I had my own reasons for wanting to reach the old mine. It was getting hotter by the hour, and I knew there would be cool shade just inside its mouth, where the hard-rock men had carved out a larger chamber for living quarters. I planned to sit out the worst of the heat there, then, toward evening, fix some coffee and a bite to eat before pushing on into the night.

I was feeling pretty achy by the time we reached the mine, and not just from the thumping I'd taken from Felix. It had been a long time since I'd sat a saddle, and my hind end felt like it had been doused in liniment, then set afire. I was determined not to make any kind of sound when I dismounted, but I had to grit my teeth to keep from it, then hang onto the saddle horn for a couple of minutes afterward while I waited for the circulation to return to my legs. I'll tell you what, that was a far cry from the man I used to be, pounding a saddle for days on end, dodging Mexican *rurales* and federal marshals alike. My only consolation—and it was actually a pretty rewarding one—

was that Del seemed to be in even more misery. He'd probably put on fifty pounds in the years since my arrest, and was showing his age in other ways, too. Although I'd yet to see him sneak a swig from a bottle, the smell of booze clung to him, and his eyes still had that watery film about them that I'd seen on functioning alcoholics.

Grinning at his hobbling, bowlegged gait, I said: "What's the matter, champ? You ain't wearing out already, are you? We've still got another four days in the saddle getting there, and five more coming back."

I don't know if Del was getting used to my needling ways, or if he was just too worn out to respond. Looking around like a man waking up in a strange bedroom, he said: "Where are we?"

I told him, then added that we'd wait there for the others to catch up. "After today," I added, "the trail's going to get rough."

Del gave me a suspicious look, then shrugged as if he didn't care one way or another.

"There should be water inside," I said. "Take your horse in with you and pull the saddle. We'll be here a while."

Del scowled. "You figure you're giving orders now?"

"I am if you want to reach Sabana before Chito Soto starts carving on Davenport's wife and kids."

Del hesitated, then led his horse toward the gaping maw of the adit. Moving alongside my bay to loosen her cinch, I noticed a faint brush of dust far to the north. My brows furrowed in annoyance, knowing that it was Davenport and the others, and that they were so far behind.

Leading the bay inside, I pulled the saddle from her back and dumped it on a piece of flat, clean ground next to the wall. Del's buckskin was standing at a wide, shallow pool of cool water about a dozen yards inside the mouth of the adit, its muzzle whiskers dribbling. The horse was still saddled, and Del was flopped on his butt against the opposite wall with his head tipped back against the cool stone, his knees cocked up like a pair of mountain peaks. His eyes were closed, and he was breathing deeply, like he was already asleep. The smell of booze was so strong in the low-ceilinged chamber I automatically glanced at the floor by his side, looking for the bottle.

"I thought I told you to unsaddle your horse," I said.

He opened one eye to squint in my direction. "I decided you could do that," he replied, then tipped his head to the side. "Put it over here where I can reach it."

"You can unsaddle your own d---ed horse."

"I can, but I ain't gonna." His grin was like a cat with the combination to the canary's cage. "I been noticing you acting more important than you really are, Latham, and it strikes me that I've maybe been too lenient. So from now on, when I tell you to jump, then, mister, you d---ed well better jump. Savvy?"

I stared back a moment, weighing my odds. Then I smiled and lifted my wrists, pulling them apart until the chain was stretched tight. "Whatever you say . . . boss."

"You'd better remember it, too," Del said, leaning back and closing his eyes.

I took my bay to the pool first and watered her, then fastened hobbles around her front legs and pulled the bridle over her head. Next I stripped the gear from Del's buckskin, dropping it where he'd instructed. I stared down at him afterward, thinking how easy it would be to drive the toe of my boot into his belly. He grinned, his eyes slitted. He probably knew exactly what I was thinking.

"Anything else . . . boss?" I asked. "Maybe some champagne or caviar?"

You might not think a bunch of cob-rough old brush-poppers from the Arizona hinterlands would know about such grub, but places like Yuma and Tucson had their fair share of sophistication, railed in on refrigerator cars via the Southern Pacific. I'd had caviar and raw oysters, and even lobster one Christmas dinner, although I'd avoided champagne on account of its high cost—ten bucks for a bottle at Frank Burgess's New York Dining Club, in Tucson.

"That smart mouth of yours is gonna earn you another lump upside your head if you ain't careful," Buchman warned.

I went over to where I'd left my own rig and settled down. I was tired, but the more I tried to relax, the more I seemed to hurt. The beatings I'd taken from both Tiny Evans and Felix Perez had exacted their toll, my wrists were chafed, and my ankle throbbed where I'd gouged it with the muzzle of Selma's semi-auto during my tussle with Felix. In fact, my ankle was giving me quite a bit of trouble that day, primarily because of my saddle. The .380 had ridden comfortably under Selma's black garter all the way from Yuma, but it was different on horseback, where the stirrup kept pressing the Colt's steel frame into the bone. I was going to have to come up with another way of carrying it soon, or risk giving away its location by limping.

I dozed fitfully, then came awake when Davenport's group hauled up in front of the mine. Pushing to my feet, I walked outside to greet them. Spence and the boys didn't look too bad, but I wanted to laugh when I saw the old man, red-faced and pouring sweat, his eyelids drooping like worn-out blinds. Licking at lips already starting to chap, he croaked: "Where's Buchman?"

"He's inside getting his rest," I replied. "I'd say you ought to do the same."

He glanced doubtfully past my shoulder. "In there?"

"It's safe, and there's water for the stock, although not much to spare. We'll squat here until things cool off, then push on through the early evening." I took the reins of Davenport's chestnut and told him to get down. "It's cool inside. You'd better get in out of this sun until you get used to it."

My words ruffled the older man. "I've been working this territory since before you were born, Latham. I don't need you or anyone else telling me how to survive in it." Then he headed unsteadily toward the adit.

Luis was grinning as he swung down from his saddle mule. "That old man's still got plenty of p--- and vinegar, eh?"

"He's lucky he didn't fall over when he dismounted."

"*Sí*, but he would have gotten right back up, and punched you in the nose if you tried to help him."

"You sound like you admire him."

"No, maybe a little. He's a tough nut, but I think I'd trust Felix before I would Davenport."

I laughed at that, but I'd soon learn—we'd all soon learn—that Luis was more right than any of us could have imagined. You can think what you want about the stories that drifted up out of Sonora in the years that followed, but I was there. I know why it all blew up in our faces.

SESSION SEVEN

The sun was low in the west when the Perez boys and Luis and I left the cool adit with our horses and mules in tow. It was still hot, but not as ravaging as earlier. It would get worse the longer we stayed in Sonora. Jorge Archuleta used to have a thermometer hanging on the north wall of his *cantina,* where the sun never reached, and it would sometimes top out at one hundred and twenty degrees through the hottest part of the summer. I didn't doubt that the actual temperature went higher, but one hundred and twenty was the maximum that instrument would register.

We took the animals out to graze, and once we had them hobbled on some good spring grass growing below the mine's entrance, I went back inside to pry the others from their slumber. Del looked aggravated that he'd been found sleeping while I wandered loose, but he didn't say anything. Spence didn't have much to say, either. He rose groggily, stretched and yawned, then went outside to check on the stock. Davenport told me to get the h--- away or he'd have me shot.

Gritting my teeth, I went outside to where Spence was standing near the mine's entrance overlooking the grazing remuda, smoking a newly rolled cigarette. He just shrugged when he saw my anger.

"The old man pays well, but he'll make ye earn ye money, sometimes just in aggravation alone."

"If he wants his wife and kids back, he's going to have to put more effort into the task. Either that or go back to Moralos and let us handle the job."

"He'll no do that, lad. Davenport's got a heap of money tied up in those 'tater-diggers and all that ammunition. He'll no be lettin' any of it out of his sight until we reach Sabana."

Making a comment not fit for public record, I went to inform Luis and the Perezes of the delay. I think the muleteers could tell from my expression that we wouldn't be pulling out any time soon.

"It's just as well," Luis replied, after I'd explained the situation to him. "The stock could use some time to graze."

He was right about that. There wasn't going to be much water or grass over the next couple of days. I just hoped the delay—a few hours here and a few hours there could add up quickly—didn't end up costing Abby Davenport or one of her kids some flesh. A lot of people don't realize how violent those days were, or how little life was valued.

While Luis and the others stayed with the mules, I climbed the hill above the mine to have a look around. That was a rugged country out there, and it was going to get even more rugged the farther south we traveled—I was going to see to that for my own selfish reasons, which I'll explain later.

The sun went down while I sat up there studying the country and enjoying the solitude. Although I didn't see any signs of intruders, I couldn't help wondering what might be standing in our way, waiting for us out there beyond the horizon. Not just Yaquis and bandits, either. There was a lot of unrest in that part of Mexico in the years leading up to the big revolution, a lot of factions vying for power and wealth. It was a volatile land, and a dangerous one for *gringos.*

While waiting for Davenport to leave his lair, I pulled off my vest and slit a gap in the lining under my left arm. I made it just big enough to hold the Colt Selma had given me, then bound both ends of the cut with thread from the little sewing kit I'd picked up in Yuma. When I was finished, I had myself a passable hide-out rig for the pistol, with just enough of a gap in the lining to slip my hand inside and grab the gun if I needed it—which I figured, sooner or later, I would.

The light was dimming rapidly when Davenport finally emerged from the mine, reminding me of a hibernating bear in both appearance and manner. Del and Spence came with him, looking rather sheepish for their tardiness. They understood the odds we were up against, even if their boss didn't appear to. Or want to.

Felix had kindled a small fire while we waited for the old man to finish his nap, and the scent of coffee caught Davenport's attention. He lifted his nose and sniffed, furthering the image of an awakening bruin. "What's for supper?" he asked briskly, striding over to the fire. "I'm famished."

"We've got tortillas we brought with us from Moralos," I said, coming up on the opposite side of the flames. "We can wrap them around some beans and eat in the saddle."

"Nonsense," Davenport replied. "We need nourishment."

"We're still four long days from Sabana, Mister Davenport, and that's only if we don't run into trouble between here and there. We're already cutting it pretty close for your family. We can't afford to waste time."

Davenport hesitated, annoyance flickering deep in his eyes. "Some coffee, then. Surely we have time for that."

"If it was me, I wouldn't," I replied.

"But it isn't you, is it?" he said coolly, then reached across the fire to where Felix was holding out a freshly poured cup.

Way down deep, I could feel my anger bubbling softly, like nitro being brought to a slow boil, and I made some pretty wild promises to myself of the things I'd do if Abby Davenport or her kids were hurt in any way. Grinning, Felix held the coffee pot toward me as if asking if I wanted some, but I knew he was just taunting me. Davenport didn't say anything, but I thought he seemed amused by my refusal.

It was well into the gloaming when Davenport finally tossed the dredges from his cup and ordered Felix to kill the fire. Walking over to where I was standing beside my bay, hanging on to the mare's lead rope while she pulled hungrily on the green grass, he broached the subject of moving on after dark.

"A bit dangerous, don't you think?" he inquired.

"A lot easier on men and animals than riding during the hottest part of the day."

He hesitated as if considering my reply. I could tell he wasn't keen on leaving with darkness closing in. "What would happen if we got an early start in the morning, took a break at midday, then rode a little farther when it cooled off in the afternoon?"

For a second I just stared, wondering if he was pulling my leg. Then I said: "You mean like today?"

Davenport's face flushed dark. "Yes, but with an earlier start in the afternoon."

"I'd rather we pushed on now. We won't have a mine to sit out the heat tomorrow, but we can likely find some mesquite to hole up under. It'll still feel like we're squatting in Satan's skillet, but it can be done." After a pause, I added: "It has to be done if you want to rescue your wife and kids."

Davenport was silent a moment, contemplating not so much my advice, but how he wanted to take it. Buchman wasn't having that problem. I could see him behind the old man, glaring at me like he wanted to slit my throat. He didn't like it that Ed Davenport was turning to me for advice. Del had been the top dog for a while, but, with my knowledge of the terrain ahead of us, I was slowly usurping that position.

Finally Davenport loudly declared: "We'll ride on until midnight, then stop for a few hours. You take the lead, Latham, and I'll expect us to make good time in the coming hours."

I didn't waste my breath with a comeback. Calling for the others to mount up, I swung a leg over the cantle of my saddle and reined out of the way. When we were ready, I headed back down the road the way we'd come until I came to a trail that wound back to the west for maybe a quarter of a mile before turning south, taking us deeper into the rugged landscape below Moralos.

The others stretched out single file behind me, Davenport next in line, then Del, followed by Luis and the Perez boys—each handling a single pack mule—then Spence bringing up the rear with a rifle across his saddle, making sure no one fell out of line or lagged behind. I kept the column moving steadily along its serpentine course, staying off the ridges as much as possible and following sandy washes when I could. I was keeping time with the moon, but Davenport was using a gold-plated pocket watch that he must have been consulting regularly, because it wasn't much past midnight by my calculations when he called a halt. Riding up beside me, he said: "Let's find a place to camp for the rest of the night. The men need a rest."

That was bull---, of course. We were all doing fine, and Davenport wouldn't have given a hoot if we weren't. But he was the boss, and if he wanted to stop, there wasn't much I could do about it. Jutting my chin toward a vee-shaped gap in a low ridge ahead of us, I said: "If I remember right, there's some chaparral over yonder where we might find some wood for a breakfast fire and grass for the stock."

It would also cover a few more miles before we stopped for the night, but Davenport had other ideas.

"What about that place over there?"

I glanced in the direction he indicated, a flat piece of ground a few hundred yards to the north, tucked up against a tall cutbank that would afford us a wall to put our backs to and shelter for a fire—assuming we could scrounge up enough fuel to kindle one.

"It's the wrong direction," I pointed out.

With a look of growing impatience, he said: "I hardly think a couple of hundred yards will make that much of a difference." Pulling his horse around, he gave it a swift jab with his spurs, breaking into a canter toward the cutbank.

"I hope you aren't regretting that decision in a few days," I said to his retreating form.

We spent the rest of that night tucked up against the cutbank, but still didn't get the early start Davenport had promised.

"We can't pack adequately in the dark," the old man argued when I went to awaken him.

"Mister Davenport, these boys could pack a mule blindfolded, and not lose a can opener," I said.

"Nonsense," the old man retorted, rolling onto his side and pulling a Navajo blanket over his shoulder. "No man is that good, Latham. Wake me when it's light."

Swearing under my breath, I walked over to where the muleteers were waiting and told them to get started. "I want those sawbucks cinched tight before first light. We can wait until dawn to load the guns and ammunition if that's what the old man wants, but I want everything ready when it's time to move out."

True to his word, Davenport refused to abandon his blankets until the first hint of gray light was spilling over the lip of the cutbank. Sitting up with a wince and a hacking snort, he stretched painfully, then reached for his boots. I motioned for the muleteers to start packing, but d---ed if the old man didn't insist on a hot breakfast before we pulled out.

"I've had enough of refried beans and tough meat wrapped in tortillas," he stated. "I want some eggs and sausage and fresh coffee, instead of the watered-down brew I was forced to drink last night."

Tight-jawed, I said: "We don't have time for breakfast, Mister Davenport, and we don't have any eggs or sausage to fix if we did."

Davenport paused with one foot booted and laced, the other still in its sock. Turning an accusatory eye on Del, he said: "You were told to pack adequately for our journey, Buchman. Aren't you familiar with the term 'adequate'?"

Del looked up from where he was squatting beside the skimpy blaze of our morning fire. "Yeah, I know what 'adequate' means, especially with the limited number of pack animals we've got. It means no heavy cast-iron skillets. It means no fragile foods, or anything that might spoil along the trail. What we've got is some jerky and hardtack, a few tins of sardines, some flour for ash cakes, salt, a smoked ham, and a little coffee . . . plus whatever tortillas and beans we've got left from Moralos. If we eat light and keep moving, like Latham wants, it'll be enough to get us where we're going. We'll have to figure out something else for our return."

Davenport's scowl deepened as Del ticked off the paltry amount of supplies we'd brought along. "You expect to feed an expedition of seven men on jerky and canned fish?"

"We didn't have enough stock to bring along extra grub," Del reminded him. "As it is, we've got Luis Vega riding a mule that was supposed to be carrying our basic supplies."

Davenport glowered toward Felix Perez, fiddling with the knots on a crate of Krag ammunition lashed to his mule's saw-buck. "That d---ed greaser wasted five days in Nogales, then came slinking back without mules or the two hundred dollars I gave him to make the purchases. He claims he was robbed, but I'd wager it was some tinhorn gambler in a poker game that did the stealing. That little thief will pay as soon as my need for him is over."

He turned to me. "Very well, then, Latham, we'll bow to your suggestion." Raising his voice to include the entire camp, he called: "Saddle up, everyone! We've got miles to cover before this d---able heat forces us to retire for the afternoon."

And that's pretty much how it went, all that day and the next one, too. Davenport remained as unpredictable as a Sonoran sandstorm, while Del seemed to grow more morose the deeper we penetrated into Mexico. Spence stayed mostly in the background and kept his thoughts to himself, while the muleteers—Mexican and *Indio* alike—became almost a separate entity, rarely included in any conversation, their opinions never sought. Of the four *gringos* within the party, only Spence and I spoke to the packers on a regular basis.

The land leveled out during the afternoon of our second day on the trail. Not flat, but more gently rolling, yet still hot and dry and furry with cactus. We made better time for a while, but I knew it wouldn't last. The roughest country lay before us, a maze of rugged cañons and rocky, sun-blasted ridges. Although we didn't see any signs of civilization, I knew there were villages and small ranches scattered on either side of us. From time to time as we crossed the low hills I'd spot the distant, snowy crowns of the Sierra Madres far to the east, like clouds riding low on the horizon.

Toward evening we passed a small herd of cattle, grazing by itself, though recently branded. They were mostly those small, black Spanish demons, with the needle-tipped horns that could gut a horse or rip a *vaquero*'s leg half off with a quick swipe of its head. If I hadn't wanted to slip through quietly, I might have been tempted to shoot a calf for meat, but the last thing we needed was some *grandee*'s fired-up cowboys coming after us with guns and nooses.

Early on the third day we entered the region I'd been warning the others about ever since we left Moralos, a land of sheer-sided *barrancos* winding between jagged, stony peaks, the sun's heat settling down in those windless cañons like a blacksmith's forge gone berserk. And it was here that I decided to finally get shuck of those d---ed cuffs that I'd been wearing for so long.

I thought it might be Davenport who called me out, but instead it was Del. We were making our way along a steep slope between a tall cliff on one side and a deep drop on the other, winding through patches of prickly pear and yucca, when he bellowed for me to haul up. I did as instructed, pushing my hat back to wipe some of the sweat from my brow. We hadn't stopped at noon because we couldn't find a place with enough grass for the stock or shade for the rest of us, and we were all fairly parched.

Del kicked his mount past Davenport's chestnut, and I could tell he was mad. "What the h--- are you trying to do, Latham?" he hollered, his question rolling on down the cañon in repeated echoes until it finally petered out several miles away.

"You might want to keep your voice down, hoss," I replied mildly. "Bandits use these *barrancos* as hide-outs. So do Yaquis, for that matter."

"What's going on, Buchman?" Davenport demanded. He was sitting his saddle loose as a goose, his face beet-red from the heat, his canteen dry since morning.

Del wasn't in much better shape. I don't know if he had any water left, but I'd seen him hitting his whiskey bottle a couple of times that day, and alcohol can take a heavy toll on a man in that kind of heat.

"I'll tell you what's going on," Del rumbled, jutting his chin toward a bald knob rising above the deep *barranco* at our side. "We passed that rock three hours ago, heading in the opposite direction. This little son-of-a-b---- is leading us in circles."

Davenport's gaze narrowed. "Is that true, Latham?"

"Yeah, it's true," I replied, trying to act nonchalant, but still ready to dive clear of my saddle if Del started shooting.

"By God, you admit it?" Del exclaimed hoarsely.

"No point in lying about it now."

If possible, Davenport's already red face turned a shade or two darker. "You'd better have a good reason for this misdirection, Latham, or I'll be tempted to leave your carcass on the side of this mountain to feed the vultures."

I raised my wrists, then pulled them apart to tighten the links between the cuffs. "I want these things off, and I want to see my pardon."

"You're hardly in a position to be making demands," Davenport said softly.

"I figure I'm in about the best position I'll ever be," I replied. "You're out of water, Mister Davenport, and the rest of us nearly are. Twenty-four hours from now, men and mules alike are going to start dropping like flies."

"Yourself included," Del growled. "I'll see to that."

"Yeah, myself included, but I figure I can last longer than either of you. When you're dead and withering away, I'll still be walking."

"Not with a bullet in both knees," Davenport pointed out.

"Then I guess I'll be dead, too, but, either way, you won't leave these cañons alive."

Davenport licked tenderly at his dry, chapped lips. He was thirsty and starting to suffer; so was Del.

"I thought we were in a rush," he said after a moment.

"We are. Every minute we lose in this cañon puts your family that much closer to Soto's thugs."

The old man came to a swift decision after that. "Release him, Buchman."

"If I pull them cuffs, Mister Davenport, we lose all control over him," Del said.

"If I intended to run, I could have done it a dozen times already," I replied. "Don't forget, I know where the water holes are out here, champ."

"Enough," Davenport said sharply. "Buchman, free the man."

Del swore mightily, but there wasn't much he could do. He dug the key from his vest pocket and tossed it to me. I snatched it deftly out of mid-air and had my wrists free in less time than it takes to tell it. After rolling my shoulders to stretch the muscles in my back, I held my wrists up where a barely noticeable breeze could soothe the badly chafed flesh.

"The water, Latham," Davenport said.

Grinning at Del, I gave the handcuffs a mighty heave. They sailed out over the edge of the cliff, the polished links glinting briefly before they disappeared into the *barranco* below.

"You son-of-a-b----," Del said.

I sent the key in a different direction, then said: "I want to see that pardon now, and I want my rifle back."

"That rifle ain't yours," Del countered.

"Show him the pardon," Davenport snapped, "then return his rifle."

Del swung to the ground with a curse, then dug the bent and partially crumpled envelope from his saddlebags. Sliding the pardon into the open, he unfolded it where I could see it from the back of my horse, the official seals like twin thumbprints at the top of the page.

"Sign it," I demanded.

"Go to h---."

"Sign it," Davenport instructed.

"Mister Davenport, that document's all we've got. . . ."

"Sign it!" The old man gave me a smoldering glare. "But Del'll keep it with him until our mission is accomplished."

"Fair enough," I agreed, although I'd already decided that if I got the chance, I'd steal the d---ed thing, and to h--- with the consequences.

"There's one last matter to discuss," Davenport said while Del rummaged through his saddlebags for something to write with.

"What's that?"

"This will be the last time I'll be held hostage to demands from anyone in this crew, and that especially means you, Latham. Attempt a stunt like this again, I'll kill you."

A chill like an Arctic wind cut through me. There wasn't a doubt in my mind that Davenport meant it. Before that day, I'd never known how seriously to take the old man's threats. Like, would he really shoot Pedro in the foot if the Moralos hostler allowed someone to steal a little gas or oil from his automobile? Spence, I recalled, had believed him, and after that day in the *barranco,* so did I.

"I want your word, Latham. Your spoken word. If you ever try this again, for any reason, I'll have Buchman gun you down where you stand. Is that understood?"

"Yeah, it's understood."

"All right." He glanced at the lawman. "Sign the pardon."

Grumbling under his breath, Del flattened the sheet of paper against the hard leather of his saddle and scratched his John Henry across the bottom in pencil. He even dated it, and I couldn't help a quick, relieved smile as I watched him return the document to his saddlebag.

"The water, Latham," Davenport said. "How far is it?"

"Not far. A couple of hours at most." Reining my horse over to Luis's pack mule, I loosened the Savage from where Del had lashed it atop one of the ammunition crates. Although Del had left the scabbard with me that day in Moralos, I don't know if he was ever aware of the cartridge belt filled with .303s that I'd kept hidden beneath my bedroll. I slid it out and strapped it around my waist, then checked the Savage's chamber. It was empty. Sliding four bottle-necked rounds from the back of the belt, I pressed them into the magazine from the top, listening to the brass cartridge counter inside the action rotate to full. After closing the action and setting the safety, I returned the gun to its scabbard just as Del swung back into his saddle.

I didn't waste any time after that. A couple of miles upcañon we came to a break in the lower wall that would take us down to the next level. It was a narrow crack, treacherous with scree that had collected there over the eons, but we made it through without injury, then reversed direction until we came to an arroyo, cutting through the rocky surface of the cañon's bench. Reining into the shallow gulch, I dragged the Savage from its scabbard and butted it to my thigh. Seeing me preparing like that, the others quickly did the same. I'm not suggesting the country we'd come through previously had been safe, but we were getting into a land frequented by both bandits and Indians, and were going to have to be doubly careful about our fires, or making any unnecessary noise.

I would have liked to have seen the faces of the men behind me as the arroyo deepened and became narrower. Soon the sides were towering above our heads, the walls closing in until there was barely enough room for the pack mules. Within a hundred yards, the cañon's sides seemed to fold in overhead, blocking out the sky, and the air turned unexpectedly cool and moist. The occasional clank of a stirrup or some piece of gear from one of the mule's packs scraping the sandstone walls seemed to grow louder in the cramped arroyo, echoing faintly before me as if scouting the way.

And then, abruptly, the cañon widened. The ceiling curved over us like a cavern and the floor turned to sand. Ahead in the dim light lay a pool of water nearly thirty feet long and a dozen across. From past visits I knew this little *mere* would be several feet deep in its middle. A shallow trough exited the far end, and beyond that was a second pool, almost as large as the first. To the right, a steady trickle of water fed the upper pond from a narrow slot in the cañon's wall.

This was my secret. This was what had made me so successful as a trader and smuggler. This was Yaqui Springs, the Cañon Where the Small Lizards Run. To the south, less than twenty-four hours away, lay the town of Sabana.

Excerpted from:
Sonora's Delightful Landscapes
by
Alice Sanchez-Harper
Ocean Front Publishing
1938

Although a rarity in Sonora, slot cañons do exist . . . [they] usually lack the vivid colors and fantastical shapes found in many slot cañons in Utah, Arizona, and New Mexico.

[They are normally] formed by the rushing waters of summer thunderstorms, cutting through sandstone over countless eons of time, but have been found in other rocks, such as granite and limestone. Creeks or streams are seldom the cause of a slot cañon's formation. . . .

These slots can be as narrow as two feet, yet rise as much as one hundred feet above the cañon's floor overhead. Occasionally near-perfect caverns can be formed . . . like that at Lizard Run Cañon State Park, north of Sabana.

SESSION EIGHT

I'd barely brought my mount to a stop when Davenport practically tumbled from his saddle in his haste to reach the pool. I grabbed the chestnut's reins and led it away.

"Keep the horses and mules out of the water," I warned the others. "There's a second pond just below us where they can drink."

Although Del was nearly reeling in his saddle from dehydration—the last few hours had been especially hard on him—he stubbornly kept his seat. I dismounted to strip the saddle from the bay's back, then the chestnut's, dumping both rigs in the sand close to the side wall. With lead ropes on their halters, I led the thirsty beasts to the second pool, then stood by patiently while they drank. One by one the others came up with their stripped-down animals, the muleteers handling both their saddle stock and pack mules.

Although it had been my intention to slake my thirst at the upper pool, I guess Del and Spence couldn't wait, and the Perezes didn't care. Glancing at Luis, I shrugged, then squatted between my two animals, hanging onto the lead ropes with my left hand while I scooped up water with my right.

You might wonder why I didn't just flop down on my belly like Del and Spence and dip my face directly into the pool, and the answer is because I'd been trained not to. With a lot of desert tribes, bellying down to drink was not only considered unseemly, it could be dangerous in a land where your enemies

might be lurking nearby, waiting for you to lower your guard—
and your guard doesn't get much lower than burying your face
in a pool of cool water.

Luis and the Perez boys drank as I did, the three of them being desert-born and attuned to their wilderness surroundings in
ways I'd never be, not even if I spent a lifetime living with the
Yaquis.

When the horses and men had taken the edge off of their
thirst, I handed the lead ropes on my bay and Davenport's
chestnut to the Perez boys.

"Hang onto them," I said. "I'm going to check out that side
cañon before we get too comfortable."

Del scrambled to his feet, water dribbling from the short
stubble of his beard as if from a kitchen sponge. I don't think
any of us had shaved since leaving Moralos.

"You don't need to worry about checking that side cañon,"
Del blustered, as if, cool and quenched, he planned to regain
some measure of his earlier authority. But h--- was going to
freeze over—not likely in that part of the country—before I allowed that to happen.

"If you're still worried about me cutting my picket pin, you
can tag along," I said.

Del hesitated, then nodded. "All right, but leave the rifle with
your gear."

"I reckon not," I replied flatly. "In fact, grab your own while
you're at it. If we run into trouble, we'll need long guns more
than revolvers."

"What kind of trouble?" Del asked, frowning.

"This is a Yaqui watering hole, and they consider it sacred. If
they find us here, they'll kill us, or die trying."

Swearing, Del tossed his lead rope to Luis. "Take care of my
horse," he growled, then stalked back to where we'd left our
gear. I retrieved my Savage, while Del yanked a bulky '95

Winchester from his saddle. "You lead, Latham. I want you in front of me the whole way."

Well, no one ever said Delmar Buchman wasn't a complete a--hole. Or maybe it was just me that said it. Sure as h---, that was my opinion of the man—had been ever since he'd slipped below the border to arrest me in Jorge Archuleta's *cantina*.

I paused beside the upper pool, where Davenport had finally crawled out of the water and was resting at the *mere*'s edge on his hands and knees. He looked green around the gills, for a fact, and I said: "If you've got to puke, don't do it in the water."

The old man raised his head high enough to glare in my direction, but he was hurting too much to put a lot of heat into it.

"I mean it," I said. "We've all got to drink from that pool for the next few days."

He just waved me away, and I went. I didn't feel like standing over him, watching out for him like some papa watching out for a toddler. He should have known better than to drink too much, too fast.

I've already mentioned that the side cañon was narrow, no more than three feet across at its mouth—like a cleft hacked into the wall by a sharp axe. It was steep, too, and in the wet season you'd be wading run-off all the way to the top, a series of short waterfalls littered with small branches and other débris from upstream.

The branches were still there, which I considered a good sign, since it seemed to indicate that nobody had been through there since last winter's rains, looking for firewood, but the stream was barely ankle-deep and no more than a foot across.

I climbed swiftly, stepping over what jams I could, pausing to clear away those I didn't think the horses could easily jump because of the slick stone bed. It was here, too, that Del began to fully appreciate the Yaqui name for the place. The scurrying claws of the brightly banded geckos and smaller whiptails sounded like the rustling of old newspapers on every side. I saw several dozen slipping into the litter along the streambed, and figured we'd both be lucky if we reached the top without some little spine-backed reptile dropping down on top of us. I hadn't seen any of the small creatures in the main cañon, but figured that would change once they became used to our presence there. Give it a day or two, and they'd start creeping back, curious as cats.

Del stayed close behind me all the way, and I could tell from the way his bloodshot eyes were darting that he was growing more and more uneasy the farther in we ventured. He probably thought it was because of the tight confines of the fissure and the vulnerability of our position in case of an attack, but I figured it was something else, and I'm not talking about Yaqui Indians or skittering lizards. I didn't say anything until we reached the top, though.

After fifteen minutes or so we came out in a box cañon maybe a quarter of a mile long and a hundred yards across. The stream spilled from a tangle of broken rocks at the far end of a grassy meadow, forming a series of shallow pools along the length of the cañon before flowing into the narrow slot to the lower cañon. There were trees in here, feather-leafed mesquite and alders growing along the stream's banks. The grass was green and lush and belly-high to a tall horse. I didn't see any evidence that it had been grazed in a long time, maybe a year or more.

It didn't take Del long to spy the object of his uneasiness. He jerked to a stop and started to shoulder his rifle, then uncertainly lowered it. "What the Christ!" he grunted.

I was staring at it, too, an ancient pictograph painted high on the cañon's south wall. Part bird and part man, it gave off an air of nearly palpable malevolence. There were smaller drawings around it, and more on the opposite wall, but none that commanded our attention like the predatorial demeanor of the ancient Thunderbird.

"I don't know his name," I said softly, almost reverently. "The Yaquis call him the big bird from *Otam Kawi,* that used to eat the people of their villages until he was killed. Now he guards the path to the other side. Or this path, at any rate."

"The other side of what?"

"Life, death. Your choice, I guess."

"With something like that guarding the entrance to h---, it's no wonder everyone's afraid to die."

"I didn't say he guarded the entrance to h---. I said he watched over one of the paths to the other side."

"The redskin's path, you mean? It sure as s--- ain't guarding the entrance to our heaven. Not some heathen symbol like that."

I glanced at him wonderingly. "You prefer Saint Peter and pearly gates watching over your entrance, Del?"

"Don't make fun of what you don't know," he replied stonily.

I shrugged and turned away. With everything else going on, I didn't see a need to drag religion into the fray. "Well, whoever he is, he can watch over our horses while we're here."

"There ain't no other way out?"

"Nope. I've never seen antelope or mustangs down here, either, although that's probably because they'd have to come in through the slot to reach it." I nodded toward the cliffs on the north side of the cañon, more broken than those to the south. "I've seen desert bighorns up there, but never down here. I don't know if they can't reach the floor, or if your ol' buddy from *Otam Kawi* keeps them away."

"Bighorn sheep ain't gonna be afraid of pictures painted on a cañon wall," Del replied, but, from his tone, I suspect the ancient Thunderbird's stare was eating at him more than he wanted to admit.

"Let's go get the horses," I said, swinging my rifle to my left hand now that I was no longer worried about finding some small band of Yaquis holed up in there.

We gathered a couple of armloads of firewood on the way back, and dumped them beside the upper pool. There were numerous old fire sites around the pond, identified by pieces of charred wood and soot stains on the curved ceiling that helped filter the smoke before it reached the surface. I told the muleteers to take the stock up the narrow fissure to the grassy cañon above and turn them loose.

"No reason to hobble them," I added. "They're not likely to wander back down here unless a cougar scares them."

Having lost a couple of pack animals to mountain lions and jaguars over the years, I knew they sometimes hunted this region, which was another reason I didn't want to hobble the stock. They'd need all the speed they could muster if one of those big cats sniffed them out.

That night, sheltered as we were deep inside the larger slot cañon, we kindled a good-size fire, then fixed a hearty supper of fried ham and ash cakes. We kept the small communal coffee pot bubbling, enough for all of us to have two cups apiece. Afterward I stretched out with my lower back against my saddle and rolled a cigarette. It felt good to have my arms free again. I'd rolled my shirt sleeves up earlier to allow the moist, cool air of the slot to soothe the angry flesh. If it had been me outfitting the group, I would have made sure we had a tin of salve along for cuts and scrapes—always a likelihood around livestock—but also for humans when the need arose, as it usually did around livestock. A little of Doctor Lester's Miracle Medical Salve or some Carter's Udder Cream would have done wonders for my itching wrists.

Davenport was looking a lot better after a good meal and a little rest. He was leaning against his own saddle, smoking one of those big black cigars that looked like it had been left behind by a sick dog, but which I've heard cost 50¢ apiece in Tucson. For the price, I would have expected a better aroma. Glancing at me over the glowing tip of his panatela, the old man asked: "How far away are we?"

"Another day and most of a night." I studied him curiously in the primeval light. "You never did say what your plans were."

"My plans were to assess the situation once we arrived at our destination, but I'd consider any suggestions you might wish to propose."

Well, as a matter of fact, I had one. I'd been considering how best to approach the ransom of Abby Davenport and her kids ever since leaving Yuma, and had come to a few conclusions along the way. I said: "If we ride in there toting those guns out in the open, there won't be much incentive for Soto to release your family."

"Hardly an original determination, Latham. I was hoping for something a little more relevant, considering your experience with the people of Sabana."

"All right, then, consider this. You've got about as much chance of riding in there and getting out again with your family as a snowball in a hot skillet. But I might be able to do it."

Davenport's expression never changed, and I'd wonder later on if this wasn't something he'd had in mind all along, one of the reasons he'd had me sprung from Yuma, rather than seeking a native guide.

"Through your past contacts, you mean?" A trace of smugness crossed his sunburned face. "Your smuggler's contacts?"

"The men I traded with, yeah."

"And you believe these men can be trusted?"

"Not all of them, but there was one older man I used to stable my burros with. I'd trust him, if he's still alive."

"Will he help us?"

"He wouldn't help you, but he might help me. Assuming I've

got something to grease his wheels with."

"Meaning money?"

"It would likely cost him his life if Soto found out what he was doing. He'd consider it treason to Castillo's revolution."

"Adolpho Castillo doesn't have a revolution," Davenport replied coolly. "He has a gang, but he's too far removed from Sabana to influence Soto's decisions, no matter what others would have you believe."

I shrugged. "Maybe, not that it would mean much to a man standing in front of one of Soto's firing squads." After a pause, I added: "You know that this isn't going to be easy, that I'm not going to be able to just ride in there and set up a trade? I'll need to keep some distance between me and Soto until I can get things set up. The guy I told you about will likely help if he can, but there'll probably be others I'll have to go through, as well."

"Cut the crap, Latham. How much?"

"Two hundred dollars. Silver or gold, if you've got it."

Davenport hesitated for so long I was beginning to think he might refuse. Then he glanced at Del. "Get it."

Del shot me a dark look, then pushed to his feet. He went to his saddlebags and withdrew the small leather pouch I'd seen him use in Yuma, and brought it back to the fire. From the edge of the darkness, I could see Carlos and Felix watching like vultures as Del passed the sack to Davenport. The old man loosened the drawstring and spilled a handful of coins into his palm. From the shadows, Carlos hissed softly.

"There's eighty dollars here," Davenport announced, pushing the coins around with a finger. "Eighty-two and thirty-five in change, to be exact." He dumped the coins back into the bag and tossed it across the flames to me.

"It'll help," I said, and dropped the pouch into a small pommel bag off my saddle horn.

"I'm going to let you take only one gun and a single case of ammunition, just enough for Soto to see what kind of firepower I've got here. Once he turns over my son, you can come back for another gun and more ammunition. Set it up for an additional mule with full packs of ammunition for the release of my wife and daughter, then the remainder of the ammunition and the final weapon when the transaction is completed." He leaned forward, his gaze intensifying. "With one non-negotiable stipulation. I want my son first."

"That isn't going to be easy. Men like Chito Soto can be. . . ."

"I am fully aware of what men like Chito Soto can be like, Latham. In this case, I don't care. With the kind of weaponry I'm supplying, he can concede this one point. Bring back my son. Bring me Charles."

I hesitated, then shrugged non-committally. I'd do what I could, but whether Davenport cared or not, men like Chito Soto had their own way of doing things. "I'll leave first thing in the morning," I said.

"But not alone," Davenport replied. "I'm sending Buchman with you."

I started at that, then shook my head. "No offense, Mister Davenport, but Del Buchman is the last person I'd want riding with me. One *gringo* is risky enough, but at least I'm known in Sabana, and I know the language a lot better than Del does, too. He'd stand out down there like a dancing bear in a flock of pelicans."

"I hate to agree with anything this little prick says," Del chimed in, "but in this case, he's right. A stranger in town is gonna get folks to talking, and word of a *gringo* stranger will likely get back to Soto and his boys before we've cleared our saddles."

"All right, then. . . ." Davenport's gaze traveled across the fire. .

"I'll take Vega," I said quickly, before the old man could make another choice. "He'll fit in better than the Perezes, and he's done this kind of thing before. He'll know the ropes better than Carlos or Felix."

"The ropes?"

"How to slip into a town without being seen, how to keep his animals quiet and on a short lead. A mule is just naturally going to want to bray as soon as it gets among its own kind, especially those it's never seen before. If I ain't wrong, Luis'll know how to muzzle a mule."

Davenport was silent as he considered my arguments. They made good sense, and while the old man might have been a first-class son-of-a-b----, he wasn't a fool. Still, I could tell the prospect of allowing me to go into Sabana with just one of the muleteers was gnawing at him. The old man didn't trust Soto, which was smart, but he didn't trust me, either. I think he finally realized he didn't have a choice.

"Very well," he said after a lengthy pause. "You and Vega. But heed me well, Latham, if either of you try to double-cross me, the flames in h--- won't be high enough to hide you."

"I'm not going to double-cross you or your family, Mister Davenport. Besides, I still want that pardon Buchman is holding. Luis and I'll leave first thing tomorrow. It'll take us most of a day and a night to get there, then however much time it takes to set up a trade. After that it'll be another twenty-four hours back here . . . longer if Soto sends trackers after us. We'll have to ditch them before coming in."

"Very well, just remember that I want my son first. I . . . there's a reason that his release is more imperative than the others."

I studied him closely in the lowering light of the dying fire, wondering what the old man's motive really was for wanting his son delivered first. If it had been me, I think I would have wanted the woman out first, but I didn't know Davenport or his family, and figured there could be any number of reasons for ransoming the boy before the others.

Switching to Spanish, I quickly outlined the situation to Luis, even though he already knew what was going on. I don't recall if I've mentioned this yet, but Luis could speak English at least as fluently as I could Spanish. Or border Spanish, at any rate, which is quite a bit different than what they teach you in high school. I don't know why he wanted to keep that little tidbit of information a secret from the others, but figured it might be for the same reason no one knew about that little Colt semi-auto I was still packing inside the lining of my vest. It ain't smart to lay all your cards on the table all at once, not if you want to walk away with a few winning hands.

"We'll pull out of here at first light," I added to Luis, who merely nodded his understanding. He was a good man, and I realized I was glad he was coming along.

Carlos and Felix exchanged glances but didn't say anything, and I could read nothing in those dark Indian eyes. Pushing abruptly to my feet, I grabbed my saddle with my bedroll still tied behind the cantle and made my way toward the upper entrance to the slot cañon. Over my shoulder, I said: "You might want to consider having a man bed down south of the lower pool, in case someone tries to slip in during the night and cut a few throats."

I was awake well before dawn the next morning, and made my way up the narrow side cañon in the dark. I found my bay in the deep grass close to the brook, and slipped a halter over her head. Luis's saddle and pack mules were standing nearby, hip-shot and dozing, and seemed to barely notice as I haltered them. Stringing them out one behind the other, lead rope-to-tail, I led them back down through the cañon to the upper pool, where Carlos Perez was feeding twigs to a fresh flame.

Del and Spence were shuffling around half asleep, while Luis and Felix puttered over an ammunition crate they'd broken open, shifting the contents—wax paper-wrapped packages of twenty rounds each—into separate panniers to help balance the new load. We'd still tote the machine-gun up high on the saw-bucks, but a single crate of ammunition would be too heavy to carry on just one side of a mule's pack. It would pull the load off balance, and rub the hide off the animal's ribs before the day was finished. There's an art to packing mules that seems to be dying a slow death in this age of modern transportation.

Davenport, I noticed, was still in his bedroll, curled on his side with his blankets pulled up over his ears. He was unmoving save for the steady rise and fall of his shoulder, and I wondered what it would take to awaken him. A trumpet? A stick of dynamite? Or maybe a Yaqui's knife, slicing through the thin flesh of his throat? Back then, a good night's sleep in that country was a luxury few men could afford.

Del came over, his woolly brows twitching in consternation. Anticipating some new threat to shackle me with, I was caught by surprise when he said: "Good luck, Latham. Get 'em outta there if you can. I met the woman once, and she's a decent sort. Just because she married a first-class jacka-- don't mean she ought to be the one to suffer for his mistake."

I hesitated, sensing more to his words than he seemed willing to acknowledge, but before I could quiz him, he stalked away. I scowled in Davenport's direction, and I swear I detected a shift in his breathing, as if he wasn't asleep any more, but wanted us to think he was. A tiny prickle of doubt eased up my spine. I shook it off and went to fetch my saddle. I was snugging up the cinch when Spence came over, munching on a piece of leftover ham slapped on a square of hardtack.

"Ye got everything ye need, laddie?" he asked.

"I could use a revolver," I replied, glancing at the one on his hip.

He nodded thoughtfully. "How about food?" He held out his piece of hardtack and ham. "I could fetch ye some crackers, if ye think ye teeth'll be rooted firmly enough to chew through it."

I shook my head. "We'll make do with what we've got." Luis and I had filled our saddlebags last night with dried meat and some leftover ash cakes, enough to get us into Sabana. After that we'd either pick up some fresh grub for the trip back, or be in too big of a hurry to think about eating.

Luis came over to tell me he was ready. I didn't insult him by asking if the load was balanced, or if the equipment was in good shape. If Luis said it was ready, it was ready.

"*Bueno*, let's get out of here."

Ed Davenport was sitting up now, the blankets puddled at his waist. He was staring at me stoically, but I didn't go over. Pulling the bay's near-side stirrup off the seat, I quickly stepped into the saddle.

While Luis went to fetch his saddle mule, Del returned with a leather case swinging from one gnarled fist. I recognized it as soon as he handed it to me. "Keep your eyes on the skyline, Latham, and don't go getting your rump shot off."

Again, his words caught me off guard. That morning, it was like his personality had done a complete flip. I'm not saying we were friends—I'll never forgive him for coming south of the border to arrest me, or the years I lost in Yuma—but for a few minutes there, while Luis and I were readying our stock, our mutual animosity seemed to cool. Not sure how to respond, I ended up lifting the binocular case in my hand, like a fish on the end of a line. "I reckon this'll help."

"Yeah, well, don't lose 'em," he replied, his tone gruff again.

"They cost me five bucks in Tucson last year."

"I'll see what I can do," I said, wrapping the heavy straps around my saddle horn. After an awkward pause, I added: "You know if we aren't back in three days, we likely won't be coming back."

"You'd d---ed well better be back," he replied. "Screwin' up ain't an option this time." Then he slapped the bay's hip with the flat of his hand, raising a powdery cloud of dust and leaving a partial imprint of his palm on the mare's hide, like an old brand nearly haired over. "Get outta here, Latham. You ain't doing nothing but wasting daylight now."

I reined the bay away from the fire, nodding to Spence as I rode past but ignoring the Perez boys. I didn't waste a rearward glance at Davenport, and he didn't call after me, either. I reckon as far as he was concerned, everything that needed saying had been said the night before.

Luis fell in behind me, a serape draped over his shoulders against the morning chill, his pack mule grunting irritably at leaving behind the comforts of the hidden camp.

The Yaqui Springs cañon is a short one, as far as cañons go, although none of the slot cañons I'm familiar were what you would call lengthy. A couple of hundred feet past the lower pool, the cañon abruptly widened to thirty feet or more, the rim flaring back, then dropping lower. Five minutes later I hauled back on the bay's reins to stare out across the rough *barrancos* and sheer-sided cliffs that were rumpled up before us.

Pulling up at my side, Luis said: "Which direction, J.T.?"

I nodded south. "See those mountains yonder? Those are the Sierra Verdes. Sabana is on the other side of them."

"They are not as far away as I'd feared."

"Not as the crow flies, but it'll take us all day to reach them, then a good chunk of the night getting over the top. There's an old game trail there nobody used to use. If it's still there, and hasn't been wiped clean by a landslide, we'll follow that over the top." I gave him a wry smile. "Now that you know my secrets, it won't be long before you're an old hand on these trails."

"Is there not enough trade for two of us?" he asked. "If not as partners, then at least we can use the same water holes without trying to shoot one another, or steal the other man's merchandise."

"No, that was never my style, but if what Archuleta says about Soto's men shutting down the Sabana breweries is true, there won't be much reason for either of us to come this far south."

"*Sí*, perhaps, but the fighting will not continue forever. When Porfirio Díaz is gone and Mexico is finally free, the trade will return."

Maybe, I thought, but it occurred to me that I was no longer interested in trading across the border—smuggling. I was tired of putting my neck on the chopping block with every trip. Even before Chito Soto took over the Sabana Valley, all that country through there had been rife with bandits and hostiles, Yaquis and Apaches alike.

I hadn't done it for the money, I'd known that from the very beginning. Slipping across the border that first time with a couple of burros laden with a case of strike-anywhere matches, a bunch of second-hand shoes, and some ladies dresses, I'd done it for the adventure, the thrill of outfoxing U.S. Marshals in the north and *Federales* to the south. But Yuma had changed me. H---, Yuma changed everyone who spent any time there, no matter which side of the bars they slept on. It turned some harder and meaner. Others swore they'd never go back, and were willing to give up their lawlessness if that's what it took. I fell into the latter category, and was determined to find another way to make a living. One that would hopefully still satisfy my need for adventure—assuming I made it out of Sabana with my head still attached to my shoulders.

Leaving the Cañon Where the Small Lizards Run, we rode more east than south for several hours, winding through narrow, rock-strewn cañons and over sharp-spined ridges, their flanks thick with cactus and scrub. Around midmorning the land began to level off into gently rolling hills. There was more grass, too, although I'd hate to think how many acres it would take to feed a single head of beef over the summer.

I wasn't following any particular trail that day, and never did when I could help it. Not even approaching the few water holes that dotted that harsh desert environment. Even Yaqui Springs had more than one approach if you knew where to look. Despite our meandering route, I wasn't worried about becoming lost, not with the Sierra Verdes rising so tall on the southern horizon. I'd spotted our destination over the mountains that morning, a low hogback ridge with twin knobs protruding from either side like the stubby horns of a two-year-old steer. The locals called it the Devil's Crown, and considered it an unlucky peak to hunt on; it was just a landmark to me, and I thanked my lucky stars that the locals were so superstitious.

The sun was just past its apex when we came to a wide, flat valley—our last barrier to the distant mountains. I pulled up, then leaned forward in my saddle to ease my sweating, aching shanks. At my side, Luis was peering about curiously.

"There is water here?" he asked.

"None that I've ever found. That's why there aren't any ranches or villages out this way."

"And the sierras?"

"Another three hours' ride, but we won't attempt it in this heat."

There was some tall chaparral off to the west. Its shade would be minimal, but better than sitting out in the open, and a lot easier on the stock than trying to cross those flats in that heat.

There's a reason the Mexicans believe in the *siesta,* and it's a practical one. Spend a day or two out in that hot Sonoran sun and you won't have to ask what it is.

We rode into the chaparral and dismounted. Slipping Del's binoculars from their case, I moved to the very edge of the flats for a closer look at the sprawling wasteland. Heat waves shimmered like burlesque dancers above the earth's surface, creating a surreal landscape where rocks seemed to float ten feet above the ground, and a trotting coyote appeared as tall as a man, its tongue lolling as it disappeared into the scrub.

To be on the safe side, I tracked backward with my glasses from where I'd seen the coyote, concerned that something might have disturbed it from its den during this hottest part of the day, but the *llano* appeared uninhabited. It wasn't, of course. Even the harshest environments can support all manner of life, but it was the human kind I was searching for, and I didn't see any sign of it.

Slipping back into the chaparral, I said: "Let's pull the head-stalls and loosen the cinches, but leave them saddled."

Luis nodded. He didn't ask about the pack mule. Like me, he would have preferred to ease the animal's burden, but we both knew that loosening the packs would invite disaster as soon as the brawny jack shifted his weight, or hooked a rope on a branch. And removing his load altogether would leave us too vulnerable if bandits or Indians showed up.

"I'll take the first watch," I volunteered, an offer Luis readily accepted.

Taking my rifle, a canteen, and Del's binoculars, I left the chaparral and made my way to the top of a nearby hill, where I'd have a better view of the terrain. Coming to a patch of bare, flinty soil surrounded by. . . .

SESSION NINE

I can see now why you warned me about your recording machine coming to the end of a disk. It makes a h--- of a racket, and I don't doubt that others have complained about it. I don't know how many people you've interviewed for this writing project the government is sponsoring, but, if they're like me, they were probably pretty deep into their memories when the d---ed thing squawked like that.

Anyway, getting back to my story, we were still about twelve hours shy of Sabana when we came to some chaparral at the edge of a wide flat and decided to hunker down for a while. We did that for two reasons. One was because it was hotter than the bottom of a skillet out there, and the other was that I didn't want to cross that open plain during the daylight hours, when we might be spotted from the Sierra Verdes. I'm not saying there was anyone up there to see us, but those are the kinds of precautions you learned to take in my old line of work.

Just sitting alone in the desert like that can get a man pondering, and that's what I was doing—thinking about my future and what I wanted to do with it. I was remembering how I'd gotten into the business, and from there it was just a hop and a skip to the conversation Spence and I had shared that first evening in Moralos, about Geronimo's capture and exile to Florida.

I hadn't mentioned this to Spence at the time, but seeing old Geronimo and his warriors outside of Holbrook that day was what inspired me to jump my own reservation—so to speak. I don't think we've discussed this yet, and maybe it isn't "germane to the plot", as the literates say, but I'm going to tell it anyway, because if it wasn't for Geronimo, I'd likely never have become a trader, or spent three years living among the Yaquis, which is what eventually led me to the Cañon Where the Small Lizards Run.

I wasn't born into an adventurous family, although I was hatched in the Prescott Valley of Arizona Territory in 1875, which I guess is somewhat better than a Connecticut farm for wild and woolly—no offense meant, in case someone from rural Connecticut ever listens to this recording, or reads a transcript of it.

Anyway, I was born near Prescott in '75, but my family moved to Holbrook during the winter of '82 or '83 to open a grocery there on Central Street. I'll confess it was a shock for me to leave what is, in my opinion, one of the most beautiful spots in all of Arizona for the flat and nearly featureless landscape surrounding Holbrook, a railroad town on the Little Colorado River and a place of perpetual wind and dust and, for some, I think, hopelessness, although it was all new when we got there, the tracks only recently laid.

It was the newness that attracted Pa. He felt there was money to be made in such a raw community, although I don't think they ever did as well there as they had in the valley. New ain't always better, if you ask me.

What made Holbrook even more miserable for me was a lack of friends my own age to run around with. Hot and lonely, it wasn't long before I began to resent the town and its people. I dreamed nightly of escaping its isolation, my goal in those tender years of my youth to become an Army scout like Al Sieber or Tom Horn. I envisioned myself leading cavalry charges against renegade Apaches and outlaws alike, wearing fringed buckskins and wide-brimmed sombreros, instead of the cheap cloth caps

137

my parents forced on me.

Those scouts were my heroes, and their exploits, brought to life in newspaper articles and cheap dime novels, provided the illusional reality I clung to when the years of stocking shelves and keeping books stretching before me became too much to bear.

And then, when I was eleven, Geronimo surrendered, and my dreams of heroism turned to ash. Barely a decade into life, and I was already a has-been, a relic of another age.

You're smiling, and the way things turned out, I know why, but you've got to remember that I was just a starry-eyed kid at the time. Still, I think I knew even then that I wasn't cut from the same bolt of cloth as my pa. I yearned for something more— adventure and danger, fast horses and fancy guns. Anything except a d---ed clerk's apron.

The Apaches had been the last hold-outs of the Indian Wars. The Sioux, the Cheyennes, and the Comanches had already succumbed to white encroachment, and manifest destiny had smothered the rest of the nation under a mantle of civilization. It was as if something wild and free within me was boarding that train to Florida, leaving behind a kid's spirit, high, dry, and wind-blown.

It's selfish and probably insulting, although I don't mean for it to be, but when I got a look at Geronimo and his men on the day the Army loaded them into railroad cars for the eastern seaboard, the expressions on their faces jelled with the feelings in my soul. For months afterward, when I wasn't in school or delivering groceries, I roamed the streets of Holbrook in a desolate frame of mind. And then, in the spring of '87, the Apache Kid cut loose on a bloody rampage that threw the entire territory into a frenzy of terror.

In looking back, I have my doubts about a lot of the atrocities we laid at the Kid's feet, but at the time we were all quick to blame just about any misdeed—including the theft of Mrs. Qualtmeyer's raisin pie from her window sill—on the nefarious murderer and his gang of wildcats, which rumor estimated in excess of thirty blood-crazed cut-throats. [*Ed. Note: Haskay-bay-nay-ntayl,* otherwise known as the Apache Kid, was born circa 1860, and may have died in either 1894 or the 1930s, depending upon the source used; his "war party" during his 1887 flight from military authority never numbered more than four followers, all of them ex-scouts like himself.]

By early summer, the Army had several detachments of the 4th Cavalry in the field to hunt him down, and I thought: *Hot d---, Dolly, here's my chance!*

It was a hot June night just after reading about one of the Kid's alleged crimes—I'm calling it "alleged" now, but figured it for a fact at the time—that I packed a cheap pasteboard suitcase with a few clothes I thought suitable for a scout's life, snuck my pa's little .32 pump-action rifle and a box of cartridges from the closet, and slipped out my bedroom window about thirty minutes before the 2:00 a.m. train to Winslow was scheduled to arrive.

I'd been watching trains roll in and out of Holbrook for several years by then—that being about the only entertainment a guy too young to visit a saloon or dance hall had in that dreary environment—and already had my escape planned. I'd hide in the shadows west of the depot, behind a pile of cross-ties that had been sitting there since the first rail had been laid through town in '82, and, when the train pulled out for Winslow, I'd make a dash for one of the cars toward the middle of the line and climb aboard.

I figured once I got away from Holbrook—meaning out of reach of my ma and pa and maybe the sheriff—I'd head south to Fort Bowie. Don't get me wrong, I never thought they'd hire a kid like me for anything, let alone a frontier scout, but I was determined to make my presence known, to hang around the men who were scouts, and to learn everything I could about the craft of guiding men in the field. Having just turned twelve years of age a few weeks earlier and still so wet behind the ears it's a wonder I didn't drown whenever I laid down, I'd decided that was the quickest way to earn my feathers.

As you might imagine, nothing worked out as I'd planned. Oh, I made good on my departure from Holbrook, and didn't go back again until I was eighteen, but I never scouted for the Army, or even made it to Fort Bowie.

I was in Phoenix when I ran out of money and had to start sleeping in barns or under porches, which I don't recommend in that country on account of snakes and scorpions and such. I finally got a job, and it probably won't surprise you to learn that it was delivering groceries. The pay was $1 a week, but the position included two meals a day and a place to sleep at night— granted, it was just a few blankets in a corner of the storeroom, but better than sharing cold dirt with a garter snake looking for something warm to curl up against.

Providing food in lieu of a higher wage may have seemed like a good idea to the pot-bellied Dutchman who ran the place, but I believe he soon came to regret the decision. A kid my age can pack away a fair amount of grub after a full day of running errands, and it wasn't long before the old skinflint wanted to put a cap on the amount of food I could have at a meal. Fortunately his wife was more kind-hearted.

Although I ate good in Phoenix, I was never really comfortable there. It always felt too close to Holbrook, so after a couple of months I drew my wages—less than $2 after personal expenses had been deducted—and hitched a ride south with a muleskinner named Henry Toomes.

Henry was an independent, meaning he contracted for his own loads that he'd haul just about anywhere a man wanted to pay to have his merchandise delivered. He drove one of those twenty-mule jerkline rigs, with two huge freighters and a water wagon hitched on back. The reason Henry consented to let me tag along was because his regular swamper had broken an arm in a saloon brawl, and he needed a man to handle the brakes on the downgrades, and to help take care of his mules in the morning and evening. I guess I did OK, because, when we got to Gila Bend, he offered me a temporary job until his regular swamper was mended.

This, finally, was the kind of work I'd been dreaming of. It wasn't scouting, but it was a close . . . well, a close fifth or sixth, I guess. Mostly it was outside, where both of us went armed, and there was the threat of real danger around every bend. Man, I loved it, and there wasn't anyone in Arizona more tickled than I was when we returned to Phoenix a couple of months later to discover that Henry's old swamper had taken a job cooking for a cattle ranch up near Flagstaff.

I had some concerns that one of Henry's contracts might eventually take us to Holbrook, but they never did. I stayed with him through my fourteenth birthday, and saw a good bit of southern Arizona and northern Mexico in that time. We even got down to Hermosillo once or twice. I'll tell you, it was grand ol' time, but it didn't last. We were coming back from Hermosillo, just outside of Magdalena and on our way to Nogales, when a war party of Yaquis jumped us as we were breaking camp one morning. I got a club upside my skull early in the fray, and didn't see what happened to Henry or his mules, but I heard about it afterward. Listening to the gory details and the eager way in which it was told, I was glad I'd been knocked senseless for the few hours it had taken them to kill poor old Henry Toomes.

Back then, the Yaquis of the Dead Horse clan were a cruel people, and torturing their enemies meant a lot to them. Like a lot of other tribes, it was almost a part of their religion, as if they took spiritual strength from watching a strong man die bravely. I'm not going to relate the methods they used to extract Henry's powerful spirit, but they must have been highly satisfied with the results by the time they were finished. It's always sobered me to realize how lucky I had been to have my own life spared. It could have easily gone the other way, and I probably would've died right there alongside of Henry if I hadn't been knocked unconscious during those first minutes of the attack.

Old Toad, whom I've already mentioned, took me in. His Yaqui name was a stretch to pronounce, and I won't even try to spell it, but it meant something like the Wise Toad That Lives Along the Big River, which to the Dead Horses, meant the Río Concepción.

I don't know if it was a coincidence that the wily old butcher so closely resembled his namesake that it could almost make you laugh to think about it. Nor do I mean to imply that the Toad was anything like a father to me. Despite the fact that he had a son about my own age, I don't believe that cold-blooded prodigy of Satan's loins had a shot glass worth of compassion in his whole body. Not for his own son, and sure as blazes not for some peach-fuzzed roustabout plucked from a freighter's camp. . . .

I was still thinking about Toad and my years among the Yaquis when I spotted Luis coming through the chaparral. He paused briefly at the edge of the scrub, then came up to where I was sitting, keeping low to the ground like the smart man he was. Dropping down beside me, he said: "*Madre,* it is hot, my friend. Like trying to sleep in an oven."

"It'll be no cooler up here."

He nodded agreement. "True, but I thought I would take over for a while." He glanced at the sky. "When do you wish to leave?"

"Sundown, I reckon. If the trail I want to use over the Verdes is still open, we ought to be in Sabana before dawn."

"A couple more hours, then?"

"Yeah, but wake me before that."

"*Sí*, I will."

Staying low, as Luis had coming up, I returned to the chaparral where my bay and the two mules stood listlessly. Despite the broiling warmth, I managed to doze a little, yet came instantly awake when I heard the clatter of branches from behind me. I rolled onto my stomach while pulling the Savage to my shoulder, but it was only Luis, making his way through the thick brush to my side. He smiled when he saw my saturated shirt and the sweat dripping from my forehead.

"I told you," he said simply.

"I believed you, too," I replied, rising. The light was softening in the east, and the sun had already dropped below the western horizon. "Did you see anything?" I asked, and, when Luis shook his head, I said: "Let's get started."

We paused again at the edge of the flats, and I took another few minutes to glass the land between us and the mountains. Not spying anything worrisome, I returned the binoculars to their case and nodded to Luis. We pushed out into the wide flat like skiffs cutting into the surf of a tawny ocean. Luis was keeping a tight lead on the pack mule, and I had my rifle across the saddle in front of me. The light drained from the sky as if tethered to the sun, and a cool breeze soon picked up. My shirt dried quickly and my flesh pimpled in the chill. Draping my reins around the bay's saddle horn, I twisted in my seat to retrieve my coat from under my bedroll and pulled it on without stopping. At my side, Luis unfolded his frayed serape and draped it over his shoulders like a blanket.

We didn't talk, but it wasn't quiet. The night is never quiet if you know how to listen. Besides the murmur of the breeze in the scrub, the far-off howl of a Mexican wolf, and the steady clop of hoof beats, there was the sandy scurry of lizards, the pad of rabbits darting out of our path, and the flutter of bat wings overhead. Twice we heard the tiny screech of an owl from the chaparral behind us, like a bow drawn shrilly across an out-of-tune fiddle.

It wasn't quite midnight when we reached the foothills below the Devil's Crown and dismounted to give our mounts a break. Stepping out of the wind, we rolled and smoked a couple of cigarettes for our meal, then pushed on into the night. The moon was sailing toward the earth's rim but the sky was clear and filled with stars. Luis, who had ridden beside me all day, had to drop back on the narrowing trail to bring up the rear.

Our path grew more treacherous the closer we got to the top, a time or two squeezing in so tight that the ammunition pouch on the pack mule's left side would scrape the stone wall, while the right-hand pouch hung out over a thousand foot drop. I could hear Luis muttering soft curses to himself. He didn't know this trail like I did, and it was making him nervous, especially in such poor light, but I'd hauled as many as eight burros up this path on darker nights than that, and never lost a load or an animal.

The wind sharpened noticeably when we finally reached the broad, grassy swale that separated the curved protrusions that gave the peak its name. The pass was dotted with lichen-covered boulders and scrawny, wind-twisted junipers, none of which were more than a few feet tall. Kicking his saddle mule alongside my mare, Luis gave me a baleful look. "I think you are trying to scare me away from this trail, *hombre.*"

I laughed and shook my head. "There's an easier one if you want to use it, but you'd never slip into Sabana that way without being seen."

"*Hijo de p---,*" he exclaimed softly. "Maybe I should get

another job. I think this one took about six months off of my life tonight."

"It ain't so bad after you've been over it a time or two." I jutted my chin toward the valley floor, where a few faint lights were still visible, even at this late hour.

"Sabana?"

"Yes."

"And the trail going down this side of the mountain?"

"Not nearly as bad," I assured him. "A little rough coming off the rim, but then we'll drop into a cañon and start making good time again."

"No more sheer cliffs?"

"Not after we get into the cañon."

He was staring grimly down the trail when a strong gust of wind slammed into us, pushing the brim of his sombrero back against the hat's tall crown. Ducking his shoulder to the icy currents, he waited until it had swept on by, then made the sign of the cross. "*Vámonos*, J.T. Let's get off of this mountain before the wind blows us back to Moralos."

The moon was down but dawn had yet to arrive when we came out of the cañon and reined up on a bench above the Sabana Valley. In Spanish, Sabana translates loosely to savannah, and you could tell right away that there was water here. A soothing moistness permeated the air, assuaging the lungs after so many days traipsing across the harsh northern desert.

Sabana's waters issued from a trio of unbelievably productive springs, roaring out of a cañon a half mile west of the one Luis and I had used coming down off the Crown. I'd been there a few times early on, and had stared in awe at a hundred-foot waterfall at the upper end of the cañon, spilling over the lip of the cliff in a rainbow of sun-glistening spray. A cool mist floated above the glade below the falls, so that, when you left, it was with droplets of moisture clinging to your cheeks like a watery beard. No doubt the place had once been sacred to the Indians who used to live there, just as the Cañon Where the Small Lizards Run had been to the Yaquis, but the Spaniards had taken over the valley who knew how many centuries before and driven out the indigenous population through disease, slavery, and outright slaughter.

The crop lands below the cañon's mouth were intersected by numerous branches of the same stream, pulling apart, then coming back together a dozen times as it made its way through the broad savannah, the rich black soil yielding a steady bounty of fruit, cotton, tobacco, and grains.

It was the grains, the barley and wheat, that provided the basis for Sabana's three major breweries, as it was the beer and tobacco that had brought me here that first time so many years before

Easing his saddle mule alongside my mare, Luis murmured: "What a beautiful valley. I could see myself settling down in a place like this someday."

"I could, too," I said, feeling a tightening in my chest to realize how much I meant it.

Then, as if to bring us back to the reality of our situation, a light came on in a flat-roofed adobe structure below us, and Luis sighed.

"Let's move out," I said, reluctant to break the valley's spell.

We took our time, keeping to back streets and alleys. Instinct urged me to hurry, and I'm sure it was eating at Luis's nerves just as voraciously, but logic told me to take my time, to feel our way along cautiously, and not draw unnecessary attention to our little convoy. Sabana wasn't a large town, but it was big enough to hide in if we were careful, and that's what I wanted to do.

We rode east along the foothills of the Sierra Verdes until we came to La Avenida de la Iglesia, one of the major arteries connecting what the locals called Little Sabana with the larger community south of the river.

The Río Sabana is wide but shallow, splitting into a dozen different channels before it reaches the mouth of the valley nearly ten miles below the town. We crossed at Dos Puentes— Twin Bridges in English—a pair of arched stone structures that had probably been built during the reign of the conquistadors, their sharp edges long since rounded off by use and weather.

The main village sat on a series of benches above the flood plain south of the river, and I felt a lot better when we got back among the squat adobe homes and outbuildings of the town. The central plaza and main business district were located higher up the slope, but I turned off well before that, winding through narrow streets that didn't seem to have any noticeable pattern until we came to a place set back amid a stand of cottonwoods, a small, flat-roofed house and a stable with a dilapidated corral out back.

Dismounting, I handed my reins to Luis, then nodded toward the stables. "Wait for me in there. If it's safe, we'll hole up here until we can figure out what's going on."

Luis nodded and led the stock away. Shifting the Savage to my left hand, I cautiously approached the house. There was a single window in the near wall, like a black, staring eye, and a chill scampered up my spine. Stepping to one side of the door, I knocked firmly—three quick raps, a pause, then a single knock, another pause, then three more.

The silence from inside seemed huge, and I wondered how much had changed since I'd last been here. I didn't even know if Ramón Gutiérrez was still alive. He'd been well into his sixties the last time I'd seen him, his narrow shoulders stooped from a lifetime of labor, his eyes red-rimmed from the dust of the brewery where he toiled. Then I heard a faint stirring at the window, and, taking a chance, I stepped back to place myself in full view of whoever was inside. A few seconds later a startled exclamation brought a quick smile to my face.

"Old friend, is that you?" a voice quavered from the small opening.

"*Sí, amigo,* it is me, come back after all these years."

SESSION TEN

Soft, cackling laughter erupted from within. "*Hombre,* you escaped that h--- hole called Yuma?"

"No, I was released, but let's talk inside. I feel like an empty whiskey bottle sitting on some target-shooter's fence out here."

"*Sí,* of course, come in, before those nosy dogs who live across the road see you, and take word to that demon who calls himself a major in Castillo's army of thieves."

I glanced across the road. Years back an elderly couple named Rameriz had lived there, he a potter at the factory in town that supplied bottles and jugs to the breweries, she a doting grandmother with a large garden and a reputation for fine jams and jellies. Before I could wonder any further, the door flew open and a time-honed face was thrust into the dim light spilling over the eastern rim of the horizon. It looked much as I remembered it, seamed and weathered, its sparse white hair in disarray atop a mostly bald pate. A claw-like hand motioned me inside. I ducked through the low door, and the old man reached up to clamp a papery hand atop my shoulder.

"I had thought I would never see you again, *amigo,*" he declared with more emotion than I had a right to expect. "Twelve years they said you were to serve, but it has not been that long, has it?" A baffled expression pinched his already narrow face as he calculated the seasons. "No, surely not twelve."

"Only four," I told him. "I was released to deliver a ransom."

Ramón's dark eyes widened. "Ah, the *gringa*?"

"Yes, do you know of her?"

"Everyone in Sabana knows of her. We thought the United States might send its army to free her, and there has been much debate as to whether that would be a good thing. Personally I do not want to see the *Norteamericanos* in my country, but there are others who say it would be worth it to pry that fat thief, Chito Soto, out of our valley."

"Is the woman safe?"

"*Sí*, I think so, and her children, too, although I do not know how long their safety can be assured. Already the major grows impatient, and threatens our people if the ransom is not soon paid."

"Your people? The villagers?"

The old man nodded soberly. "At first it was the woman and her children Soto promised to harm, but lately it has been the people of Sabana, as if he blames us for the long silence from the north."

"*Señor* Davenport sent a man to Tres Pinos a couple of weeks ago to negotiate a ransom. That man's head was sent back to Tucson without its body."

"But with an extra hole in its skull?"

"That's what I heard."

"This Da- . . . Davort." He spoke slowly, mangling the unfamiliar word with its strange, harsh accent. "He is the woman's husband?"

"Yes. He's waiting in the hills for me to bring her back."

Ramón was quiet for a moment, then said: "You risk much, my friend."

"A woman's life is at stake, and her children's. Would you do any less?"

He sighed heavily. "Today, I don't know, but when I was younger." Then he grinned, his eyes sparkling in the dim light. "When I was younger, I would have gone up to that fat *bandido*

150

and cut his ugly throat."

I laughed, and I believed him, too.

"Is it safe here, and can we stay?"

He shrugged. "It is as safe here as anywhere in the Sabana Valley, and for maybe five days' ride in any direction from it. Of course you may stay. Did you bring the ransom for the woman?"

"Part of it. Enough for one of the children."

"A wise decision, I think. This Major Chito Soto is not a man I would trust. Not if my life depended upon it, and believe me, *amigo,* yours does."

I nodded. I'd known Ramón Gutiérrez for a good many years by then, and trusted him when he said my life was at stake. But I wasn't surprised. I'd known the odds when I'd accepted the job.

"I have a horse and two mules in your stables, and another man who I trust."

"Your animals will be safe if your man can keep them quiet."

"They've come a long way and are very tired. They won't make any noise if they aren't disturbed."

"*Bueno.*" He moved to the table in a shuffling gait and struck a spark into a piece of black char cloth with his flint and steel. He used the char to light a piece of tinder, the tinder to light a candle sitting in a base of its own wax in the middle of the table. Pinching out the char's spark with a thumb and forefinger, he returned the fire-making kit to a brass container and set it out of the way. "You are hungry?"

"Not if it's jerky or hard crackers."

Ramón smiled and went to kneel before the corner fireplace. While he fixed breakfast, I went outside to help Luis unsaddle the animals and remove the machine-gun and ammunition from the pack mule.

"You trust this old man?" Luis asked as we loosened the ropes holding the machine-gun in place.

"I've known him a long time. I trust him like a father."

Luis studied me for a minute, then said: "My father cut my mother's throat when he caught her with another man, then kicked me out of the house when I was fourteen."

"I left home early, too, but it wasn't because of my father. It was because of what he did for a living."

"Bad?"

"Pretty bad."

After a moment's reflection, Luis said: "A politician?"

"A grocer."

The slim Mexican shrugged. "That does not sound so bad."

"He wanted me to become one, too," I replied, and Luis shuddered.

"You made the right decision," he assured me as we lowered the machine-gun's crate to the ground.

"Even with four years in Yuma?"

"*Si,* even with four years. That kind of life might be pleasing for some, but for men like you and me, it would be even worse than Yuma."

I didn't argue, having come to more or less the same conclusion years earlier. We set the heavy container on the ground in a shadowy corner of the stable and stepped back.

"I think maybe we should hide it," Luis said.

I shrugged. It seemed like a wasted effort to me, and likely only to draw attention to the crate if anyone saw it. I glanced around curiously. When I'd known Ramón before Yuma, he'd kept his goats and chickens penned up in here, but, from the look of the dung littering the dirt floor, it didn't appear that any livestock had been in the stable for at least a year. Still, there was dried manure and old straw, and I told Luis to shovel some over the top of the crate.

"Not much," I cautioned. "Just enough to make it look like it's been sitting there a while. Same with the cartridge pouches.

When you're done, come on in. Ramón is fixing breakfast."

The sky was noticeably lighter when I returned to the old Mexican's small house. Cocks were crowing all over town, and the morning air was pleasantly cool, although I held no illusions about what the day would bring. The good waters of the Río Sabana kept the valley air moist, but it didn't filter out the heat worth a d---. By midday the sun would be blazing down, the village all the more miserable for the humidity.

Ramón had bacon sizzling in a cast-iron spider, and a dozen eggs laid out for frying. Coffee brewed in a white enamel pot on the opposite side of the flame, its red trim chipped and nearly worn away with age, its bottom blackened beyond recovery. The old man motioned toward a trio of pewter mugs sitting on the table.

"The coffee is hot, and the meat will soon be ready."

"Smells good," I said, hunkering down at the old man's side to pour myself a mug. Replacing the pot at the edge of the flames, I wandered over to a stout, hand-carved bench I remembered from my very first visit there. Studying the elderly man's features in the light of the fire, I reflected on how much he'd changed over the years, and especially how much he'd changed since his wife's death, a few months before my last trip to Sabana. She'd been a vibrant woman, I recalled, bringing color and vitality to the small house, making it more of a home than merely the place to eat and sleep that it had become.

"How are your daughters?" I asked after a bit, just to make conversation.

"They exist, but barely, since the *bandidos* came. *Gracias a Dios* they were born ugly, like their father. Too many young women have been taken into Soto's stronghold to satisfy the lusts of those brutes he calls soldiers."

"Can't the *Federales* do anything?

"Ramón sadly shook his head. "There was a small garrison

here when Soto arrived, but they were no match for the bandits. The local *comandante* negotiated a surrender, but Soto broke its terms as soon as the garrison was disarmed." He shifted around to stare at me with brooding eyes. "Soto gave the *Federales* a choice. Join his forces, purportedly under the banner of General Castillo's Army of Liberation, or face a firing squad. To be certain that the men of the garrison understood the consequences of their decision, he had the *comandante* and a young captain placed against the side of the garrison's wall, then shot like rabid wolves." He shook his head in disgust, then spat into the flame.

I stared at the hard-packed dirt floor between my boots. Jorge Archuleta had told me basically the same story in Moralos, only with a couple of lieutenants instead of a captain.

Back in those days, I still figured Porfirio Díaz had a firm hold on the country, and that it was only a matter of time before he got around to eradicating troublemakers like Chito Soto and Adolpho Castillo. But I guess there were too many smaller revolutions going on for him to get a rope around all of them, and it wouldn't be very many more years before men like Pancho Villa and Emiliano Zapata finished what the smaller fry like Soto and Castillo started.

"What became of the rest of the garrison?" I asked quietly.

"As you would expect. They are all now good soldiers under the major's command. After the garrison was disarmed, Soto ordered his soldiers to go through the village and confiscate the arms of the people. I'll tell you, *hombre,* they caught us by surprise with that one. The *alcalde* and some of his minions went to Soto to protest. They told him we still needed our guns as protection against Indians and thieves, but Soto just laughed at them. He promised that he would provide all the protection we needed." Ramón snorted contemptuously. "It is true that he has made good on his vow to protect us from the Yaquis and Pimas, but he has left us defenseless against his own men. [*Ed. Note:* Gutiérrez is probably referring to the Lower Pimas, or *Pima Bajos* here.] Women have been raped, and others, men and women alike, have disappeared entirely. Cattle, goats, and hogs have gone to feed the major's growing army, while the wheat fields that once supplied the breweries have been turned over to other crops to feed Soto's men and horses." He chuckled ruefully. "You should have heard the major's outrage when he learned there was no more beer for him and his men, that they would be forced to drink the common mescal of the common man. They say his wailing could be heard from the horns of Diablo's Crown."

There was a soft rap at the door, and Luis warily poked his head inside.

"Welcome, friend of Latham, who he says I can trust," Ramón called, pushing to his bare feet to greet the younger man. "I am Ramón Gutiérrez, former manager of the *Ceverza Grande* Brewery warehouse, on la Quinta."

"The warehouse manager?" Luis gave me a look of grudging respect. "Now I know how you obtained such fine beer for the trade." He moved across the room to shake the older man's hand. "I am Luis Vega, of Nogales. Like our good friend, I was also a trader along the border, although without his source for beer."

We settled in to eat, Luis and I sharing the bench, Ramón squatting Indian-fashion beside the fireplace where he could keep an eye on the coffee. There were no forks, and the spoons were all made from goat's horn. Luis and I were hungry, and didn't speak until we'd cleaned up all the eggs and bacon, and drained the coffee pot. Afterward, while Luis scrubbed the dishes, Ramón and I sat at the table and discussed my options.

"Soto and his men have taken over the *Federale* garrison," Ramón told me. "They keep the *gringa* and her *muchachos* there, in one of the back rooms. They are sometimes allowed outside, in the yard behind the barracks, but never without at least two guards."

"Can I get to him, talk to him?"

"Soto?" Ramón shrugged. "Perhaps. He is expecting the guns, but his men are not true soldiers. They lack discipline. It might be wiser to have someone else approach the fat bandit first."

"You?"

"Me?" The old man chuckled, then shook his head. "No, not for all the guns in your packs, *amigo*. You will have to find someone else."

"Who?"

Ramón's brows furrowed in thought. After a couple of minutes, he said: "There is someone . . . maybe. You know of Poco Guille?"

I frowned, remembering a kid who used to hang out at some of the *cantinas* across the river in Little Sabana. He hadn't been more than seventeen or eighteen at the time, always around, always underfoot. He'd wanted to go into the trading business with me, but I'd never taken him seriously. No one had, as I recalled.

"What was his name?" I asked. "Not Poco Guille."

"Guillermo Calderón."

Maybe I ought to explain here that Guillermo is the Spanish equivalent of William, and that Poco Guille translates loosely to Little Billy. Little Billy Calderón.

"Is he still around?" I asked.

"*Sí*, if Soto's men haven't shot him since yesterday afternoon, when I saw him down by the river with Juan Kaspar's daughter. His being shot is a possibility, although I didn't hear any gunfire from the garrison. Usually I can, if it's an official execution. Of course, there is always the chance that Juan Kaspar shot him, for hanging around his daughter."

"I can understand why this man Kaspar might want to shoot a brash young fool," Luis said, "but why would Soto's men want to shoot him?"

"Because Poco Guille is a thief, a rascal, and a rake." Ramón smiled, the flesh around his eyes crinkling into deep *barrancos*. "But he is well-liked, especially by the women."

"Is he trustworthy?"

"Like a coyote in a hen house," Ramón assured us.

Luis was scowling fiercely by this time, looking at me. "He is not the man for us, J.T. We need someone we can trust. Our mission here is too important to risk on a scallywag."

But I wasn't so sure.

Watching me curiously, Ramón said: "You know Poco Guille, don't you?"

"Some. He wanted to ride the border with me for a while. I told him no."

Actually I'd told him to p--- off, but I was hoping he wouldn't remember that.

"If he is such a great thief, why doesn't he ride for Chito Soto?" Luis demanded, drying his hands on a piece of coarse brown *jerga*.

"Because Poco Guille is not a killer, and Soto knows that," Ramón answered solemnly. "Probably one of the *Federales* who joined Soto's army warned him away from Guille, because when he tried to join Soto's army, he was told to leave immediately or be shot. He was also ordered to leave his guns behind. Later, one of Soto's lieutenant's put him to work in the fields west of town, but Guille disappeared before the day was half over. He has been dodging Soto's men ever since, but he won't leave Sabana. It is said he hates Chito Soto, but I think he likes being a thorn in the old dog's side."

I was smiling by the time Ramón finished. That was Little Billy to the core, I thought, as reckless as he was independent.

"Does he still hang out around the Loro Azul *Cantina*?" I asked.

"Sadly no. El Loro's whores were moved into the garrison last year, and the mescal and *pulque* was confiscated by Soto's men. El Loro has sat empty ever since, waiting for the day Soto's men leave the country for good. It is also unfortunately true that Poco Guille is now a wanted man. He was seen stealing a revolver off of one of Soto's guards late one night, the guard sleeping drunk at the front entrance to the garrison. There is no reward, but Soto was said to be very angry, and had the guard flogged. Billy is to be brought into the garrison to stand trial for his theft if captured, then he is to be shot as a traitor to the revolution."

"But he's still around?"

"*Sí, el chamaco loco.*"

Crazy kid or not, I thought he could still be our best bet for making contact with Soto. If not directly, then through a friend. Men like Poco Guille usually had friends crawling out of the woodwork. "Can you get word to him?" I asked.

Ramón nodded. "Yes, I think so."

You might be wondering why we didn't just ride up to the former *Federale* garrison and announce our presence, and I'll admit we might have gotten away with it. But I'll also put it to you this way. Chito Soto was like a king in that part of Sonora, and you don't just ride up to a king and start chatting. You've got to go through channels. You've got to know who to approach, and how to approach them. And in a situation like we were facing there in Sabana, approaching the wrong man could have gotten us killed real quick, while the man or men who committed our murders confiscated the Colt-Browning machine-gun for themselves and tried to work their own deal with the bandit chief. Those weren't risks I wanted to take if I didn't have to. Not with my life or any of the Davenports'.

I dug a single, silver eagle from the poke Davenport had given me and spun it across the table. "I need to talk to Poco Guille, the sooner the better."

Ramón studied the coin for a moment, then slipped it into his pocket. I considered him a friend, but he was also a business-man, and from the very beginning our relationship had been built on graft and the illicit exchange of goods. I wouldn't expect him to involve himself in my problems without compensation.

"Stay here, and stay out of sight," he instructed. "If Soto's men find out I am hiding you, I'll be shot." He went to the window to study the street in front of his house. "One of you should return to the stables to watch over your stock. It is known that I no longer own a jackass, and it would be bad if a mule's bray was heard from my stable."

"Luis," I said, nodding toward the door.

"*Sí.*" He grabbed a clay *olla* filled with water and hurried out the door.

"Why would your neighbors want to turn you into Soto's men?" I asked.

"Because they are frightened. The fat dog keeps them that way with periodic executions. He claims that to betray his wishes is to betray the coming revolution, but we all know he is a liar. Still, some feel it is better to remain loyal to a liar than to risk one's life on a bandit's whimsy."

"Then Luis and I should leave?"

Ramón sighed. "*Sí,* but not today. It is already too late to risk it today. Maybe tonight, after dark, if we are not all already dead."

He pulled on a pair of leather sandals, an old palm-leaf sombrero, and draped a serape over his shoulders, then stepped outside without further comment. I went to the window to watch him trudge up the hill toward the plaza. Gray light and the quivering purr of nesting hens from the old Rameriz place

159

filled the narrow street. Despite the early hour, the town seemed unusually quiet, and that, too, was Chito Soto's doing.

For the next several hours I kept up a nervous ambulation, moving from one window to the next, one room to the other. Ramón's house was small, a front room that took up half of the entire structure, a small bedroom consisting of a chest of drawers and a rope-strung bunk with a nearly flat cornhusk mattress, and a small storage room, its shelves once filled with the produce of a large garden and solid employment, now cluttered with dust and spider webs.

Around midday I stretched out on the old man's bunk and closed my eyes. I kept my vest on, the semi-auto a solid weight under my left arm, and placed the Savage on the mattress at my side. I slept fitfully, and was awake when Ramón returned. He grinned at my rumpled appearance, then stepped aside to allow another man to enter. I lowered the Savage's muzzle when I recognized Poco Guille, standing in the doorway with a wide grin on his face, an old Hopkins & Allen top break revolver thrust into the waistband of his trousers.

"*Buenas tardes,* my friend," Guille sang out cheerfully. His quick smile and perpetual good humor was one of the things I remembered best about Little Billy Calderón. It was also one of the reasons I'd told him to get lost that night in El Loro Azul, when he asked to join me on my next trip north of the border. Back then I didn't believe he had the temperament to be a successful smuggler, and I wondered that day at Ramón's if I was making a mistake.

"*Hola,*" I greeted in return, then glanced at the older man. "Everything all right?"

"Yes, fate smiled on my efforts."

"Maybe it will smile on mine, as well," Guille added. "You remember me, *Señor* Latham?"

"Yeah, I remember you. That's why I asked for you."

160

"Good, I am glad you have finally realized my potential. This old man says you need my help. Soon you will know how useful I can be." Then he leaned closer to peer at my face, the marks from Tiny Evans and Felix Perez still visible. *"¡Ay, chihuahua! What happened, amigo? Did you fall off el Diablo's corona?"*

I glanced at Ramón, who laughed softly. Tucking a couple of cold tamales under his shirt, the old Mexican headed for the door. "I will see if Luis is hungry, and say hello to your mules. It has been a long time since I've had guests in my stables, and I miss the smells of an active barn."

He went out, pulling the door closed behind him. Motioning to the table, I told Guille to sit down. "Did Ramón tell you why I wanted to see you?"

"No. He did not even tell me it was you until we were at his door, although I warned him when we left the plaza that if he tried to double-cross me, I would blow his brains out." He tapped the Hopkins & Allen as if to assure me he was capable of carrying out his threat. It made me remember what Ramón said of the younger man that morning.

Poco Guille is not a killer, and Soto knows that.

I was guessing that most of Sabana knew it, too, otherwise the cocky little *chamaco* would have been turned into Soto long before I arrived in town.

Still, it wasn't Guille's skills with a gun that I was seeking, and I swiftly outlined my reasons for being there, my need for the younger man's talents. When I finished, I said: "Can I trust you, *amigo?*"

He laughed, white teeth flashing in the dimly lit interior of the small adobe house. "You would not have sent for me if you didn't know you could trust me," he replied glibly.

"All right, are you interested?"

"Maybe." He leaned forward, elbows on the table. "I am tired of this town, Latham. There is no future here for a man of my many abilities. I have been looking for another job for a long time. Not work." He waved a hand as if scattering cigarette smoke. "I've never been fond of anything that raises a sweat on a daily basis, but I've never cared for stealing, either. These people are my friends and countrymen. They are like family to me, and what kind of man steals from his family? No, I have thought about this for a long time, and the kind of job I seek requires adventure, and maybe a little danger."

I guffawed softly, which brought a scowl to the younger man's face. "You find that funny, *amigo*?"

"Only because I once felt the same way. But I'm older now, and no longer have a need for danger. Maybe it's time for me to step aside for a younger man."

Guille's eyes widened in eagerness. "For someone like me, perhaps?"

"Maybe, you and another man who also seeks adventure."

"Who?" Guille asked suspiciously.

"Luis Vega. Do you know him?"

"No. He is from Sabana?"

"He's from Nogales, but he knows the business as well as I do. I think the two of you would work well together."

The younger man shook his head. "No, it is you, Latham, who I wish to learn this trade from."

"It's too late to learn it from me, *amigo*. When this job is finished, I'm leaving the border country."

After a short pause, Guille exhaled loudly. "And this Luis Vega, he will stay?"

"Yes."

"And he is even now the man in the stable, eating tamales with Ramón Gutiérrez?"

"He is. You'll meet him later today, but first I want to hear about Chito Soto. Can you get me to him?"

"Yes, that won't be a problem. My cousin Felipe is a corporal in Soto's command. He can get word to the major."

That brought an immediate sense of relief. I'd been worried that Ramón had overstated the kid's connections that morning.

"Have your cousin tell Soto that the guns are nearby, and that I'll be at Dos Puentes with the first one tonight at sundown. Tell him that if he wants it, he'd better be there with the woman. Emphasize that, Guille. Make sure he understands that I want the woman first, not either of the kids. Got it?"

"Sure, I've got it, but I doubt if Soto is going to like it."

The fact is, I was counting on him *not* liking it. For whatever reason, Ed Davenport wanted his son ransomed first, but I couldn't count on Soto giving in to the rich *gringo*'s demands. It just didn't work that way. Soto would expect Davenport to order his wife's release first, so that he could get her away from the leering, lecherous bandits who guarded her. That made perfect sense to me, and I figured it would to Chito Soto, too. Which was why he'd want to hang onto the woman until he had all the guns and ammunition. It's also why I'd demand Abby Davenport's release before the others, as convinced as I was the bandit chief would do the opposite of whatever Ed Davenport dictated.

"Just tell him," I said. "Dos Puentes, tonight at sundown."

"Sure." Guille pushed to his feet, then hesitated as a smile rippled across his dusky cheeks. "You know something, J.T.? It's going to feel good to make that fat buzzard swallow a little of his own crap for a change."

I looked up warningly. "Don't push him. We aren't here for revenge. All we want is to get that woman and those kids out of there."

"Sure," Guille agreed, though lightly, and on his way to the door. "But there is no reason we can't rub his nose in it a little, too, eh?"

"Guille!" I shouted, jumping to my feet, but he'd already

darted through the door. I watched from the window as he swung astride a raw-boned gray.

"Tonight at Dos Puentes," he promised.

"Don't botch this, kid. That woman's husband'll kill you just as quick as Soto would if something goes wrong."

"Sure," Guille replied, tossing me a quick wave as he reined away from the house. "But don't worry, nothing will go wrong with Poco Guille in charge." Then, laughing, he kicked his horse into a rough canter and disappeared around the corner.

I cursed softly and stepped away from the window. Needing to get away—for some reason, Ramón's little house was starting to remind me of my iron-strapped cell back at Yuma—I took my rifle and slipped outside, then made my way quickly to the stable.

Luis and Ramón were sitting on the machine-gun crate when I walked in, but Ramón immediately stood up and left the stable. Luis was watching me closely. I think he must have sensed my doubts about the kid.

"Do you trust him, J.T.?"

"He'll do fine," I replied, feigning more confidence than I really felt. Nodding toward the crate, I said: "Do you know how to shoot that thing?"

"No, I don't even know what it looks like. Do you?"

"I know how it works in theory, but I've never handled one. What say we break it out and set it up? It might be a good idea if we know how it works . . . just in case something goes wrong tonight."

Session Eleven

It's funny how your mind works. Sitting here drinking cup after cup of Folger's, remembering what it was like down there in Mexico, how terribly afraid we all were, even if none of us would admit it, it's like I'm reliving those days all over again. Then I go to the window and look outside and I can barely make out the street light for the blowing snow. There's at least six inches on the ground right now, and more coming down, and the streets look like a sheet of ice. You might want to consider spending the night if it doesn't let up soon. There's a spare room upstairs, and we've got plenty of blankets. Plus, if you don't mind, I'd like to keep recording for a while. I've got to admit I don't want to stop just yet.

Anyway, the memories keep coming back, and not just what happened or what was said, but the *sensation* of it all, you know? Like with the sun being so hot I could feel it even through the fabric of my vest, and how heavy Sabana's humidity felt settling in my lungs while I waited at Dos Puentes for Soto to show up.

He was on time, which kind of surprised me, but he also brought along a lot of men. I'd counted on that, too, which is why I didn't have the Colt-Browning with me. Earlier that afternoon, after Guille got back, I had him and Luis take the big gun out west of town and set it up on a little grassy flat where I used to graze my burros. There was a tall cutbank on the south side of the river they could put their backs to if the major tried anything underhanded, and plenty of open space on

165

every side in case it came to a fight.

Luis and I had put the gun together in the stable that afternoon, then filled the sturdy cloth ammunition belts with cartridges that we fed experimentally into the receiver. Luis actually chambered a round, but didn't squeeze the trigger. Later on, when I saw what the Colt-Browning was capable of, I was glad he hadn't. We'd have likely blasted out the side of Ramón's stable.

Satisfied that we had the gun figured out, we tore it down and repacked it. We were just lashing it to the mule when Guille returned. Feeling uneasy about the look on his face, I asked him what the problem was.

"Felipe says Soto refuses to bring the woman. He says you can have the boy in trade, or he'll keep all three hostages and take the gun you have. He is afraid you only have the one, you see?" After a pause, he added: "I told you Soto wouldn't like it."

"That's all right," I said, relieved that he'd taken the bait. I glanced at Luis. "There's a chance Soto had some of his men follow Guille, so you'd better start riding. Get that gun ready to fire. I'll be along as soon as Soto shows up." Switching to English, I added: "I don't have any reason not to trust this kid, but stay sharp, and if he looks like he's trying to double-cross us, shoot him."

"*Sí*, I will," Luis agreed.

Turning to Guille, I switched back to Spanish. "Do you know that little flat where I used to set up camp?"

"*Sí*, the Smuggler's Glade."

That took me aback for a moment, then I laughed softly. "All right. Take Luis there, then stay with him. Help out where you can. He's in charge, so you do what he says."

Guille's gaze drifted to the pack mule. "Are you going to fight Soto for the woman and children?"

"You just do what Luis says, and don't give him any grief. I'll meet Soto at Dos Puentes, and, if I like what he has to say, I'll take him out to the glade."

The kid shrugged but nodded, and after they were gone, I led my mare outside and tightened the cinch. I didn't see Ramón, and I didn't go looking for him. Swinging a leg over the cantle, I reined onto a narrow cart track behind the stable and made my way back to Little Sabana, across the river.

Holed up inside the abandoned Loro Azul *Cantina*, I waited tensely for the evening shade to creep across the valley floor. As the time of my meeting with Soto drew near, I left my perch at a boarded-up window and led my horse outside. Dos Puentes was less than two hundred yards away, and it took only a few minutes to reach the low hump of rocky soil between the two ancient bridges. My gaze swept the southern shore. Sabana's streets were deserted. Apparently word of my rendezvous with Chito Soto had already spread throughout the community, and the townspeople were staying inside, out of the line of fire.

I was there only a few minutes when a band of horsemen trotted out from behind a low-roofed adobe house behind me, cutting off escape to the north. Moments later a second group of horsemen appeared on the opposite bank. As the two parties converged, my mare shifted restlessly, sensing my apprehension.

From all the talk I'd heard since leaving Yuma, I was expecting a greasy, ox-like bandit in ragged clothing, loaded down with revolvers and machetes, but the man I saw riding at the head of the second column didn't come close to that description. Major Francisco "Chito" Soto, of the Army of Liberation, was certainly a big man, but he wasn't sloppy fat. He was short and beefy and wore a red-trimmed khaki uniform with a tall, military-style kepi held in place with a slim chin strap. A single handgun rode in a flapped holster at his side, carried butt forward in a military manner, along with a saber on his other hip, its decorative hilt highly gilded. Soto's boots, like those of his men, were polished beneath a normal haze of dust, and his hair was recently trimmed.

As far as his men, well, they wouldn't have been mistaken for a troop of U.S. cavalry in parade dress, but there was a semblance of order in their movement, a sense of conformity in their uniforms, mostly of the same khaki twill as Soto's attire, although without the crimson piping. There were blue chevrons on a couple of sleeves, and a lieutenant's bars on the shoulders of a ramrod-stiff man riding at the major's side. A quick count netted twenty soldiers, plus half a dozen others to my rear, led by a corporal with a thin mustache. Behind the lieutenant was a stocky sergeant in a battered sombrero. I remember that sombrero well because it was so out of character with the rest of the *soldados,* and because of a bullet hole in its crown.

The two squads reined up at the outer abutments of the twin bridges, and, after a moment's pause, Soto motioned the lieutenant and five others forward. I stayed where I was, keeping both hands in plain sight. The lieutenant's gaze shifted suspiciously to either side as he crossed the larger bridge, and my guts kind of shriveled up as I took in his bearing, the hard authority of his eyes. It was like watching the Grim Reaper enter the room carrying a card with your name on it, and knowing you'd waited too long to make a run for it.

Halting a few yards away, the lieutenant said: "You are alone?"

"I am."

"And the gun, this creation of the famous John Browning?"

"It's safe."

My reply didn't set well with the hard-shelled Mexican, but I went on before he could reply.

"I came here to speak with Chito Soto," I said, deliberately leaving off the man's rank. "Not his errand boy."

The tall man's expression never changed. "I am Lieutenant José Alvarez, and, for the moment, you will deal with me. Where is the gun?"

"Where is the woman?"

A smile curled lazily at the corner of the lieutenant's mouth. He raised a hand, and from an alley about a block away, a third squad of horsemen appeared. It took only a moment to pick out the sandy-haired youth of about nine, riding behind a soldier on a bay shaded similarly to my own.

"The boy first," Alvarez said. "Not the woman. Your man, Guillermo Calderón, has already explained this to you, no?"

I nodded that he had. "I'll take Soto and five men with me to where the gun is waiting. The boy comes with us, but I want to talk to him first, make sure he is who you say he is. You and the rest of Soto's men will wait here for the major's return."

A look of disdain burned across the lieutenant's face. "*Señor* Latham, do you take me for a fool? I already know where the gun is located. I maintain this façade of civility only because Major Soto wishes to assure you of his sincerity in our dealings. But do not think that I can be toyed with like a ball of yarn under a kitten's paws. We will go to this place you have chosen for our trade and examine the gun that Edward Davenport has sent to us. If it is satisfactory, the child will be turned over to you, and you will be allowed to leave Sabana to retrieve the other guns and the ammunition. But be assured, *hombre,* that if you do not wish to complete this initial exchange in a timely manner, if you attempt to needlessly delay our transaction, I can have you shot here, and deal with Vega personally. Perhaps he will not be as difficult if I brought him your head as proof of my determination in this matter."

Although I managed to preserve an air of indifference, I swear it felt as if my heart had momentarily seized up. If Soto knew our names, then Alvarez probably wasn't bluffing when he said they also knew the location of the machine-gun. Someone had betrayed us, and I didn't believe the traitor was Guille. My thoughts turned to Ramón Gutiérrez, who likely figured he was covering his own b--- by going to the major.

You might think I'm going to say something like: *Well, I couldn't blame Ramón for looking out for himself,* or, *I might've done the same,* but I'm not. I'd given that old thief a silver eagle—$10—to keep his d---ed mouth shut, and then he turned around and double-crossed us before the afternoon was out. I was just thankful we'd left those other two Colt-Brownings behind; otherwise you might be interviewing my ghost tonight, instead of blood and bone.

Alvarez's icy demeanor never changed. "Your decision, *señor?*"

Leaning forward in my saddle to speak past gritted teeth, I said: "Well, h---, champ, let's ride."

With Alvarez at my side and his men, including the corporal's small bunch from north of the river, falling in behind, we rode over to where Soto calmly waited. The child had been brought up while the lieutenant and I did our haggling, and I didn't need to question the youth to know he was Edward Davenport's son. The old man's features were stamped all over him, but especially in that slightly thrusting jaw that was so intimidating on the father.

Soto eyed me with quiet curiosity as I hauled up in front of him, my mare's nose nearly touching the muzzle of his sorrel gelding. I nodded a howdy, not quite sure how to proceed.

Returning the nod courteously, Soto said: "It is my pleasure, *Señor* Latham, to finally make the acquaintance of the famous Zorro Yanqui." [*Ed. Note:* Spanish for Yankee Fox; it probably refers to Latham's reputation as a smuggler.]

My puzzled expression seemed to amuse him. "Were you not aware of your fame among the citizens of Sabana, *señor?*"

"I'm afraid I wasn't, especially after being away for so many years."

"The legend of el Zorro Yanqui is well-known among my

people," he informed me in surprisingly gentle tones. "They speak also of the cove along the river where you used to pasture your burros. The Smuggler's Glade, I believe it is called." He smiled amiably. "It is also told that you have been detained for several years within the *gringo* prison at Yuma. Is that true?"

"It's true."

The major nodded solemnly. "Let us hope that these crimes that caused you to be imprisoned for so long are not crimes that can lead to your execution in Sonora."

I didn't respond to that. Soto didn't intend for me to. Nor was he making idle conversation. He was telling me he knew all about me, a warning of sorts that I figured I'd better heed if I didn't want to end up in front of a firing squad.

Glancing toward the Sierra Verdes, their rocky flanks purpling with twilight, the major said: "Perhaps we should be on our way to this glade where Davenport's machine-gun awaits our inspection. Darkness approaches, and I know you wish to return for the other guns as soon as possible."

Well, that wasn't any secret. I'd purposely set up a sundown meeting just so I'd have the element of nightfall to count on if something went wrong. And to help throw off pursuit, or at least delay it, if Soto sent trackers after us on our return to Yaqui Springs.

It was a thirty-minute ride at a short lope to the little meadow the locals called Smuggler's Glade. No one spoke because of the pace, but I snuck more than a few glances at young Davenport, wondering what was going on with him. Although dirty, as you'd expect from someone in his predicament, he didn't appear to be physically injured, yet there was a look in his eyes that troubled me. A kind of a vacant stare, like I'd seen on some of the men I'd done time with at Yuma, lost and alone and not quite all the way there. I hoped for young Charles's sake that it was only a temporary problem, brought on by the anxiety of his captivity and his concern for his mother and sister, but it was worrisome.

We were still several hundred yards short of the glade when Alvarez called a halt, likely out of respect for the Colt-Browning's range. He glanced at Soto, who merely nodded, and Alvarez hooked a finger at me.

"You will ride at my side, *señor,* while six of my best marksmen follow close behind with their carbines trained on your heart. Should any attempt at treachery be made toward me or my men, your death will be instantaneous."

"We came here to make a trade," I replied curtly. "Let's get at it."

Alvarez nodded and we rode forward at a walk, leaving young Davenport with Soto and the main body of troopers.

Luis and Guille had the Colt-Browning set up and ready to fire, although thankfully its muzzle was pointed toward the cutbank, and neither man was standing overly close to the trigger. Dismounting some distance away, we left our horses with one of Alvarez's men and went the rest of the way on foot. Luis and Guille were watching me attentively, as if searching for any sign of trouble, but so far, with the exception of Ramón's little knife in my back, it was all going about as smooth as something like this ever did.

"So this is what all the fuss is about, eh?" Alvarez said when we came to a halt at the gun's side.

I gave him a searching glance, wondering if he was aware of what the Colt-Browning was capable of, or that there were armies throughout the world that would have given up an entire troop of cavalrymen for just one of these weapons.

Alvarez dropped to one knee behind the machine-gun. An ammunition belt was already threaded into place, and with brisk efficiency that convinced me he'd handled similar weapons before, he threw the under lever, grasped the pistol grip lightly with one hand and the top of the gun with the other, and squeezed off a burst of fire with spectacular results. At least two score of .30-caliber rounds raked the side of the cutbank within a matter of seconds, punching fist-sized cavities several inches into the damp sod. Guille leaped back with a squawk silenced by the roar of the machine-gun, and the frightened pack mule nearly threw itself in its hobbles. I think even my own head might have rocked back a little in awe of the weapon's capabilities. I'd seen a Gatling gun fired up at Fort Lowell many years before, but it was nothing compared to John Browning's masterpiece of precision.

Rising smoothly, Alvarez took a handkerchief from his pocket and calmly wiped a trace of gun oil from his fingers. "It would appear to be adequate," he stated casually.

"I'd say that's a little more than adequate," I replied.

"It would depend on the situation," Alvarez countered. "A jammed or disabled firearm is of little value during a desperate struggle." Then he turned to me with a faint smile, the first I'd seen from him. "But do not become alarmed, *señor*. I am satisfied with the gun's performance." He raised a hand toward the main body of *soldados*, and I guess I was expecting him to motion the major in. I think that's what Luis and Guille were expecting, too, so it caught all of us by surprise when the men who had accompanied Alvarez and me to the glade suddenly leveled their carbines at our bellies. The stocky sergeant with the gun-shot sombrero barked a command for us to raise our hands, drawing his revolver as he did and jabbing its muzzle against my spine.

"I would suggest, *Señor* Latham, that you do as Sergeant Marcos instructs," Alvarez stated coolly. "He has been ordered to fire if he suspects noncompliance."

With my jaw clenched in anger, I grudgingly lifted both hands to the height of my shoulders. Stepping back, the sergeant motioned for Luis to join me, while a couple of troopers quickly bound Guille's wrists behind his back. Realizing what was happening, I said: "He's with me, Lieutenant."

"No," Alvarez corrected mildly. "Guillermo Calderón is under the jurisdiction of the Army of Liberation, and is charged with the theft of a revolver. He was ordered to be executed by firing squad upon the authority of Major Francisco Soto."

Even as the lieutenant was speaking, the troopers who had secured Guille's wrists started shoving him toward the cutbank. I think we all realized at the same time what was about to happen.

"God d--- it, Lieutenant!" I shouted. "Calderón is with me. Either he rides back with. . . ."

That was as far as I got when a rifle butt slammed into my kidneys. My insides seemed to explode with a pain that shredded me from top to bottom. I cried out and my legs buckled, dropping me to my knees in the soft spring grass. I would have tumbled onto on my face if the sergeant hadn't grabbed my collar and pulled me back. A couple of soldiers grabbed me under my arms and hoisted me to my feet.

I might have been standing, but my brain was skidding back and forth like a California seismograph. The world spun dizzily—violet sky and dark green pasture, the sounds of the river and wind and barked commands, the taste of my own bile like acid at the back of my throat—all of it fusing into an abstract reality that I finally had to close my eyes against to escape. Focusing on my breathing, the surge of my pulse gradually leveled out, but it was several minutes before I felt confident that I wasn't going to lose the eggs and side pork Ramón had fixed for breakfast that morning.

"You must remain silent and respectful, *señor*," the sergeant whispered in my ear. "This is a very sad occasion for many of us. I myself know this man you call Poco Guille, and consider him a friend."

I opened my eyes. Guille was standing braced against the side of the cutbank, his arms bound in front, twin bayonets pinning him to the dirt wall. They weren't piercing the flesh, but had been driven into the dirt under his armpits to keep him from collapsing, while the troopers who had placed him there were moving hurriedly out of the line of fire. Jutting my chin toward the macabre scene, I said: "Is this the way you treat your friends, Sergeant?"

"No," the sergeant replied with what sounded like genuine regret. "This is what happens to men who steal from General Castillo's Army of Liberation. It saddens me, but one must do his duty, else he faces the same fate."

Soto was there. He must have ridden up with the rest of his men while I'd been struggling against unconsciousness. Young Davenport was at the major's side. I wanted to protest the youth's presence but the words wouldn't come, and my gaze was involuntarily drawn back to the cutbank, the sounds of Guille's sobs. It was then that I noticed Lieutenant Alvarez kneeling behind the Colt-Browning. This time there was no mistaking the smile on his face. He was watching Soto, who was staring at me, waiting for my undivided attention. When he had it, he tipped his head forward in a silent directive, and Alvarez's smile seemed to spread across his face. There was no—"Ready, Aim, Fire."—no final request or last cigarette. He just pointed the Colt-Browning's muzzle at Guille's chest and pulled back firmly on the trigger.

The ammunition belts we had with us in Mexico held one-hundred and forty rounds apiece. Alvarez had fired about forty into the side of the cutbank earlier. He emptied the rest of the belt into Guillermo Calderón's chest that evening on the banks of the Río Sabana. It's an image that twists in my guts to this day.

Session Twelve

I thought about this a lot last night, and I've decided that I'm not going to say anything more on the subject of Guille's death. He was gone, and that's all there is to it.

Luis and I were given our horses and Charles Davenport, and told that we were free to go. It was Sergeant Marcos who lifted the boy onto the saddle in front of me. Keeping my free hand flat against the kid's shrunken stomach, we got our hind ends out of there. Not fast, mind you—you don't run from a pack of blood-crazed dogs without inviting chase—but we didn't tarry, either. It was full dark by the time we got back to Sabana, and although I gave serious thought to swinging past Ramón's house long enough to pick up some extra food, then blow the b------'s brains all over the wall, I decided I didn't have the energy for it.

We made our way cautiously to the top of the Sierra Verdes, stopped briefly below the Devil's Crown to rest our stock, then pushed on to the north. Our mounts were worn to a frazzle, and I made up my mind that we'd leave them behind on our return trip to Sabana, and use someone else's horses. I personally intended to commandeer Davenport's fine-looking chestnut for my own, and was enjoying the mental image of his irritation as we made our way out of the Sierra Verdes and started across the arid flats toward the Cañon Where the Small Lizards Run.

Our horses were stumbling frequently as we approached the mouth of the slot cañon late the next day. Davenport must have had someone watching for us, because we were still a couple of hundred yards shy of the entrance when the old man came spurring out of the gorge. Del Buchman, Spencer McKenzie, and Felix Perez were riding close behind.

I hauled back on the bay mare's reins, stone-jawed and numb of mind, observing their approach as if through a set of foggy lenses. Reaching our side, Davenport jumped from his saddle with a much younger man's agility and swept the boy into his arms, and d---ed if there weren't tears in the old buzzard's eyes. But the kid, well, that shell-shocked look hadn't left him, which Davenport was quick to notice. Turning an accusing eye on me, he said: "What happened?"

"I couldn't say. He was like that when Soto turned him over to us. He's skinny and he's got to be hungry. Maybe some decent food and a little rest will perk him up."

I didn't mention that the boy had been witness to Poco Guille's gruesome execution.

"You saw Soto?"

"I saw him."

"And everything went off as planned?"

Again, I kept the news of Guille's death to myself. "No problems," I replied.

"Were you followed?"

"I don't think so."

"You don't *think* so?"

"I reckon we're tired, Mister Davenport, and maybe not as sharp as we could have been, but we weren't asleep in our saddles, either. Soto is expecting us back with more guns and ammunition to trade for your wife and little girl. He doesn't have a reason to send trackers after us."

Looking unaccountably relieved, the old man turned toward his horse, the boy held tight in his arms. As he passed Del, he said—"Do it."—but kept walking.

Del's gaze hardened at the old man's words. Drawing the Remington from its shoulder rig, he leveled it at Luis and me. I remember my eyes narrowing as I studied the .45's yawning bore, not so much surprised as confused.

"Drop that hogleg, Vega," Del rumbled, and while Luis did that, Spence kicked his mount alongside mine and yanked the Savage from its scabbard. He flicked the safety off with a thumb, then turned the muzzle on me.

"The rifle, too," Del instructed Luis.

I heard Luis's Winchester clatter to the rocky ground alongside his revolver, but kept my gaze fixed on Davenport as he rode away. The old man was returning to the cañon's mouth at a leisurely pace, the boy cradled in his arms like a fragile vase. From his poise, you might have thought he was just taking a pleasant jaunt around the park on a Sunday afternoon.

Turning to Del, I said: "What's going on?"

"There's been a change of plans," he replied sullenly, then motioned for Felix to pick up Luis's rifle and revolver.

"Oh, I doubt that, Delmar," Spence interjected. "Was ye to ask me, I'd say the old bugger's been plannin' this all along."

"Ain't nobody asking you, McKenzie, so shut your trap," Del growled.

"What kind of change of plans?" I demanded.

Del gritted his teeth and refused to answer. It was Spence who enlightened us.

"It appears the old boy's got another deal set up for those two remainin' potato diggers," he announced. "Seems he won't be needin' ye services any longer."

"What about his wife and daughter?" I asked, having trouble wrapping my mind around everything that was happening.

"Shut up," Del said harshly, and I realized that whatever was going on, it was eating at him a lot worse than it was Spence. Glaring at me as if the anguish he felt was somehow my fault,

he added: "This ain't my doing, Latham. I didn't know s---
about any of this until after you and the Mex there had already
left for Sabana. I wouldn't have pulled you outta Yuma if I
had."

"Well, I can't say I won't hold it against you," I replied
heavily. I looked at Spence, puzzled by his unruffled manner. "I
thought you and I were friends."

"Aye, lad, we are, but 'tis business we're speakin' of now. A
bloody cruel business, to be sure, but unfortunately inescap-
able. I'm sure ye understand."

I shook my head. "I don't reckon I do . . . *amigo.*"

Spence shrugged dispassionately. "Well, 'twill give ye
something to mull on then, these few minutes ye've got remainin'." He nodded to the trail behind us. "Mister Davenport has
requested that we complete our errand yonder, lads. He's
afeared buzzards may give away ye position, once Soto figures
out he's been dealt a crooked hand and comes huntin' ven-
geance."

My gaze shifted to Felix Perez. He had been sitting his pinto
silently some distance away, as if not sure what was going on.
He hadn't drawn his revolver, but he had Luis's pistol shoved in
his belt, and was balancing the Winchester across his saddle.
He'd be no help, but I wasn't sure yet what his part in all of
this would be.

"Let's go, lads," Spence persisted, bobbling the Savage's
muzzle to attract our attention. He took a peek at Buchman.
"Are ye comin', Delmar, or don't ye have the stomach for such
doin's?"

Del was quiet for a long minute, then abruptly holstered his
Remington. "You go ahead, you cold-hearted son-of-a-b----," he
snarled, then yanked his buckskin around and started back
toward Yaqui Springs. He pointed a finger at Perez as he rode
past, indicating the wiry little *Indio* should follow him.

Over the years I've often wondered about Del's actions that day. Did he have another motive when he so drastically lowered the odds against Luis and me? Or was it just a thoughtless gesture, an unconscious concession to their need to pack up and move on as quickly as possible, before Soto's men came after them?

When there was just Spence and Luis and myself, I abruptly tugged the bay's head around and started back down the trail. After a startled pause, Luis heeled his mule after me. Spence fell in a few rods behind, keeping the Savage in his right hand, its muzzle swaying easily with the gait of his horse but never leaving either Luis or me. After half a mile I started to ease back on the reins. Not enough to stop my mare, but just to slow her down, allowing Luis to catch up and closing the gap between us and Spence. After another hundred yards I stopped altogether, reining partway around to block the path. Thankfully Luis had the presence of mind to guide his mule out of my way. Spence pulled up, his eyes darting distrustfully from one side of the trail to the other.

"What's the problem, lad?"

"I figured this was far enough."

After a pause, Spence chuckled amiably. "Ye're bein' an accommodatin' sport about this, laddie, and, aye, I believe ye be right. 'Tis far enough. Now to pick a likely spot."

"We probably ought to find a gully where you can dump our bodies," I suggested. "You'll want to roll some stones over us, too. I'm not suggesting you waste valuable time on a decent burial, but enough so that Soto's men will have to wonder where the stench is coming from."

Luis was watching me curiously, wondering what I was up to, and Spence's smile had disappeared. He swung the Savage's front sight toward my belly. At the angle I was sitting, he couldn't see me slide my right hand inside the small opening in my vest's lining, or notice the bulge of my fist as I curled my fingers around the semi-auto's hard rubber grips.

"I'll no ask ye for the courtesy of making me job easier," Spence said. "I'd rather ye ride to wherever we end up, and enjoy what remains of this fine but warm day, but 'tis your choice, lad, and enough that ye know I'll shoot ye where ye sit if ye try anything funny."

"I've got to know, Spence. Why? H---, man, we've shared a hard trail together. Shared campfires and poor grub and tobacco, and I know you don't care for Davenport or his heavy-handed ways. So why are you doing this when you don't have to?"

A baffled expression crossed the Scotsman's face. "I work for the man, lad. Surely ye'd do the same, was the old bugger to order me killed."

I've thought about that comment a lot over the years, and I'm no closer to understanding Spencer McKenzie's reasoning now than I was then. It just seemed too simple a conclusion to be embraced by an individual I'd considered reasonably intelligent. Not knowing how to respond, and figuring my time was swiftly running its string, I said: "It ain't much of an answer, Spence, but I guess it'll have to do." Then I thumbed the Colt's hammer back and squeezed the trigger, firing through the vest because I didn't want to risk the pistol snagging on the lining if I tried to pull it out.

I wasn't more than twenty feet away when I fired, and even though I hadn't properly aimed, my bullet caught Spence solidly in the side. He grunted loudly at the slug's impact, the Savage bucking in his fist as his finger instinctively tightened on the trigger. The rifle's round sailed harmlessly over my shoulder, whistling off into the distance, but I flinched anyway. Then I fired again.

The echo of gunfire crashed deafeningly back and forth

between the cañon's walls, and Spence's leggy roan jumped and spun and nearly threw its rider. The Savage tumbled from the Scotsman's fist as he grabbed for the saddle horn. I got off two more rounds before the semi-auto's slide caught the vest's shredded fabric and jammed. Spence didn't know that, though. Yanking his horse around, he drove his heels into the animal's ribs. Already spooked, the roan took off as if shot from a cannon. By the time I was able to rip the pistol free, then clear the slide, horse and rider were gone, the reverberation of the roan's hoofs ebbing into a silence that seemed almost unnatural after the chaos of a moment before. Then I swore and began beating out a small fire that had ignited the tattered corduroy at one of the exit holes in the vest's front panel. Preoccupied with extinguishing the flame, I reacted instinctively when I saw Luis jump to the ground and hurry toward the Savage. Leveling the Colt, I shouted: "Leave it be!"

Luis jerked to a stop, then quickly backed away. There was fear in his eyes at first, then understanding, followed by anger. "You think you cannot trust me, J.T., after all that we have been through?"

"No, but I didn't think McKenzie would turn on me, either." I dismounted and led the bay over to retrieve the Savage. "It ain't anything personal," I tried to assure him, but I could tell my words didn't have much effect.

"*Sí,* of course not," Luis replied contemptuously. He motioned toward his mule. "Do I get on, or will you shoot me here?"

"I'm not going to shoot you," I snapped. "Go ahead and mount up."

I was staring upcañon, toward the spot where Spence and his roan had disappeared. Only shimmering heat waves and the hesitant call of a quail from higher up the slope disturbed the heat-seared atmosphere. Luis's rig creaked loudly as he climbed into the seat. He sat there a moment, fiddling with his reins, then said: "What do you intend to do about the woman?"

At that moment I didn't have the foggiest idea of what we could do to help her, but I knew we couldn't just ride away. Luis knew it, too; otherwise he wouldn't have asked the question. After a lengthy silence, I said: "I know a way around that slot cañon. It's pretty rough, but it'll take us above the upper entrance. If Davenport tries to go out the way we came in, we might be able to cut him off."

"And do what?"

I looked at him. "I don't know. Do you have a better idea?"

Luis sighed and shook his head. "No, unfortunately I don't. Lead the way, my friend."

I smiled and nodded—but I didn't give him my rifle or the handgun.

There are a lot of trails through those *barrancos* north of the Sierra Verdes. Some of them go somewhere, many don't. There isn't much grass for your stock, and there isn't much water. It's a fiercely harsh land, and although people lived there, most of them didn't do it by choice. In that part of the world there's no better place to get lost in, which isn't a bad thing if you're trying to shake a troop of *Federales*, but not much good if you're just wanting to pass through.

I didn't know what Davenport's knowledge was of the terrain around there. He had that map he'd showed me in Moralos, but it hadn't been very good. Maybe he was counting on the Perez boys to get him out of there. Or maybe he'd already arranged another meeting with some other rag-tag group calling itself an army, one that could provide him with gold or silver, rather than a woman and a child.

I knew those trails fairly well because of my years living with the Yaquis, then afterward running my burros between Sabana and Nogales. It wasn't like I'd grown up there and knew every bush and rock, as the saying sometimes goes, but I could get along. Especially near the water holes, which is always your destination in the desert—the next spring or rock tank where you can find enough sustenance to push on to the one after that.

The trail I'd told Luis about was a few miles east of the Cañon Where the Small Lizards Run. Little more than a débris-filled arroyo, it cut through the sheer cliff above us to the sloping bench we'd used to reach the slot cañon's upper entrance. I found it easily enough, but it was steeper and more treacherous than I remembered, and we had to dismount about halfway up and lead our mounts the rest of the way.

The sky was growing dim, the air losing some of its earlier heat, by the time we climbed back into our saddles. Knowing from experience that full dark would descend on us faster down here than up above where the land was more open, I urged my weary mare into a shuffling jog, about all she had left by then.

Luis kept up, but I could tell from the cant of his mule's ears that that big jack wouldn't allow himself to be pushed much farther. A horse will just about kill itself doing what you want it to, but there's a reason terms like "mule-headed" and "stubborn as a jackass" keep floating around out there—although I'd always thought their stubbornness was more from intelligence than contrariness.

Luckily we didn't have far to go once we got up above, and there was still plenty of light to see by when we dismounted several hundred yards east of the slot cañon's upper entrance. Taking along the binoculars Del had loaned me, Luis and I crept as near as we dared to the cañon's head. Nothing stirred nearby, but after a couple of minutes I spotted a whiff of dust far to the west, following along the same slanted bench where Luis and I were crouched. There was a trail leading in that direction, I recalled, although not the one I'd used bringing us down from Moralos. I lowered my glasses, scowling in concentration.

"Did you see something?"

"Take a look just below that splinter of rock leaning toward the cañon's floor, about three miles out." I handed Luis the glasses and he adjusted the focus to suit his eyes. After studying the distant haze for a couple of minutes, he brought them down.

"What do you think?" I asked.

"I think it is Davenport and the guns. I think he must have expected our arrival today, and was waiting with the horses and mules already saddled and packed." He looked at me. "They're running, *amigo.*"

I nodded thoughtfully, having come to the same conclusion. But I hadn't noticed Spence anywhere along that cañon trail, and I should have.

"Still down below with those d---ed lizards?" Luis stated, as if reading my mind.

I thought of Spence down there, armed and wounded. Running my tongue over dry lips, I said: "There's only one way to know if he's still there."

He graced me with an unsympathetic look. "Sadly, my friend, I do not possess a rifle, or even a pistol. If I did, I would gladly volunteer to go first."

Well, he had me there, but I still wasn't going to give up one of my guns. "Fetch the horses," I said. "I'll do down and see what's afoot. I'll give a shout if it's safe."

I headed for the slot cañon's entrance. I was nervous about going in, but I would have felt more vulnerable following after Davenport and those guns without knowing where Spence was, or how badly he was injured.

Placing my feet with care and avoiding the side walls out of respect for how well sound carried through the narrow passage, I moved into the deepening twilight of the cañon as swiftly as possible. It didn't take long to reach the main chamber. Keeping my finger tight on the Savage's trigger, I stepped onto the sandy beach along the upper pond.

Spence was there, slumped against the far wall with his head twisted to the side. His horse stood nearby, ears perked forward as it monitored my approach. Fortunately the tall roan recognized me and didn't bolt, although my stealthy advance was making it skittish. Halting at the edge of the pond, I said loudly: "McKenzie, Spencer McKenzie."

He opened his eyes to look at me, and I took an involuntary step back. His lips peeled away from his bloody gums in what was either a grimace or a grin, I couldn't tell which. "Ah, lad, there ye be. I was afeared I'd have to die alone in this god-forsaken hole."

"You aren't hurt that bad," I said. "Stand up where I can see you."

"Ye'll have to do ye lookin' from there, J.T., for I'll no be movin' from this spot unless ye see fit to bury me proper-like."

"Like you were going to do for Luis and me?"

Spence chuckled, bringing up a fresh gout of blood that misted the front of his already sodden shirt. I realized then that he wasn't lying about the seriousness of his wound. Not that I trusted him enough to lower my rifle. Wading across the pool, I yanked a Smith & Wesson revolver from his holster and tossed it over beside our old campfire. Spence's rifle, a sturdy Marlin in .45-70, was still on his saddle.

"That Smith the only gun you're carrying?"

"The only one on me. I've a pocket pistol in me saddlebags, plus the rifle ye see yonder."

Edging forward with the Savage pointed unwaveringly on his chest, I loosened the buckle, then slid the gun belt out from under him and tossed it after the revolver.

"Just how bad is that wound?" I asked, stepping back.

"Enough to kill me, I'd wager. Ye bullet hit a lung, laddie, I know that for sure. What else it tore up, I couldn't say."

"You'll understand if I don't offer my condolences."

"Ye'd be a d---ed fool if ye did," he agreed weakly.

An iron horseshoe scraped the slot cañon's floor, and I knew Luis would soon be there. Moving back across the pond without taking my eyes off the wounded man, I caught the roan's reins. Leading the horse over to our old fire, I picked up the Smith & Wesson and brushed off the sand as best I could, vowing to clean it more thoroughly later on. After strapping the gun belt around my waist, I checked the revolver's cylinder to make sure it was fully loaded, then dropped it in its holster. Even though I'd been carrying the Savage for a while by then, it felt good to have a handgun on me again, something I could grab in a hurry. I liked that it was a brawny .44 caliber, too. If I'd had a .44 or a .45, rather than the .38, Spence would still be out on the trail where I'd shot him, and probably not talking, either.

Luis came warily into the chamber, glanced briefly at Spence, then at me. There was a guarded look on his face as he led my bay mare and his black mule to water. "That is quite a collection of guns," he observed, hanging onto the reins while our mounts drank.

I walked over to shove the Savage into its scabbard on the bay, then pulled the belt of .303s from around my waist and I draped it over the saddle, like a dead snake waiting to be skinned for supper. "I'm thinking that mule is about to quit on you," I said. "You can have my bay, and the rifle, too."

That seemed to appease him somewhat, like maybe he wasn't feeling so much like a prisoner as a partner again. He didn't question me keeping the better mount and firearms for myself, either; we both knew he would have done the same had the situation been reversed.

You might wonder why I didn't keep the Savage, since I'd

more or less laid claim to it when Felix brought it back from the desert. Fact is, that .303 is a sweet little cartridge, but it's got a limited range and not much punch compared to Spence's Model '95 Marlin. Plus the Savage only holds four rounds, even with a cartridge chambered, and that's a definite disadvantage when bullets are flying back and forth too fast to keep track of who's shooting—the kind of situation it isn't all that hard to find yourself in when you're dealing with a man like Chito Soto. Or Ed Davenport, as it turned out.

It would be nice to tell you that Spence passed away quietly while Luis and I were there, and that we buried him in a nice shady spot, marking the grave with a stone that had his name scratched into the surface. But that's not what happened. It was getting real dark down there in that sandy chamber, and Luis and I both knew Davenport was moving steadily away from us. We didn't have time, or much inclination, to wait around for Spence to punch his ticket. Still, I was caught off guard when Luis slid the Savage from its scabbard and headed for the wounded man with a determined look on his face.

"What are you doing?" I asked.

He gave me a puzzled look. "I am going to finish the job."

"Like h--- you are," I said, dropping my hand to the holstered Smith.

Luis was watching me closely, wondering if I was serious. I knew what he was thinking. It was obvious to Luis that Spence wasn't going to survive, but he didn't want to just ride off and leave him to suffer alone. And I'll tell you what, there were an awful lot of men in those days who would have shared his feelings. Men who would have condemned us for not "finishing the job," as Luis put it. But I wasn't one of them. In my mind it was better to let a person play out his own string. And who knew, maybe someone would come along after we were gone and nurse him back to health. I've seen stranger things happen in Mexico.

Luis, though, felt differently, and he felt it strongly. "We cannot just ride away, J.T.," he said. "Do you want that on your conscience?"

I told him about my theory of someone coming along after we'd left and rescuing Spence, but my arguments sounded pretty flimsy in the slot cañon's thickening shadows.

"It is more likely a jaguar would find him," Luis said, "and there would be no mercy in that meeting."

"We can't just shoot him."

"He is already dead," Luis argued, his words tinged with impatience. "Would you walk away from a horse or a dog as badly wounded?"

I was silent for a moment, then I said—"No, we aren't going to shoot him."—and this time, there wasn't any doubt in my words. "Get on that bay horse and let's ride."

Luis hesitated for so long I started to worry that he might swing his rifle on me. Then he turned away with a curse, kicking up showers of sand as he stalked toward the bay. It was too dark by then to tell if Spence was conscious, but I could still hear the raw, wheezing suck of his wound every time he inhaled, so I knew he was alive.

Now I'm going to ask you—what would you have done? Did I do the right thing, the moral thing? Or did I take a coward's way out? It's a question that was going haunt me before our journey was finished—but there I go again, getting ahead of myself.

That roan gelding of Spence's was a lot fresher than my mare, and it wasn't long before I began to pull ahead of Luis. There was only one path wide enough for saddle stock heading in the same westerly direction I'd spied the dust earlier, and the tracks along it were newly planted, so I was confident we were following the right trail.

The light finally faded out and the cañon's walls resembled ink flows. Although I could hear the occasional clop of one of the bay's hoofs, I could no longer see Luis or the mare. Overhead the pale ribbon of the sky was like looking at the underside of a river, although populated with bats instead of fish, and once an owl passed so close overhead I could have almost touched it, yet it was so silent I wouldn't have known it was there if I hadn't spotted it from the corner of my eye. We'd gone maybe five miles when I heard a voice up ahead, and pulled the roan to a stop.

"McKenzie, that is you?" the voice called softly in Spanish.

My heart kicked into a higher gear, and my scalp did a little dance across the top of my head. I was pretty sure that was Felix, and I was betting Davenport had sent him back to see what was keeping Spence.

"McKenzie?"

"*Sí, muchacho,*" I replied in a clumsy attempt to reproduce Spence's Scottish accent—in Spanish.

I was sure now that it was Felix Perez who was calling to me, and not very far away, either. Unfortunately my efforts to mimic Spence's familiar—"Aye, laddie."—didn't fool him, and a shot rang out, pinging off a nearby stone. Kicking free of the roan's stirrups, I dropped to the ground, then to one knee. From this lower angle, and probably because Felix was moving so fast, it took only a moment to spot him scrambling up the incline on my right. I snapped off two quick rounds, then threw myself off the trail as a second bullet from Felix's rifle crackled through the brush at my side.

I moved deeper into the thick scrub flanking the trail, my left hand held before me to ward off any thorny branches that might want to claw at my eyes, or sweep my hat from my head. The heavy Marlin, held before me like a pistol, was a strain on the muscles of my right arm.

It's an odd sensation to move through the dark like that, knowing there's someone out there hunting you, wanting to end your life. For Felix, I knew it would be personal. He'd never forgiven me for laying into him that night in Moralos, then taking away the spoils of what I was certain was his ambush of the motorcycle rider I'd seen leaving Archuleta's. Felix Perez wanted revenge; his ego demanded it.

The minutes ticked past like a clock dipped in molasses, and after a while I decided to just stop and let Perez come to me. Coming to a low boulder with a flat top, I settled down to wait. You might recall me mentioning earlier how even the quietest night can seem noisy when you're really listening. The next twenty or so minutes in that cañon was no exception. I swear I heard a snake crawl past on my left, and the flutter of bats' wings was like a softer version of Midwestern cicadas.

Even concentrating as intently as I was, I was caught off guard when I heard the echoing roar of a gunshot from above me, its muzzle flash briefly illuminating the cañon's walls. Two more shots rang out from higher up. Then, hearing another shout and the clatter of hoofs, I shoved to my feet and raced toward where I'd left the roan.

My horse was gone, of course. I don't know if it had ever been trained to stand ground-tied, but I wouldn't have expected any animal to hold its position with everything that was going on around it that night. There were more shots from upcañon, then a shrill cursing I recognized as Felix's. The next thing I knew, the *Indio*'s pinto was bursting out of the scrub not forty yards away. I swung instinctively toward it, shouldering the Marlin but not pulling the trigger. I guess I didn't shoot because somewhere deep in my mind I knew it wasn't Perez racing the paint horse toward me.

"Luis!" I shouted.

Vega spotted me and reined the pinto in my direction. Felix was still shooting wildly from above, and I'll swear one shot came so close I felt it ruffle the brim of my hat. Shifting the Marlin to my right hand, I reached out with my left as Luis wheeled the pinto in a tight arc around me. I caught his arm up high, near the bicep, and he caught mine in the same place, and it was like we'd been training for this moment our entire lives. I jumped, swinging my right leg over the pinto's hips while Luis leaned to the offside to help vault me up behind him. Then we were racing down the cañon, the pinto's hoofs pounding the hard ground while Felix's shouts faded behind us.

We found the roan about a quarter of a mile back down the trail. It had bolted with all the gunfire, but stopped when it came across my trail-weary bay mare, hitched in the scrub alongside the trail. Luis hauled up and I slid from the saddle's skirting. The roan acted like it might take off again, but I managed to sweet-talk it into letting me grab the reins. Stepping into the saddle, I rode back to where Luis was sitting his new mount in the middle of the trail, listening for pursuit.

"Anything?" I asked.

He shook his head, although I doubted if he could have heard much over the creaking of leather and the puffing of our horses.

Returning the Marlin to its scabbard, I said: "What happened back there?"

"When I heard your shots, I decided to leave the bay here and make my way up on foot. I spotted Felix where he was slipping down through the brush, but then I saw the pinto. He had it tied off in a little arroyo coming down off the side wall. I decided I wanted the horse more than I wanted to kill Felix Perez, so I went after it instead of him. Felix saw me, but I think he was afraid of hitting the horse, and pulled his shot at the last minute. I didn't have that concern, and I'm pretty sure I got him in the leg. I saw him fall, but then he wiggled off into the brush like the belly-dragger that he is. I didn't go after him."

I considered Luis's reply, about as much as I'd ever heard him say in one sitting. I also thought about Felix Perez, alone up there and wounded, but probably no less dangerous because of it.

"We'll never catch up, not in time," Luis said quietly. "Even if we did, we'd have to get the guns away from Davenport and the others. By the time we got back to Sabana, Soto would know. Even if we could get the guns and ammunition, it would be too late for the woman and the *niña.*"

I nodded agreement. "Felix was coming back to look for Spence, I'd bet money on that. When he doesn't return, Davenport will know something went wrong. He'll be waiting for us."

"They may have even heard the shots."

"We've got to go back, find another way to get Abby Davenport and that little girl out of there." I looked at Luis, not knowing what else to say. The task seemed monumental—impossible.

"There may be a way," Luis ventured tentatively. "While Guille and I waited for you at the glade, he told me about the garrison. He seemed certain that Soto would double-cross us, although I don't think he expected what ultimately happened."

No, I thought grimly, he couldn't have. None of us had.

"Guille was convinced we'd have to go in after the woman, and he already had it planned out in his mind," Luis continued.

"Did he tell you what he was thinking?"

"*Sí,* in detail." He smiled. "He was a talker, that one."

"Can it be done?"

"Possibly. It would be dangerous, very dangerous, but it is possible."

I could feel my resolve hardening. Davenport might have

abandoned his wife and daughter, but Luis and I hadn't. Pulling the roan's head around, I said: "Let's go get her."

SESSION THIRTEEN

We rode back past Yaqui Springs, but didn't use that route to reach the cañon floor. If it had been daylight we might have tried it, but we were both a little uneasy with the idea of Spence McKenzie still lying down there. I'm not speaking of haunts, mind you, but because I hadn't searched him more thoroughly after pulling the Smith & Wesson off of him. It would be just like the back-stabber to take a shot at us as we came through assuming he was still alive.

We used the same rugged arroyo going down as we had coming up. At first the bay—Luis was riding the pinto now, with the mare tagging along of its own accord—refused to follow us, but eventually its fear of being abandoned in cougar and jaguar country overcame its reluctance to negotiate the scree-filled gulch, and it came bounding down after us, squealing and snorting her displeasure. In case you're wondering, we'd left the mule in the Cañon Where the Small Lizards Run; the last I'd seen of it, it had been sniffing curiously at the entrance to the narrow side cañon that led to the grassy meadow above the pools. If it went on up, it could have lived out its life there in comfortable solitude.

I've already described the route between the slot cañon and Sabana. The only difference this time was our early evening start, which put us on top of the Sierra Verdes a couple of hours before sunset. Rather than risk being spotted by dropping down off the mountain while it was still light, we reined into a tiny vale out of the wind and stripped the saddles from our horses.

Luis had left Felix's old hulk back in the *barranco,* but had brought along the Indian's saddlebags. He dumped the contents on the ground while we chewed on hardtack and cold ham. The bags held the usual items you'd find in any drifter's war bag—extra clothing, some odds and ends of food and cooking utensils, a couple of boxes of old Henry rimfire ammunition that I didn't even know they still made. Then Luis opened a worn leather sack that had been crammed down at the bottom of the bags and upended it. A cold shiver ran down my spine as I stared at the items spilled before us. There were women's rings, pocket watches, money clips, odds and ends of photos, a woman's lacy red garter—and a leather thong strung with human ears.

"Jesus," Luis breathed, staring numbly at the hard, rubbery appendages.

I tentatively pulled the blood-blackened cord away from the rest of the trove. I counted fourteen ears, and with a sickening clarity, realized they were all right ears.

"That boy's been busy," I said dryly, then pulled the thong around so that the freshest ear lay separate from the rest. "What do you think, a week old?"

"About that," Luis agreed.

In my mind I saw the Wagner motorcycle leaving Moralos, the thin rooster tails of dust kicked up from its tires, the way its lanky rider had leaned forward over the handlebars as he guided the bike through a thorny forest of ocotillo and prickly pear. Dragging the leather string with its grisly catch out of the way, I went through the rest of Felix's illicit cache, but couldn't find any kind of identification, other than an inscription inside the lid of one of the pocket watches: *To my Darling Husband,* and below that, at the bottom, *Your Loving Sarah.*

"Makes me wish we'd taken time to root that hog out of the

brush," Luis said. "For this I would have gladly killed him."

"Fate will catch up with Felix Perez soon enough," I predicted. I said that figuring a wounded man alone in that country didn't stand much of a chance, unless Davenport sent someone back to look for him, and I couldn't fathom the old man having that much compassion.

Luis picked up the string of ears and threw them over the edge of the mountain. Then he scooped up the other items—the pocket watches and rings and all the rest—and tossed them after the ears. I can still see those photos caught in an updraft, swirling above our heads for several seconds before the wind finally scattered them.

We moved out again at dusk, and reached Sabana shortly after midnight. I led through the town's winding streets until we were within a couple of blocks of the former garrison, then turned into an empty lot behind an abandoned tinsmith's shop. There was a small corral set back in the shadows that didn't looked like it had been used since Castillo's Army of Liberation had taken over the town, and we hitched our horses to the railing.

"We should have kept the pinto's saddle for this one," Luis lamented as he guided the bay mare into the corral with a hand on her jaw.

"I didn't think she'd follow us this far," I confessed.

"She is loyal," Luis replied, patting the mare's neck affectionately, "but I think she is also too tired to make another hard run. We will need a fresh mount for the woman." He looked at me. "If we can get her out."

"We'll need to be ready if we do," I agreed.

We walked back to the street, staring toward the central plaza. The garrison was to the south of the plaza and above it by twenty-five or thirty feet—I think I've already mentioned that the town was built on a series of benches rising above the river.

Only the church sat higher, a towering adobe structure whose bell used to toll with irritating regularly at midnight and noon.

"What do you think?" Luis asked, nodding toward a still-open *cantina* on the far side of the plaza where several horses were standing patiently, swatting listlessly at flies.

"I reckon if they catch us, they'll put us in front of a firing squad no matter what we do. Might as well be shot for stealing a horse as trying to break out a prisoner." I gave Luis's arm a gentle poke. "Pick a good one," I said, then walked back to where our own mounts waited and began examining the riggings as best I could in the dark. With luck we'd be able to slip inside the garrison, then back out again with the woman and child, without disturbing a soul, but we'd need to be ready, too. Just in case h--- started to pop.

It took Luis only a couple of minutes to return with a sturdy-looking dun, a heavy *vaquero*'s saddle cinched to its back. Grinning self-consciously, he said: "If I had known stealing horses was so easy, I might have taken it up years ago."

"Looks like you've got an eye for it," I replied, running my hand over the dun's shoulder and down its forearm, admiring its strength and the sleekness of its hide. It was a good horse that had been well taken care of. Someone was going to be almighty ticked off when they discovered it missing.

I loosened the Smith & Wesson in its holster but left the Marlin behind, figuring a couple of men walking up the street too heavily armed might draw unwanted attention, but I felt peculiar without it. Like I'd left the house without my pants on. A handgun, if you'll pardon the pun, is handy to have around, but I'd always preferred a rifle, being a better shot with a long gun than a revolver.

We went to the plaza, then turned south toward the garrison. It was uphill all the way, and I was sweating heavily before we were halfway there, although I suspect it was as much from nerves as it was the climb. We took our time, just a couple of *amigos* heading home late from a night on the town. Luis had the side closest to the street, where his sombrero would help mask my lighter colored Stetson and *gringo* features. At the next block we stopped catty-corner from the garrison and rolled a couple of cigarettes, studying the bandit stronghold from the corners of our eyes.

The former *Federale* garrison was a sprawling complex surrounded by thick adobe walls eight feet high. The main entrance was set in the middle of the lower wall, double gates of solid oak planks that could be swung back wide enough to allow a good-size supply wagon to be driven inside. Or a company of Mexican cavalry. On that night there was a heavy-set man standing loosely at attention to one side of the entrance. A lantern hanging from an iron spike driven into the wall above his head illuminated a good portion of the street in front of him.

"Have you ever been inside?" Luis asked, thumbing a match into flame.

I shook my head as I accepted the light. My credentials as a trader, even this far south, were tarnished by my refusal to buy a license or pay an import or export fee, but I guess Guille had been inside numerous times, and had explained the layout to Luis in some detail.

"Let's go around back," Luis said.

We moved on, drawing on our cigarettes and conversing quietly, in the manner of men-about-town everywhere. The guard at the front gate graced us with barely a glance, and I told Luis that, if we had to, we could probably force our way past him.

"It will be better in back," Luis assured me.

It was, too. The rear of the post appeared even more vulnerable than the front. The entry was smaller, for one thing, more like a large door than a gate, and the single guard leaning against the rough mud wall looked as if he had been fighting sleep for quite some time. There was a lantern there, as well, but it was sitting on the ground instead of hanging from a peg, and its glass was nearly black with soot. The guard's carbine, one of those stubby single-shot Remingtons that were so popular in Mexico during those turbulent years, was propped against the wall at his side.

We halted behind what I at first thought was a buckboard with its front wheels chocked against the grade, parked across the side street from the garrison, but a second glance revealed that it was an automobile. More crudely built than others I'd seen, but gasoline-powered nonetheless, and I remember thinking with some surprise: *Even here.*

Trying to remain unobtrusive, we dropped our half-smoked cigarettes and ground them out under our heels. The guard hadn't noticed us yet, and I wanted to keep it that way for as long as possible.

"Did Guille say when they changed sentries?"

"No, unfortunately he did not."

"From the way that *hombre*'s head is bobbing, I'd say he's been there a while."

"Then we should not tarry."

I chewed thoughtfully at my lower lip, wondering if there was some way we could approach on the sly and not be spotted. Then Luis motioned toward one of the rocks shoved against the front wheel of the automobile.

"Bring that," he said. "I have an idea."

I didn't question him. Kicking the head-size stone free, I tucked it under my arm like a football and we sauntered back down the side street until we were no longer in the guard's view. Once out of sight, we hurried across the dark street. At the garrison's wall, Luis said: "If I can get on top, I can follow it around to where the sentry dozes."

"It's worth a try," I agreed.

Lacing my fingers together like a stirrup, I lifted him high enough to scramble on up. Then I hoisted the stone overhead, and he plucked it from my fingers. Rising cautiously atop the humped crown of the wall, he flashed me a quick but apprehensive grin, then took off in an almost dainty stride, the heavy rock carried in both hands in front of his stomach, his toes pointed out against the slanted crest.

I followed as far as the garrison corner, then removed my broad-brimmed hat to peer around the edge. I couldn't see Luis from where I was standing, and the wait seemed to stretch on for so long that I started to get worried. Then a pair of brown hands extended out over the wall, and for a moment I felt a pang of doubt about what we were doing. That rock probably weighed ten pounds or more, and it occurred to me that it could kill the man if it struck him right. Then I thought of Guille, and who knew how many others who had been gunned down by Soto and his hooligans, and brushed my qualms aside. Luis hands parted slightly and the stone plummeted toward the ground. Hearing the melon-like thump of the rock striking the sentry's head, I quickly darted around the corner.

Luis's aim had been true. A broad gash above the guard's brows was pumping blood across his craggy features, and his eyes had rolled back in his head. But he was still alive, and I felt oddly pleased that we hadn't killed him.

The guard's leather-brimmed kepi had been knocked off by the stone. I kicked it aside, then hurriedly stripped off his jacket before it became saturated with blood. A hand-forged key hung from the man's neck by a slim cotton cord, and I took that and a plain Colt revolver in a scarred flap holster, as well. Then I hauled him into a sitting position with his back to the wall, his knees bent up to just under his nose. Grabbing a double handful of collar, I tugged his loose-fitting shirt up in back, then down over his lacerated scalp. Standing back, I studied my work with some satisfaction. From a distance the sentry would look like he was sitting down on the job, but with his head hooked back like it was, it wouldn't appear as if he were asleep. Or worse, that he was unconscious. And it didn't hurt, I decided, that the heavy cotton fabric would help staunch the flow of blood.

"J.T.!"

I looked up. Luis was perched on his hands and knees atop the humped wall, staring down anxiously. I held up the key, and he exhaled in obvious relief.

"Open the gate," he whispered. "I can crawl down that way."

I inserted the key in the lock, the simple tumbler inside flipping back with a barely audible click, and the gate swung inward. I stopped it where Luis could grab the top, then swing down to catch a cross-support with his toes. From there it was an easy drop to the ground. As soon as he was down, I shut the gate, but didn't lock it.

Most of the enclosed compounds that I've been in had the bulk of their dwellings butted up against the inner walls, but the garrison at Sabana was different. Its outer walls were bare on the inside, without even a walkway along the top to keep watch from. Its buildings were clustered in the center of the enclosure like a bunch of mud blocks. Lamplight burned in a few of the windows, but there were no guards.

"Where's the woman?" I asked.

Luis's eyes were darting back and forth, trying to mesh the picture Guille had painted in his mind with the reality of what he saw before him. After a moment's hesitation, he jutted his chin toward a low building near the west wall. "That one, I think."

We took off at a swift walk, neither of us wishing to linger outside any longer than was necessary. As we crossed the empty space between the gate and the flat-roofed structure Luis had pointed out, I started handing him the items I'd taken off the guard. He put on the revolver and holster first, then the jacket and the kepi hat, handing me his sombrero to carry. The last thing I gave him was the Remington carbine, with its heavy cartridge belt of 7×57 ammunition, the same gun Soto's men had carried at Dos Puentes.

We paused at the door with the natural reluctance of someone about to blindly stick their hand in a dark hole without knowing what was inside. Neither of us spoke. I think we were so deep into the mire by then that words had become irrelevant. Then Luis tugged resolutely on his jacket's lapels, and I tripped the latch and stepped back. Our plan was that if there was anyone inside, Luis would try to pass himself off as one of Soto's latest recruits, but thankfully the door opened on a long, empty hallway, running down the center of the building. We slipped inside and I closed the door. There was a candle burning in a sconce at the far end of the corridor, but otherwise the narrow passage was bare, without even a bench or a runner to break its brittle sterility. Not counting the second exit at the far end of the hall, there were six closed doors before us, three on either side.

"Guille said she would probably be in one of the rooms on our left, but he didn't know which one," Luis breathed.

We began inching our way down the corridor. The floor was planed oak, darkly polished and worn nearly smooth as glass by the thousands of boots that had scuffed its length over the years. Coming to the first door, I cautiously pressed down on the latch. It opened easily, and from the darkness within a masculine voice sleepily grumbled: "Who is it?"

"Luis," Luis replied quietly. "Go back to sleep."

I pulled the door closed and stepped back, my heart like a wildcat on the end of a short leash. We waited and listened, but when we didn't hear anything more from inside, we moved on to the next room.

None of the doors had locks, but this one had a long iron stake—he kind trail cooks used to use to suspend their kettles over a fire—braced behind the latch in a way that made it impossible to open from inside. I removed the bar as quietly as possible. I think we both had a fair idea of what we'd find on the other side, but, after our experience at the first door, we went in softly, our fingers wrapped around the grips of our revolvers.

There was a candle burning in here, too. Its flame guttered briefly as I opened the door, then rose back to its full height, revealing a cramped room with a bunk, a table and bench, and a shuttered window in the outside wall.

Despite our efforts at silence, the woman was awake. Perhaps she'd never been asleep, although the hour was late. She sat fully dressed on the edge of the bunk, clutching a small, brown-haired child to her breast. The woman's eyes were wide with alarm, although she didn't cry out. The little girl's face was pressed into her mother's shoulder as if trying to hide. In English, I said: "Abby Davenport?"

"Who are you?"

"My name's Latham, this is Vega. Your husband sent us to get you out of here."

"Charles," she said, her voice trembling with uncertainty. "Have you seen . . . ?"

"He's with your husband, ma'am. He's safe."

Some of the rigidness seemed to go out of her with my words, and her eyes misted over. Luis and I stepped inside, and Luis closed the door. I'd brought the iron bar with us, and quietly set it out of the way.

I'll admit right here that Abby Davenport wasn't what I'd envisioned. Considering her husband's wealth and influential connections, I'd expected someone younger and higherbosomed, with a golden mane and a flawless peaches-and-cream complexion. Even taking into account her recent ordeal, the woman sitting in front of me would never be considered classically beautiful. She was stoutly built with a plain round face and sandy hair, parted in the middle, then pulled back and coiled in what remained of a once fashionable coiffure. She wore a cornflower blue traveling dress, the sharp-pointed toes of a pair of black shoes peeking out from beneath its grimy hem like the unblinking eyes of a mouse. To be honest, if I hadn't known better, I would have mistaken her for a handsome but work-worn farm wife, rather than the spouse of a prosperous American merchant.

Moving deeper into the room, Luis said: "Are you all right, *señora?*"

"Yes, we're fine." She was stroking the little girl's tousled hair. "Hungry and frightened, but unharmed. You . . . you said Edward is here?"

"No, he didn't come into Sabana with us," Luis explained, then, after a moment's pause, added what wasn't really a lie, but was still mighty shy of the truth: "He is in the hills north of town with your son."

Abby looked momentarily perplexed, then shook her head as if to physically dislodge any further questions regarding her husband's whereabouts. "How do we get out of here?" she asked pragmatically.

"With a little luck, we'll just walk out," I replied. "You need to know that we weren't able to work out a ransom for you and your daughter. We're going to try to sneak you out the back way, but we'll have to be quick about it, and quiet."

"I understand," she said, then added: "In case . . . in case something happens and I'm not able to express this later, I want to thank both of you for what you are attempting. I shall always be grateful."

My throat tightened unexpectedly. It's amazing what a simple statement of appreciation can do to a person's morale. "You'd best save your thanks for when we get back to Arizona," I said huskily. "We'll have more time then."

It was a warm moment between the three of us—the four of us, really, for the child, Susan, was staring at us in wonder—but it didn't last. A door banged open in the hall, and a voice demanded to know who had removed the iron bar from the outer latch. The color seemed to drain from Abby's face. I suspect it did from mine, as well. Muttering under his breath, Luis headed for the door, while I palmed the Smith & Wesson on my way to the window.

Luis flung the door open and stepped into the hall. "What is all this commotion?" he demanded authoritatively.

An angry curse was his answer, and he ducked inside a second before a gun thundered in the narrow passageway, its bullet raking the wall like a giant fingernail. Luis slammed the door closed and threw me a desperate look. I was pushing at the shutter, but it was nailed shut. "J.T.!" he hissed.

Returning the Smith & Wesson to its holster, I grabbed the bench from beside the table and raised it above my shoulder. I wasn't even thinking at that point, just reacting. At the bunk, Abby was readying her daughter for flight, wrapping a blanket around her and grabbing the girl's shoes off the floor. I slammed the bench into the middle of the shutter with everything I had, and it crashed open with a hideous screech as a pair of nails were ripped from the wood. I tossed the bench aside. Luis had propped the iron bar against the door, but we both knew it wouldn't buy us much time—a couple of minutes, at most. Yanking the now useless kepi from his head, he threw it aside and grabbed his sombrero off the table. I snapped my finger and the woman rushed to my side. No, it wasn't polite, but she wasn't complaining. Lifting the girl from her arms, I practically tossed her to Luis.

"Susan!" Abby cried, but I spun her toward the window before she could say any more.

"Outside," I barked, then slipped one arm under her shoulder and the other under her knees and swept her off her feet like a bride at the threshold. There wasn't anything romantic in my actions, though. I carried her to the window and nearly poured her through. She squawked when she hit the ground, but was back in the bat of an eye to accept her daughter from Luis.

"You first," I said, shoving Luis toward the window. He didn't argue, but dived through, headfirst, although wrapping one arm around the sill on his way through so that he'd be able to spin around on the outside and land on his feet. I was right behind him, the hall door shuddering under blows from the far side, but still holding as the four of us made a dash for the rear gate.

The alarm was being raised all over the garrison, although in a haphazard manner. I could hear confused shouting from several quarters, then a voice from another building demanding to know what was going on. Then someone fired a shot into the air, and I knew the fat was in the fire.

We made it to the gate, but there were others behind us. As Luis yanked the big door open, a panicky *soldado* called for us to halt. I palmed the Smith & Wesson and snapped a round into the dirt at his feet, and heard the other soldiers scatter.

The echo of the report had barely died when the rear door to the building where the Davenports had been held was flung open. A burly man wearing only trousers and a jacket with sergeant's stripes stepped into the frame. Taking the situation in with a glance, he bellowed for us to stop and lay down our weapons, even as he lifted his own. Knowing I couldn't take a chance with this one, I squeezed off a round that caught the heavy-set man in the gut, and he staggered backward with a hoarse cry.

We were through the gate in a flash after that, darting around the corner to the side street and making a run for the plaza, but we hadn't covered even half the block when the sentry from the front gate came busting around the lower corner of the garrison. Shots from both Luis and me drove him back, but we knew that route had just been closed. Nodding toward a complex of corrals, open-faced stock sheds, and small holding pens across the street, I said: "That way."

I'd guess there were seventy or eighty head of horses penned inside those corrals, already growing agitated from the sound of gunfire and shouting from the garrison. We scampered down an alleyway where *vaqueros* had once run cattle and horses from one pen to another. I could hear Susan crying fearfully from beneath the blanket, while Abby tried to control the volume of her sobs so as to not give away our location. The front-gate sentry was shouting that we were hiding in the corrals, but not a lot of men were listening to him. Taking advantage of the pandemonium, Luis, Abby, and I ducked through the railing on the north side of the complex and ran across an empty, weed-choked lot to the mouth of the alley that would take us, two blocks down, to where we'd left our horses behind the abandoned tinsmith shop.

It was dark as pitch along the alley, with only the stars above us, like buckshot fired into a coal-black ceiling. Our progress was slowed by the junk we kept stumbling into—a smashed wagon wheel, scraps of lumber set aside for some future project or the winter stove, mounds of old ash shoveled out of fireplaces and ovens. A dog, some kind of knee-high mongrel, lunged at us from one of the lightless doorways, and Luis swung the carbine solidly into the animal's nose, sending it howling out the far end of the alley. We rushed after it, making it as far as the southwest corner of the central plaza before we were halted by a squad of Soto's men, racing past on foot.

I grabbed Abby and hauled her back out of sight, the three of us flattening ourselves against the rear wall of whatever building we'd been stopped behind. The dog Luis had struck had already raced across the street, and one of the soldiers shouted: "This way, I saw them go in here!"

That dog probably saved our lives that night, but it also led Soto's men into the darkness behind the row of businesses lining the west side of the plaza, of which the tinsmith was one.

We'd lost our horses.

Standing with our backs pressed tightly against the rough adobe, Luis panted: "What now?"

As if in response, a voice from the far end of the block shouted that he'd found our mounts.

"The horses in the corral," I said. "If we can get even a bridle on a couple of them, we can make a break for it." I glanced at Abby. Her eyes were wide in the starlight, frightened but not panicked. "Can you make it?"

"I can do whatever I have to do," she assured me, and we pushed away from the building and started back toward the corrals. Unfortunately that route was also cut off. We paused at the edge of the empty lot, listening to the front-gate sentry insisting that we'd gone in here, meaning the corrals. This time he was starting to garner some interest.

We crouched among the tall weeds, sucking wind but trying to keep the sound down. Susan was still snuffling, but more quietly now, her face pressed into her mother's shoulder. At my side, Luis whispered: "Which way, J.T.?"

"I don't know."

"West?"

"Into the desert?"

"Into the fields, the barley and wheat and tobacco. It is our only hope."

"They'd find us in those fields. Maybe not right away, but as soon as it's light. We've got to stay in town where there are more places to hide."

"They will find us here, too," he insisted. "They will organize search parties, and comb every corner, invade every home."

"We can't stay here," Abby cried softly, probably wondering what kind of mess she'd gotten herself into. "There must be some place we can hide."

"The. . . ." Luis paused, staring uncertainly into my eyes. "*Amigo*, would they search their own quarters?"

"Maybe, eventually," I replied, but I had to admit it was a better idea than any I was coming up with.

Keeping low, we skirted the corrals on the desert side, then swung back toward the garrison. I could see the sentry and a handful of others moving through the pens, pushing the horses out of their way as they poked under the feed troughs with their carbines and used pitchforks to probe the haystacks. But they weren't paying any attention to what was going on outside the corrals, and we were soon back to where Luis and I had started, crouched behind the motorized buckboard with its remaining chocked wheel. My fingers tightened on the Smith's grips when I saw the knot of men clustered around the still unconscious guard at the rear gate. That route, too, was plugged.

I turned to Luis, searching his face for some sign that he'd come up with an alternative to fleeing blindly into the desert, that there was a way out of this mess that I was overlooking. He shook his head.

"Mister Latham?"

I glanced at the woman. "Yeah?"

"This." She had her free hand on the side of the automobile, and gave it a small push. The car was so flimsily built that it rocked easily under her hand. "Why can't we take this?"

I leaned back to study the machine more closely. I'd realized from the first that it was crudely made, but it wasn't until I took time to really study it that I realized it was actually a barn-crafted vehicle, a bastardized buckboard hammered together by some enterprising blacksmith or mechanic.

The name *Watson Masner* was painted on the sideboards in gold script, but I don't know if that was the buckboard's maker, or the name of the mechanic who had converted it into a motor-ized vehicle. [*Ed. Note:* A James V. Watson was listed in the El Paso, Texas, city directory as proprietor of Watson Wagon Works, on Río Arriba Road, from 1898 to 1925, with Franklin W. Mas-ner cited as manager of that company from 1914 to 1922; no other combination of Watson and Masner, in association with either wagon or automotive manufacturing, could be located; it is duly noted that the above dates do not correspond with Latham's journey into Sonora in 1907.]

The engine was slung under the bed from iron brackets, with a sturdy bicycle-style chain running from the flywheel to a large steel sprocket that girdled the rear axle. The wagon's tongue had been removed, and a metal shaft run through the straps that bound the hounds to the coupling pole; the shaft extended up through the floorboards to terminate in a nearly horizontal wooden steering wheel.

I recognized the pedals on the floorboard from my experi-ence with the Berkshire, but the other gadgets I knew only vaguely—choke, spark, fuel mixture. The throttle was fastened to the steering column like an upside-down pie tin, with a lever jutting from the right-hand side to adjust the speed; pull it all the way back to open it up, then forward to close it.

As I studied the various mechanisms, it dawned on me that I could probably drive this thing if I could get it started. Unfortunately I didn't have a clue how to start it, and I was almost positive Luis didn't, either.

"Unless you know how to operate all those levers so we can get it running, about the best we could hope for would be to roll it downhill, and that wouldn't get us very far," I told the woman.

"But, I do know how to start it. At least I think I do." She was standing beside the Watson Masner, seemingly mindless of the *soldados* gathered at the rear gate, or of those still searching the corrals below us. She ran a hand over the levers and knobs with growing excitement. "I've watched Mister McKenzie start Edward's Berkshire I don't know how many times in Tucson, and my father's chauffeur in New York even let me drive our family Ford around Central Park on several occasions. This is really no different than either of those vehicles. This is the clutch, and that's the throttle, and this brass things controls the timing. . . ."

"Wait a minute," I cut in. "You can start this machine? Are you sure?"

"I'm certain of it."

Hope flared briefly, then drifted back like a receding tide as I recalled the ear-numbing racket of the Berkshire when we started it in that sandy wash north of Moralos. We'd never get away with anything like that in Sabana, not with Soto's men swarming on every side. I told Abby my reasoning, but she had another idea.

"Randolph, my father's chauffeur, explained it to me while we were watching another driver start his vehicle that way."

"Quicker than turning the engine over with a hand crank?" I asked doubtfully.

"Considerably so," she assured me. "Here." She handed Susan to Luis, reminding her to remain quiet when the youngster started to whimper. Then she bent forward to study the engine, silhouetted against the lights of the garrison. Reaching toward a tiny, knurled knob under a tank located beneath the modified buckboard's single seat, she confidently backed it open. The faint gurgle of gasoline running through the copper tubing brought a quick smile to my face. I was feeling better already. I'd have never known you needed to open a valve so that the fuel could reach what I'd eventually learn was the carburetor, but Abby did, and my confidence in her rose.

She studied the engine another minute, then turned her attention to the steering column. She pulled the choke all the way out, adjusted the spark about midway, then nodded solemnly. "I think that's it." She looked at me with a hesitant smile. "Shall we try it?"

I glanced at Luis. He stared back wordlessly. Knowing I'd ridden in an automobile before, he was letting me make the call. What Abby was proposing was as crazy as h---, but I didn't know what other choice we had. "I say we try it."

Luis nodded and started tucking the blanket more tightly around the child.

"What do you want me to do?" I asked Abby.

"Let me get into the driver's seat and prepare myself. When I'm ready, please remove that rock from under the front wheel. Then I want you and Mister Vega to get behind the carriage and push it as fast as you can." She smiled at my puzzled expression. "I do indeed intend to roll it downhill, Mister Latham, but only partway. If things work as I believe they will, we shall have ignition before we reach the plaza, and can proceed from there under full power."

"Through the plaza?"

"I shall have to depend upon you for guidance. I'm afraid my thoughts were in something of a turmoil when I was brought here."

I nodded soberly. Luis set the girl in the buckboard and pushed her under the seat behind her mother's legs—the most sheltered spot he could find. Then he moved around behind the automobile and placed the Remington carbine on the bed in front of him. I looked at Abby and asked her if she was ready.

"As ready as I shall ever be," she replied, no trace of her earlier smile remaining.

I moved around in front of the snub-nosed vehicle. "Say the word," I whispered.

"Mister Latham, let us fly."

SESSION FOURTEEN

Mister Latham, let us fly!

I'm going to remember those words until the day they put me in my grave, but I didn't have much time to appreciate them that night in Sabana. After kicking the remaining stone out from under the buckboard's front wheel, I hurried around back to help Luis. The wagon had rolled only imperceptibly forward under its own weight, but quickly picked up speed with the two of us pushing it. We managed to cover about ten feet before one of the men at the garrison's rear gate spotted us. They immediately shouted for us to halt, while simultaneously opening fire on us with their carbines.

Although we caught a moment's reprieve as soon as we rattled past the corner of the garrison's rear wall, it was a short-lived clemency. Hearing the shouting and shooting, the men combing the corrals immediately raced after us. They started firing as soon as they saw us, but had to aim high because of the latticework of railing between them and the street. Their bullets peppered the garrison's adobe wall, raining a mud-colored shower over the road.

It went on that way for the next three blocks, everything happening so fast I could barely keep track of it all. Luis and I were pushing with everything we had, our bodies nearly parallel to the ground as we strained at the recalcitrant vehicle. We were picking up quite a bit of speed, too. Enough that, for a fraction of a second, right there at the end, I was afraid we'd gone too far and were going to lose our footing before we could clamber aboard.

I remember gasping for Luis to jump, but I think he'd already started. I heaved myself toward the tailgate, scrambling over the top, then wiggling into the bed. Bullets were raking the air on every side, the dull smack of lead clawing at the vehicle's sideboards like the beating of drums. We shot past the lower corner of the garrison so quick that a lot of the men standing at the front gate never even got off a shot. Then, just about the time I thought we were on our way, Abby released the clutch, and the Watson Masner lurched to a near halt.

Luis and I, caught unaware, started skidding wildly toward the front of the vehicle. Susan screamed in terror as we flew past her mother's feet and crashed into the footboard in a tangle of arms and legs. The child immediately started wailing, while Luis and I resorted to a more adult version of tears, and began cursing loudly and colorfully as we attempted to extract ourselves from the buckboard's clutch and brake pedals.

But a funny thing happened, too, and if you've ever driven an automobile, I suspect you already know what it was. Abby had jump-started the car, just as Randolph had instructed her back in New York City's Central Park all those years before. It wasn't a smooth start—I thought for a second the engine had been torn loose from the undercarriage—but then it caught with a violent chatter of valves and pistons, followed by a great belching of smoke and enough fire from the exhaust to mimic a cannon's blast. Abby jammed the clutch to the floor, briefly pinning Luis's left arm to the footboard in the process, then began a rapid flurry of leg and arm movements during which I believe she managed to readjust just about every pedal, knob, and lever the Watson Masner offered.

The vehicle—I never have been able to decide whether it was an automobile or a buckboard, and usually refer to it in whatever manner seems natural at the time—lurched forward with a jerk that seemed to nearly tear it in half. But then we were rolling forward again, under the engine's power this time, rather than gravity's.

All that happened in about five seconds, if not less, and before any of us other than Abby really knew what was going on, we were barreling through the plaza with even more guns going off on every side, flying through there so fast I was still clawing for my revolver when Abby leaned hard on the wheel and we shot into a side street that took us northwest toward the river. Twisting partway around, Abby shouted: "Where to, Mister Latham? Where do we go from here?"

I crawled forward on my hands and knees until I could grab the back of the seat. Maybe I should have explained this earlier, but one of the characteristics of a buckboard—where the vehicle got its name, in fact—was that there were no springs on the bed to soften the ride, no thorough braces to rock the wagon's body back and forth like stagecoaches used to use. In later years, manufacturers would add leaf springs under the buckboard's single seat, but a lot of the earlier models had just a wooden plank nailed across the body toward the front of the bed. If you're curious about where the word "buck" comes from, think about the last rodeo you attended, and rest assured the ride was similar.

I was clinging to the back of the buckboard's seat for dear life as we sped through Sabana's narrow, winding streets. There was no point in directing Abby toward the Dos Puentes, since there would be nowhere to go on the other side even if she could negotiate those two pinched spans over the Río Sabana at the speeds she was driving, and we'd already missed the eastbound road to Tres Pinos. It seemed to me that our best bet would be to follow the main road west out of town, past the grain fields of the Sabana Valley and into the harsh desert toward the Sea of Cortez. [*Ed. Note:* The Sea of Cortez is more commonly known today as the Gulf of California.]

You might wonder why I didn't have Abby turn around and make a run for Tres Pinos, where we could maybe catch the Ferrocarril del Pacifico to Nogales. There were two reasons. One was that we didn't have any way of knowing when the next northbound train might pass through Tres Pinos, or if it would even stop when it did. But the main reason we didn't go back was the simplest. We were already heading west. Turning around would mean going right back through a town filled with angry *soldados*.

So we went west, the road running straight between broad fields of grains and tobacco. Our way was wide but rutted, and I hung on until my fingers ached from the strain. Luis was huddled at my side, cradling the child as best he could from the worst jolts. I remember looking behind us at one point and seeing the pale stretch of road empty of pursuit, and hollering for Abby to slow down, but she only shook her head and continued on at full throttle.

"You're going to wreck us!" I shouted above the roar of the unbaffled engine, and she replied, without looking around or loosening her white-knuckled grip on the wheel: "The throttle seems to be stuck, Mister Latham. I'm afraid I can't slow down."

My heart sank a little with that new information, and my fingers tightened on the back of the seat. I remember glancing at Luis. He was in a fetal position on the floor by then, the child clutched tightly to his chest. I could tell he hadn't heard Abby's announcement, and decided that was for the best.

The road continued on into the night, its few curves gentle and sweeping. Our route followed the center of the valley, even after we left the largest fields behind. We continued to pass a few small adobe houses along the way, each with its own tiny garden patch and maybe a few acres of grain or tobacco, but by dawn even those sporadic gasps of civilization had petered out. The land became more rugged as we approached a low mountain range that choked off the western tip of the valley. Spying a gap in the hills that I remembered from my time with the Yaquis, I tapped Abby's shoulder and told her to stop.

"There's a sharp curve up ahead that you're never going to make at this speed," I shouted, and she nodded in tight-lipped understanding.

"As soon as I push in on the clutch, reach over the side, and pull that heavy black wire from the engine. That should stop us."

I crawled to the edge of the buckboard's narrow bed. I think we must have been flying along at about fifteen or twenty miles an hour at that point, and staring at the ground flashing past in a tan blur just a couple of feet below my face sent a rush of emotion squirreling up my spine. Not fear, but excitement. Remember me mentioning that Coney Island roller coaster the other night, when I was telling you about our drive south from Sentinel? It was like that, a kind of hang-on-and-scream-at-the-top-of-your-lungs moment, although I kept those bubbling emotions to myself.

"Are you ready, Mister Latham?" Abby called.

"I'm ready, Missus Davenport."

"Now!" she shouted, and shoved the clutch pedal to the floor.

The engine screamed as the tension between the flywheel and the rear axle was released. I grabbed the center wire off what I would eventually learn was the magneto's distributor cap and gave it a yank, yelping at the unexpected electrical shock that traveled up my arm like a couple of dozen fleet-footed centipedes to explode in my armpit. My fingers instinctively popped open, dropping the wire as I rolled away, and the engine clattered to a stop. The automobile kept rolling, and lying on my back in the middle of the wagon bed, I told Abby to hit the brake.

"I'm afraid the brake doesn't work, either," she informed me.

I stared incredulously at the back of her head. "How long have we been traveling without brakes?"

"Ever since we left Sabana."

"Jesus," I breathed, exchanging a dumbfounded look with Luis.

"That lady's got more grit than my socks," he said, though keeping his voice low so that she wouldn't overhear and be offended.

I crawled back to the seat and grabbed on. "We've come all this way without brakes?"

"I fear that we have," she admitted, disengaging the transmission and allowing the vehicle to coast to a stop. It didn't take long in that sandy soil. When we finally rolled to a halt, Luis gently set the girl on the floor, then crawled out the back of the wagon box and dropped to his hands and knees in the middle of the road.

"You all right?" I asked him.

"*Sí*, I'm just going to kneel here a moment and say a prayer to the Virgin."

I started to laugh, then clamped it off. Dropping over the sideboard, I hobbled up to where Abby was preparing to dismount and helped her to the ground.

"Mama?" the little girl said, and the woman quickly brushed past me to lift the child into her arms—the adventuress gone, vanished in the blink of an eye, the mother returned.

"It's OK, baby," she soothed, then took the youngster off into the rocks to do whatever it was she thought needed doing.

Walking back to where Luis was now sitting on the ground, staring into the distance, I pulled the makings from my pocket and started a cigarette. "Well, this ain't hardly what I had in mind," I remarked.

"We are still alive, my friend. Not so long ago, I wouldn't have bet on our living to see the light of this fine new day."

Plopping down beside him, I handed him the cigarette, then started a second one for myself. "I doubt if we'd be here if not for Missus Davenport."

Luis nodded admiringly. "She was something to see, was she not? It makes me wonder how someone could turn his back on such a woman."

"The old man?"

"*Sí.*"

"I hope to get the chance to ask him that someday," I said softly.

"It is a question that burns in my mind, as well, but not as much as wondering what we should do now."

I didn't have an answer for that, not right away. After putting the finishing touches on my cigarette, Luis struck a match and lit his and mine, then shoved the match head into the dirt beside his boot. I rubbed my knees. They were really hurting after the pounding they'd taken while I clung to the back of the buckboard's seat.

"You told the woman there was a sharp curve before us," Luis said after a bit. "You know this road?"

"A long time ago. Back then, this road led over the top to another valley where there used to be good grass and decent water. There was a horse operation headquartered in a little side cañon to the south, and a couple of families of *vaqueros* who hunted mustangs that they sold to the ranches around Tres Pinos. If it's still there, we might be able to trade for some horses, then make a run for Arizona."

"How long ago was that?"

"It's been a good many years," I admitted, but didn't add that I'd still been traveling with the Yaquis then, and that we'd raided the Vaquero Springs *rancho* for fresh mounts. There had been survivors when we pulled out, but I didn't know if they'd stayed after we were gone.

We were finishing our cigarettes when Abby returned with the girl. I've already described what Mrs. Davenport looked like, but I haven't mentioned the child. Susan Davenport was just a few weeks shy of her seventh birthday when she was snatched off that train with her mother and brother. She was a cute kid with a round face and curly brown hair several shades darker than her mama's sandy tresses. She wore a white satin traveling dress with a frilly pink trim that was now tattered and stained, and plain black Oxfords, scuffed to bare leather at the toes. Her stockings were white with pink stripes that matched the ribbon in her unruly hair, and there were dark circles under her red-rimmed eyes—like her mother's. Both of them were obviously exhausted, yet trying hard not to show it.

The woman paused some distance away as if gathering her courage, then strode purposefully forward. "Might I ask if there is any food? Susan hasn't eaten since yesterday noon, and that was little enough."

I pushed gingerly to my feet, my knees still protesting the beating they'd taken from the Watson Masner. "I'm afraid what little food we had is still with our horses, but if we can get this contraption running again"—I rapped the automobile's sideboard with a knuckle—"there used to be a ranch over those hills yonder that might have some grub to spare."

She smiled apologetically. "Of course, and I don't mean to be a bother. I just wanted to inquire."

Luis was fumbling inside one of the pockets on his vest. "I have a little something," he said. "It is dirty, but it might take the edge off the *niña*'s hunger." He brought out a broken square of hardtack and a palm-sized chunk of cold ham, both sprinkled liberally with pocket lint.

"Thank you," Abby said gratefully, accepting Luis's offering, then kneeling at her daughter's side as she picked off the worst of the débris.

"We will all need food soon," Luis told me quietly. "Water, too."

"There should be plenty of water at the springs, even if the *vaqueros* who used to live there have moved on." I glanced at the carbine he'd brought with him from the garrison. "If we've got enough time, we might find a deer or a stray calf. Even a rabbit would help."

While the girl munched hungrily on her meat and cracker, Abby came over with a weary smile. "That all sounds so delicious," she said, meaning the possibility of fresh meat. "Shall we take a look at our transportation and see if it can be made to function again?"

"Tell me what you need."

"I was thinking we should check the gasoline and oil. Randolph always did that before we began any journey. And I'd like to fix the throttle and brake if possible."

At that time I didn't have a clue how to fix a throttle, but I'd watched Spence check the oil and refill the Berkshire's gas tank on the way down from Sentinel, and figured I could handle those chores. Whatever was troubling the brakes would be relatively easy to track down, too, being the same friction-block set-up as any other small wagon—at least once the main brake rod left the mechanism under the bed.

While Luis went around the far side of the buckboard to have a look at the brake, I took off in search of a clean, dry limb to poke inside the gas tank. While we were doing that, Abby headed for the engine. I could tell by the tentativeness of her approach that she didn't really know any more about the workings of a gasoline-powered motor than I did, but she seemed determined to do as much as she could.

It didn't take long to track down most of the problems, and we were soon back at the tailgate comparing notes. The news wasn't good. The gas tank, a ten-gallon iron keg strapped on its side under the seat, held less than two inches of fuel, and the oil was also low. The brake was unfixable, the hinge in front of the wooden pad having been sheared in half at some earlier date; it was Luis's opinion that the bracket would have to be either completely replaced or welded by a blacksmith to be functional again, neither a task we were capable of completing in the field.

Fortunately the news from the engine wasn't as dire. By tracking the metal rod backward from the steering column, Abby had discovered a missing bolt where the slim shaft connected to the carburetor's throttle arm.

"It had to have come off on the road," she stated. "I'm certain it was working while I was making adjustments prior to our starting the vehicle in Sabana."

"It doesn't matter when it came off, can it be fixed?" I asked.

"It already is," she beamed. "I used a hairpin to reconnect the two pieces." Then her smiled faded. "I don't know how long it will last, though. I'm worried the pin's strength will be inadequate for the rigors of an automobile's engine."

"With the gas tank so low, it won't have to last long," I predicted glumly.

"What about the brake?" Luis asked. "Can we drive it without that?"

"Since the throttle is no longer stuck wide open, we should be able to slow down enough to coast to a stop," Abby said.

"We might be able to rig up some kind of a drag for downhill," I added, eyeing the distant crest of the low mountains we still had to cross. It was several miles from where we'd stopped to the divide, but, if I remembered correctly, a fairly short but steep plunge down the other side. Turning to Abby, I said: "Let's see if we can get this machine running."

Starting an engine, even those old hand-cranked models, isn't as complicated as you might think, but I'll be the first to admit that I was more than a little intimidated by the process that first time behind the wheel. Abby was using words like "fuel mixture" and "spark" and "choke", terms that seemed overwhelming as I climbed into the seat, as did the need to keep the vehicle in "neutral" while someone cranked on the engine. What the heck was a *neutral*, anyway, and how did I get something as big as a buckboard inside of one?

You can go ahead and laugh if you want. It won't hurt my feelings. Nowadays I can start those old engines alone and blindfolded, but back then it was a two-person chore, with a lot of tension in the air surrounding that rattletrap of an automobile as we sorted it all out together.

Sitting alone in the middle of the seat with Abby standing beside the vehicle to tell me what to push and what to pull and what to turn, and Luis fitting the heavy crank to the main shaft, I got that now-familiar lump of excitement in my throat as we prepared to start the engine. Up front, Luis gave me a chary look and said he was ready. I told him to: "Give it a whirl."

On the third spin the engine bucked so wildly the entire vehicle seemed to lift off the ground. Abby jumped back with a startled exclamation, and Luis swore colorfully in Spanish, a language I was pretty sure neither Abby nor her daughter understood, although I suspect they could have easily grasped the essence of his words from the passion in which they were uttered.

"It is going to explode!" Luis shouted, backing away with the crank dangling from one hand.

"It's not going to explode," Abby replied. Making a quick spinning motion with her hand, she said: "Try it again."

Again turned out to be the magic number. The motor sputtered to life with a hoarse, barking cough, accompanied by a cloud of stinking gray exhaust from a too-rich fuel mixture. We had a few missteps getting everything adjusted, but the engine was warm and forgiving, and was soon running strongly.

Clapping her hands in delight, Abby placed Susan in the bed, then crawled in after her. Luis jumped in behind Abby and made himself as comfortable as possible with his legs dangling over the end of the lowered tailgate, the carbine riding handily across his lap, its cartridge belt curled up at his side. I asked if everyone was ready, and, when I got an affirmative from the rear, I eased the vehicle into gear and carefully released the clutch.

I was lucky in that my first efforts at driving had been under Spencer McKenzie's tutelage. Recalling his instructions and my own clumsy accomplishments in that sandy wash above Moralos, I was able to get the Watson Masner moving along without bogging it down or killing the engine. I don't want to imply that I started out as a great driver, because I didn't, but I did manage to keep the vehicle on the road, and only occasionally clipped some of the cholla and ocotillo that lined our route.

We started climbing almost immediately, and our speed slowed to a crawl, the engine straining loudly. I was aware of Luis throwing me nervous glances, and of Abby Davenport's tight-lipped scrutiny of our progress. I've already mentioned how the Watson Masner was so haphazardly built, probably some blacksmith's first attempt at mating a gasoline-powered engine to something with wheels, and the gearing—what little there was of it—was too high for mountain grades. Even those overgrown hills west of Sabana were proving to be a challenge for it.

The temperature rose steadily hotter as the morning progressed, an indicator of the approaching summer season, and the heat from our overworked engine was seeping up through the vehicle's floorboards. Down below I'd envisioned making the same great time we had after leaving Sabana, but it didn't take long to realize that wasn't going to happen. At least not until we reached level ground again.

We were almost at the top when the engine began to sputter, our already laborious pace slowing to a crawl. I glanced questioningly at Abby, but she could only shake her head in helpless ignorance. We managed another couple of hundred feet before the vehicle finally lurched to a halt.

Luis jumped to the ground and shoved a rock under one of the wheels to keep the auto from rolling backward. Abby and I were slower getting out, and for a while the three of us just stood there without a clue as to what had gone wrong. It was Luis who suggested a second check of the fuel, and that turned out to be the problem. We weren't out, but with a gravity-fed tank and the road's constant upward grade, gasoline was no longer reaching the forward-mounted valve.

I swallowed back a frustrated curse. If I'd had a wrench I could have loosened the metal straps holding the tank in place, then we could have tipped it forward so that the gas once again reached the valve, but the bolts were too firmly drawn into the wood to be loosened by our fingers, and the floorboards were too tightly nailed to be kicked free. I lifted my eyes to stare morosely at our destination, less than half a mile away.

"We almost made it," Abby said wistfully.

"Should we walk?" Luis asked.

After a moment's deliberation, I shook my head. "We should push. It's at least four miles from the top of the pass to the springs on the other side. That'd take us several hours on foot in this kind of country, but it should be pretty easy to coast on in from the divide, even if we can't get the car started again. And if we do get it started, we could be there in under an hour."

Luis looked doubtful. "That is a pretty long push, my friend."

"It is, but the grade isn't as steep as it has been, and it'll be quicker than walking in the long run." I turned to the woman. "Would you steer while Luis and I push?"

"Of course."

The girl roused at her mother's voice, then sat up with a grumpy expression just short of full-blown tears. Abby went to fetch her before the crying began. I felt a moment's unaccountable jealousy when the child's gaze fell on Luis and her snuffling abruptly stopped. I'd already picked up on her shyness around me, but that was the first time I realized how much she had taken to Luis. I suppose her affection came from his efforts to protect her on our wild ride through the dark Sabana Valley the night before, but I couldn't help feeling a bit left out.

Abby took a moment to comfort the child, then set her in the seat behind the wheel with the request that she assist with the navigation. "You can help guide me around the big rocks," she said, and what remained of the girl's crabby demeanor vanished behind a smile.

Abby took the car out of gear, meaning she put it in neutral—and I'll say here that for the amount of time invested, I think I learned more about automobiles on that trip from Sabana to Vaquero Springs than I have in all the years since—while Luis kicked the rock out from behind the wheel.

A buckboard is a light vehicle. One man can easily lift either the rear or front if he needs to get it off the ground to work on something. Even the addition of a raucous four-stroke engine, a nearly empty gas tank, and all the levers, gears, and pedals up front didn't add all that much weight. But the road before us that morning, although not overly steep, was still uphill, and the Watson Masner's narrow wheels seemed to want to dig into the soil, making our journey all the more difficult. Thankfully Abby hadn't followed Susan onto the wagon's seat, and was instead walking alongside the auto, handling the steering with her right hand and helping push where she could with her left.

Still, the bulk of the labor fell to Luis and me, and we were both sweating buckets by the time we'd cover a hundred yards. At twice that distance the thin desert air was stabbing at my lungs, and the muscles in my calves were starting to cramp. The top of the pass was still another five hundred yards away when Luis uttered a low but spirited curse and quit pushing.

"Jesus, Luis," I grunted, throwing myself against the tailgate to keep the buckboard from rolling backward. I expected him to grab a rock to shove behind the wheel, but instead he stood there, staring back the way we'd come. It was Abby who hurriedly rolled a small boulder behind the front wheel. I stepped back, breathing heavily, but any thought of further complaint was cut off by the view behind us.

"Is it them?" Abby asked quietly.

Susan whimpered softly, no doubt sensing her mother's apprehension. Far below, a cloud of dust hung over the desert plain like a blemish.

"I think it must be," Luis replied.

After a few seconds, she said: "They are following the road, aren't they?"

No one replied to that. The road ran east across the arid landscape, the dust clinging to it as if tethered. A rough estimate put them perhaps an hour behind us, certainly no more than twice that.

"Well, we knew they'd be coming," I said heavily, although to be honest, I hadn't expected them this soon. Not at the speeds we'd been traveling after leaving Sabana.

I could feel Luis's eyes on me. Abby was also watching me, waiting for my decision. Silently I d---ed the mantle of responsibility I felt settling over my shoulders, yet their expectations were understandable. After all, it was me Ed Davenport had hired to rescue his family—or at least the male element of it. I was also the one who supposedly knew this country like the back of my hand, as the old man had put it that night in Moralos.

"J.T.," Luis said gently.

I took a deep breath, then turned to the Watson Masner. "Let's keep pushing. It's our only chance now."

After a moment's hesitation, Luis joined me on the tailgate and Abby moved up to take the wheel. Susan said: "Mama, can I push?"—but Abby shook her head.

"I need your help on the wheel, sweetie. You're going to have to take a tighter grip until we get to the top."

Although we redoubled our efforts, the results were disappointing. As gradual as the grade had appeared, it was still too steep to make much time. On top of that, the lack of food and water—especially water—was beginning to take its toll. I don't know how the others handled it, but I soon reached a point where I just kept my eyes on the ground under the tailgate, wearily swinging one foot in front of the other. I was so lost in my focus on the backward crawl of the earth that when Abby called out that we'd made it, I hardly knew what she was talking about.

Luis collapsed under the buckboard, his shirt and hair, even his trousers around the waistband, soaked with perspiration. I wasn't any better. Only the stiffness of my battered knees kept me from dropping to his side. Abby tried to kick a stone under the front wheel, but the coffee pot-size chunk of rock refused to co-operate. Finally Susan jumped down to wedge the tiny boulder in place. With the vehicle secured, Abby seemed to let go, sagging to the ground with an agonized moan. Susan went to her side, crying softly as these two stalwarts of her recent life—her mother and Luis—seemed to emotionally fade away.

I kept my feet, but just barely. My limbs trembled as I stood braced against the vehicle's tailgate. The impulse to let go, to fall hard, then wiggle into the shade of the Watson Masner like a dying slug dominated my thoughts. Only the memory of the men coming up from behind kept me from giving in. After a couple of minutes of rest, I staggered over to where I could view our rearward trail. The dust from the pursuing horsemen was closer than I'd anticipated, already beginning its climb. They would have to slow down as the grade increased, but I suspected their delay would be minimal.

They won't have to get behind their horses and push, I reflected bitterly.

Although still too far away to make out any details, I estimated at least a dozen riders urging their mounts up the steepening incline. I doubted if Soto was among them, but I wondered about Lieutenant Alvarez. My thoughts flashed back to Poco Guille. The image of his shredded form, hanging limply between those twin bayonets plunged into the side of the cutbank, was burned into my brain. I mouthed the word—B——— then turned away.

My legs were still wobbly as I walked over for a better look at the road cutting down the far side of the mountain. I stared in bewilderment at the narrow, winding track. The last time I'd seen it had been from below, and I guess the passage of years had distorted my memory. I'd remembered only one sharp curve in the road on this side of the divide, but that recollection had been made from a horseman's perspective. Even in my limited experience with automobiles, I knew we'd never be able to negotiate that rutted trail without good brakes.

I couldn't see the *jacales* or the corrals at Vaquero Springs, but I could make out the mouth of the side cañon where they were located. That was also farther away than I recollected, and I felt a moment's irritation for the way things were turning out. The scrape of boots on the rocky soil distracted me from the difficulty of the road. Luis halted at my side, his expression registering initial curiosity, then disbelief, and finally anger. For the first time since leaving Moralos, I saw incrimination in his eyes. In Abby, who had followed with Susan, I saw only hopelessness.

"D--- you, J.T.," Luis blurted.

"Please," Abby quickly interjected. "Arguing at this point won't gain us anything."

"And what will?" Luis demanded.

I stared back silently, caught off guard by the fire in his words, his willingness to loosen his tongue not only in front of the woman, but also the child; he hadn't been this vehement even when facing Spence McKenzie's gun, back in the *barranco* below the Cañon Where the Small Lizards Run.

"I didn't remember it this way," I said vaguely, trying to explain. "I've only been through here once, and that was a long time. . . ."

"To h--- with you," he interrupted hotly.

"Please," Abby repeated, her voice rising in agitation. "We are all tired and . . . and frightened, but we can't allow our feelings to come between us. We can't let Susan be taken. Major Soto was very clear regarding our futures if Edward should fail to come through with the ransom."

Tears sprang to the woman's eyes, and that was surprising, too. She'd been so resolute all along, so strong and unflinching, no matter how desperate the odds.

My gaze swept the mountainside with growing urgency, a willingness to consider now what I might have dismissed as impossible under other circumstances. In that frame of mind, I paused as my eyes traced a path through the cactus and rocks, not so much a trail as a series of open spaces between the divide and where the road began to level out so far below. Struggling to harness my scattered thoughts into a coherent line, I studied the passage with growing excitement. It could be done, I thought, dangerous but possible. Yet when I turned to share my discovery with the others, they were gone.

I went back to the buckboard, where Luis was strapping the carbine's cartridge belt around his waist. Watching silently, Abby didn't even look around when I came up. In a voice harsher than I intended, I said: "You think you can stop them with a single-shot rifle and a six-shooter?"

"I intend to try," Luis replied with equal punch. Glaring at me from beneath the brim of his sombrero, he added: "Or die like a man, if death is my only option."

"It may not be."

He made a curt, dismissing motion with his free hand, accompanied by a growl of disdain. "I have listened to you enough for one day. If I am to die. . . ."

"Yeah, you're going to do it like a man," I cut in. "I reckon I'll keep going."

"Then go!"

But Abby, always the practical one, interrupted our argument before it became irreparable. "What are you suggesting, Mister Latham?"

I hooked a thumb over my shoulder, toward the far side of the ridge. "I think I've found a way down. It's going to be rough as a cob and it'll probably break our necks, but the odds will be better than trying to make a stand here."

Luis hesitated. "Where?" he demanded.

"Just about straight down the side," I said.

After a long pause, he said: "You're crazy, *hombre*. It cannot be done. Not straight down."

"You're probably right," I replied, and couldn't say to this day whether I was agreeing that I was crazy, or that it couldn't be done. "What do you say? Want to give it try?"

He glanced at Abby, whose eyes had regained their spark of hope. "I don't want to perish out here, Mister Vega," she said, "but I believe I would rather take a chance at escape, no matter how depressing the odds, than surrender to Soto's murderers. And I believe that standing our ground here, even if we are to die in the end, would be the same as surrendering."

"Jesus, J.T.," Luis said softly, then shook his head as if dealing with an idiot. "To tell you the truth, I would like just one more drink of water before I die."

"Well, h---, let's go get it," I said.

SESSION FIFTEEN

Do you want to hear about that ride down the side of the mountain? About me sitting up there like a king and hanging onto the steering wheel like it was a bucket of gold, while Luis and Abby and Susan clung to each other—or whatever else they could find—screaming and hollering and being nearly thrown free of the careening vehicle at least a dozen times each before we regained the road near the bottom?

Or is that what I just did, in my own roundabout manner? Sorry, didn't mean to laugh, it's just that I'm not really sure how to describe that crazy voyage in a way that anyone listening to these recordings would believe.

We made it, all of us in one piece and not a broken bone among us, although with fresh bruises, new cuts and scrapes, and a rekindled appreciation of having both feet planted solidly on the ground again. Luis's left arm was quilled from elbow to shoulder with thorns from a cholla plant that we toppled along the way, no small feat since he'd been clinging to the right-hand side of the wagon bed at the time. I don't know if it was a broken limb that was flipped through the air to strike his left arm, or if it happened during one of his brief, low-level flights after hitting a bump.

The Watson Masner took an even worse beating than its cargo. The right rear hub had splintered skidding into a boulder about halfway down, and both front wheels suffered broken spokes from one of our hardest, nose-first landings—I think we were probably completely airborne at least three times. Several teeth on the rear axle sprocket had been chipped off, as well, although the gear itself was large enough that it didn't affect the auto's drive.

When the slope gentled out about two hundred feet from the bottom, I ran the Watson Masner into a creosote bush along the road to slow it down, then into soft sand to bring it to a stop. Sitting up and looking around, Susan suddenly began laughing with a child's delight, as if the ride had been her greatest thrill since the roller coaster—a comparison I realize I've made more than once, but which always seems to come closest to fitting the moment.

I started laughing myself, happy, I suppose, to have made it to the bottom without killing anyone. I'd like to say that Luis and Abby shared in our joy, but neither cracked a smile, and Abby was watching her daughter closely, as if expecting her to burst into tears at any moment.

We got out long enough to inspect the Watson Masner for damage, and for Abby to pluck nearly a dozen cactus thorns from Luis's shoulder, her tongue unconsciously probing a small cut on her own lower lip. Deciding the automobile was still serviceable, we wrestled it back onto the road and pointed its nose toward the valley floor. The remaining descent was relatively gradual, and with the gas in the tank once more reaching the value, I popped the clutch about halfway down and the vehicle sputtered familiarly to life. Susan and I both cheered, and I eased the throttle open until we were chugging along at probably twenty miles an hour.

Without steady traffic beating at the sod, the road here was in better condition than it had been on the Sabana side of the mountains, and although the center hump was grown over with low scrub, we made good time. I glanced over my shoulder just before we entered the brush-lined cañon, but the mountain pass was empty.

The little *rancho* was tucked up close to the head of the draw, its adobe walls blending almost perfectly with the surrounding landscape. There hadn't been much to the place when Old Toad's Yaquis had descended on it all those years ago, and time hadn't been especially kind. There was a two-room house, its *portico* constructed from the ribs of saguaro cactus, and a couple of small *jacales* off to one side. A corral about eighty yards in front of the nearest building was starting to sag from neglect. The stone-lined tank that marked the location of the spring stood between the corral and the dwellings, its walls less than a foot high and dark from seepage. A verdant hue hung over the shallow cañon, reminiscent of the Sabana Valley, although on a much smaller scale.

A sizable herd of horses was grazing across the low hills that flanked the springs, looking fat and sassy in the early morning light, and a pale ribbon of smoke curled from a cook fire in front of the house. Nudging my shoulder, Luis nodded toward a pair of horsemen coming down off a squatty hill on our right.

"Better slow down," he said.

A third man rose from beside the fire in front of the two-roomed shack, a thumb tucked almost casually behind a cartridge belt at his waist, scant inches from his revolver, and a Remington carbine, identical to the one Luis was carrying, leaned against the side of the house just a few paces away. He'd been tending a fire-blackened stew kettle hanging over low flames when we came into view. At least I hoped it was stew. Only the fact that we were all about as desiccated as an old boot had kept us from dwelling too much on the emptiness of our bellies.

I eased the hand throttle forward until we were barely crawling along, a prickly sensation skittering up and down my spine.

Although these men weren't outfitted in the uniform of Adolpho Castillo's Army of Liberation, they didn't look like *vaqueros,* either. Fact is, they reminded me of the bandits I used to dodge during my earlier forays into Mexico, lining up goods to haul back to Arizona—lean-as-slat figures, shabbily dressed, and heavily armed. Behind me, Abby gently pulled her daughter down to her side, half shielding the child's body with her own.

"Three is all I count," Luis said quietly.

"Three'll be more than enough if we aren't careful," I replied, allowing the Watson Masner to coast to a stop near the corral gate. I disengaged the drive but left the engine idling in case we had to make a run for it.

After warning Abby and the child to stay in the vehicle and keep their heads down, I slid cautiously from behind the wheel. Luis eased to the ground on the other side, affecting a wide, friendly grin and making a big production of placing the Remington on the buckboard's seat before stepping away from the auto.

"Hey, *amigos!*" he called amiably. "We are looking for some water, and maybe a little food if you have some to spare. Enough for the *niña,* at least, eh?"

The man at the fire stayed where he was, but the two horsemen were approaching warily, their eyes skimming the hilltops for signs of an ambush, their hands seemingly fused to the revolvers holstered at their waists. Eyeing the number of guns the men were carrying, I felt fairly confident they weren't *vaqueros.* Not in the traditional sense, at any rate.

Apparently deciding that we were alone and probably harmless, they kicked their horses forward, converging on the Watson Masner with cocky grins and making sure that Luis and I were aware of the appreciative manner in which they were studying Abby Davenport.

"Welcome," the taller of the two men said expansively. "You

are lost, no?" His gaze flitted briefly to the battered automobile, and I felt a moment's concern that he might recognize it from Sabana, but his expression remained unchanged, and after a brief detour to Abby's chest, he brought his eyes back to Luis. "You are the *Americanos*' guide?"

"*Si,* we are on our way to Puerto Penasco, but need horses to complete our journey."

The taller man's eyes widened. "Puerto Penasco? That is a long way, *amigo,* and there isn't anything there except a few Seri fishermen. I think you will need more than horses to complete that journey."

"Sure, some food and water . . . and more arms." Luis tipped his head toward the bandit's waist. "I notice that you seem to have plenty."

The taller man chuckled. "A few perhaps, but not enough for trade." His gaze darted once more to Abby, his hunger for her—for any woman, I suspect—like coals buried deep in his eyes. I'm sure she was aware of his interest, but she maintained an artfully cool demeanor as she studied the horses wandering down off the slopes to inspect our arrival.

"Perhaps there is something we have need for," the tall man murmured.

"I don't think so," the shorter man interjected scornfully.

"Hey, my friends, you are making me a little nervous," Luis said. "Surely with so many horses, you can spare a few for this fine automobile. Some horses and a little food, and we will be on our way."

"These horses belong to Major Soto, and are not for trade," the shorter man replied brusquely.

"Ah." Luis nodded in understanding. These were Soto's remounts, probably switched out every few weeks so that his men always had fresh riding stock.

Swaying back with a smile, Luis seemed to relax, his voice

taking on a deceptively compliant tone. Standing a few feet away, I swallowed hard, but kept my stupid grin beaming toward the bandits as if I hadn't a clue in the world as to what was happening.

"Are you sure about the horses?" Luis asked mildly. "We have gold, if you don't want the automobile."

That was as pretty a lie as any I'd ever heard, and it slipped off of Luis's tongue like butter from a hot knife, but Soto's men fell for it completely. They didn't even bat an eye in doubt. While they were exchanging broad, congratulatory grins, Luis and I palmed our revolvers so quick we had them pointed at the bandits before they even knew what we were up to.

The man at the shack had been too far away to hear Luis's fabrication, but he saw the results before the horsemen did, and shouted a warning as he raced for his carbine. Up close, the bandits' eyes widened as they stared into the bores of our revolvers, their own guns still uselessly holstered. Surprising the two horsemen even more, I told them in Spanish not to move a muscle.

"Don't even quiver," I added.

At the house, the cook had paused with his carbine in hand, waiting to see what we intended to do.

Speaking to the taller horseman, I said: "I want you to pull your pistol real slow and let it fall to the ground. If you try anything funny, or if I even think you're trying something funny, I'm going to put a bullet through your heart. Savvy?"

Head bobbing, he delicately plucked a double-action Colt from his holster and let it drop beside his mount's forelegs, then followed it with a pair of older model single-action revolvers of the same caliber and a little hide-out gun stashed inside his shirt that I hadn't even considered. After a questioning glance, he left a Winchester booted.

"Now get down and walk over to the corral."

He did as he was told without taking his eyes off of me. Judging from his expression, I had no doubts about what he'd do to me if he got the chance, but that wasn't my first shindig, either, and I kept the Smith & Wesson on him all the way, fully committed to pulling the trigger if I had to.

"Now get down on your belly," I ordered, and, after he'd complied, I had Abby fetch the lariat from his saddle. Handing her my little sodbuster's knife, I told her to cut off a four-foot section, then go inside the corral and tie the man's hands to the bottom rail. It took her only a couple of minutes to complete the task.

With the first outlaw bound and out of the way, we turned to the second man. While Abby and I were doing that, Luis led the horses around the far side of the Watson Masner and hitched them to the bed. Afterward Abby lifted a gourd canteen off of the taller man's saddle horn and took it to Susan. Luis and I stood off to one side, studying the man at the house and wondering what to do about him.

"If we try getting any closer, he'll start shooting," I pointed out.

"*Sí*, I think you are right." Raising his voice, Luis called: "You should come over here and let us tie you. We don't want to hurt you, but we need horses and food."

The man shook his head but didn't move. He was standing before the door with his carbine held protectively across his chest, watching us with equal patience. Luis glanced at me. "We could probably shoot him before he got inside."

"Maybe we could, but, if we missed and he did get inside, we'd never get close to that stew pot or the spring."

"Mister Latham," Abby said loudly, and I spun around at the urgency in her voice. She was staring toward the mountains we'd crossed that morning. Although I couldn't see the low saddle from where we were, the cloud of dust rising above it couldn't be mistaken for anything other than what it was. At my side, Luis swore softly.

"How long before they get here?" Abby asked.

Picturing the route in my mind, I knew it would be too soon for what we needed to accomplish. "Half an hour, at most," I replied.

"Then . . . ?"

I was staring at the loose horses watching us from the surrounding hills. A few of the more curious animals had descended all the way to the cañon's floor, but were keeping their distance.

Horses aren't the dumb brutes some people make them out to be. They can sense trouble, and likely these remounts of Soto's were well aware of the tension hanging over our little band, not to mention the odd behavior of the two bandits stretched out on the ground with their hands tied to the bottom rail of the corral. Although we could have used a third mount for Abby and the girl, my bigger concern at that moment was leaving behind fresh horses for our pursuers.

"If we had more time . . . ," I started to say.

"We can't wait," Luis replied.

"Can we take the extra horses with us?" Abby asked, sensing our dilemma.

"Not without spending an hour or so bringing them down from the hills," I remarked.

"Perhaps there is another . . . way," Abby said, her sentence ending with an odd hitch. She turned to Luis and me. "It's important that we take as many of these mounts with us as possible, isn't it?"

"Either that or scatter them so that Soto's men can't use them for a while," I replied.

"Then you must promise not to laugh."

I've got to admit she'd piqued my interest. With an armed bandit standing not eighty yards away and a troop of *soldados* bearing down on us from above, she seemed more concerned with looking foolish than she did with our swiftly deteriorating predicament.

"Whatever you must do, *señora,* you must do it quickly," Luis said kindly. "I promise, neither of us will laugh."

With her cheeks flushing prettily, Abby stepped between the bandits' mounts and, cupping her hands around her mouth, emitted a near-perfect imitation of a colt's terrified whinny, followed by the harsh barking of what sounded like a vicious dog. The result from the hills was instantaneous, the remounts—the mares in particular—came plunging frantically through the brush as they raced toward the Watson Masner and the unseen colt under attack.

At my side, Luis was laughing like a child at Christmas.

"Mama!" Susan cried as the herd swept toward us, and Luis stepped quickly forward to lift the child from the buckboard's narrow bed.

"Don't worry, little one," he cooed reassuringly. "Your *madrecita* knows what she is doing."

I reckon she did, too. The horses, all of them, were gathered around the Watson Masner in less than five minutes, milling nervously as they searched for the now-silent colt they had instinctively rushed to protect.

Over by the corral, the two bandits were straining their necks to keep an eye on the high-strung remuda, while at the adobe shack the third bandit had ducked inside while our attention was diverted by the horses. I watched one of the shutters swing partway open and felt a chill clamber up my back as I recalled the last time I'd stood out here, the gun barrels bristling from the *jacales* like quills from a porcupine's spine, and Old Toad's rage as the tide turned against us—but that's getting ahead of myself, which I've noticed I've had a tendency to do during these recordings. I'll try to watch that in the future.

Excerpted from:
Despots and Dictators—A Detailed Description of
Tyranny Within the United Mexican States
by
Herbert Carlton Matthews
Broken Mill Press
1930

Chapter Eight
Sonora: The Díaz Years

[*Ed. Note:* José de la Cruz Porfirio Díaz (September 15, 1830 -
July 2, 1915) was an eight-term president of Mexico, ruling for
thirty-five of the forty-year interim between 1876 and 1916.
Viewed largely as a dictator by outsiders and countrymen alike,
his administration was one of constant internal conflict and cor-
ruption, resulting in national economic instability and often
brutal oppression. He was forced from office during the
Mexican Revolution of 1910 to 1920.]

. . . [T]hese smaller insurrections, a direct response to the heavy-
handedness of the Díaz administration, continued in the west
with men like . . . Juan Adolpho Castillo and the bandit chief

"Chito" Soto [becoming] a constant thorn in the government's side.

[Castillo was a] disenfranchised landowner from the state of Durango before taking up arms against the Díaz regime in the late 1890s. Although never a threat on the level of men like Emiliano Zapata or Pancho Villa, Castillo's Army of Liberation was estimated at numbers between twelve hundred and fifteen hundred men . . . [and] struck terror throughout the states of Durango, Chihuahua, Sinaloa, and southern Sonora.

Adolpho Castillo's own brief regime was put down by Díaz's troops on March 4, 1908, at the Battle of Sini, in Sinaloa. He was tried by military tribunal, found guilty of treason, and executed by firing squad at dawn on March 5, 1908.

On a smaller scale were men like Francisco "Chito" Soto, who early on was a staunch supporter of the Castillo polity. Yet in the end, even he turned his back on the General [Castillo].

Unlike Castillo, Soto did not come from wealthy ancestry. His parents were laborers in the sawmills of Tierras Aradas . . . with the younger Soto displaying at a tender age the resentment toward the upper classes that was so prevalent among early supporters of the revolution.

Although rumors persisted for many years that Soto was banished to the Sabana Valley of Sonora because of Castillo's fear that the bandit's popularity among the men might eventually undermine his own authority, Soto was never able to raise more than two hundred and fifty men on his own . . . [and] it seems unlikely he would have ever posed a serious threat to the general's power.

"Chito" Soto was killed at the Battle of Celaya on April 13, 1915; he was a captain in Villa's *División del Norte*.

SESSION SIXTEEN

There wasn't going to be enough time to pry that third bandit out of his adobe hide-away, which meant we were going to have to give up our goal of packing along any extra food, finding a third saddle, or plunging our heads under the cool waters of the mossy tank. I think it was the latter I regretted the most.

We took the bandits' guns along, as well as the shorter man's sombrero for Abby—protection against the burning Sonoran sun. Luis gave Susan his bright green bandanna, which she wore over her head like a shawl, much to her pride and Luis's delight. Abby studied the sombrero doubtfully, but after a careful examination for vermin, she put it on. I also gave her the taller man's double-action Colt, along with its holster, which I stripped from his waist; the belt was a loose fit, even pulled up to its last notch, but I figured we could punch some new holes in it that night if we were still alive.

All of this was accomplished within minutes. Then Luis swung into the shorter man's saddle and went after a horse for Abby, while I confiscated the taller man's leggy claybank, with its heavy *vaquero*'s rig decorated with tarnished silver *conchos*, a horn as big around as a dinner plate, and sweeping *tapaderos*. Noticing a series of long, curving welts along the horse's ribs spawned an urge to rip the massive spurs from the bandit's heels and do a little gouging of my own. A lot of those old-time cowboys from both sides of the border were pretty heartless when it came to bit and spur, but I'd never felt a need to dominate an animal that way.

Although I was keeping a wary eye on the adobe shack, that third jasper never showed himself. From time to time I'd catch a glimpse of a rifle barrel poking out the window, but I think he was doing that more to remind us that he was still there, and that he wouldn't be trifled with. If he'd pointed it at us, I would have hit the dirt fast, and taken Abby and Susan with me, but he seemed content to let us go about our business as long as we didn't pay him any mind.

As it turned out, our efforts to take the remuda with us, or at least frighten and scatter it, was nearly our undoing. When Abby'd asked me earlier how much time I thought we had, I'd estimated thirty minutes. Taking into account not only the number of miles between the divide and the mouth of the side cañon, but also the steepness of the road as it wound down off the mountain, I figured we'd have at least that long, but I'd either lost track of time or Soto's men were pushing their horses a lot harder than I'd anticipated.

Luis was just riding up with a dappled gray in tow for Abby when I swear his face turned as pale as whey. His lips parted, but no words came. Abby and I both instantly knew what he'd seen, and didn't waste time taking peeks for ourselves. Grabbing the woman around the waist, I tossed her onto the gray's back, then grabbed the girl from behind the Watson Masner and shoved her into her mother's arms.

"Can you ride?" I shouted—kind of a moot question at that point, I suppose, although the woman was nodding frantically that she could. She tucked the child in front of her while I looped the free end of the lariat around the gray's muzzle, then tucked it back through the noose to fashion a simple, single-reined bridle. Handing her the rope's loose end, I swung into the claybank's saddle without touching the stirrups, then heeled my mount alongside of Abby's.

"Mister Latham," she gasped, nodding toward the wider valley behind me, where the pounding of hoofs from the direction of the road were rapidly increasing in volume. Grabbing Susan, I plunked her down in the saddle in front of me.

"I'll take care of her," I told Abby. "You just concentrate on hanging on."

I'll tell you what, my respect for that woman just kept on growing. There was no fussing, no demands that I return her daughter, just a grim acceptance of what needed to be done if we were to survive. Abby Davenport knew when to raise h---, but she also knew when to keep her mouth shut and do what she was told.

Luis had already capered his long, lean sorrel behind the remounts and was spurring his horse among them, screaming like a mountain lion. When he fired his single-shot Remington into the air, the whole herd bolted toward the open valley. Luis rode hard on their heels with Abby close behind him, leaning low over the gray's neck. Swinging the claybank in at her side, we made our break for the distant wastelands.

I got my first good look at Soto's men as we exited the side cañon. I counted twelve mounted soldiers racing after us, but could have missed one or two. Alvarez was there. So was the stocky sergeant, Marcos, who I thought—apparently mistakenly—I'd shot back at the garrison.

We came out of the side cañon hugging its western flank, Soto's men pounding after us from the east, not quite three hundred yards away. The Remingtons they were carrying were easily capable of reaching us from that range, but thankfully Alvarez didn't halt his command to have them dismount and fire, and d---ed few shooters could have come even remotely close to us with anything other than a wildly lucky shot at that distance and from the back of a running horse. By keeping his men in their saddles, Alvarez lost an opportunity to stop us cold.

The remuda began to break apart almost as soon as we were out of the wide draw. Luis couldn't keep them together by himself, and Abby and I were too far back to be of much help. At a gesture from me, Abby did swing her gray to the left while I reined to the right, and between the three of us we made a sort of inverted funnel that kept the herd loosely together for perhaps another half mile. Then a chance shot from one of Soto's men clipped the leather on my right-hand tap, and I said the h--- with it and shouted for Abby and Luis to let the horses scatter.

Without us pushing them, the remounts quickly spread out in front of us like an opening blossom. Coming together in a wedge, the three of us forged a path through its center, squinting our eyes against the dust and ducking our shoulders to the pebbles and clods of earth flung up by the hard-digging hoofs. Soto's men were lost behind us, and we took advantage of our temporary camouflage to veer to the north.

We stayed with a fragment of the herd for close to a mile before it also became too scattered to afford us further protection. Reining free of its embrace, we slowed to a canter. Luis glanced to our rear, then whooped loudly. I couldn't help a smile of my own when I spotted what was left of Alvarez's troop, spread out across the plain far to the south and still moving in a westerly direction. I didn't see the lieutenant anywhere, and thought that was to our advantage, as well.

After a few more miles, we slowed to a walk. The three of us were riding alone by then, the handful of remounts that had followed us for a ways having finally dropped out and turned back. None of us believed Alvarez would quit, but, by spooking the remuda, then stampeding it over such a wide range of country, I figured we'd bought ourselves a little time. And it was right in there that I began to realize that if we were going to make it out of Mexico alive, it would have to be just that way—no big cessa-tion of hostilities, no breaking off of pursuit. We'd just always have to stay out front, one step ahead of the nearest bullet.

We continued on at a walk, Susan struggling in my arms until I handed her over to her mother. Luis teased her about being afraid of the hairy *gringo*. It hadn't occurred to me that the grooming I'd enjoyed my last night in Yuma might have worn off by then, although I suppose it should have, if for no other reason than Luis's shaggy, unkempt appearance.

Spying a low hill a couple of miles away, we turned our horses toward it. Although I kept glancing over my shoulder for signs of pursuit, none materialized, and I began to think maybe our efforts at scattering the remounts had done more good than I'd hoped.

That hill was probably no more than twenty feet above the valley floor, but it offered us a good view in every direction. While Abby took Susan off in search of some privacy and I made myself comfortable in the shelter of a tall yucca to watch our back trail, Luis loosened the cinches on the two saddled horses, then began going through their bags. I wasn't overly optimistic about him finding anything useful, but dang if he didn't soon let go of a triumphant yell.

"Food!" he exclaimed, holding up a loaf of bread and a brick of orange cheese. There was also coffee, a wedge of hard chocolate, a bundle of jerky, and a couple of cloth bags, one containing raisins, the other filled with parched corn. It was all good trail food, and, along with a pair of nearly full gourd canteens strapped to our saddles, it made me think the two bandits must have been on their way out when we showed up.

Luis brought one of the canteens and the bread and cheese over and flopped down at my side. Taking a folding knife from his pocket, he carved off several fist-size chunks of cheese, then quartered the bread and set it aside.

"There is enough food to last us for several days," he said, "but we will have to find more water soon." He shook the canteen, listening to its slosh. "Two days, with our horses, then we will be in trouble."

Abby and Susan returned, the girl racing toward Luis when she saw the bread and cheese. Even Abby's face brightened as she took in the feast sitting in the dirt between Luis and me.

"Heavens, it looks delicious," she declared, settling down nearby.

Luis doled out equal portions of food, while I twisted the wooden stopper from the canteen and handed it to Abby.

"Just a sip," she told her daughter, although I noticed she didn't say anything when Susan snuck in several swallows, rather than just one.

Although we took it easy on the water, we still managed to drain about three-quarters of the gourd by the time we were finished. It was to be expected, I suppose, as it had been a while since our last drink, but it was still worrisome.

Pushing to his feet, Luis mumbled—"I'll go see what else I can find."—and headed for the horses. Susan went with him, the two of them sitting in the dirt between the animals' legs, discussing the items they pulled from the saddlebags.

After a short silence, Abby said: "I hope you aren't regretting your decision to return for Susan and me."

"No, not at all."

Her smile was grateful but strained. "Thank you for saying so."

I didn't reply, wasn't even sure if I was going to for a while, but then decided I didn't want to leave it hanging in the air like that.

"I wouldn't have said it if I didn't mean it."

Outwardly her expression never changed, but I thought she seemed more relaxed after my reply, and maybe sort of relieved, too. After a moment's reflection, she said: "Were you telling me the truth when you said Charles was safe?"

"He was the last time I saw him."

"And his . . . health?"

Recalling the vacant look in the boy's eyes and his apathetic manner, I knew she wasn't talking about his physical strength. Trying to be gentle, I said: "Probably a few days rest and he'll be as good as new. Your husband seemed concerned."

"Yes, he would be." She scooped up a handful of pebbles that she arranged in her palm so that she could toss them, one at a time, into the dry flora below us. "Charles fulfills Edward's need to leave behind a legacy, you see? An heir not just to his wealth, but to his name. That's important to Edward, that sense of immortality. I've never really understood it myself, but I suppose I have my own share of quirks that Edward has never quite comprehended."

"Seems like quirks go with being part of a family," I said.

"That's true, but I think some couples, just by virtue of their contrasting personalities, generate more of these than can be considered normal. Edward and I have always been that way. At one point our differences were what attracted me to him, and I'd thought perhaps it was what attracted him to me, but I've come to the sad realization that Edward's goals for our marriage have always been contrary to my own." She stopped then, looking at me with something akin to horror, and quickly added: "I apologize, Mister Latham. I didn't mean to burden you with my issues. I suppose I felt I should . . . warn you, perhaps, of Edward's peculiarities. For instance, that I was aware he intended to abandon Susan and myself down here."

I gave a start at that. "Did Luis say something?" I asked, not knowing how else she could have found out.

"Oh, heavens no. Mister Vega is far too much of a gentleman to reveal such an ugly truth, not that any of us have had a free moment to even consider sharing our personal fears. No, I suspected as much when Charles was taken from my room . . . how many days ago was that?" She laughed, the genuineness of the sound bringing a hesitant smile to my face. "I'm afraid my time in Mexico, at least since our removal from the Ferrocarril del Pacifico, has become rather a blur," she confessed.

"It's been that way for me, too," I admitted, thinking that the clanging of the sally port gate as it closed behind me at Yuma seemed a decade in the past now.

There was another pause between us, although more comfortable this time. Wanting to keep it that way, I said: "You've got to tell me how you learned to call horses."

Her cheeks flushed with embarrassment. "Rather an unusual talent for a girl born and bred in a fashionable neighborhood like Harlem, wouldn't you say?"

"I couldn't, but it sure pulled our fat out of the fire. I'm glad you knew how to do it."

"It was Randolph who taught me."

"Randolph? Your chauffeur?"

"Yes. He'd escorted me to a riding stable in Central Park where my father kept several horses. I was being taught the art of the side-saddle, but one day when we arrived, we discovered that the horses had gotten loose and were scattered throughout the park. The men were all afoot, and chasing horses, as I'm sure you are aware, is a tedious project, nearly impossible to accomplish when the animals are frightened." She looked at me with a smile. "The men in Central Park were having a rather difficult time of it. That's when Randolph went off some little distance away and actually called the horses in. I suppose you already know his secret?"

"Mimicking a young colt in trouble?"

"Yes, although I would find out it is a trick of limited allocation. A case of the adage . . . Fool me once, shame on you, fool me twice, shame on me. Apparently the employees at the stables were so overjoyed by Randolph's trick that they assumed they could turn their horses out at any time, and simply call them back when they were needed, but it didn't work that way."

"A feed bucket works best for that," I said, smiling.

She nodded. "An appropriate reward has its advantages."

The scuff of boots on the flinty soil interrupted our conversation. Luis and Susan were returning, the girl carrying a leather tube that she solemnly handed to me.

"Tell him," Luis urged.

I didn't know it at the time, but Luis had picked up on the girl's reticence toward me, and was trying to break down that barrier of shyness.

"Telescope," she said, the word so softly spoken I barely heard it.

"*Gracias,*" I replied solemnly, and she hurried to her mother's side as if I'd hollered "Shoo!"

Luis laughed and called her a silly pickle, which brought smiles to all of our faces; the girl was bringing out a side of Vega I'd never seen before.

I examined the case. It was nearly two inches in diameter and probably fourteen inches long. The latch had been broken off years before, judging from the patina covering the thin metal clasp, but the lid was still in place. Upending the hard leather capsule, an ancient eyepiece slid into my hand. Its body was brass, with a worn leather sheath over the main tube, the entire instrument dented and gouged and tarnished almost black. After extending it as far as it would go—a good thirty-six inches—I eyed the obvious downward sag in the scope's three sections with skepticism. Abby laughed outright at the cartoonish image, which in turn elicited a giggle from Susan, a happy sound that—along with full bellies and no pursuit in sight— seemed to lighten all of our moods.

"Does it work?" Luis asked.

I put the instrument to my eye, located a tall cholla about a hundred yards out, and slowly compressed the loosely-fitted sections until the furry limbs of the cactus crept into view. I grunted favorably. Compared to the binoculars Del had loaned me in the Cañon Where the Small Lizards Run, the quality was poor, but opposed to the naked eye, it was an improvement. I handed the scope to Luis.

"See what you can find."

I didn't have to explain what I was looking for. After readjusting the focus, he began scouring the horizon for Alvarez's men. I'll confess I was more than a little apprehensive when he closed it several minutes later without having spotted any sign of the lieutenant's troops. Shaking his head in a troubled manner, he said: "It is as if they have gone to ground."

"Wouldn't that be a good thing?" Abby asked. She seemed puzzled by our reaction.

"It would be a very good thing if it were true," Luis told her.

"Then you don't believe Lieutenant Alvarez has ceased pursuit?"

Luis shook his head. "I don't," he admitted.

We hunkered on that little knoll for another hour or so, taking turns keeping an eye on our surroundings with the telescope while the horses grazed, then moved on at an easy walk. Susan rode behind her mother astride the gray, clinging sleepily to the woman's waist. Luis and I had commandeered the saddles. I suppose it wasn't very gentlemanly of us, but we were carrying most of the guns and the bulk of the ammunition, and needed something solid to hang them from.

Luis had tossed the Remington after firing its single round into the air to stampede Soto's remounts, but with the two Winchesters, the double-action Colt I'd given to Abby, the Frontier Model Colt Luis had taken off the shorter bandit, and my Smith

& Wesson, we were actually pretty well armed for a change. Our horses were tough range stock that had been well-grazed and were rested, and we were carrying enough food to last us for several days if we didn't get hoggish. Our only real concern—outside of the certain knowledge that Chito Soto's renegades were still out there somewhere looking for us—was water. Those gourd canteens held a fair amount, but we were four thirsty individuals, plus a trio of hard-working horses, and what we had wasn't going to take us far in that heat. Unfortunately the only reliable water holes I knew of were those favored by the Yaquis, and, although I wasn't keen on pushing our luck in that direction, I figured that, sooner or later, we'd have to.

We slogged on through the growing heat. That country between Moralos and Sabana was harsh, but this was like the bottom rung of Hades, a blistering trial of endurance. It brought to mind the stories I'd heard of this land in the cool *cantinas* of Arizona and Sonora, of eyes boiling in their sockets and tongues swelling up thick enough to choke a person. We wouldn't find any *Federales* out here, and d---ed few bandits. This was Yaqui country for the most part, so designated because it was just about their last place of refuge, a land not even Díaz's troops would venture into to root out the few remaining broncos. [*Ed. Note:* Although traditionally used in reference to wild, unbroken horses of the American West, the word *bronco* was sometimes used to denote an American Indian who refused to surrender to military authorities; in its indigenous attribution, it is primarily a Southwestern term.]

Looking back the way we'd come, I realized we'd been climbing steadily for a couple of hours, an almost imperceptible upward tilting of the land that I hadn't noticed until I saw how the country behind us seemed so open. We were moving mostly west and a little north now, toward a rocky escarpment I recalled from my years with the Yaquis, a geological rift in the desert's floor maybe eight or ten miles long and no more than a couple of hundred feet at its highest point. Those cliffs were pocked with a series of tanks along its westward-facing rim, natural basins that held anywhere from fifty to several thousand gallons of water well into the summer. I wasn't exactly sure where we were at that point, but I took the fact that we were moving upward as a good sign.

We were still in our saddles—those of us who had them—when dusk swept across the land like a gust of wind from a slamming door. I looked up in surprise, eyes gritty from the abuse they'd taken all day, my temples throbbing. The relief was small but immediate, and I looked around to see if the others were also feeling it. Susan was asleep in her mother's arms, her skinny legs hanging down on either side of the gray's sweating withers like pink and white striped barber poles, but Abby and Luis had taken note of the abrupt change, and were exchanging uncertain glances. I studied the skies to the west in search of an approaching storm, but the horizon was bare, not a cloud in sight.

With the heat lessening, I pulled up and stepped down. My legs teetered briefly when I hit the ground, and Luis gave me a questioning glance, but I shook my head and slid the telescope from the claybank's saddlebags. Dropping the sorrel's reins, Luis went to help Abby and Susan dismount.

Stepping away from the horses, I pulled the scope from its case, then spent the next few minutes examining our back trail. It wasn't the first time that day that I'd stopped to glass the country behind us, but the view was always the same—cactus, rock, and scrub, the white alkali nearly blinding in the waves of heat that shimmered above the desert floor in a mocking dance. No men, no horses. Not even a vulture hanging motionless in the washed-out sky. I closed the telescope and put it away.

"Mister Latham, Mister Vega." We turned at Abby's words.

She was holding her daughter, whose facial expression conjured up a quick image of Charles's vacant stare. "Please, could she have some water?"

Luis cursed and yanked the canteen from his saddle. I hovered at his side, strangely angered by the girl's suffering, brought on by the greed and weaknesses of others. I'd glanced at her only moments before and she'd looked fine, tired but clear-eyed after having been roused from her slumber, but I'd forgotten how quickly that country could get to you if you weren't careful. Or if you're young and vulnerable.

"How are you, ma'am?" I asked Abby.

"I'm all right," she tried to assure me, but Luis nodded toward the claybank even as he splashed water over Susan's face, and I went to fetch the second canteen.

"We'd all better have a couple of swallows," I said, handing her the leather-cradled gourd.

Her whole carriage seemed to shift almost imperceptibly, like a pin had been pulled loose from inside. "Well, perhaps a drop."

"Make it four long, slow swallows," I replied. "Take your time, and let it soothe your throat on the way down."

She nodded and did as she was told. I was watching the horses, noticing the hungry way they were eyeing the canteens, smelling the water but unable to reach it. I'd thought earlier that we could probably make it as far as the bluffs with what we had. At that moment, I wasn't as sure.

Susan came around quickly enough, and Abby was also looking vastly improved. Luis and I drank while Abby took Susan into the bushes. When we were alone, Luis said: "I think maybe we need to be a little more careful tomorrow, *amigo.*"

I nodded distractedly and didn't reply. My attention had been drawn to a line of hills several miles to the southwest. A frown creased my brow, tightening the sun-parched flesh between my eyes. Sliding the telescope from my saddle, I focused it on the rocky knobs.

"You see something?" Luis asked.

"Maybe." I handed him the glasses. "Take a look at those hills over there?"

He aimed the scope in the direction I'd indicated. "What about them?" he asked after a minute.

"You notice anything unusual toward their middle, right at the base?"

His eye narrowed on the lens, but after a moment he shook his head. "I don't see anything." He looked at me. "What do you see?"

I swore quietly, accepting the scope and returning it to its case. "Nothing, something . . . I don't know. Let's not say anything to Missus Davenport, but I'd like to ride over there and have a look around."

I kept telling myself it was probably nothing, but, when I stepped into the claybank's saddle, I eased the Winchester from its scabbard, lowered the lever enough to reassure myself that there was still a live round chambered, then placed the gun across the pommel in front of me—just in case.

SESSION SEVENTEEN

Although only a few miles away, the light was fading by the time we neared the low range of hills that had caught my attention earlier. Not wanting to unduly frighten the women, Luis and I tried to keep our manner casual, but I suspect Abby knew something was amiss as soon as we pulled our rifles.

We were still a couple of hundred yards away when I noticed a clump of greenery at the mouth of an arroyo near the center of the ridge, barely discernible in the weakening light. The patchy verdure and the horses' increasing restlessness raised my hopes for a spring or small tank, although not enough to lower my guard. Not even when an errant breeze brought us the scent of moist earth and new foliage.

Hauling up several hundred feet away, I motioned for Luis and the women to stay back, while I made a final reconnoiter of the area surrounding the arroyo. Butting the Winchester to my thigh, I tapped the sides of my heavy wooden stirrups against the claybank's ribs and reined south, away from the spot of green. I couldn't explain my edginess, but I trusted it, and was ready to either kick the claybank into a run or make a dive for the scrub at the first hint of trouble.

I rode into the hills probably a quarter of a mile south of the arroyo, then turned north. The range of hills wasn't large, and paled in comparison to the Sierra Verdes, or even the highlands we'd crossed that morning in the Watson Masner. I'm guessing no more than a couple of miles long and half a mile across, the tallest peak barely a hundred feet above the surrounding desert.

Even in the thickening gloom I could see the tracks of antelope, mustangs, quail, javelinas, and coyotes that had come there for water, but it wasn't until I reached the mouth of the arroyo, where a watery seep had turned the ground soft, that I saw my first sign of human occupation. Dismounting, I pushed into the thorny fortress, using the Winchester's muzzle to part the branches before me. The moccasin tracks were easily spotted in the moist soil—pale blades of grass flattened in the muck, limbs snapped or bent out of the way. There were dozens of prints in a variety of shapes and sizes—feet, knees, hands, knuckles, even the bottom of some kind of kettle—scattered up and down the arroyo, but they were thickest at the pool's black edge, a kind of primitive art stamped into the mud.

My pulse surged rhythmically as I traced a number of the shallow impressions with my fingers. They were several days' old, at least, and there was no proof that they had been left behind by Yaquis, although I found it disquieting that none of the tracks seemed to have been made by women or children. Nor was there any evidence of horses or dogs among the wayfarers. A war party might travel that way, I knew; without livestock, they could be nearly as soundless as the stars.

A shiver racked my spine as I kneeled there staring at the tracks. Darkness closed in around me like stalking goblins, and the moon hung overhead with a lop-sided smirk. I probably crouched there for ten minutes before the claybank poked its nose through the arrow weeds to sniff out the shallow pool. Smiling tepidly, I creaked to my feet and loosened the reins from around the saddle horn so that the horse could drink. When it was finished, I led it out of the scrub and stepped into the saddle. It was too dark to see very far, but I took off my hat and waved it above my head, figuring Luis would spot the movement. Seconds later the delicate call of a nighthawk broke the stillness, and I called back to let them know that it was safe to come in.

We made a cold camp at the mouth of the arroyo, and while Abby whipped up an inelegant meal of parched corn and cheese, I took my rifle and the telescope and made my way into the hills. The tallest peak in the range was a knob of volcanic rock, protruding from the top of the ridge like a broken thumb. I didn't try to climb it, but found a surprisingly cool slab of stone at its base and settled down with the Winchester at my side, the telescope across my lap. It was probably an hour later when I heard Luis coming up through the scrub. I guided him over with a low whistle, and he sank down on the other side of my rifle.

"Do you realize it's been over twelve hours since anyone has taken a shot at us?" he asked, switching to Spanish as if needing a break from the English language. I knew the feeling well; it was one of the reasons I'd always looked forward to returning to Arizona after a trip to Sabana, where I had to rely on my border Spanish.

"If it would make you feel any better, you could go stand out there a ways and I could pop off a few rounds."

Luis chuckled and pulled the makings from his pocket. "No, I believe I will decline your gracious offer," he replied as he started a cigarette. "I would hate to put you to so much trouble when others are begging for the opportunity."

I laughed softly, tipping my head back against the stone monolith and listening to the crinkle of squared-off cornhusk Luis preferred to store-bought paper. He finished his own, then offered me the makings, which I accepted. He didn't light his smoke right away. Even in 1907, matches were rare enough that we didn't waste them if we didn't have to; I'd light both cigarettes from the same stick, and maybe not be left wanting somewhere down the trail.

"How are the horses?" I asked, fashioning a trough in the husk with a finger.

"They are still strong. If we can continue to find water. . . ." His words trailed off. "Do you see that?"

"I see it."

"How long has it been there?"

He was referring to a faint yellow glow far to the east, like a bowl turned bottom side up. I'd been keeping an eye on it ever since I'd gotten there, and it hadn't come any closer or grown any larger. By that time I didn't expect it to. Although I thought I knew what it was, there was no way of being certain. Not without riding back to investigate, and I had no intention of doing that.

"It looks kind of like the lights of a town."

"It does, but it isn't."

He gave me a curious look. "An Indian village?"

"I thought about that, too, but I don't think so. It's too big for a village."

His voice softened. "Alvarez?"

"That's what I'm thinking. Of course, I could be wrong." I returned the tobacco pouch, then drew a match from my vest pocket and leaned close. Striking a flame, I lit both our cigarettes, then drew in a lungful of smoke. It was my first cigarette in nearly twenty-four hours, and that inaugural inhalation sliced through the tension constricting my muscles like wind through a whistle.

Bent forward with his elbows on his knees, his sombrero pushed back to reveal a thick mop of black hair falling over his forehead, Luis said: "That fat b------ of a major must have sent an entire regiment."

"Maybe, but I doubt it."

He turned to study me in the thin moonlight. "You think he has lost interest in the woman and *niña?*"

"No, I think he still wants them, but I reckon by now he's realized the old man has double-crossed him. I doubt if he suspects us, because he knows we don't have those other two machine-guns. But he knows the guns exist because of his spies in Nogales and Tucson, and maybe even in Moralos. He'll figure Davenport has them, and that he must have gotten a better offer from someone else."

Luis spat in disgust. "A week ago I would have pointed out a very obvious flaw in your thinking, my friend, which is that no man would abandon his family for money. I wish I was still that naïve."

"Yeah, me, too." I was silent a moment, thinking back to Abby Davenport's partial explanation that morning of why her husband had turned his back on her. She hadn't offered much in the way of clarification, and I hadn't pushed for more. I think mostly I didn't want to know what the old man's reasoning might be. I didn't want to believe there might be a legitimate argument for turning your back on someone you'd promised your life to.

"What about that?" Luis asked, nodding toward the distant cap of light.

"That's got to be twenty miles away."

"*Sí.*" He was silent, waiting for me to go on.

"One of the things I've been wondering about is why would Soto send so many men after us when he knows we don't have the guns, and I can't think of a solitary reason. How many men did you count at Vaquero Springs this morning?"

"Not many. A dozen, perhaps fourteen."

"That's about what I counted. So where were the rest of them . . . if they were even there?"

"Ah," Luis breathed, finally seeing where my own thoughts had so slowly taken me. "You believe this fire belongs to Alvarez and his men, and is a ruse?"

"Why would a dozen men need that much fire if they aren't burning down a town?"

Luis shook his head in growing exasperation. "My friend, your thoughts wander worse than my grandmother's. Don't ask me any more questions, tell me what you think."

I laughed. "All right. I could be wrong, and I probably am, but what if Alvarez kept a few men back to create a diversion, try to make us think he was farther away than he really is?"

"Another question?" He shrugged. "All right, then he might expect us to lower our guard?"

"It's possible. I think Soto still wants us, especially the woman and child. I think Alvarez wants us, too, although maybe for different reasons. We made him look like a fool this morning, and he'll take that personally."

"And our plans? Do they change?"

"Maybe." I scratched absently at the dark stubble along my jaw. "Alvarez could be pretty close, waiting for us to make a mistake, give ourselves away."

"Like starting a fire or shooting something for our supper? They might even know about this water, and be sitting out there now."

"That's a point," I agreed, then came to a decision. "Let's not wait until morning. We'll give the horses a few hours to rest, then push on. I'd like to have another twelve or fifteen miles between us and here when the sun comes up."

Luis nodded and ground out his cigarette. "I will tell the woman and the *niña* of our plans," he said, pushing to his feet. He paused before moving off, staring back at me. "You will be all right here?"

"I'll be fine."

"Then perhaps I will try to catch a few hours' sleep. I will wake you around midnight."

I watched him go, marveling at how silently he could move in the darkness, how quickly he vanished. I leaned back to make myself as comfortable as the rocky terrain would allow, but I knew better than to become too complacent. Sleep was an ally of Alvarez, not mine; it was a stalker who lurked on the sidelines, waiting for me to lower my guard.

Judging from the slant of the moon and the stars, I figured we left that low ridge around 3 a.m. As worn out as we all were, I was pretty pleased with our start. I'd even managed a couple of hours of sleep myself, thanks to Luis, and felt more refreshed than I had a right to expect.

Our horses, being in better shape than we were, moved out smartly in the cool morning air, as frisky as colts after just a few hours' rest and a final trip inside the brush-lined arroyo for a last drink. Another day or two of pushing across the hot desert would take some of the starch out of them, but I was hoping by then we'd no longer have Alvarez or his men to contend with.

The fact is, I was feeling pretty confident about our situation, and was even visualizing a possible route back to Arizona, when my expectations started to unravel. What happened was, we were riding single file in a northwesterly direction with dawn still a couple of hours away, when I heard a voice not too far away. Luis, riding up front, jerked his horse to a stop, and Abby's gray bumped into it in the dark. My hand flashed back to cover the Smith's grips, but I didn't pull it. Reining off the trail, Luis waited for me to come up.

"You heard that?" he whispered.

"I heard it, but I couldn't make out where it came from."

"It came from behind us," Abby said, pulling her horse around to stare back the way we'd come. Sitting behind her, Susan's eyes were large in the starlight. "I couldn't make out the words, though."

"It was Spanish," Luis explained. "He said . . . *They're gone!*"

My scalp was crawling as I twisted around in my saddle to

study the low ridge of hills, no more than a mile away. I couldn't see anyone—the light was too weak, the scrub too thick—but I knew they were there. I was guessing probably a dozen of them.

"What do we do, J.T.?"

"We keep riding," I replied. "We stay off the ridges and the high spots, and we don't make any more noise than we have to." I gave him a look and a nod. "You're leading, let's get going."

We kept our horses to a walk, albeit a fast one after that, and, by the time the darkness began to dissolve, we'd probably covered another ten miles. As the light strengthened, I was relieved to note that we were still gently climbing, and I figured that escarpment I mentioned in our last recording session couldn't be too far ahead.

We stopped just short of sunup and I hauled out my telescope for a quick look to the rear, but the land seemed empty as far as I could see. Not even a wisp of dust marked the possible location of Alvarez's soldiers.

The sun came up and the chill from the night before quickly became just a pleasant memory. I thought the grade was steepening, and the sweat showing up along the claybank's cinch seemed to bear that out, although the horse didn't seem to be hurting. We continued to stop every hour or so to scope the surrounding countryside, but I never saw a thing. To tell you the truth, the lack of pursuit was starting to bother me. There should have been something out there—a flash of color, a haze of dust, movement—something.

Late that morning we came to a rocky glade surrounded by catclaw and decided to stop. The horses needed a break, and so did we. Although we didn't pull our saddles, we did slip the bits, then hobbled all three horses and turned them loose to graze.

While the horses picked listlessly at the sparse grass, the rest of us crawled under the thorny branches of a catclaw, more out of habit than logic, I think, since there wasn't enough shade to cover a mouse. We took our canteens and some cheese and jerky, and engaged in what was probably the most pathetic excuse for a picnic that part of Sonora has ever seen. Afterward Luis and Susan stretched out for a nap, but I knew I wouldn't be able sleep. Taking my rifle and the telescope, I crawled back through the catclaw until I could see a large segment of the country to the east and north. It wasn't long before I heard Abby following me through the scrub. She sank down at my side with a muffled *umphf,* kicking up a spurt of dust we might have chuckled about had we known one another better.

After an awkward pause, she said: "I thought you might like some company."

"I would," I said, but didn't know where to go from there.

Staring out across the land, she said: "I once thought this country was beautiful in a primitive sort of way. It's amazing how one's attitude can be so radically changed by simply stepping out from behind the glass of a railroad coach window."

"It's got its own beauty," I argued mildly. "Your introduction to it has been a little rough, is all."

"I sha'n't quibble such a trifling point with someone who has risked his life to save my own, but you'll have to offer proof of your point of view to change my opinion. You haven't so far."

I chuckled but didn't push it. An awkward silence settled between us. I could tell something was eating at her, but didn't know what to say to draw it out. It took several minutes before she screwed up enough courage to ask her question.

"Be honest, Mister Latham. What are our chances?"

Talk about getting banged on the blind side. I drew in a deep breath, staring at the stony soil in front of my boots and wishing I could drill a hole in the dirt with my eyes, then crawl into it. Abby was peering intently into my face, waiting for my answer, only gradually realizing that silence was my reply.

"Oh," she said quietly. Then, after another stretch of quiet, she added: "Please accept my apology. I've put you in a horribly untenable position, and I had no right to do that."

"There's no need to apologize," I said. "We're all here together, and doing our best to go home. The odds are long, but that's just the way the river runs sometimes. It doesn't mean we won't make it."

She smiled, and the transformation was immediate; fear and uncertainty were bulldozed into rubble, hope soared like bottle rockets. It made me feel about fifty pounds lighter to see her that way again, and it would be another dozen years before it dawned on me that she'd done it on purpose, burying her own doubts in an effort to ease mine. Man, I adored that woman. I did then, and I still do today.

I heard movement behind us. Luis making his way smoothly through the catclaw, avoiding its grabbing thorns like a kid playing tag.

Abby sat up with a look of alarm. "Where's Susan?"

"Don't worry, *madrecita*," he replied with a reassuring smile. "She is safe. I left her with the horses."

Jumping to her feet, Abby hurried back through the catclaw with considerably less dexterity than Luis had displayed coming in. Dropping to one knee, he glanced toward the cactus-studded plain to the east.

"Anything?"

"Not even a speck of dust."

His brows furrowed. "Then soon, I think."

I gave him a curious look. "Why?"

"Because I feel it, *amigo*, like a worm twisting in my gut. They are out there, creeping toward us as the fox stalks a dozing chicken."

A chill crept up my spine. I'd never known Luis to speak so

prophetically, but I knew him well enough to trust what he was saying. Pushing to my feet, I said: "Let's ride."

SESSION EIGHTEEN

The sun rose, then started down again, but the heat kept climbing. Our horses were still in good shape, but you could tell the desert was taking its toll. The d---ed desert always claims its share, one way or another.

Far ahead I could see a line of boulders jumbled up along the horizon like an old logging chain fallen from the back of a wagon. It was our destination, the top of the bluffs. I figured we'd be there by dusk if nothing got in our way, but had no idea how long it would take to locate one of the tanks cupped down among the rocks.

Luis had the lead again. Susan was riding with him, perched on the coarse wool scrape tied behind his cantle, her little fingers clinging to the cartridge-lined gun belt at his waist. She'd begged her mother to ride with him before we left the glade among the catclaw, and Abby had consented once Luis assured her the girl wouldn't be a bother. Abby rode beside them for a few miles, then fell back with me, smiling pleasantly.

"I believe I am getting used to this heat, Mister Latham."

"It's survivable if you've got enough water and know what you're doing." I didn't add that we'd been pretty lucky so far. If I hadn't spotted that seep the night before, we would have been in bad shape.

"Susan was asking this morning how much longer it would be until we could go home. I think she has a vague awareness of our danger, but only a child's cognizance of what it means."

"If I told you four days, it could be a lie."

She looked surprised. "Really, that long? I had thought we might be closer."

"With good horses and plenty of water we could be there in forty-eight hours," I replied, although that might have been stretching it. I've looked at a couple of maps of Sonora since then, and we were pretty deep into the state at the point.

"But we don't have good horses or plenty of water?"

"I've got no complaint with the horses, other than I'd like to have a saddle for your gray. As far as reaching Arizona, water will be a problem. An even bigger obstacle will be Alvarez and his men, not to mention the possibility of Indians."

"Yaquis?"

"Those and others."

"Mister Vega hinted that you were familiar with the Yaqui Indians."

"About that."

"About what?"

"About familiar, I'd say."

She gave me a doubting look, like she thought I was trying to be flippant, but I wasn't. It was just that, even though I'd lived with the tribe for three years, I'd never really come close to understanding them. You'd have to be born a Yaqui, or captured within the first few months of your life and raised by them, to really comprehend their ways. I was familiar with them, but that was about all.

"Mister Vega mentioned a chief called Old Toad. He said the man was quite dangerous, but I'm not sure he wasn't making a joke at my expense, exploiting my ignorance of the country and its people."

"No, Old Toad is real enough. He's the war chief of a bunch that calls itself the Dead Horses, after a branch of the Río Concepción where they used to winter. It's a small band, but meaner than most. Toad hates White Eyes as much as he does Mexicans, and that's a lot. We'd be better off falling into Soto's hands than running into him or any of his Dead Horses."

Her expression sobered. "I would dislike having to consider either of those options," she admitted. "Was . . . is this Toad fellow the Indian who abducted you as a child?"

"I wasn't much of a child by Sonoran standards," I explained. "I was fourteen when Toad's warriors jumped us in a freighter's camp outside of Magdalena. That was back in 'Eighty-Eight, and I was working for a muleskinner named Henry Toomes, who was a good enough man, though reckless to be in that country with just a kid to cover his backside." I was dimly aware of my anger—never very far away when the subject of Old Toad came up—and of the growing sharpness of my words. "There were close to twenty of them, and only the two of us," I continued. "They were on us before we even knew they were around. I was knocked unconscious pretty quick, but they caught Henry and. . . ."

My words trailed off as I recalled what Toad's bloodsuckers had done to poor old Henry. What they'd done to others, too, over the years that I ran with them. But when I glanced at Abby, I was startled by the look on her face, a kind of morbid reluctance that made me aware of my own blackening mood.

Looking away with a self-conscious chuckle, I rolled my shoulders as if I could work the anger loose like tight muscles. Deciding to change the subject before my fury toward both Old Toad and Henry led me to reveal the kind of graphic details a woman of Abby Davenport's refinement had no business hearing, I said: "Anyway, I was pretty old to be taken captive."

And fortunate, too, I've reflected a thousand times since then. Lucky not to have been gutted and burned alongside Henry, or hauled back to Toad's village as a slave, or fodder for their dogs.

"I'm sorry," Abby said softly. "I shouldn't have pried."

"You weren't prying," I assured her, but I was glad when she let the matter drop, and even more relieved a few minutes later when she urged her horse back up beside Luis's. I wish I could get rid of the memories that easily.

The Yaquis called me White Dog, but it wasn't a compliment, or even a descriptive name, like Crazy Horse or Sitting Bull. It was just a coarse description of a scared but combative youth, and when you transcribe these recordings, you could easily lower-case both words and still be correct.

I've mentioned my anger toward the Yaquis a couple of times now. A lot of people believe getting mad is a waste of time and energy, but I'd argue that it was my antagonism toward my captors, and Old Toad in particular, that kept me alive during those first chaotic weeks of my capture. It's also what kept me out of the clutches of the women, who would have made my life a living h--- as a slave, fetching wood and water and fighting the dogs for scraps of food. In my defiance, I think Toad saw the potential for a warrior, another defender of an already badly decimated nation.

The others never saw me that way, and I suspect in time even Old Toad came to regret his decision. Oh, I was fighter enough. Even a fourteen-year-old can take up the Yaqui cause when there's a *Federale* on the other end of a gun trying to kill him, but my heart was never in it. I wanted to live, which is about as basic a desire as exists, but I didn't care whether or not the Yaquis did. Argue all you want about the abomination of genocide, but my feelings toward the Dead Horses were cemented when I learned what they'd done to Henry Toomes during the final hours of his life.

I lived with them, I hunted with them, I even raided with them. And I learned the country, all along the coast and as far inland as the Sierra Madres. Not as intimately as the Yaquis, but better than any other man, white or Mexican, that I've ever met. I didn't know all the water holes—the tanks and seeps and springs—but I knew a lot of them, including the Cañon Where the Small Lizards Run, which is what opened up a previously unforgiving country to regular business trips between Nogales and Sabana.

My thoughts were still running with the Yaquis when I heard a warning shout from Luis. Jerking my head around, I was struck nearly dumb by the sight of half a dozen *soldados*, all but one of them wearing the tall caps and khaki uniforms of the Army of Liberation, pouring from the mouth of a draw to the northeast like milk from a broken jar. They were still pretty far away—a mile, at least—but I guess they'd decided they weren't likely to get any closer before nightfall, and didn't want to risk losing our trail again in the dark.

I shouted for the others to make a run for it, but they were way ahead of me. Luis had wheeled his sorrel behind Abby's gray and was lashing its rump with the loose ends of his reins. I slammed my heavy stirrups into the claybank's sides, and the horse practically lunged out from under me. We were heading for the line of rocks I'd spotted earlier, and that I was convinced was part of the upper lip of the escarpment.

I yanked the Winchester from its scabbard, but didn't even consider taking a shot at that range. Up ahead, with Abby's gray darting through the cactus like a fleeing jack rabbit, Luis had also drawn his long gun. He was staying close to the woman, though, which I appreciated. If the need arose, I could fall back or split off, and not have to worry about Abby's safety.

Those rocks I've been telling you about, they weren't that far away when Alvarez's men jumped us. Maybe three miles to the top, and with another couple of hours of daylight left, too. We were going to have to find a place to hole up real quick when we got there, though, before the *soldados* could pin us down. And we'd need to be close to water when we did, because those soldiers weren't going to give us time to poke around for the most likely spot to defend.

We rode silently for the most part, with just the wind rushing past our ears and the pounding of our horses' hoofs beating a desperate cadence against the hard dirt. Alvarez's troopers weren't yelling, which bothered me for some reason. I mean, what kind of men don't holler and shout when they attack, if only to bolster their own courage?

Me, I was cussing a blue streak under my breath as we raced through the scrub, and I won't apologize for it, either. I don't know why, but, as we made that dash for the rocks, I was more afraid than I'd been at any time since breaking Abby and Susan out of the garrison at Sabana. Bent low over the broad horn of my Mexican saddle, the Winchester at my side like a sawed-off lance, the curses just kept jolting out of me with the claybank's every forward lunge.

We were still a couple of hundred yards shy of the rim when I heard the first report of a rifle. I twisted around in my saddle in disbelief. The khaki-clad horsemen were still at least a mile off. They wouldn't waste a shot at that distance. Then I heard another shot, and swung back just as Luis howled and jerked his left hand back, shaking his fingers as if they'd gone to sleep. One of his reins had fallen and was whipping through the brush like a striking rattler. Gunsmoke drifted from the rocks in front of us. Abby glanced wildly over her shoulder, and I pointed the Winchester's muzzle toward a jumble of gray stones a couple of hundred yards south of where the shooter was crouched. Taking a rearward peek, I saw Alvarez's men slowing their mounts, as puzzled by the rifle fire coming from the rim of the bluff as we were.

Abby was racing toward our second destination with Luis crowding the gray's tail, his loose rein recovered. Susan was bouncing up and down on the saddle's skirting, hanging on for dear life. Then, even as I watched, another shot rang out from the bluff, and Abby's dappled gray went down in an explosion of dust and shattered brush. Luis, right behind her, couldn't stop. His sorrel made a valiant effort to leap the tumbling gray, but came down on top of it, instead.

After that, everything was a blur, like a series of out-of-focus snapshots. I remember a pinwheel image of Abby's skirt, its twin spokes clad in a pair of frilly pantaloons; Luis flying low through the desert scrub, both hands stretched in front of him with his palms raised against the rapidly approaching earth; horses' legs flailing—at one point I think all eight of them were pointed skyward at the same time—and a sombrero sailing clear of the wreckage like a hawk in flight.

Of Susan I saw nothing, not even a splash of white satin, and my heart sank as the mass of horses, of man and woman—and somewhere in that hodge-podge of death and destruction, a child—spun across the desert before me.

It was all over in a handful of seconds. I jerked the claybank to a dirt-showering stop and jumped clear of the saddle. A cloud of dust hung over the crash site. The gray was on its side, squealing and kicking, but Luis's sorrel wasn't moving; its neck was broken, tucked back almost under its body.

Susan, thankfully, was sitting spraddle-legged on the far side of the pile-up, screaming her beautiful brown eyes out at the indignities that had befallen her young life. There were shallow abrasions on one cheek and a prickly pear pad clinging securely to her thigh through the fabric of her dress, but otherwise she seemed fine.

Abby was also sitting up, although with her hands braced flat on the ground behind her. She looked dazed, and, having survived more than a few wrecks myself over the years, I could appreciate her confusion. Her hair had finally come completely undone and was hanging loosely around her face and shoulders in a way that did nothing to distract from her looks, and her clothing, although in a disarray and revealing several new tears, appeared bloodless.

Luis was standing with his legs spread wide for balance, both hands—the palms bloody from where he'd tried to stop his fall—held out to the side while the world spun around him. I knew that feeling, too. Then a fourth shot exploded from the rocks, and Luis's jacket twitched as the bullet passed through its hem. I grabbed him around the waist and threw him to the ground, then dropped to my knee at his side, corkscrewing partway around and snapping off probably the luckiest shot I've ever made in my life.

Up in the rocks, our ambusher was spun violently to one side. He tumbled into a boulder and was starting to fall when he suddenly caught himself, then pushed to his feet and darted into the stone forest at his rear. Although Luis was cursing vehemently in Spanish, the bullet had missed and he was unharmed save for the raw flesh of his palms. Abby had crawled over to Susan's side and plucked the cactus pad from the youngster's thigh. She was holding the child in her lap, rocking her gently and murmuring in her ear.

My claybank was heading back to Vaquero Springs at a running trot, its head and tail held high, reins trailing uselessly. The gray had ceased its pitiful cries and now lay stretched out on its side; blood bubbled from its nostrils in a pink mist, and a thumb-size, scarlet-rimmed crater just behind its shoulder implied a bad lung wound and almost certain death. Out on the desert floor, the soldiers had brought their horses to a stop and were just sitting there, watching and waiting. They were about five hundred yards away by then, and a grim smile played across my lips when I recognized the stocky sergeant in the bullet-pocked sombrero among them. Marcos had already dispatched a rider to fetch Alvarez, and seemed content at this point to keep us corralled until the lieutenant could come up with the rest of his men.

I took all this in at a glance, then grabbed Luis's arm and hauled him to his feet. "Find your rifle and get the women out of here," I barked, then turned to the sorrel.

Although the claybank was gone, taking one of the gourd canteens and about half our ammunition with it, the rest was on the sorrel. I quickly stripped what I thought we'd need from the saddle and carried it over to the gray's side. Gritting my teeth in regret, I drew the Smith & Wesson and put a round through the animal's head. Then I took off after Luis and Abby, who were making a dash for the rocks a couple of hundred yards away.

I was only a few seconds behind them when they reached the top. This was the escarpment I'd been aiming for ever since we left that little knoll west of Vaquero Springs. The edge of the cliff was about twenty yards away, the emptiness beyond both ominous and awe-inspiring. A strong breeze curling up over the lip of the precipice flicked annoyingly at the brim of my Stetson.

Dropping the sorrel's canteen and saddlebags at Luis's side, I told him to stay with the woman and child, then rummaged under the offside flap for a box of cartridges for my Winchester. Both our rifles and Luis's Frontier Model Colt shot the same .44-40 round, but we had only a single, twenty-round box of ammunition left.

Luis watched me refill the long tube under the Winchester's octagon barrel. He knew what I had to do, and I could tell it bothered him to remain behind, but somebody had to stay with Abby and Susan, not to mention keep an eye on those *soldados*.

Not knowing what to say to Luis or Abby, I didn't say anything. Slipping out of the tangle of rocks where we were holed up, I made my way north along the rim of the bluff, staying low but moving fast. Without any idea of how seriously our ambusher had been wounded, I was taking some foolish chances. But he had to be rooted out of that high ground; we were going to need it when Alvarez showed up with the rest of his men.

As pressed for time as I was, I couldn't prevent myself from slowing down as I neared our assailant's location—instinct battling instinct, I suppose, with the more immediate danger winning out. I crept forward, hugging the edge of the cliff while the wind tugged at my clothing, threatening to snatch my hat from my head. I spotted an open space in the jumble of boulders ahead of me, like a clearing in a forest, and intuitively headed toward it. What I saw when I cautiously eased around a slab of stone jutting toward the cliff's face stopped me cold.

It was a clearing all right, with a body lying on its side beside a bed of ashes from a cook fire. Although the man's back was to me, I recognized him instantly. He wasn't moving, and there was no one else around. Stepping into the clearing, I said loudly: "Carlos! Carlos Perez!"

I don't know if the wiry little son-of-a-b---- had been faking it or not, but he whirled quick as a diamondback at my words, his revolver spitting a cloud of smoke and a chunk of lead before I came close to reacting. I felt the hot pull of the bullet across the top of my shoulder even as I pulled the Winchester's trigger.

Carlos's bullet didn't miss, but it didn't stop me, either. My return shot was dead on, striking the little turncoat square in the chest.

I stood there a moment, my jaw agape at the rapidity of what had just occurred. I don't remember dropping to a crouch when I fired, but I guess I did. Straightening slowly, I levered a fresh round into the Winchester's chamber. Carlos was on his back now, both arms above his head, his revolver lying a good foot above the outstretched fingers of his right hand. I stepped warily into the clearing, but no one else showed up. Somehow I knew they wouldn't. I don't know why I felt so certain Perez was alone out there, but I didn't question it.

There were a few acres of well-watered grass not too far away, with Carlos's seal brown gelding and Ed Davenport's pack mules picketed in its middle. The crates carrying the potato diggers and ammunition had been tucked under a low overhang at the camp's edge, partially covered with a piece of canvas.

I was still standing there absorbing the scene when I heard a shout from the desert. Startled, I hurried through the rocks to where Carlos had set up his ambush. It was a natural spot for anyone wanting to cover the entire eastern approach to the clearing, with plenty of cover and an open field of fire for several hundred yards. Staring past the bodies of our dead horses, I watched a second group of horsemen hook up with Marcos's smaller bunch. José Alvarez was easy to spot. Even after forty-eight grueling hours in the saddle, he sat his horse tall and ramrod-straight, his chiseled features like a chunk of cured oak. With his men stopped, I was finally able to get an accurate count—thirteen altogether, including the two officers.

I sank back under a cloud of hopelessness. Thirteen men against the two of us. Three if you counted Abby, although I wasn't sure I wanted to do that. Not if she was going to have to face Alvarez alone after our deaths. Thirteen heavily armed soldiers, their bandoleers sagging with ammunition, against a pair of Winchesters and a half-empty box of cartridges. I closed my eyes, feeling the burn of the sun through the fabric of my shirt, its heat cooking the deep blue finish of the rifle's barrel. Then I opened them with a start, laughing softly as the heaviness lifted from my shoulders, wondering what the h--- I'd been thinking.

I hurried back to the clearing. There was a short camp axe sitting beside a pile of dried cholla limbs next to the fire. I grabbed it on my way to the overhang where Carlos had stacked the cases of guns and ammunition. Yanking the canvas aside, I attacked a crate containing one of the Colt-Browning machine-guns first, prying off its lid and spilling the bulky cargo into the dirt. It was already fully assembled except for the tripod, although smeared with a thin layer of packing grease I wouldn't take time to clean off. I opened an ammunition crate next and yanked out a pair of cloth belts that I quickly began filling with .30-40s.

Each belt held a hundred and forty rounds. You might recall me mentioning that a few sessions back, when I told you about Alvarez pumping the last hundred rounds into Poco Guille at that little cove outside of Sabana. As much as I resented its intrusion, that was the image occupying my thoughts as I shoved cartridge after cartridge into the Colt-Browning's belt.

"¡Hijo de p---!"

I glanced over my shoulder. Luis and Abby were standing at the edge of the clearing, just about where I'd been when I shot Carlos Perez. Susan stood at her mother's side with her face buried in the woman's skirt, her back to the clearing and the bloody corpse in its center. After that quick burst of Spanish profanity, Luis hurried over to start filling the second belt. Abby led Susan to the stack of munitions, still partially covered with canvas, and told her in no uncertain terms to stay put until she or Luis or I came to fetch her. Susan ducked under the canvas shelter like a frightened rabbit, and Abby came over to relieve Luis of the task of filling the second belt. I had the first belt finished by then, and, with that draped over my shoulders, Luis and I picked up the Colt-Browning and carried it into the rocks where Carlos had launched his ambush.

"A good place," Luis declared, glancing around as I spread the tripod's legs and adjusted them for height. Luis eased the machine-gun onto the narrow, channel-like platform, and I started tightening the lug while he held the gun steady. After watching me work for a couple of seconds, he said: "How bad is your wound?"

I looked up, puzzled at first, then gradually becoming aware of a dull stinging at the junction of my neck and shoulder, accompanied by a warm dampness soaking into the fabric of my shirt. I twisted my head around in an attempt to view the damage, but the wound was too close to get a fix on it without a mirror. Luis moved my collar aside with a brown finger to examine the injury.

"Not so bad," he announced. "A crease only, although it will leave a scar. If we are not all dead by then, I can look at it closer tonight."

"How about your hands?" I asked, nodding toward the torn flesh of his palms and recalling how he'd used his forearms to lower the Colt-Browning onto the tripod.

He turned them over to show me. The right one was worse, with small pebbles ground under the skin. They both looked raw and sore, but not necessarily debilitating.

"My hands are as your shoulder," he said. "They can wait."

While I made a few final adjustments to the tripod, Luis fed the belt through the machine-gun's action, then rocked the lever under the barrel to chamber the first round. I strung the ammunition belt out at the machine-gun's side so that it would feed smoothly, without hanging up or jamming. When Abby got there, we hooked the second belt to the free end of the first one, and I showed her how to keep them straight, and help advance them through the gun. We were still getting everything squared away when Alvarez shouted at us from the desert.

"You men there, surrender at once or face the consequences!"

I smiled, grateful that he wanted to dicker. It would give us a few more minutes to ready ourselves for his attack. Leaving Abby and Luis to handle the potato digger, I ran a crooked path back to camp, where I grabbed the Winchesters and the half-empty box of ammunition. I took just a moment to peek inside the canvas cavern where Susan was crouched, fresh tears washing down her cheeks. I repeated her mama's admonition to stay down and out of sight, then hurried back to where Luis and Abby were listening to a new batch of demands from Alvarez.

"What's he want?" I asked.

"The woman and the *niña*."

"Did you tell him no?"

"Not yet. Should I?"

I glanced to the west, where the sun had already set. It would be full dark in another hour. We were running out of time.

"Better do it," I said, then crawled out of the cramped pocket to find my own place from which to fight.

I won't relate the entire exchange that took place between Luis and Alvarez over the next several minutes. You can probably guess most of it, anyway. Alvarez wanted the woman and child and me and Luis, and if he'd known we had Davenport's guns, he would have wanted those, too. Luis kept telling him no, until Alvarez finally told us we had five minutes to make up our minds. If we hadn't sent Abby and Susan out by then, he would be obliged to attack, which would not only risk the lives of the women, but also ensure our own deaths.

"There will be no quarter given if we are forced to charge your position," he added, as if the outcome would have been different if we had co-operated—which none of us believed for a second.

"It is about time you grew some *cojones*!" Luis shouted back. "I am becoming weary of this futile exchange of words."

I glanced at Abby, grateful that she didn't understand what was being said. Luis's insulting replies to Alvarez had been getting more and more inventive, not to mention crude. [*Ed. Note:*

At the time of her abduction, Abigail Davenport [sic] was fluent in several languages, including French, German, and Spanish.]

Alvarez didn't reply, although he did make a big production of dragging something out of his pocket—presumably a watch, although it was too far away to be sure—and quietly staring at it. At Marcos's command, the troopers spread out on either side of the lieutenant, then quietly sat their mounts with their carbines butted to their thighs. I was lying on top of a sloping boulder a few feet to the left of where Luis and Abby were crouched, with a clear field of fire and probably the best view of the coming attack as anyone.

"You two ready?" I asked the pair below me. They both nodded stiffly, and I added: "I don't know what kind of range that potato digger's got, so let's let 'em get real close before you open up."

Luis gave me an uncertain look. "When you want me to fire, you say so. Until then, I won't pull the trigger." He leaned back from sighting along the Colt-Browning's barrel. "Just remember, *amigo*, I've never fired one of these things before. If something goes wrong. . . ."

He let his words trail off, but he'd made a good point. Still, I wanted Alvarez's men as close as possible before we started shooting. I figured we'd only get one chance to break their charge before they realized we had a machine-gun. If we hadn't made a big dent in their ranks by then, their tactics would immediately change, and we'd lose whatever edge we had.

Alvarez's voice drifted in from the desert. "Two minutes."

Shouldering a Winchester, I settled in against the gentle slope of the rock.

"One minute, *señores*. Please, make this easier on all of us and capitulate. Surely you realize it is our victory which is inevitable."

Michael Zimmer

I said: "That's mighty big talk for a bandit, don't you think, Luis?"

"*Sí,* but that is what happens when you put some men in uniforms. I have always believed it is the tightness of their collars that swells their heads."

Abby and I both laughed. Out on the desert floor, Alvarez raised his hand above his head. The picture lacked only a saber to make it romantic.

"You know, *amigo,* we have come pretty far, you and I," Luis said.

"We've been bucking the odds ever since we left Moralos, for a fact."

"It's been a good fight, a good effort." He looked at me and grinned. "To tell you the truth, *hombre,* we've made it a lot farther than I expected."

"You two," Abby scolded. "You're acting like we've lost this battle before it's even begun."

From the desert, I heard Alvarez give the command to advance.

"No, *señora,*" Luis assured her. "This battle is not lost, but I think it is good that we appreciate what we have accomplished. Just in case, you know?"

We turned our attention to the desert. Alvarez was riding out front, I'll give him that. He'd kicked his horse into a short lope, and was really eating up the ground. The rough terrain was forcing his men to spread out behind him, but they were making an effort to stay as close as possible, which would be to our advantage. My smile faded as I tucked the Winchester into my shoulder. I've heard men insist a .44-40 is good for five hundred yards if the shooter knows what he's doing, but I've always thought two hundred yards was stretching the cartridge's limits. Alvarez's men were right at two hundred yards when I thumbed the Winchester's hammer to full cock.

"Not yet," I told the others.

Sweat was rolling off my brow, needling the corner of my right eye. I pulled my hand away just long enough to knuckle the worst of it aside, then returned my finger to the trigger.

"Not yet," I repeated as Alvarez's men swept past the one hundred-yard mark.

"D--- it, J.T," a voice cursed, and I realized with a little jolt of surprise that it was Abby who was speaking, not Luis.

"Let 'em have it!" I shouted in reply, squeezing off a round that took that son-of-a-b---- José Alvarez square in the gut.

Before I could lever another round, the Colt-Browning seemed to explode at my side. That first burst of a dozen or so rounds went so high I figured only the farmers in Sabana needed to worry about them. Then Luis found the machine-gun's rhythm, and ran a hail of lead across the desert floor. At less than eighty yards, the carnage was as immediate as it was horrific. Luis skimmed the machine-gun from left to right, then back again, two slow passes that emptied the first belt completely and moved twenty or thirty rounds into the second before he finally took his finger off the trigger. In all, I'd estimate he maintained a steady barrage for no more than ten seconds. I'd fired a solitary round. Out in the field, only a few of the horses remained standing.

For a long time, maybe two or three minutes, we stared silently at the destruction we'd wrought. After a while I looked at Luis, and the expression on his face was like nothing I've seen before or since. Abby's countenance was more despairing than frightened; she looked like she was about to collapse from the weight of her involvement. As for me, it was like being encased in fog; I had to force myself to pull my hand away from the Winchester's trigger, and then I didn't know what to do with it when I had.

Luis was the first to rise, breaking the spell. After making a quick sign of the cross, he motioned for his rifle. I tossed it to him, then slid to the ground. Luis was already heading toward the killing ground. Abby took off in the opposite direction, back to the clearing to find Susan. She hadn't spoken a word since I gave the command to fire.

I walked out with Luis, the Winchester like an anvil in my fists. Our destruction wasn't as complete as I'd thought from the rocks, and it wasn't clean, either. Several of the horses had been killed outright, but a couple were badly wounded, standing broken and bleeding within the scrub. The rest of the troopers' mounts had taken off after my claybank as if they knew where they were going, and I had no doubt that they would eventually find their way back to Vaquero Springs, where Soto's men would tend to any lighter wounds, and wonder what had become of their riders.

Drawing my revolver, I quickly put both of the wounded animals out of their misery, as I'd done earlier with Abby's gray. Then I began stripping the extra canteens from their saddles. I left the single-shot Remington carbines where they'd fallen, and was just slinging the last canteen over my shoulder when I heard the thunder of Luis's revolver echo across the desert. I spun around to find him standing above a soldier.

"Hey!" I shouted, dropping the canteens and running over. He was already moving on to the next man when I stepped in front of him. "What the h--- are you doing?" I demanded, putting my left hand out like a traffic cop.

He motioned toward a stocky individual sprawled on the ground a few feet away, his stomach ripped open, face waxy with pain. I swore when I recognized Marcos, then turned back to Luis. "You can't do that. He's a human being."

Luis stared back dully. "You would have me leave him here for the vultures?"

"He deserves a chance, no matter how bad the wound or

how long the odds."

"Bull----," Luis flared, his jaws knotting with . . . what? Anguish? Rage? Then he spun his revolver to thrust it toward me butt first. "You do it," he said flatly. "You finish this job that we started."

"I didn't start it, Luis. Davenport did. Or Soto. Or Alvarez. Take your pick."

"I pick you, J.T.," he said coldly, the .44 unwavering in his hand. "Finish the job, or get out of my way and let me finish it."

"Let him . . . do it."

I turned back to the figure on the ground. I'd thought Marcos was too far gone to understand what we were arguing about, but he was staring at me with a quiet intensity, a silent plea. He knew what was going on, what his odds of survival were; I guess it was a gamble he didn't want to take. My mind struggled for a reply, but there wasn't any. Shoving me aside, Luis stepped over to the man's side, flipped the revolver back into his own hand, cocked the hammer, and fired in one fluid motion. Marcos grunted at the bullet's impact, momentarily stiffened, then abruptly relaxed, his face taking on a strangely peaceful cast.

Death isn't pretty, but some are worse than others, and what happened out there in the desert west of Sabana was about as ugly as it gets. I just needed to tell you that, so that you'll have a better understanding of what happened later on.

SESSION NINETEEN

It was just about dark when we got back to the little clearing among the rocks. Abby had dragged Carlos's body into a nearby crevice, then covered it with a piece of tarp. She was going through the Mexican's packs when we got there, setting out ham and hardtack and tins of sardines. Susan was perched on a crate at her side, staring out over the edge of the cliff. She didn't even look around as we walked into the camp.

Luis and I stood quietly, watching Abby prepare a simple meal. Nobody spoke, and, after a couple of minutes, Luis leaned his rifle against the crate behind Susan and walked back into the rocks. He returned a few minutes later cradling the Colt-Browning in both arms. Abby stopped what she was doing as Luis walked across the clearing. I think it caught both of us off guard when he awkwardly tossed the machine-gun over the edge, then stood there watching it fall.

It took a while for the heavy gun to reach the bottom, but you could hear the crash even from beside the cold ashes of the campfire. It didn't stop there, though. The Colt-Browning hit the boulder-strewn scree at the bottom of the cliff, then rolled and tumbled all the way to the bottom, generating its own little rock slide as it went. A few seconds later a thin cloud of dust curled up over the lip of the bluff, riding the currents.

Turning away from the cliff, Luis eyed me speculatively, waiting, I suppose, to see what I'd say. Wordlessly I walked over to the cache of arms and dragged the crate containing the second

Colt-Browning from the stack. After using the camp axe to pry off the lid, Luis and I carried the gun to the cliff's edge and, on the third swing, sent it sailing into the gloam. We waited for the sounds of the crash to subside, then went back for the ammunition, breaking open each box separately and smashing the pasteboard cartons until the cartridges were heaped in the bottom of the crate like a pirate's booty. Hauling the cases to the edge of the cliff, we heaved them out one after the other, the brass twinkling like fire-lit confetti as it vanished into the shadows far below.

When we were done, we staggered back to the cold fire where Abby dressed our wounds—my neck and Luis's hands—as best she could, then fed us a skimpy meal of ham and sardines on hardtack. I've eaten worse.

We didn't bury Carlos or the *soldados,* figuring Chito Soto would send out a troop when Alvarez's horses showed up, and that they could do as they wished with the dead. We brought the stock in before dawn the next morning, and were saddled up and ready to ride by first light. Abby used Carlos's rig on the *Indio*'s seal brown, while Luis used the saddle from his sorrel on one of the mules. I brought in an old U.S.-made McClellan from one of the dead horses on the battlefield, using the breeching off a pack saddle to keep the rig in place atop the witherless animal.

We brought along all the food we could carry, filled the canteens at a long, shallow tank still half full from last winter's rains, then moved out as before, with Luis up front, then Abby and Susan, and me bringing up the rear. Other than what was necessary, we still weren't speaking much.

We'd been traveling more west than north ever since leaving Sabana, but that was largely on account of Alvarez. With the lieutenant no longer a concern and our canteens full, we turned north along the rim of the escarpment. Our destination was the

Río Concepción, where I was fairly confident we'd find water. I was also worried that we might run into some Yaquis or Southern Pimas there, but hoping we'd see them in time to avoid an encounter. My plan was to refill our canteens at the river, then make a final push for Arizona. It would be tough haul, but we needed to get out of Mexico—all of us, but especially Susan.

About three miles north of the clearing we came to a split in the cliff's rim, with a trail winding down to the bottom maybe one hundred and fifty feet below. We halted on top when Luis spotted the tracks of other horses in the dirt. He dismounted to examine them more closely, running his fingers lightly over the ridges of loose soil. After a couple of minutes he stood and returned to his mule.

"I think two," he said, throwing a leg over his cantle.

"Davenport and Buchman?" I asked.

There was no reaction from Abby at mention of her husband's name, which seemed odd at the time.

"*Sí*, I would think so."

"How far ahead?"

"Yesterday morning." He was looking east, calculating our route from Sabana, as I was doing from the Cañon Where the Small Lizards Run. It would come out just about right, I decided.

"That means Carlos probably didn't double-cross them," I said.

"It would seem so," Luis agreed.

"Are you saying Edward and another man are somewhere ahead of us?" Abby asked doubtfully.

"That's the way I read it," I replied.

"They are not traveling fast," Luis observed. He was looking at me now, his expression pulled into a frown as he tried to make sense of the old man's plans. "Perhaps they have gone to meet someone."

"Someone wanting to buy his guns?"

"It is possible, no?"

I glanced at Abby. Her lips were a pencil-thin line scratched across her face, her eyes as hard as cherry pits.

"It doesn't matter," I said abruptly. "If they're ahead of us, we'll watch out for them, but we're heading for Arizona."

Luis nodded and reined his mule toward the cañon's rim. Abby and I followed close behind, our mounts' hoofs setting off little avalanches of pebbles and dust. At the bottom we turned just west of due north and settled into the ride.

The sun rose warm, then turned hot, but there was a thin haze in the air that blunted the worst of the heat. Later that morning the clouds thickened and the wind picked up, kicking sand in our faces like a Mr. Atlas beach bully, and the stock— Abby's seal brown in particular—turned fractious.

Luis and I pulled our hats down to shield our faces, but Abby had lost her sombrero when her horse was shot out from under her, and had to use a blanket drawn over her head like a shawl. Susan used it, too, crawling underneath, then pulling her legs up out of the blowing sand until she was nothing more than a lump along her mother's spine.

The wind died late in the afternoon, but the clouds remained. Although the temperature wasn't as brutal with the sun's rays filtered by a buttermilk sky, the humidity rose noticeably, making our progress even more miserable than when we'd suffered the full brunt of a cloudless day.

We made another cold camp that night, then pushed on the following morning in a cheerless silence. With the wind down, the stock became easier to manage again, and we started pushing a little, eager to reach the Río Concepción and fresh water.

I think for the others, as well as myself, the Concepción had become more than just another water hole. It was our final bar-

rier, the United States—or at least one of its territories—
beckoning seductively from the other side. We were still several
hours away when Luis suddenly hauled back on his reins. I
heeled my mule forward, my hand dropping to the Smith &
Wesson's scarred walnut grips.

"What is it?" I asked.

He pointed with his chin toward a clump of catclaw about a
hundred yards to our left. "I saw something."

"Man or animal?"

"I couldn't tell."

Then Abby gasped. Following the direction of her gaze, I saw
a man standing in the brush on our right. He was short and
dark and pot-bellied, the way the hungry sometimes are, with
coal-black hair cut straight at the brow and shoulders, and bare,
spindly legs. He wore a breechcloth made of *jerga,* ankle-high
moccasins, and a necklace of javelina tusks strung between
wooden beads. He was carrying a spear in his right hand, its
butt digging into the ground at his side.

"You recognize him?" Luis asked. He meant the Indian's
nationality. Although in these parts he could have been Pima or
Apache or even one of the coastal tribes, I knew he wasn't. I
think Luis knew it, too. That's why he started to ease his hand
toward the revolver riding on his hip, although in fairness I
don't think he intended to draw it. He just wanted to be ready.
Unfortunately it was too late for that.

And me? I sat there with my hope puddled on the ground
under my mule like so much urine. Placing my hand lightly on
Luis's arm, I croaked: "Don't."

He gave me a searching glance. "Why not?"

I nodded toward the clumps of chaparral that surrounded us
on every side. Three more Yaquis had joined the first. They were
all dressed similarly, the earthen tones of their clothing and the
reddish-brown hue of their skin blending into the landscape like

chameleons. These three were carrying bows, with arrows nocked but as yet undrawn. I wasn't falling for their little attempt at chicanery, though. They were testing us, putting out a poorly armed bait to see how we'd react, but I knew that if Luis drew his gun, we'd all be dead before he could cock it.

"Leave off," I murmured. "We're outnumbered."

"There are only four of them," Abby pointed out. She was probably wondering what had me so spooked when I'd faced worse odds against Chito Soto and his goons. I nodded toward the chaparral, and Abby cried out softly. I counted eight men loosely surrounding us, three of them toting cocked rifles. Shifting around in my saddle for a look to the rear, I added another dozen warriors to the total, and said quietly: "They've got us, and they'll kill us if we try to fight or make a run for it."

"What do we do?" Abby asked, patting Susan's hand in a futile attempt at reassurance.

"Do what you're told to do, and nothing you aren't," I replied tersely. Then, in Yaqui as rusty as the hinges on an abandoned barn door, I called to the man who had first stepped forward. "I am White Dog, a friend of the *Yoemem,* who I once lived with. We come in peace, and wish only to pass through your country as quickly as possible. Except for water and air, we will take nothing that belongs to the People." [*Ed. Note: Yoemem* is Yaqui for "The People", which is how they historically referred to themselves.]

"I know who you are, White Dog," the man replied coolly, "and you are no longer welcome among us."

The fact is, I'd never been all that welcome among the Yaquis, even when I lived with them. An outsider from the get-go, I'd been tolerated solely because of Old Toad's unusual attachment to me.

"We wish only to pass through," I persisted. "When we leave, we will never return."

"That promise was made once before," the Indian pointed out. I remembered him then. His name was Ghost, because of his ability to move silently through the brush, neither seen nor heard. Early in my stay with the Dead Horse clan, in a fit of teenage frustration, I'd blurted to Ghost that if I ever escaped, I'd never come back. Apparently he hadn't forgotten.

Ghost wasn't coming any closer, but some of the others were. Rifles were held at the ready, and those men armed with bows had finally drawn their arrows. Tipping his spear toward us, Ghost said: "Remove your guns."

I took another quick look around. The numbers were increasing. I counted nineteen now, and figured there were still a few more in hiding in the chaparral. Real easy, I loosened the buckle on my gun belt and let it fall. Luis and Abby did the same, although I could tell Luis was hesitant to comply. I could appreciate his feelings, remembering the hatred of Mexicans that had burned in the breasts of so many Yaquis.

With our revolvers on the ground, the Indians sprang forward. Clutching hands hauled me roughly from my saddle. My arms were pulled back and my wrists—still tender from Del Buchman's cuffs—were lashed with short lengths of rawhide. Through a forest of thin brown legs I caught glimpses of others doing the same to Luis and Abby, and I could hear Susan wailing as she was carried away.

Abby was screaming for them to return her child, kicking and twisting wildly. I shouted for her to let it go, that the girl would be all right, but she didn't hear me, and probably wouldn't have stopped if she had. She fought like a demon, and if she'd been a man, they would have bashed her skull in and left her for the vultures. Instead they found her desperate struggles humorous, and laughed and joked as they forced her to the ground, then bound her wrists behind her back. It took five of them to do it.

Luis's face was the bloodiest when we were all brought back

to our feet, the near-perfect shape of a rifle butt already starting to swell the flesh under his right eye. I knew it would go harder on him than either Abby or me because of Porfirio Díaz's eradication policy toward the Yaquis.

Abby had ceased her resistance and stood with her head bowed, her chest heaving. Tears glistened along both cheeks, cutting narrow channels through the dirt. The warrior who had snatched Susan had also confiscated the seal brown, and was riding west at a swift gallop, the girl clamped firmly in his arms. Her cries floated back to us long after she and her captor had disappeared, like claws slashing at her mother's heart.

Mine, too, for that matter.

Others had mounted the two mules and were circling behind us like cowboys gathering strays. A branch torn from a creosote bush came down on my shoulders like a strip of fire. I cried out a guttural protest and spun around, staring into the laughing eyes of a young man who couldn't have been more than fifteen or sixteen. The smile faded from his lips when he saw my expression, and I won't deny a desire to pull him from the mule's saddle and wring his scrawny neck, no matter his age.

"Before I leave, I'll cut your throat," I swore darkly, although my Yaqui was so poor and my anger so hot, I'm not sure he understood my words.

Ghost stepped in front of me, his eyes blazing with their own special hatred. "You run, White Dog," he growled in Spanish. "All of you run, or we will gut you on the trail and leave you as live bait for the coyotes."

He meant it, too. I'd seen him do it to a Mexican family the Yaquis had caught harvesting salt from the Sea of Cortez, my first year living with them. Luis already knew what we were facing, but I translated Ghost's threats to Abby so that she also understood the situation.

"It's going to get real bad," I told her. "But you've got to hold on. For Susan's sake."

She'd kept her face hidden behind the screen of her long hair while I repeated Ghost's truculent promises, but raised her eyes to meet mine when I mentioned Susan.

"You are lying, Mister Latham," she said softly. "I shall never see my darling baby again."

"I'm not lying, ma'am. The odds aren't good, but they're there, and we've got to take them. We've got to keep on taking them, until we just can't take them any more."

She was staring deep into my eyes. I could tell she wanted to believe me. Finally, uncertainly she nodded. "All right, sir, you sha'n't find me lagging. I give you my word."

I reckon that's about all you can ask for in a case like ours.

Just being real blunt, what followed after that was a nightmare of pain and humiliation. The majority of the Yaquis continued on east on whatever business had brought them out there to begin with, but Abby, Luis, and I were herded toward the setting sun like so many sheep, the two young men on our mules acting as cruel shepherds. They kept us moving in a tottering, graceless run, and I'll swear they picked the scabbiest patches of earth they could find to drive us over. My legs started to cramp soon after starting, and my lungs were straining within the hour. Sweat poured into my eyes like rivers of salt, nearly blinding me. I stumbled once and went to my knees, and the kid with the creosote switch sent me flying, nose first, into the dirt by running the shoulder of his mule into my back. He swung around even as I struggled to rise, striking at me again and again with that whip-thin limb until I got my legs under me and started running.

If it was hard for Luis and me, it was even worse for Abby, encumbered as she was by her wide-sweeping skirts and whatever trappings she had under it, petticoats and bloomers and who knew what else. At one point she fell and refused to get up. One of the kids returned to whip his mule back and forth over her. The sturdy jack tried hard not to step on the mushy figure beneath him, knowing the loose footing would likely throw him, but he couldn't help clipping the woman several times with his iron-shod hoofs.

Finally the kid jumped down and in exasperation began beating Abby across the back and shoulders with the flat of his mesquite wood bow, until she forced one knee up, then the other, and surged to her feet. She stood there a moment, her nose bleeding, her jacket nearly ripped from her back, glaring at the youth as he remounted the mule. The kid stopped the jack in front of her, grinning broadly, then pointed the tip of his bow to the west.

Abby started off without comment, passing between Luis and me with barely a glance. We fell in silently behind her. I hated what that kid did to her, but I'm even more embarrassed to admit how much I savored the break her fall had given me. It was a chance to catch my wind, and allow my heart to slow its rapid pounding. I could see that Luis felt the same way in the subdued cast of his face when his eyes met mine, then darted away.

There were still a couple of hours of cloudy daylight left when we reached the Río Concepción. We stumbled down its sloping bank like trail drovers at the end of a three-day spree, staggering and glassy-eyed from fatigue, our bodies aching from our run. I was vaguely aware of a village on our left, but too exhausted to care, too parched to take my eyes off the gentle flow of water before us.

The Concepción was always a small river, but never to be dismissed in that arid wasteland. At that time of year—it was still the middle of May, remember?—the river was running a good twenty feet wide and several inches deep, rippling swiftly and purposefully over its sandy shoals.

I dropped to my knees in the wet sand—the h--- with scooping water up in my hand like a true warrior—and flopped forward onto my belly to dip my face in the surprisingly cool water, letting it flow over my sun-burned cheeks and split lips. Abby and Luis were doing the same on either side of me, the three of us wallowing in the life-giving shallows of the Concepción like hogs in a mud hole. After a while the kid with the creosote quirt jumped to the ground and started beating us over our shoulders to keep us from drinking too much, but we refused to be driven away. It wasn't until several middle-aged men from the village came down to forcibly drag us out of the water that I finally started to take note of my surroundings.

The village was fairly large for 1907. I estimated at least two dozen dwellings, strewn like overturned bowls throughout the mesquite that grew along a low bench overlooking the Concepción. The older men stood above us while the kid who had given us so much grief on the trail explained our presence in a loud and agitated manner, his right arm gesticulating wildly. After a minute or so of listening to the youth's rambling, one of the older men quieted him with an upraised hand, then spoke briefly to another man, who rolled me onto my back with his toe. I didn't recognize him, although in fairness I was still half blinded from the sweat and dirt rimming my swollen eyes, despite the dunking I'd given them in the river.

The older man's words were too agile for my poor Yaqui to follow, although I heard Ghost's name mentioned a couple of times, as well as Toad's. I wondered if the old war chief lived there, if he was even still alive. Then the two youths who had driven us to the village suddenly quirted their mules and raced away, while a couple of the older men hauled me to my feet. They half led, half dragged me up the bank to an abandoned wickiup, where they dumped me against the wall like a piece of firewood. They had my legs bent back and my ankles hitched to my wrists in about as much time as it takes to tell, then strode off talking conversationally about, as near as I could follow, what one of the men's wife was making for dinner that night.

The sun set and night came on. I lay there alone and uncovered, so stiff from my afternoon run that I could barely move. I was half starved and near about froze, but the worst part about that whole night were the cramps. My legs and arms and along my spine, even the muscles across my stomach, kinked and contracted all the way through to dawn.

I know you've had a charley-horse, or that cramp where your big toe wants to veer away from the others. Imagine enduring that all night long and not being able to jump out of bed to pace or stretch your muscles back to normal. It was h--- with a capital H, although I never lost sight of the fact that, as bad as it was, I was still alive.

The sun was barely up the next morning when a young man in his late teens came to fetch me. He was wearing a heavy butcher knife in a brass-tacked sheath, and sneered as he stood above me fingering the weapon's chipped scales. He was looking for a reaction, preferably fear, but I'd lived among the Yaquis for too many years to give him that kind of satisfaction. I turned my head away as if bored, and he laughed and whipped out the blade. I couldn't help a small, grating moan as my limbs were freed. My hands had turned purple from a lack of circulation, and I couldn't feel anything below my knees. The youth, predictably, appeared unconcerned with my disability.

"On your feet, dog," he commanded.

I tried, but my limbs wouldn't co-operate. My legs wobbled and bowed, and I had to look to where I wanted my hands to go, then kind of flop them in that direction. The Yaqui's contempt for me deepened as he watched.

"Are all white men as feeble as you?" he asked.

"Did your mother enjoy copulating with the skunk that sired

you?" I replied.

I guess my Yaqui was improving, because he gave me a kick in my ribs that sent me spinning across the ground. His reply came faster than I could follow, although I didn't have any trouble interpreting his feelings, especially with that butcher knife jacked back over his shoulder. That ol' boy wanted to cut me open so bad, he could taste it, but I just laughed at him. You might think me foolish for doing so, but a man didn't get far with those desert tribes by groveling.

"Why don't you go find a snake to copulate with?" I suggested.

"I will cut out your tongue, then laugh when you try to howl at the moon."

That might not sound too impressive to a *gringo,* but it was pretty bold talk for a Yaqui. It was also buying me some time, so that while he was making similar promises for my future, I actually managed to climb to my feet, as shaky as they might have been. I stood there, swaying and light-headed, rubbing feeling back into my wrists, until he started to wind down. When he finally sputtered out of prophecies, I said: "Where?"

He didn't like me, not one bit, but he was finished making threats, and turned away without answering my question. He took off at a swift walk I couldn't come close to matching in my faltering gait, although I did my best. He was about fifty yards out front when he abruptly turned toward a low-domed wickiup made of willow saplings and arrow weed, held together with plaited yucca leaves. Batting aside an antelope hide hanging over the lodge's entrance, he disappeared inside.

With a destination in sight, I slowed down to have a look around. I didn't see Luis or Abby anywhere, but there was a *ramada* some distance beyond the wickiup where the young Yaqui had disappeared that caught my eye. Several women were sitting in its shade, grinding some kind of grain or nut into flour with a pestle. A number of children were playing in the dirt in front of the open-sided structure, and I felt a huge wave of relief when I recognized Susan among them, wearing a simple *jerga* shift and holding what looked like a grass-stuffed leather doll. She grinned real big when she saw me and started to come over, but one of the women spoke a sharp reprimand, and the girl quickly backed away, her face clouding over as if she wanted to bawl but was afraid to.

I smiled and winked to show her it was all right, and she smiled back. Turning toward the wickiup, I was only peripherally aware of another white child standing in the shadows behind the women, a boy a few years older than Susan, wearing a breechcloth and moccasins. Then I brushed the antelope skin aside and ducked into the darkness.

The wickiup's interior was similar to just about every other Yaqui lodge I'd been in over the years—bigger than it looked from the outside, with rolled-up reed sleeping mats and blankets pushed against the walls, rawhide bags and leather pouches stuffed with food and other belongings hanging from the structure's willow frame. A Krag-Jorgensen rifle, the kind our boys had used so well in Cuba in '98, leaned against a fancy Mexican saddle propped up on its horn, and there was a squat figure sitting behind a small blaze in the middle of the lodge. Staring at the old man's features, cast to a bronze hue by the flickering embers of the fire, I remember thinking: *He hasn't changed much.*

I sat down cross-legged on the man's right, as befitted a guest rather than a prisoner. Old Toad must have been in his sixties by then, an advanced age for a Yaqui in those days, but his resemblance to the amphibian he was named after was as startling as ever. The way he sat enhanced the image—his knees up and out, arms usually folded between them. He had a wide face with heavy jowls and small black eyes that never seemed to blink. The only thing that was really different about him was his hair, a steel-gray now, where it had been only lightly streaked in my youth.

Toad was holding a cigar between the fingers of his left hand that looked vaguely familiar. At first I thought it might have been one of the brands I used to smuggle north across the border, but I couldn't place the name. He continued to study the slim panatela as if I wasn't there, and after a few seconds the young brave who'd cut me loose took the hint and left. When he was gone, Toad spoke.

"You have fared well, White Dog," the old man said without looking up.

I didn't know if that was a question or an observation, although, judging from my bedraggled appearance, I was guessing the former. I didn't reply. Poking a rolled-up piece of heavy paper into the fire, Toad lit the stogie. His movements were slow and deliberate, and he pinched the flame out afterward and set the paper aside for reuse. Closing his eyes in appreciation of the undiluted tobacco—pure leaf was hard to get for a bronco in those days—he drew in a lungful of smoke. He held it for almost a full minute, then tipped his head back to exhale a slim stream of blue toward the ceiling. My eyes followed the pother as it entwined itself in a lattice of arrow weed. Taking a deep breath, Toad brought his gaze back to the fire, as if seeking answers in the pulse of its coals.

"I did not expect you," he confessed after a bit.

"It was not my idea."

"You broke the sacred trust of the Cañon Where the Small Lizards Run."

I winced at that, but wasn't really surprised that he knew. I didn't ask how, figuring he'd just give me some nonsense like a gecko told him. I never understood the Indian way of thinking, but I never bought into its mysticism, either. At the time, it was my punishment for revealing the slot cañon's location to outsiders that had my bowels threatening to turn to water, my knees to jelly.

"The woman, she is yours?"

I hesitated only a moment, then said that she was, hoping both Abby and Susan's situation might be marginally better if Toad thought she was my wife. Of course, I could have just as easily made things worse. Most of the decisions I had to make down there were a crap shoot, at best.

"And the child?"

"She is also mine."

He nodded thoughtfully, though having yet to look directly at me. After taking another drag on the cigar, he began to speak, his words low, almost gentle.

"In a dream, long before you came to live with us, I saw you kill the soldiers who tried to take away the life of my son. Later I saw him rise from the killing ground to become a great warrior of the People. So when you left us that day, I knew the truth of my dream, and that the time had come for you to go back to your own kind. Now my thoughts are like the whirlwind because I did not foresee your return. I don't know if the right thing to do is to kill you as an enemy, or let you live as before."

"You didn't let me live that day at Vaquero Springs," I reminded him. "I stole that Mexican's horse and left before you could make that decision."

Toad considered my argument for a moment. In his own cutthroat way I knew he wanted to do the right thing, to please his spirit guides and his gods. But I also understood his hatred of all white men, and in his mind there was little difference between the Mexicans who had invaded his country from the south and east, and the Americans who came from the north.

"In my dream, you went away after freeing my son." He paused for nearly a minute, then shook his head in indecision.

"I will have to think about this some more," he said, then motioned toward the door. "You are free to go, but not to leave. If you try to run away, the others will hunt you down, and I will not be able to stop them if they decide to end your life."

I nodded silently, knowing there was nothing I could say that would influence the old warrior's decision. He would make up his own mind regarding my fate. I just hoped that d---ed gecko stayed out of it.

Before I left, I leaned over to pick up the piece of paper he'd used to light his cigar. I stuck it in my pocket, then stood and walked out, never having once looked into the old man's eyes, or he into mine.

Excerpted from:

Despots and Dictators—A Detailed Description of
Tyranny Within the United Mexican States

by

Herbert Carlton Matthews

Broken Mill Press

1930

Chapter Seventeen
The Yaqui Solution

[*Ed. Note:* A true understanding of Yaqui/Mexican relations cannot be contained within a single volume, let alone excerpts from
only one source, but a basic understanding of the conflict
between these cultures is necessary to comprehend the mind set
of men like Ghost and Old Toad. For readers who wish to know
more about early Spanish interaction with the Yaqui nation, two
excellent sources of information are Evelyn Hu-DeHart's: *Mis-
sionaries, Miners and Indians: Spanish Contact with the Yaqui Nation of Northwestern New Spain, 1533-1820,* and *Yaqui Resistance
and Survival: The Struggle for Land and Autonomy, 1821-1920.*]

It should be noted that the often contentious entanglement of
these two nations—one native; the other seeking new worlds to

conquer and new wealth to claim—began as soon as the first Spaniard entered the Yaqui River Valley of Sonora in 1533, and was immediately ordered to leave . . . a battle ensued and the Spaniards withdrew, but the lines had been drawn, both figuratively and literally.

Although largely agrarian and fiercely protective of their land, which the Yaquis believed was granted to them by their Creator, their relationship with Spanish authority didn't begin to seriously deteriorate for another two hundred years, when civilians in search of new lands to farm and mineral wealth to mine, began to encroach upon the almost sacred Yaqui River Valley in ever larger numbers . . . [which] resulted in a revolt in 1740 between the Yaqui/Mayo alliance and the invading Spaniards, and the loss of thousands of lives on both sides.

. . . [An] uneasy truce, marred by numerous skirmishes, existed between the two nations for another eighty years, until Mexican independence was won from Spain in 1821 . . ʻ. [after which] further attempts to control the Yaqui tribe led to increased hostilities.

Brutality, always a hallmark of war, marred the conflict in Sonora from beginning to end. [As examples] in 1868, the Army first shelled, then burned, a Catholic church with approximately one hundred and fifty Yaquis inside; in 1903, Yaquis reportedly sawed the feet off of scout "California Dan" Ryan, and made him walk on his bloody stumps until he expired.

Thousands of Yaquis fled to the deserts and mountains during this time, waging guerrilla warfare against the government.

By the end of the 19th Century, [Porfirio] Díaz was rapidly increasing his efforts to modernize the more rural areas of the country . . . [by] openly seeking backers from the United States and Europe who were willing to invest in Mexico's infrastructure. . . .

By 1903, Díaz had grown impatient with the still-warring Yaqui resistance. Viewing it as a major obstacle to the progress he sought, and especially to the development of *Hiakim* [the Yaqui name for their homeland], he initiated what amounted to an eradication policy toward the Yaqui people. In 1904, Sonoran governor Rafael Izábal was ordered to oversee a series of state-wide "round-ups" of the remaining Yaquis . . . [and by] 1909, between ten thousand and fifteen thousand Yaquis had been captured and deported. Some were sent to Bolivia or the United States, but most were sent to other parts of Mexico to work in near slave-like conditions on henequen, sugar cane, and sisal plantations in Yucatán and Oaxaca. An estimated sixty percent of these people died within their first year of confinement due to the harsh, unfamiliar climate and inhumane conditions of these plantations.

SESSION TWENTY

The women were still under the *ramada* when I left Old Toad's wickiup, but the children were gone. Remembering the boy I'd seen in the shadows brought a scowl to my face. Was it possible? I'd caught barely a glimpse of the lad, and at the time I hadn't even considered the prospect of him being Abby's son, but now I wasn't so sure. If it had been him—and, mind you, I wasn't convinced at that point that it was—then where were Del Buchman and the kid's father? Could Old Toad's village have been Ed Davenport's objective all along? I hardly thought so. The Yaquis had never possessed the kind of wealth the old man would demand for his potato diggers. Which meant, perhaps, capture—and, ultimately, torture and death.

Assuming the kid I'd seen was Charles.

Free to roam, I headed for the Río Concepción. Although I'd drunk some yesterday when we reached the river, my thirst had hardly been quenched. Kneeling at its banks with the morning sun just peeking through the mesquite, I scooped handful after handful of cool water down my raw throat. I drank until I thought I was going to vomit, but I still wasn't satisfied. My stomach was full, but it was going to take time to satisfy the rest of my system.

Crossing the shallow stream, I sank to the ground with my back to the soft bank, the sun's rays—the same ones I'd cursed with such passion through the preceding days—warming my still-chilled frame. I was hungry, and would go looking for food soon, but first I wanted to think. I wanted to remember that incident Old Toad had related to me, and review it again from my memory, rather than his.

I was seventeen at the time, and as close to a pure-quill Yaqui as a captive White Eye was ever likely to get. About forty of us had been on a raid along the foothills of the Sierra Madres, far to the east. We were heading home with a dozen plunder-laden pack horses and a couple of prisoners—women we would keep alive and assimilate into the clan, or kill if they resisted too strongly.

We'd skirted the Sabana Valley because of the *Federale* garrison there, but went out of our way to attack the little *rancho* at Vaquero Springs. We wanted the horses we knew the Mexican mustangers would have in their corral, and whatever loot we could find. We hadn't known the soldiers—mounted *Federales*, not Adolpho Castillo's collection of misfits and thieves—were approaching from Sabana until it was too late.

The *Federales* had hit us from the east, much like Alvarez's men had done to Luis and Abby and me, striking our flank with an element of surprise that nearly overwhelmed us. We fell back, but we didn't scatter or make a run for it. We had our booty to protect, you see, culled from isolated homes and tiny villages all along the front range of the Madres. Old Toad sent a handful of boys ahead with the stolen stock, of which I suppose you might consider our captives a part of, while the rest of us hung back to fight a delaying action.

The *Federales* were all over us. They had us outnumbered by at least four to one, and were better armed, to boot. We couldn't hold out for long, and we knew it. All we wanted to do was keep the soldiers off balance, keep our own retreat organized. We would break apart, then come together again a few hundred yards down the trail, little pockets of resistance the Mexicans couldn't contain. Like stinging wasps, we'd hit them from every side, then duck back into the chaparral before they could mount a counterattack.

I didn't have any doubts about what my fate would be if the Mexican soldiers caught me. I might have started out a captive, but I'd be a warrior in their eyes. Nor would it help that I was carrying an old single-shot muzzleloading rifle taken off a California-bound immigrant the Yaquis had captured and butchered many years before. I hadn't killed anyone with it, but that was only because I hadn't needed to. If faced with the choice, I would have pulled the trigger without deliberation—it was a pretty nebulous line I walked in those days.

We were probably forty-five minutes into the fighting when the soldiers finally overran us, and, for a while there, it was chaos everywhere you turned. Powder smoke hung over the battlefield in a tattered, swirling fog, and men and horses were screaming and dying on every side. I got separated from the others, and out of the blue it occurred to me that an opportunity for escape could finally be at hand. Warrior or not, I'd never given up on the idea of someday making my way back to my own people.

There were soldiers everywhere, but none that seemed to be paying me any special attention, so with my heart pounding at my ribs, I took off for the chaparral. I'd just about made it when I heard yelling from behind me. Fearing the worst, I spun around and dropped to one knee, shouldering the old caplock with practiced ease. I figured I'd been had for sure, but it was Old Toad's son, Slayer, who they'd brought to bay.

There were at least four *Federales* on top of Slayer, and I knew he wouldn't last long against those odds. A Mexican hates a Yaqui about as much as a Yaqui hates a Mexican, and those soldiers had blood in their eyes. For a moment I just kneeled there, staring. You've heard the term . . . *frozen with indecision?*

That was me. The chaparral was beckoning. I could be in it and out of sight within seconds, and not a soul to stop me, but Slayer . . . well, he wasn't really a friend, not by *gringo* standards, but he was as close to one as I'd had in my years among the Yaquis. I'd trained alongside him under Old Toad's tutelage, and we'd developed a guarded respect for one another's abilities, if not a brotherly affection. There's not a doubt in my mind that if I'd abandoned him that day, he would have been dead before I reached the chaparral.

Deciding to go back wasn't a conscious choice. Fact is, I don't know that it was a choice at all; it's just what I did. Yelling a frustrated curse that could have easily been mistaken for a war cry, I bolted toward where Slayer and the troopers were fighting hand-to-hand. I don't recall now if I was screaming in Yaqui, Spanish, or English, but I do know the sounds I was making that day were coming from my soul.

I fired on the run and my ball flew true, spinning a hapless soldier out of my way and opening a path into the center of the brawl. One of the soldiers on top of Slayer saw me coming and shouted a warning. He was a short, broad-shouldered man with lank black hair sweat-plastered across his forehead, a huge ebony mustache nearly obscuring his mouth. He rushed to meet me with a bull-like roar, but I deflected the downward blur of his saber with my rifle, then drove its butt into his paunch. He dropped to his knees with a wheezing screech, and I lifted the rifle above my head and brought it down like a club. I can still hear the ripe-melon thunk of the steel butt plate connecting with the soldier's skull, the look of astonishment on his face as he crumpled at my feet.

With a crazy, garbled yell, I jumped over the dead soldier and slammed into the two *Federales* still struggling with Slayer. Swinging my rifle like a bat, I caught the taller of the two troopers on the back of his neck and dropped him like bucket of hot coals. He fell as the first two had, with a startled grunt and a look of utter surprise.

Slayer was wiggling out from beneath the fourth soldier by the time I got there. The *Federale* was already dead from several powerful knife thrusts to his chest, but Slayer was also badly injured. Blood had soaked his shirt a dark crimson, and a gash running from his eyebrow all the way down and across his jaw was deep enough that I could see his teeth through the laceration.

Although our own battle had been won, the fighting continued. It rolled back over us in clouds of dust and débris, kicked up by the shod hoofs of the troopers' mounts. My route into the chaparral was cut off by a dozen or more *Federales,* their sabers glinting in the sunlight as they hacked at the swarming Yaquis.

I grabbed Slayer by the arm and yanked him to his feet. We couldn't stay where we were, but there were an awful lot of *soldados* between us and where Old Toad was fighting with a large contingent of his warriors. My rifle had been lost in the fray, but I spotted another not too far away. Briefly leaving Slayer to fend for himself, I made a dash for the gun. It was a double-barreled shotgun, its battered stock decorated with brass tacks in a series of whirling wind designs. [*Ed. Note:* The "whirling wind" pattern Latham references here is probably the swastika, an ancient symbol of power, strength, and good fortune that has been used by numerous cultures around the world for more than three thousand years; its current negative connotation stems from its more recent adaptation by Nazi Germany, under Adolf Hitler's Third Reich.]

Snatching it from the ground, I turned back just in time to see a knot of *Federales* spurring their horses toward us. I shouted a warning to Slayer, then threw the shotgun to my shoulder and tripped the hammer on the left-hand barrel. I'd been more than a little concerned that the gun might be empty, but its shoulder-rocking kick dispelled that fear.

If that first round proved fatal to anyone, it had to have happened later on, because it sure didn't unhorse anybody at the time. Still, it was a good shot. Three of the troopers hollered loudly as they grabbed at their faces and shoulders, slapping at the peppering sting of the lead shot.

The charge from the left-hand barrel slowed the Mexicans' assault, but it didn't stop it. Two of the soldiers who had been galloping toward Slayer and me escaped the blast entirely, and were frantically spurring toward our position. I fired again, and by then the Mexicans were close enough to absorb the bulk of the shot. The nearest rider screamed as his right arm blossomed red from shoulder to elbow, while the soldier next to him was sent tumbling from his saddle. The second man's horse went down with its rider, the trooper hanging up in the stirrup, then tangling himself with the animal's legs, causing the horse to fall hard only a few yards away.

Although badly wounded, Slayer instinctively threw himself at the first horseman, the one with the pulpy arm. Dragging him from his saddle, Slayer pinned the man to the ground with a single plunge of his blade. The trooper cried out once, the sound shrill but short. Staggering to his feet, Slayer headed for the second horseman, but the youth's wounds were finally catching up with him. His knees buckled and he might have gone down if I hadn't grabbed him. Slipping a shoulder under the Yaqui's midsection, I headed for the first trooper's horse. Slayer struggled briefly, then abruptly went limp, for which I was grateful. Grabbing the animal's reins, I was trying to heave the injured warrior across the saddle when he unexpectedly regained consciousness.

"Put me down," he yelled weakly. "Let me die as a man."

"Shut up and get on this horse," I grunted, shrugging him,

belly first, over the saddle. "Go help the others. Your responsibility is to the People and their protection, not to collect more scalps for your wickiup."

"You are a coward, White Dog. I spit on your bow."

"Go spit on someone else's bow," I snapped, suddenly out of patience with the whole Yaqui experience. "Go on, go help the others before it is too late."

I got Slayer's leg over the saddle, then slapped the horse's rump with the flat of my hand. It wasn't much of a blow, but it didn't take much, as jumpy as it was. As the horse bolted toward its new life as a Yaqui, I could still hear Slayer's sibilant battle cry, all the more pitiful for the way he clung to the saddle horn with both hands, tossing like a rag in the wind.

That was the last I saw of Slayer, and good riddance was my thought at the time. I walked over to where the second horse was still on its side in the dirt, the *Federale*'s leg pinned beneath it. He was hanging onto the reins, and had the animal's head pulled so far around its muzzle was nearly touching the cinch. I think even as seriously injured as the trooper was, he understood that if he lost his horse, his life would soon follow. I didn't care, and kicked him hard in the face. He let go of the reins and the horse lunged to its feet, the trooper spilling free.

I grabbed the reins and pulled the horse around. The space between me and the chaparral had opened up again, a bare but bloody piece of earth, marred only by the litter of the battle— military hats and guidons, a crushed bugle, a dead horse, a handful of discarded weapons I wouldn't take time to search through. The heart of the fighting had moved to the west, maybe two hundred desert-hardened warriors, some of them in dusty uniforms splotchy with blood, others nearly naked, fighting to preserve their homeland.

And within the midst of the battle was the hate-twisted face of the Yaqui's war chief. Old Toad had stepped away from the swirling dust and confusion, and was standing quietly with a Mexican saber in one hand, a revolver in the other. The warrior's eyes were fixed on me as if welded there. I think he knew I was going to run before I did, and I was almost certain he'd try to kill me first. After three long years there was no love lost between us, no unexpected moment of warmth. To me, Toad had never been anything other than pure evil. Then the old cutthroat swung back into the fighting as if I didn't exist, and I climbed onto my confiscated steed and raced out of there as fast as that horse could carry me.

Six days later, both of us more dead than alive, we arrived in Nogales in the chill of an early December evening. I was wearing a *Federale*'s jacket and spare shirt, cotton trousers the Yaquis favored in cooler weather, and moccasins worn nearly through from all the miles I'd walked, leading my horse and trying to keep both of us alive in that harsh wilderness.

And after all that, here I was, once again sitting on the banks of the Río Concepción, still trying to understand that wily old man's thinking. Had he really seen me in a dream before I'd been captured? I doubted it. Toad had another motive in mind. I just didn't know what it was.

Feeling more restless than rested, I pushed to my feet and returned to the village. The sun was well up by then, the wide street, if you want to call it that, busy with people. I was keenly aware of the hostile gazes that followed me, the distrust and hatred that dogged my every step.

I went to the *ramada* where I'd seen Susan and the white boy earlier, but they were no longer around. I didn't really expect them. More than likely they were being hidden somewhere, which is what the Yaquis usually did when there were strangers in their village. Hide the captives and the plunder, and profess their innocence to anyone stupid enough to . . . wow, there's that anger again. I don't guess it will ever totally go away, but I won't dwell on it.

There was a stew of some kind bubbling in an iron kettle on the fire, and tortillas warming on a large flat stone next to it. I didn't wait for an invitation, having learned during my earlier captivity to either help myself or starve. Squatting nearby, I spooned a concoction of meat, wild onions, and squash onto a tortilla and started shoveling it down my gullet. The women had discreetly vanished when I walked in, which suited me just fine. I ate my fill, and I'm not ashamed to admit that kettle was considerably lighter when I finally walked away. I was heading toward the center of the village when the kid who had cut me loose that morning stepped into my path. I stopped warily, expecting trouble, but he was only there to deliver a message.

"Grandfather has made his decision. He wishes to speak with you."

Grandfather? My eyes narrowed as I studied the youth's features. As far as I knew, Old Toad had only the one child, Slayer. Could this be Slayer's son, or was the boy merely showing respect for an older warrior's wisdom and leadership?

I followed the young man silently—it would have been rude of me to ask about his father straight-out—and ducked through the entrance to the lodge. This time the kid left immediately, pulling the antelope covering over the door to afford us some privacy.

Old Toad was sitting in the same spot as before, and motioned me to a place on his right, which I took as a good sign. I sank down cross-legged, studying the old man's profile in the dim light.

"You have eaten?"

I nodded, surprised by the question.

"I saw the way you were studying my grandson. You wonder if he is the son of my son?"

"They look the same."

"That is because he is who you think he is."

I felt a peculiar sadness creep through me. "You haven't mentioned his name," I remarked, knowing he probably wouldn't if Slayer was dead.

Toad nodded, almost sadly, I thought, then dismissed the possibility. Old Toad wasn't capable of those kinds of emotion.

"When did he cross to the Other Side?" I asked quietly.

"In the battle with the soldiers at the *rancho*."

Something in my reaction must have given away my surprise. Toad finally looked up, our eyes meeting for the first time.

"It was the wounds he received from the soldiers," the old man explained. "But because of you, I was able to bring him home, and the soldiers did not cut away his scalp or mutilate his body." He sighed loudly, and his gaze dropped back to the whispering flames of the fire. "For a long time after you left, after my son went away, I wondered about my dream. I wondered what it meant when I saw him rising from the field afterward to become a great warrior. I finally decided that my son is still fighting, leading his people in the land on the Other Side, where I will someday go to meet him. He would not be able to do that if his body had been desecrated, and so my prophecy was correct. For that reason, White Dog, I have decided that you may leave our village and return to the land above the line that only the Mexicans can see." [*Ed. Note:* Old Toad is referring to the International Border between the United States and Mexico here.]

Toad was watching me with the smile of an iron-fisted patriarch handing out gifts at Christmas. His offer seemed generous enough, but I suspected treachery. I always anticipated the worst where that old butcher was concerned.

"And the woman and our children?"

He started to reply, then hesitated as the meaning of my

words reached him.

"The boy is also mine," I stated flatly. "The one I saw with the girl this morning."

Old Toad shook his head. "There is no boy, and the woman and girl are to remain here." He sounded irritated that I wasn't satisfied with my own life, and I guess he had a point. D---ed few white men ever got the kind of gift Old Toad was offering me, not among the Dead Horses.

"The woman and children are mine, as is the Mexican called Luis. I will have them before I leave."

The old Indian's eyes narrowed dangerously. "You demand much for a man with nothing to barter."

I didn't reply at first. Then for some reason I remembered the rifle, still propped against the Mexican saddle. Rising, I walked over to pick it up. Toad smiled derisively as I turned back to the fire.

"My death will only bring about your own," he asserted calmly. "There are but a few bullets for that rifle, yet a thousand arrows for a hundred bows. You will be hunted down and killed."

"I am not seeking your death," I replied, returning to my seat with the Krag across my lap.

Old Toad's thin brows furrowed as I drew a figure in the dirt between us, a circle with the initials *REM-UMC* in the top arch, and in the rocker, *.30 USA*. Working the side-action bolt, I extracted a live round that landed at the old man's feet. Sitting the rifle aside, I picked up the cartridge and turned the base toward him so that he could see the headstamp. I knew he couldn't read the letters, or have any idea what they meant, but he could see that they were the same as in my drawing.

"These markings identify the cartridge as belonging to this rifle," I said, my finger tracing the letters and numbers in the brass. "You say you have only a few, but I know where there are many, all of them identical to this one. There are thousands, as many as the stars in the sky."

Taking the cartridge from my fingers, Toad turned it over slowly, as if really seeing it for the first time. In the past he'd simply mated a cartridge to a rifle based on the shape and size of the round. I don't think it had ever occurred to him that there might be other ways of determining a cartridge's fit.

"As many as the stars in the sky?"

"Guns, too," I said, remembering the Remington carbines we'd left among the dead. The cartridges, of course, were the crates of ammunition Luis and I had tossed over the side of the cliff, the .30-40 Krag rounds used in Davenport's machine-guns, but which would also fit Toad's rifle.

The old Indian was watching me closely, searching for any hint of deceit. I met his gaze evenly, waiting for his decision.

"Where?" he finally asked.

"For the woman and children."

"The woman only. The child we have need of."

I shook my head. "The woman and both children and the Mexican."

Toad eyed the fire silently for several minutes. I didn't speak, knowing better than to disturb his ruminations. Finally he pushed creakily to his feet—showing his age, I thought—and told me to come along.

We exited the lodge and Toad paused to face the still-hazy light of the sun, breathing deeply of the mesquite-tinged air. "It is good to live," he murmured, then turned to me with a wry smile. "You should not be so eager to give that up, White Dog."

"I am not," I replied coolly.

We headed east toward the rising sun—downwind, it would later occur to me. Leaving the river's influence, the mesquite and willows soon petered out and the landscape turned hot and dry, studded with cactus. Just outside the village we came to a clearing, and it was as if my heart slammed into my throat, choking off my wind. Half a dozen Yaqui men were standing around, casually talking and smoking. Occasionally one of them would go check on three figures staked to the flinty soil. Old Toad led me to the nearest one first. I recognized Ed Davenport, though just barely, as the Yaquis had been working on him for a while.

I'm not going to take any pleasure in telling you this, but like some of the other things I've mentioned, it's important for you to understand exactly what happened down there, what the options were, if you want to understand the decisions I made.

Ed was stripped naked and spread-eagled, and someone had built a small fire at his side, its blaze turning the skin along his lower ribs black, the flesh peeling back like the hide on a piece of pork left too long in a skillet. But that's not why they built the fire there. I think it was just a matter of convenience, like a doctor keeping his tools close by during an operation.

In addition to the deep searing along Davenport's ribs, hot coals had been placed between the toes of his bare feet, and a single coal, as big around as a man's fist, had been inserted inside his mouth and his jaws tied shut. I saw that because the sizzling burl had burned a silver dollar-sized hole in the man's cheek.

There were other holes containing burned-out cinders and gray ash—in his stomach and along both thighs, and at the base of his neck. There were cuts everywhere, little slices of skin peeled off and probably fed to the dogs—I'd seen them do that. Other wounds had been left raw and open. His fingers had been pulled back and broken, and coals had been added to each nostril.

The worst part was that he was still alive. Not by much—I doubt if he would have recognized me if I'd spoken to him—but his chest was rising and falling in irregular spasms, although I suspect his capacity to feel pain had long since dissolved.

That was probably why the Yaquis had moved on to their next victim. They'd been working on him for a while, too, although Del's features had yet to be so altered that I couldn't identify him. Someone had cut away his eyelids, allowing the sun to boil the orbs to a gray mush. They'd also broken both shins so that the jagged ends of the bones were jutting obscenely in different directions. They'd just started the skinning process, but hadn't yet gotten to the fire.

Del was still feeling the pain; like rats chewing at his every nerve, it was stripping away his sanity in thin layers.

When Old Toad motioned toward the third figure, the chill I'd felt along my spine when I saw Ed and Del turned into a river of ice. Luis Vega was stretched out farthest from the village, and looked like he'd been there since we were brought in the day before. The green rawhide they'd used on his arms and legs was still drying in the sun, pulling tighter with every passing hour. His face and torso was swirled with bruises, and there were already a few small cuts along his legs. But the Yaquis hadn't really started torturing him, not seriously. Of course part of his torment, as I knew it had been for Del, was the anticipation, watching the Indians work on other prisoners and getting an idea of what was in store.

I'd lived among the Yaquis for three years, and I'd seen this more than once. The first time—a *vaquero*—had turned me nearly numb, until I'd thought I might be the one to lose my mind. By the time I left, I still hadn't become used to it, but I no longer became physically ill after witnessing a three- or four-day session of cruciation. Like I've said before, torture was a part of the Dead Horses' culture, a means of extracting a portion of their enemies' strength, while also making sure to cripple the man's spirit on the Other Side. The side where Slayer was even then doing battle, if what Old Toad believed was true.

Luis watched my approach with a look of abject acceptance,

but no recrimination, for which I've always somehow felt guilty. He'd wanted to fight when Ghost first stepped out of the brush, but I'd nixed the idea, believing we stood a better chance if we surrendered. Now Luis was about to pay a horrible price for my mistake, and there wasn't a d---ed thing I could do to stop it. As far as my negotiations were concerned, Luis Vega was off the table.

"How do I know you are telling the truth about the bullets?" Toad asked softly.

Staring into Luis's eyes, I said: "You know I would not lie to you. Have I ever?"

Toad thought about my reply for a moment, but I knew he'd eventually have to concede the truth of my words. I'd hated the man, but I'd never lied to him.

"How many guns?"

I held up all ten fingers four times—forty guns, more or less, counting carbines and revolvers. The Colt-Brownings had been destroyed in their long fall off the top of the bluff, and would be useless to the Dead Horses.

"And the bullets?"

"As many as the stars."

He nodded, satisfied at last. "Your life I have already given to you. For the guns and the bullets, I will trade the woman and both children. But not the Mexican. He belongs to the People, and will pay for the many wrongs his tribe has caused us."

Ignoring the watching Indians, I told Luis about the trade. I spoke in Spanish, which I knew Toad understood, so that the old war chief wouldn't think I was trying anything underhanded. When I finished, I said: "I am sorry, *amigo.*"

"*De nada.* It is for the *niña* and her *madrecita.*"

"And the *niño.* The boy is also here."

Luis nodded. He understood. My decision had been the only one I could've made, the situation being what it was. I started to turn away, but Luis called me back.

"Don't leave me like this, J.T.," he said in English.

I swallowed hard but didn't reply. He knew I didn't have a choice. What did he expect me to do, slip him in my pocket before I left? I started toward the village, but his voice reeled me back.

"J.T.!"

"God d---it," I practically shouted. "There ain't nothing I can do!"

But there was. Luis's gaze dropped to the bullet-shredded vest that hung limply from my gaunt frame, his eyes pleading, and my mouth turned to cotton. At my side, Old Toad watched in fascination. He didn't know about the semi-auto that still resided within the lining of my vest; it had been there for so long I was barely conscious of it myself.

"For the love of God, *hombre*, you know what they are going to do to me. *Finish the job!*"

And that, finally, was what it all came down to. Finishing the job.

I turned to Toad, my voice harsh. "Our deal is completed, is it not? I will tell you where to find the guns and ammunition, and then I will take the woman and children and go."

He nodded suspiciously, his distrust returning when Luis and I began speaking in English. "The Mexican stays," he said.

"Yes, the Mexican stays." Then I told him where to find the munitions. I told him about the dead *soldados* under José Alvarez's command that we had left on the battlefield, and that seemed to please him. He knew the place I was talking about, and told me he had killed a jaguar along that very bluff when he was a young man, not much older than his grandson.

"You are satisfied?" I asked when our conversation came to an end.

"Yes. The woman and children are waiting at the *ramada* with a horse and some food. Go there and get them. My people will not stop you."

I nodded stiffly, then walked over to where Luis was lying on his back with his eyes closed. His lips were moving rapidly in what I assumed was a prayer. I didn't dare risk giving him time to finish. With my back to the Toad, I drew the semi-auto from the lining of my vest, rocked the hammer to full cock, and pulled the trigger.

So now you know, and I guess soon enough the rest of the world will, too. I . . . I asked you this question once before, when I told you how I wouldn't let Luis kill Spencer McKenzie. Now I'm going to ask it again. Am I a hero, or a coward? A saint or a sinner? Was what I did an act of mercy, or murder? I'd like to know, because I've lived with that d---ed question since the day I walked away from Luis Vega's body, past Old Toad's stunned face to find Abby and Charles and Susan and take them home.

SESSION TWENTY-ONE

Old Toad had lied . . . somewhat. There was no horse waiting for us at the *ramada,* but Abby and the kids were there, and Charles was looking a heck of a lot better than the last time I'd seen him.

Not knowing how Toad or the others would react to my killing Luis, taking away something that was important to them in a way most *gringos* could never understand, I didn't want to push my luck by demanding a mount. There was a canvas water bag hanging from one of the *ramada*'s posts, dripping fresh from the Río Concepción, and I grabbed it and tossed it to Abby and told her to bring it along.

"What's happening?" she asked, obviously surprised to see me.

"Just take the god d---ed water bag and your kids and start walking," I replied in such a cutting manner I think she might have actually blanched. She was a swift-thinking woman, though, and didn't take offense or ask a bunch of foolish questions. Slinging the bag's strap over her shoulder, she swung Susan onto her hip with one hand and grabbed Charles with the other, practically yanking him along as she followed me out of the village.

I'd picked out a spot on the horizon just about due north of the *ramada,* and headed for it in swift, purposeful strides. When Abby tried to come up beside me, I barked for her to stay back.

"Get behind me and keep your eyes on the ground," I

snapped, and she immediately complied.

I had no doubts that we were being watched. I could feel the cold eyes of the People fixed on us like gunsights, but I didn't look back, or reveal any inclination I might have had to run. Not even when a howl of rage engulfed the village as word of my treachery spread through the community.

We crossed the Concepción about a mile north of the village and continued on in as straight of a line as that scabrous terrain would allow. After about five miles of steady tramping, I veered west toward the Sea of Cortez. A hard push for Arizona was out of the question now. Without horses, we'd never get close. But we'd been moving more west than north ever since leaving Sabana, and I knew we couldn't be far from the Gulf. There weren't any real towns along the coast that I knew of, but there used to be a few trading posts and fishing camps, and I was hoping we might find one of those, and that it would be inhabited.

We kept moving for another couple of hours before I finally ordered a stop. Abby promptly sank to the ground, then scuttled into the mostly illusionary shade of a Wait-a-Minute bush, pulling her kids in with her. I remained on my feet, staring back the way we'd come. The land in that part of Sonora is about as flat as the bottom of a skillet, and, if not for the chaparral, I'm pretty sure I could have still seen the Yaqui village. Or at least the low rise of land it sat on. Instead my view was limited to thorny scrub and cactus. I knew it wouldn't be difficult for a few hotheads to slip out on the sly and come after us, but an instinct honed by years of smuggling beer and tobacco into the American markets told me that we weren't being followed. Toad had given his word that we wouldn't be molested, and I felt confident the People would honor the old man's promise— whether they agreed with it or not.

I don't know how much you want to hear about the next few

days. They weren't very exciting compared with what we'd already been through, although they were certainly death-defying. In spite of all the hardships we'd endured since leaving Arizona, none of it really compared to that last sixty or so miles to the Gulf.

Just so you know, I'd told Abby to stay behind me with the kids and the water because that was the proper position for a woman of the Dead Horse clan, but once we started for the coast in earnest, things returned to normal. Abby still walked behind me most of the way, but that was only because I was following the path of least resistance, and she was following me. She kept her kids close the whole way. I think after nearly losing them to the Yaquis, she would have chained them to her if she could have.

Those were good kids, Charles and Susan, but they weren't Yaqui. They lacked the stamina of a desert-born people. They did OK that first day, and even into the second, but by the third day it was as if they'd hit a brick wall. They couldn't go on, and Abby and I weren't doing much better. She was carrying Susan almost constantly by then, and I had Charles with me, riding on my shoulders. The water bag was empty, and the few tortillas Abby had managed to snatch on her way out of the *ramada* had long since been consumed.

By the fourth day our situation was getting desperate. We'd been crossing one sandy swell after another since dawn, trudging numbly forward under a cloudy sky, when all of a sudden I heard Abby stumble and fall. I staggered to a halt, took a moment to be sure of my balance, then slowly turned. Charles swayed limply above me, barely hanging on. Abby lay curled on her side, while Susan crawled around her as if looking for a niche to snuggle up in, something safe and familiar.

Very carefully, so that I didn't end up on the ground at Abby's side, I eased Charles from my shoulders. He immediately dropped down beside his mother. His eyes were closed and his lips were parted, and I thought his breathing seemed shallow and maybe a little irregular. I wanted to tell Abby of my concerns for him, but she wouldn't have heard me.

For a long time, maybe ten minutes or so, I stood there in an indecisive daze of my own. A voice in my head was urging me to keep walking, insisting that I'd done all I could, and that I needed to think about my own safety. But something else was probing at my brain, like the niggling sensation of a fly walking across your face when you're trying to nap. I turned to the west. A breeze rustled the limbs of a burro bush at my side, and a brackish odor toyed with my sinuses. From somewhere up ahead I heard a faint but rhythmic pounding. When I finally realized what it was, I told Abby to get on her feet.

"Come on," I croaked around a tongue that felt twice its normal size. "We've made it." When she didn't respond, I nudged her with my toe. "Come on, now, we're almost there." She still didn't move, and I kicked her lightly on the hip, loosening an unintelligible mumble, but nothing else. Running out of patience, I hoarsely shouted: "D--- it, woman, get up!" Then I kicked her harder. That time she groaned as the pain wormed through the dehydration and exhaustion blanketing her mind. Her eyelids fluttered open, and her gaze kind of wandered over to settle on my face.

"We're there," I said. "Just a little farther."

For a moment she stared at me as she might a stranger, and I wondered what I'd do if she refused to go on. Then she sat up and looked around as if awakening from a deep sleep. "Where?" she asked in a voice nearly as unrecognizable as my own, and I motioned vaguely to the west.

"Over yonder."

She thought about my reply for a moment, then struggled to her feet. It was just about all she could do to pick up Susan, and it didn't occur to me until she already had the girl in her arms that I could have helped. Like I said, I was feeling more than a little off-plumb myself.

Being careful not to lose my balance, I gathered Charles in my arms, then slung him over my shoulder like a sack of grain. After a glance at Abby to assure myself that she was ready, we struck out across the low dunes, pushing forward one slow, dragging step at a time. Twenty minutes later we were standing ankle-deep in the Sea of Cortez, staring up the coast toward a rambling collection of adobe shacks and brush-and-mud *jacales*.

"Mister Latham," Abby rasped. "I believe we have made it."

SESSION TWENTY-TWO

I just got off the phone with Iowa Electric. The guy said the outage was caused by ice dragging down a power line, but they've got it fixed. I'm just glad it didn't hurt your Dictaphone.

We don't normally get a lot of power failures out here, but it's been a bad storm. I checked the thermometer and it's thirteen degrees outside, which is funny, because before the electricity went out, I would have sworn it was the hottest part of summer. I guess that's what happens when you get too deep into your memories.

Those buildings Missus Davenport and I saw, they belonged to a German named Hans Gruder, who traded with the Seris. The Seris were a coastal tribe that used to hunt and fish throughout that region, and kept the Yaquis mostly inland, along the riverways.

We stayed with Gruder for nearly a week, recuperating under the able care of his Seri wife Lola. We'd been lucky after leaving Toad's village in that the sky had remained overcast the whole way, shielding us from the worst of the sun. If not for that, I don't think we would have made it.

Gruder had a flagpole in front of his trading post, and would run a triangular red pennant to its top when he wanted to flag a passing ship. That's how we caught a ride on a stern-wheeler called the *San Angelo,* six days after stumbling into Gruder's post more dead than alive.

Other than the lingering effects from the sun, we were all looking halfway decent by the time we boarded the *San Angelo*. I was freshly shaved, recently bathed, and decked out in a new suit of clothes that Gruder sent a bill along for, and which Abby promised to make good on when we got back to the States. Because her face was still peeling, she insisted on wearing a veil to hide her features from the other passengers, although no one seemed to care. They were fascinated by our tale of desert survival, but likely would have been appalled, if not outraged, had they known what we left out. Three days later we docked at Yuma, the prison sitting on the hill above town like an accusing eye. Or at least that was my take on it.

If you're wondering how Missus Davenport and I got along after our return to civilization, it was probably about what you'd expect if you aren't romantically inclined. I reckon Abby had a lot of emotional garbage to sort through, and kept mostly to herself. From what I heard, she seldom let her children out of her sight. As soon as she got in, she telephoned her family in New York and had them wire her funds to take care of her needs while in Arizona, which included a suite of rooms at the Riverside Hotel. She also tried to pay me a reward for rescuing her and the kids, but I refused. I guess I had my own baggage to deal with.

Last night while we were waiting for the electricity to come back on, you asked me to think about some of the things I've left hanging—like why Old Toad allowed me to walk away after I shot Luis, and why he didn't punish me for revealing the location of the Cañon Where the Small Lizards Run—but I've already said I never understood an Indian's way of thinking, and that especially applied to Toad. Still, I've thought about it over the years, and I've come to some conclusions that may or may not be anywhere near the truth.

The deal Old Toad had made with me was that in exchange

for the information on the munitions, I'd get to leave with Abby and the kids, but I'd also have to leave Luis behind—and that's what I did. That I'd also cheated the Dead Horses out of their fun, not to mention whatever spiritual gains the clan might have harvested from Luis's torture and death . . . well, I always figured Old Toad admired my audacity for that. I'd beat him at his own game, so to speak. It was something the old cut-throat might have done himself, and I think it kind of made him proud that I'd pulled the same stunt on him, made him feel like he'd done right in my training.

As far as the Cañon Where the Small Lizards Run, it's true I'd revealed its location to others, but the only person left alive by then—if you don't count what remained of Ed Davenport or Del Buchman—was Charles, and, despite his claims to the contrary, I don't think Toad wanted anything to do with the boy. Charles Davenport's name comes up in the newspapers every once in a while, and he's a pretty sharp politician from what I can tell, but back then he was still walking in that shadowy land between the living and the dead, and that had the Yaquis spooked. H---, it had me spooked, if you recall.

Spencer McKenzie died there in the Cañon Where the Small Lizards Run, I'm convinced of that, but I don't know what became of Felix Perez. I never saw or heard of him again. I doubt if he survived, but who can say? He was a tough ol' bird, I know that. [*Ed. Note:* A Felix Perez was located in an Internet search as having been sentenced in Guaymas, Sonora, on February 6, 1909, to life in the Federal Penitentiary at Islas Marías for the murders of Fillipe and Joséfina Cartol; there was no way to confirm if this is the same Felix Perez of whom Latham speaks.]

If you're wondering what Ed Davenport and Del Buchman were up to when they cached their munitions at the escarpment, your guess would be as good as mine. I'd always assumed

Davenport had another buyer lined up somewhere, but I don't know who it was, or where they were supposed to meet. Unless you've run across something I haven't, I suppose that's a mystery that will never be solved. Not that I've ever tried.

After saying good bye to Abby Davenport, I hopped a Southern Pacific freight train heading east. It wasn't the first train I ever hoboed, having left Holbrook the same way in '87. You might think my circumstances dire, but they weren't. I still had the semi-auto Selma Metzler had given me—and no, I didn't go see her before leaving Yuma that last time—and I also had my pardon, only partially burned when Old Toad had used it to light his cigar that day on the Río Concepción. Both Del's signature and the governor's were still legible, and I had the document checked by an attorney a few years later just to reassure myself that it was legal. It is, and I've got it locked away in a fireproof safe right now, if some government official runs across this transcript and wants to see it.

I left the S.P. at Tucson, then hitched a ride south in a Model A Ford that had been cut down into a delivery truck. The driver was hauling a load of oranges to Nogales, where I used to outfit from, back in my smuggling days. And if you're wondering, h--- yeah, I talked him into letting me get behind the wheel. The novelty of operating a motor vehicle had long since worn off for him, but it never has for me.

In Nogales I looked up a man named Esteban Rivera, who ran a small livery down in the Mexican part of town where I used to stable my horse and burros. His jaw just about hit the floor when I walked in, but I told him he didn't have anything to worry about. Esteban had sold my stock when I was sentenced to a twelve-year stretch in Yuma, and I don't guess he'd heard of my release. Not many folks had at that time. Anyway, he figured I'd come back for the money he'd gotten for my animals and all the gear, the pack saddles and panniers and such, but that wasn't why I was there.

"You keep that money," I told him. "Use it to repair your stable wall."

He looked puzzled by my suggestion, and followed at a distance as I walked to the rear wall where I used to store my goods before taking them south into Mexico. Using a grubbing hoe, I tore out a section of adobe until I came to a metal box buried inside. I'd put it there late one night after Esteban had gone home to his wife and kids, then hidden the repaired wall behind a broken pack saddle until the mud dried. Inside the box was a fully loaded snub-nosed revolver, a leather poke containing $200 in gold and silver coins, and a bank book wrapped in oilcloth. Wishing Esteban a long and prosperous life, I walked over to the Central Bank of Nogales and withdrew my entire savings—more than $8,000 that I took in small bills.

I got a shave and a bath and a better set of duds than the one Gruder had sold me, and was on my way to the Grand Hotel, one of the better establishments in town at the time, when I saw the guy I'd hitched the ride south with. He was cranking on the Ford's engine like he was just about cranked out, sweat-soaked and gasping but too bull-headed to quit or try to think the problem through. I asked if he was having trouble, and received a reply vicious enough to strike sparks off a stone fence.

"Want to sell it?" I asked.

He paused, leaning against the radiator to keep from falling over, and glared at me for probably a full minute. "Yeah, I'll sell the son-of-a-b----, if you're dumb enough to want it."

"I want it," I said simply

I ended up forking over $300 for the modified Ford. It seemed like a heck of a deal to me, although Ford would introduce its Model T to the public the following year for less new than what I paid for the Model A used. Still, I never regretted buying the A. Truth is, I wish I still had it.

Instead of getting a room at the Grand, I got an outfit for camping—a tent and blankets and cooking gear—plus four five-gallon cans of gasoline and a gallon of motor oil and some basic tools—a set of wrenches, screwdrivers, and pliers, that kind of stuff. After strapping everything down in the A's bed, I went to a grocery and bought enough food to last me a week. I left the A where it was while I did my shopping, and, when I got back, I started fiddling with the various knobs and gears and levers as I'd seen Spence and Abby do. I had the auto running on the sixth crank, while the guy I bought it from stood in the door of a nearby saloon shooting daggers my way.

Not sure of the legality of my pardon at the time, I decided not to hang around Arizona. I followed the old Butterfield Stage route east to Silver City, New Mexico Territory, then turned north. I motored through Albuquerque and Santa Fe, then over Raton Pass into Trinidad, Colorado. I just kept driving, moving from place to place and seeing the sights—Pike's Peak and Yellowstone National Park and the site where Custer and his men were wiped out by the Sioux. I went east and saw Chicago and St. Louis and New Orleans, then wound back north in the face of autumn. Winter caught me in Davenport. I've been here ever since.

End Transcript

Great Plains Racing Journal
Vol. 10, No. 6, 1957
The Rallying Point
by
Bill Macklin

Rarely have I faced these pages with the degree of melancholy I feel today, having just learned from my good friend, Jason Terhoure, that the automotive world lost one of its pioneers yesterday. James "J.T." Latham, 82, was killed when his souped-up 1953 Ford Coupe, "Fast Fawn", lost control on the second turn at the Three Hills Race Track outside of Moline, Illinois, on May 17[th.]

Latham, of Davenport, Iowa, was racing on a closed track when witnesses said it appeared as if the steering mechanism on his recently rebuilt coupe suddenly locked up about halfway through the second bend of the famed "Moline S" and spun into the fence. Terhoure, who witnessed the accident along with other automotive specialists and racing fans, told me that Latham was taken to the hospital in Moline, where he was pronounced dead at 3:30 p.m.

For those of you who never had the pleasure of meeting J.T., be assured that his reputation as a "gentleman on the track and a rascal off of it" was well-deserved. Latham and his wife, Barbara May, were famous for their off-tracks hijinks, and were frequent hosts of after-race "shindigs" at their home south of Davenport. Although J.T. had quit racing professionally many years ago, he still liked to take a fast car onto the track when possible.

The Lathams were prominent figures on the racing scene across the Upper Midwest, and were co-owners of Yuma Racing, of Davenport, a manufacturer of high-end racing components, including the Yuma-Five Camshaft™, which was popular some years back. Latham, through Yuma Racing, was the sponsor of the Three Hills Three Hundred, held annually on the third weekend of September.

J.T. retired from Yuma Racing in 1954, after the untimely death of his wife to cancer. The business was taken over by Latham's children, including son "Fast Jimmy" Latham, last year's winner of the Three Hills Three Hundred and a prominent member of the NASCAR racing circuit.

A full feature on Yuma Racing, J.T., and Barbara May will appear in the next issue of *The Journal*. Cards and condolences to the family—son Jimmy, and daughters Clare, Rebecca, and Erin—may be sent to the Yuma Racing facility in Davenport.

R.I.P., Old Friend

ABOUT THE AUTHOR

Michael Zimmer is the author of twelve previous novels. His work has been praised by *Booklist*, *Library Journal*, Historical Novel Society, and others. *City of Rocks*, chosen by *Booklist* as one of the top ten Western novels of 2012, was a Finalist for the Western Writers of America Spur Award. Born in Indiana, and raised there and in Colorado, Zimmer now resides in Utah with his wife, Vanessa, and their two dogs. His website is http://www.michael-zimmer.com.